OLENA NIKITIN

POISONED

SECRETS OF DAGOME

KINGDOM

Contents

Dear Reader,

We appreciate that everyone has a different level of sensitivity and may be triggered by different topics. It is up to your discretion whether you can handle the content in our books.

The book is intended for a mature audience of particular interests. It contains a certain amount of **coarse language, graphic sex scenes in MF pairings, as well as sexual innuendo and BDSM-related power play.**

You can also find **scenes of attempted SA, physical violence, poisoning and medical conditions** *that you might find triggering.*

The book is based loosely on Slavic mythology and Eastern European culture.

To enhance your experience, please check the **MAP** *or the* **GLOSSARY** *for unfamiliar words and terms (the definition may be different from what you can find in an external search as I've adopted several terms to fit the story).*

The book is written in British English but contains specific Slavic words with intentional Polish spelling and pronunciation.

CARE'TA VOS EMPIRE (DARK FAE)
WIOSNA
DWARVEN HILLS
PIRAN SWAMP
KLINCH
LUMIVITAE KINGDOM (LIGHT FAE)
TIVALARA

VODIANKA
ZDROJC
KINGDOME OF DAGOME
TRUSO
HIPWRECK COVE

Chapter 1

Roksana

I'd drawn the sigil correctly. The diagram looked exactly the same as the textbook, but the shimmering aether I'd been weaving between my fingers fizzled out without warning. The incomplete spell sent the distillery apparatus ringing, and my frustration emerged as a curse that would make a dwarf's ears curl.

'Whoever wrote this drivel, you've cost me a month's wages, you blabbing moron!' I slammed the book closed with such force that a few pages fluttered free. Angry tears stained my cheeks. I was risking so much by casting spells in the dwarven kingdom, but if there was even a slight chance I wouldn't have to see another patient die, it was worth it.

Fire spells are supposed to be easy, so why won't any of them work? How can I move on to healing if I can't even light a fire?

The sigil's glow fluctuated gently before dimming, my outburst making no difference. My second sight faded as I relaxed, the life-giving aether disappearing into the background while I wished the bitter taste of a failure would vanish just as easily.

Magic was my last resort for saving the injured dwarves, but nothing worked. With each failed spell, the ambition to teach myself how to weave aether became more of a ridiculous joke. Worse, I had no idea what I was doing wrong.

At least no one's here to witness my crime, I thought, wiping sweat from my brow, hoping Perun, the god of thunder, would bless this evening with rain.

Looking up, I could see that the sun hung low over the horizon. Its rays penetrated the high, stained glass window, burning my skin. The crude stone walls of my infirmary's office warded off most of the heat, but not enough to feel fully comfortable. Summer was always stifling in the dwarven kingdom, but this year, the blistering heat was relentless, and the drought affected even the tall oaks outside.

I shifted my chair away from the patch of light and rubbed my neck, stretching until the tired muscles eased and the knots in my shoulders loosened.

'Why don't you just go home and rest? You can't help anyone if you work yourself to death.'

Tova's voice made me jump, and, swallowing an embarrassing yelp, I forced a smile as I turned to greet my friend.

'I'm fine. It's hot in here, that's all,' I said, ignoring his raised eyebrow. The dwarf studied me closely whilst balancing some haphazardly stacked medical equipment on a metal tray in one hand and holding two tankards in the other.

'Of course you are. So, should I ignore what the maids have told me about how many hours you've been working? Or that I almost tripped over the tray of food they swore had been left for you first thing this morning?' Tova sighed, shaking his head, but didn't stop scolding me. 'Sana, for fuck's sake, you're human; your body can't go days without food like a dwarf's.' He placed his hands on his hips, glaring at me through narrowed eyes. 'They had to call me at work to check on you because I'm the only one who can open this bloody door.'

I looked down, attempting to appear contrite. Nature hadn't gifted Tova Orenson with the features necessary for a serious argument, and I struggled to look chastened as he frowned. Despite being five years older than me, his pale blue eyes and wavy strawberry-blond hair gave him an innocent and gentle look, no matter what emotion he meant to convey. His full lips were permanently pursed into a sensual pout that his long, dense beard did nothing to cover up, which didn't help the cause. He looked, as his late mother used to say, striking.

I smirked, thinking of another who had also made it his life's mission to scold and feed me. *If Irsha were here, these two would have a blast berating me together.* The memories of my childhood friend, bittersweet as they were, filled me with homesickness, even though I knew I had burned that bridge when I left Truso five years ago.

'I'm sorry they bothered you. I just . . . I acquired some new books and wanted to see if they were useful.' I couldn't tell him about my magic. The fear of being discovered didn't go away simply because I'd found a safe place to live . . . Well, it *had* been safe. Recently, the king had decreed that all magic and mages were to be banished from the kingdom. I sighed. 'Why does the king need so much srebrec, Tova? How much magical ore does Młot need to feel safe?'

The haunted look in my friend's eyes instantly made me regret my outburst. Both of his parents had perished mining the srebrec ore, and even after several years, his wounded heart was still raw.

'I don't know, Sana. I don't understand him anymore,' he said quietly, adding to my guilt.

'I didn't mean to . . . It's just . . . we're running out of time. The cave-in was a catastrophe. Add in the aether flux caused by that much unstable metal, and there aren't enough hours in the day to treat this many injured. This shit is never-ending; even the bloody weather is affected,' I answered, walking towards him and taking a tankard from his hand. 'Mead?' When he nodded, I tipped it back, emptying it in a few long gulps.

An insistent knock startled me, and Tova answered while I bent over, choking on my drink.

'My lady, another soul is in the final stages,' said the woman.

My heart sank, but I couldn't let whoever it was suffer to spare myself the heartache. I grabbed a vial from my desk and headed for the exit while Tova silently followed. The short distance between my office and the infirmary felt endless, each of my steps a dull thud echoing off the stone walls.

How many times have I walked through this corridor with death in my hands? I thought, promising myself that tomorrow I would try harder, maybe with a different spell. *Something* had to work. Fate couldn't be so cruel as to give me the ability to see aether without the means to use it.

The nurse led me to a cot that was surrounded by a privacy screen near the end of the large infirmary. The dwarf lying there was another victim of Młot's obsession with srebrec. I gently took his hand, uncaring of the pus leaking from his dead, grey skin or the stench that, after these long months, no longer turned my stomach.

'You know what I've come to offer you,' I said softly when his fingers twitched.

'Please, my lady. Death is better than rotting alive . . . please end the pain . . .' His voice was weak, but the dwarf's eyes were focused intently on my face.

I helped my patient to sit up and put the vial to his lips, wishing I could drag Młot here. The bastard deserved to see the mangled flesh of his people, to look them in the eyes and tell them it was worth it.

Not that I had any hopes of him feeling a shred of guilt.

As soon as the poison touched the dying dwarf's lips, the miner sighed, a smile ghosting his features for the first time. His eyes glossed over, affected by the extract of nivale root, while he reached for me, calling me a name I didn't recognise.

'His wife. She died a few months back, but we never retrieved the body,' Tova said from my side, and I let the man feel a touch of happiness before he died in my arms, just like the many before him. I hummed my mother's lullaby, easing him past the Veil with a song about a world of talking trees where cruelty and greed had not yet tainted nature.

I felt the heaviness of his body when death took him.

Strange how what's left behind always weighs more when there is no soul to lighten its steps. Have a peaceful journey, my friend. May Veles welcome you to a better place.

Closing his eyes, I slowly lowered the body on the cot, finally free of suffering.

'Take care of his remains,' I said as I walked to a side room to wash my hands and change into clean clothes.

Alone in private, I pressed my head to the cold stone sink and let my tears fall, taking a moment to compose myself. 'I gave him peace. His death is not my fault,' I whispered, repeating it over and over again until his face faded into the crowd of those that had died by my hands. Only then was I ready to rejoin Tova.

When we returned to my office, I noticed it'd been cleaned. The maids had used my absence to neatly stack the books on the shelves, while loose paperwork had been piled up on the desk, ready to be read. I grabbed the second tankard Tova had brought and finished it without taking my lips from the edge.

'You don't have to hide your tears from me,' Tova said, gently stroking my back. 'The king wasn't like this before the war. That is, he was always short-tempered, but he allowed mages to help his men, and the gods as my witnesses, you need that help.'

'Tova Orenson, you want me to believe there was a time our noble Młot wasn't a paranoid twat waffle who believed evil mages weren't out to get him? How naïve do you think I am?' Bitter laughter escaped my lips, but Tova didn't join in.

'You don't know what war's like, Sana. It changes you,' he said quietly.

The Battle of the Rift, the bloodiest conflict of the Second Necromancer's War, was fought five years ago, just as I had left my old life in Truso to settle here. I'd only ever heard the rumours of the blood and gore that covered the battlefield when a conduit mage had levelled the mountains to kill our immortal enemy. I couldn't imagine what that was like.

'I'm guessing when one's seen true carnage, a few bodies pulled from a mining shaft must feel insignificant. Still, they are his people, and they deserve more from their king,' I snapped. Over the past three months, death had hung over the dwarven capital like a thundercloud. Hatred for mages had blinded the king, fuelling his rising paranoia. Now, he believed that only srebrec weapons could protect him. Meanwhile, the victims of his fear kept dying on my watch.

'You're right, but what can we do? Now that he's discovered another vein, there'll be even more casualties.'

'What? Blasted idiot, does he want to kill us all?' I cursed, rubbing the bridge of my nose. 'Even the dwarven furnaces can't smelt so much srebrec into augurec[1]. You already can't walk through his court without tripping over those weird cubes that are supposed to shield him from mages. He'll end up slicing his own foot off one of these days.'

'He's started selling it.'

---

1. **Augurec** — inert srebrec alloy used to create shackles and collars that suppress magic.

Now, that news made me gasp. 'To whom? The mages?' I didn't know who else could, or would, buy srebrec. Only mages or those who wanted to control them or other magical beings had a use for it. It was too soft for making swords or armour, and too unstable to be worn as jewellery.

'Be serious.' Tova's voice was laced with bitter amusement. 'He found a buyer in the south. Someone who hates Dagome and their mages as much as he does, so expect the worst.'

'I always do, but I don't know how to find any reason in this madness,' I said with a shrug, inhaling deeply to clear my mind. The smell of herbal remedies was overpowering but reminded me I still had more salve to make. I'd slacked off today, too engrossed in studying.

Examining the dwarf's muscular body, I grinned.

'Since you're here, Master Artificer, would you help this poor, besieged woman whose arms are as weak as spring twigs with all the burdens she bears?'

Tova's brow shot up as I pushed a mortar and pestle filled with half-crushed herbs into his hands.

'Sana, you're a bloody menace. I came to get you to stop working, not to do your work for you . . .'

When I patted his shoulder, my friend fell silent. 'You can do both. The sooner it's done, the sooner I leave. Please, just one batch, then we can go to the tavern. I'll even buy you a beer . . .' I taunted.

'Fine! But not a *word* to anyone. I mean it, drah'sa.[2] I don't want anyone knowing that the best artificer in Wiosna is mashing herbs like a hedge witch.'

I nodded eagerly, grateful for his help. It was a never-ending need I could barely fulfil. The salve and potion didn't cure those affected by

---

2. **Drah'sa** — a dwarven term of endearment meaning 'little sister,' used for one considered a family member.

aether flux. However, the nivale oil and other herbs provided my patients a peaceful, painless death. It was a better alternative to them writhing in sweat-soaked beds, chafing swollen grey skin full of bleeding pustules that didn't heal.

Because death always comes.

All I could do was ease their passing.

A flashback of my recent patient's face forced a frustrated curse from my mouth. I'd never been trained. Even admitting to being able to see aether could be a death sentence—one, if not issued by my old master, then by the mages who wouldn't tolerate me working independently. Młot, who'd banished every aether user from his kingdom, would certainly have my head.

My only magical achievements were being able to influence aether to purge poisons and the ability to resist psychic manipulations. Neither of those had come from books. With poisons, I was always balancing on the edge of death, and instinct took over. And after a certain psychic arsehole had tried to force his suggestions into my mind, I had spent months working with a dark fae learning to set up a mental barrier.

I'm bloody useless. A wave of helplessness crashed over me, and I smashed the herbs I was working on with such force that the paste splashed onto the table.

'Should I ask what brought that on? If you want, I can give you this mortar too, so you'll have more ways to channel your anger,' Tova said with a smirk.

'I'm incompetent. It angers me. How did I end up here when the king must have had more qualified healers apply?' I snapped, unwilling to disclose my thoughts even to Tova.

'As if.' He shrugged, placing his mortar with perfectly blended herbs on the table. 'Dwarves aren't healers. He banished the mages, so he had to choose the least smelly human who wanted the position,' he finished with a shit-eating grin.

I turned, intending to playfully smack him, but a sudden draft from the door opening startled me, and I accidentally knocked an inkwell onto the floor.

'My lady, what are you . . .?'

I looked up from the black pool at my feet to the servant standing in the doorway, staring at me with horror in her eyes. 'The king wants to see you immediately, my lady. But your dress . . . It's all ruined. Gods, that will never wash out.'

'No worries, I'll just scrub it with some vinegar and brewing powder. That'll remove the stain. Do you know what the king wants?' I asked, removing my apron and placing it neatly aside.

'No, only that he wants to see you right now,' she said, still gazing at the mess. 'The messenger looked scared and had a black eye.'

Tova patted my back. 'You need to go, Sana. His tantrums have been getting worse lately; the longer we delay, the more excuses he'll find to punish you for some imaginary transgression.'

Młot barely tolerated his own kin, and I was like a rock in his shoe. He endured my presence because my knowledge of herbal remedies brought him some relief, even if only Tova and I knew those remedies contained an unhealthy dose of sedatives.

I nodded, turning to the servant. 'Don't wait for me. The salve is almost ready. Just mix it with lard and take it to the sick while I see what our ever-so-patient monarch wants,' I said, washing my hands and glancing in the mirror to ensure my unruly waves were neatly plaited in a tight braid.

'You must've fallen off your perch and hit your head if you think I'll be mixing anything with lard.' Tova scoffed, offering me his arm. 'I'll escort you to the king.'

'I wasn't asking you, tinkerer, but well . . . thank you.' I forced a smile as we left my little sanctuary.

'Fuck, how can you endure it?' Tova whispered when the stench of death once again assaulted our senses. I shrugged, looking around the crowded hall where row after row of the cave-in victims and those affected by aether flux lay suffering slow, agonising deaths. 'The way you held him . . . no one could ask for more.'

'I've seen worse. Besides, someone has to help them. I'm doing my best even if it's barely enough,' I said, swallowing hard, painfully aware of my own inadequacies.

Tova squeezed my hand, comforting me the best he could. 'I know, drah'sa. I know. I wish I could help, but as you said, I'm just a tinkerer. A good one, but I know nothing about the body. If they were machines to fix . . .'

'Then you'd be the first person I'd call,' I said, heading toward the infirmary's exit.

We left the building, and the blistering heat hit me so hard it took a moment to notice the sounds of crickets and the scent of night flowers.

The streets were peaceful. Only a few stalls were open, the goods of metal, wood, or gems lacking the variety a bustling market should have had. But it hadn't always been like this. I remembered Wiosna on the day of my arrival. The capital was bursting at the seams with laughter and rowdy haggling, children running around causing lighthearted mayhem. Now, the only people here were rushing silently about their business, rarely stopping to even look at the stalls.

Wiosna, the dwarven city that gave its name to the entire country, was supposed to be just a brief stop in my travels. A place to rest, since I wasn't allowed to return to Truso. But then it became the place where I could forget about my old life. Yet, lately, what had felt like my safe haven made me feel a stagnant dread. More often than not, I found myself considering whether I had made a mistake in throwing my past away.

'Halt! Who goes there?' shouted the guard when we neared the entrance to the dwarven court.

'Sana Regnav. The king wanted to see me,' I said.

'And Tova Orenson. I don't need an invitation.'

Tova's cocky smirk didn't go unnoticed.

'Enter, Lady Healer. Orenson, best be mindful of your tongue. The king's in a foul mood today,' the guard warned.

Tova shrugged. 'Is he ever in a good one?'

The question was left unanswered as we stepped into a metal cage, the door closing behind us. It felt like being lowered into a grave as the lift slowly dropped into the bowels of the earth.

Minutes later, we stood before the gates of King Młot's palace, and I had an awful feeling that this time, I might be buried there.

Chapter 2

Roksana

The doors opened soundlessly, and we passed through seemingly endless corridors before standing in front of the ornate gates of the throne room. My presence must have been anticipated because with a loud, '*Where is this bloody wench?!*' the gates swung open.

I took a deep breath before entering the room. The underground court was a place of stunning beauty if you could bear the thought of tonnes of rock above your head. As I stared at the intricate carvings, glittering with countless gemstones that sparkled in the light of a thousand candles, I had to admit it was awe-inspiring. But it didn't change the fact that I always felt uneasy coming here. I was too used to life aboveground to ever be comfortable at these depths, especially now with the strange srebrec weapons everywhere. Unfortunately, I couldn't refuse a summons from the king, so here I was, ready to deal with whatever the annoying bastard wanted this time.

'Come, healer! You have some explaining to do.'

I tightened my jaw at the curt command, but after a small curtsy, I approached the man sitting on the throne.

'What would you like explaining, sire?' I asked, taking a few cautious steps.

His eyes narrowed at my question. 'When will my men be returning to work? The quotas aren't being fulfilled, and the latest order isn't ready.'

'Err, never? The accident was severe, and your miners are dying. You can't expect me to—' I stopped speaking, attempting to rein in my anger. 'Their condition is irreversible,' I finished, tightening my fists.

Młot just sat there, a sneer marring his features. 'Dying? You promised me you could heal my men if I gave you the resources requested. I demand you fulfil your part of the bargain,' he said, deceptively calm, but the way he said the last word made me shiver. Did he think I could perform miracles?

'Your Majesty, I've used all my knowledge and resources, searched through every book I could get my hands on, but all I've found is a way to ease their pain. Your problem is not my lack of knowledge but the fact that you're dealing with aether-enriched ore without mage protection. Their condition is irreversible, and despite that, I'm still trying to—'

'Roksana, my dear, what a surprise to see you here. Truly the last place in the Lowland Kingdoms I expected to find my apprentice.'

I stuttered to a halt as a tall, slim man stepped out from the shadows. I knew that silhouette, and an old fear sank its claws into my heart. If the Dark Brotherhood's poison chapter master was here, whatever life I'd built for myself was decidedly over.

'Jagon. Whatever ill fate brought you here, stay away from this.' The warning in my tone should have been enough, but my former master wasn't done.

The bastard turned towards Młot while I stood frozen in place, shaking like a leaf. 'My king, I may have the answer for your healer's inability to heal. She cannot. The woman standing before you, who claims to have the skills needed for the job, is my apprentice. The infamous Deadly Nightshade, who sadly disappeared from the Dark Brotherhood a few years ago. I would be grateful if she could be returned to me.'

'Sana?' Tova's voice and his warm hand on my back steadied me enough to answer, anger replacing the fear.

'Returned? I'm free, Jagon. I didn't disappear. I paid my dues and handed over every single coin required to end my contract. You witnessed the grand master taking it and burning my scroll. What I do after that is none of your business.' I sneered at the bounder who had ruled my life since I joined the Brotherhood, whose obsession had almost broken me. I was lucky I'd realised his intentions and escaped before he had forced me to warm his bed.

Unfortunately, I was so focused on Jagon that I failed to notice Młot's reaction. His face was turning purple with anger as his advisor passed him some books. When I finally did give him my attention, it was too late.

'You *lying wench*, how do you explain this?' Młot yelled, throwing the tomes at my feet. Pages fluttered across the floor, each one showing spell sigils and magical techniques, the same pages I had studied earlier today before the maids had cleaned my workshop.

'I can explain . . .' I stuttered, but it was pointless.

Młot flew into a fit of rage. 'You lied to me! You're a mage . . . *a bloody mage*! My men died because of your insidious lies, and now you're raising your voice in my throne room? I don't care if you're the infamous Nightshade or a failed hedge witch! Your time in Wiosna is done!' Spittle flew from Młot's mouth as he shouted, and I knew this blind fury all too well.

He was past listening. In his mind, I was his enemy, a wretched mage who had come here to kill him, the sole reason for his men's demise. He conveniently forgot *he* was the one forcing them to work in such dangerous conditions, and that the aether flux the mining caused was killing even more on the mine's surface.

Tova's hand fell from my back as he stepped to the side. 'Dark Brotherhood? Nightshade? *You're* the Deadly Nightshade?' he whispered, shaking his head.

I stepped closer, but he shifted back. His rejection hurt more than I'd admit, and I swore that if I survived this, I would explain everything to him—about my life, about what happened fifteen years ago—but right now, I had to keep my head on my shoulders.

'Your Majesty, I left my life in the Brotherhood behind, and I work hard . . . I'm no mage, but I was investigating the aether to help your people. You know that raw srebrec ore creates the flux that is corrupting their bodies. I was just trying to find a way to protect them.' I tried to offer an explanation he could accept. 'I'll resign from the position as soon as you find someone to replace me. There are still many dying in the hospital.'

I looked at Jagon, memorising the smirk on his narrow face. He thought he'd won, but I was going to fight for my cause until the end.

'As if I'd let a mage anywhere near my miners. The place for liars and criminals is the dungeon.' He gestured to the men behind my back. 'Guards! Take her to the darkest cell you can find.'

The cruelty in his voice was startling when he sneered at me, 'I hope you've had your fill of sunlight, healer, because you'll never see it again.' Młot was beyond reason, but his orders were still being followed as several guards rushed in my direction.

'My lord, the apprentice belongs to me . . . If you agree, I can remove her from your presence in exchange for access to the trade—' Jagon started.

Młot waved him off. 'I'll double the next order, but she will pay for lying to me! You can stay for the execution or return to Dagome and your Brotherhood before I execute you for aiding mages as well,' he spat out.

'May I at least be allowed one last conversation to say goodbye?' Jagon asked.

'Fine, you can visit her in the dungeon but be careful. Any problems, and you'll be sharing her fate,' Młot answered dismissively.

Jagon bowed before he exited the throne room. 'Of course, Your Majesty.'

I backed away from the approaching guards, assessing my chances.

I could fight reasonably well, but I was trained to be a master of poison, not blade. Facing ten well-armed adversaries dressed in steel, I was at a disadvantage. *It's easier to escape if I'm uninjured,* I thought, raising my arms in surrender, praying that it wasn't the worst mistake I'd made in my life.

Still, as long as I had friends outside, there was hope that my time in the dungeon would be short. I winced when a guard twisted my arms, forcing me to my knees. Turning my head, I hoped to catch Tova's eye—only to see the dwarf who had been like a brother to me for the last five years striding from the throne room without a single backwards glance.

Młot hadn't been joking when he said I'd be visiting a dark dungeon, but his ordering my execution was shocking. Previously, he'd only exiled mages, occasionally beating them in his fury.

Is his paranoia getting worse?

It was scary to witness the mind of the man who commanded the entire dwarven army slowly fall apart. The enemy who threatened his people was *him*, and his fear delivered a steady stream of souls to Veles' cauldron.

My understanding didn't change the situation. I was as good as dead unless I found a way out of this prison. Bracketed between two frowning guards, the journey seemed to take forever. Eventually, we turned a corner, and I was confronted by a dim corridor, its sides lined with ominous barred doors. I was sure it made no difference which cell they chose, but the guards dragged me to the farthest, darkest cell, prying its door open with a screech of unused hinges.

Their retreating footsteps thumped the tolling of the death bell until the sound faded away into the distance.

'Is anyone here, or am I the only one lucky enough to have free bed and board in this exclusive dwarven inn?' I shouted loud enough to be heard all the way down the corridor. As expected, no one answered. Dwarves liked their justice swift and bloody, and if I didn't come up with something soon, I'd be another ghost lingering in the abandoned cell.

Time to plan, Sana. You can't sit around waiting for Młot to smash your skull in with his hammer.

'The idiots didn't even search me,' I muttered to myself, grateful that Młot's outrage had trampled over logic this one time. I still had a means of escape. My belt was intact, and I sighed with relief as I pulled a package wrapped in oiled paper from one of its pouches.

I'd kept a few items from my old life on me; I'd had to cut and run too many times not to be prepared. Most notably, I had a long hairpin that doubled as a weapon, its jewelled tip concealing a button that released a small dose of my deadliest poison. Tucked away with it were a set of lockpicks and a small vial of *merciful sleep*, a last resort that granted a painless death if all else failed.

I secured the hairpin in my braid for easy access and put the poison back in the pouch before kneeling in front of the lock, determined to free myself.

Unfortunately, I'd underestimated dwarven craftsmanship, and hours later, I was sweaty and close to tears.

'Fuck! I should have fought my way out,' I groaned when the last lockpick broke, the metal stressed from my incessant twisting. That had been my last chance. Now, I could only sit here waiting for someone to drag me away.

My thoughts drifted to Tova and his shock at the revelation of my identity.

Not you, my tinkerer.

A deep ache squeezed my chest as I swallowed hard. I didn't have many friends, as the Dark Brotherhood had taught me to trust no one. Those who laughed with you over a tankard of mead could just as easily sink a knife in your back for a handful of gold. Besides, even those I had trusted, I'd left behind.

And yet, that awkward dwarf and his easy friendship had slipped past the walls around my heart. We'd been thick as thieves since I'd healed him after he went to the mines to rescue his parents, only to find them dead under a pile of rocks. Tova turning his back on me hurt more than a broken lockpick and the threat of execution.

'I will not cry,' I whispered, pressing my forehead to the rusty metal bars. 'This is just another obstacle. They'll need to take me out of this cell eventually . . . then I'll have my chance.'

I was wallowing in self-pity when a flicker of light caught my attention. A moment later, I heard the thumping of heavy boots right before Jagon appeared, accompanied by Młot's guards.

'I would like to speak with my apprentice alone, if you please,' he said politely while I shifted as far away from the bars as I could.

When the guards disappeared around the corner, he approached the locked door. 'So, this is where you've been hiding. Aren't you going to welcome me, Roksana? Surely all those years as your mentor merit a handshake at the very least.'

'Welcome you? I'd slit your throat with a rusty butter knife given half the chance.' I scoffed, happy I no longer had to play at being his coy apprentice. 'Why did you get involved? Why the *fuck* do you *always* have to destroy everything I try to build? Couldn't you have just stayed quiet instead of telling them who I was?'

My outburst made him slowly withdraw, curling his fingers into a fist.

'So much venom. You should be grateful I intervened. A maid found your books, Roksana—*that's* why he summoned you. That little shit came to him with your papers, begging for her brother to be released from the mines.'

I winced, feeling the sting of my maid's betrayal. 'Did the king at least let her brother go?' I asked.

'Oh yes, but she won't enjoy the family reunion for long,' he replied with a smirk. 'A servant who betrays her master must die. My men are handling it—I gave the order the moment I realised the scrawny healer Młot intended to punish was you. Seeing your face has reminded me just how much I missed you.'

I rolled my eyes. 'Of course you did. Who wouldn't miss the foolish girl who'd eliminate your enemies while you stood by, leering behind her back? And you call *this* help? If you wanted to see me broken and miserable, then here I am. Take your fill and get lost. Gods, why did you even come?' I asked, looking him straight in the eye.

'You're breaking my heart, Roksana. But fine. I came here on business. Now, imagine my surprise at seeing my best apprentice accused of being a mage . . . How could I stand idly by? It was like fate's touch, especially since I have a task that seemed impossible until I realised someone with your unique skills could easily complete it.'

I tilted my head, studying my former mentor. Jagon had always enjoyed manipulating me, but the slight twitch of his fingers gave away his unease.

'I'm not the Deadly Nightshade anymore. If your task requires a poison master, you can do it yourself. Or did you forget how?'

'My charms are not quite suited to giving a man the kiss of death, my dear,' he said. I froze. Noticing my frown, Jagon smirked. 'Did you think I didn't know about your little hobby? I know you killed Ignac Tivala, but I've kept your secret. A small jar of lip gloss, red as your lips, and so poisonous that it'd kill anyone who touches it . . . How inventive. I saved it as a memento, thinking I'd never see you again, yet here we are.'

'He was a killer who deserved to die. I did what the Brotherhood should have done if they'd had the guts.' I didn't have an ounce of regret in me for killing the man who only got hard when he made women suffer and bleed. I didn't even care that he was the only male heir of the most powerful noble in Dagome.

'Oh, I'm not judging, but you know the creed: the heart does not steer the knife.' Jagon's condescending tone made me wonder why I'd ever considered him my superior.

'And you wonder why I left. But go on, tell me. Who is it that even the master of the Brotherhood's poison chapter cannot kill?' I shouldn't have asked, but my curiosity betrayed me.

'No one *yet* . . . but the time might come, and you would be the perfect tool for eliminating the king of Dagome.'

'Are you out of your mind?' My voice echoed down the empty corridor before I could stop myself. 'The War King? *Why*? Has Boyan authorised this? And what about the covenant with the Crown? You will destroy us, meddling in political affairs.'

'I'm trying to *save* us. Dagome's changing; alliances are shifting now that there's no Lich King forcing the kingdoms to work together. We'll die off if we continue to adhere to old agreements in the face of emerging unknown forces. Reynard won't be sitting on his throne for long, and the Brotherhood has a history of siding with the winner. But just in case he clings to his position . . . Well, we can always send you.'

'You're delusional if you think the man who outmanoeuvred the Lich King will be easy to depose. And why would you even want to kill the person who granted the Brotherhood its freedom?'

I didn't know the new king, but if Jagon hated him, I already liked him. I'd left Truso before the uprising that had placed him on the throne, but I'd heard he was ruthless and calculating. I doubted many could outsmart him.

'I've been honest with you for a reason. Your choice is simple: work for me or die. Return to the Brotherhood, and I will free you, no matter the consequences. Refuse me and . . . well, you know how Młot likes to execute those he thinks wronged him. I don't want to see you dead, Roksana,' he said.

I huffed in response. 'It wouldn't be a problem if you hadn't tattled about my past. And how would you stop me from killing *you* at my earliest convenience?'

'I misjudged Młot's anger, a mistake I can easily rectify. As for that other matter, I have a way to guarantee your loyalty.' His smirk widened as he trailed long slender fingers over the cell's bars. 'Tivala's family is still looking for the killer; if you betray me, I may accidentally insinuate it was a certain courtesan who ordered the assassination. I'm curious as to what the old duke would do if he found out a whore had been behind the demise of his heir . . .'

I threw myself at the bars, fists reaching out to pulverise that smug grin. 'Leave Liliana out of this, you treacherous bastard.'

'How predictable.' Jagon stepped away with a knowing smirk. 'Hate me all you want, but if you want to live—if you want *her* to live—be ready at dawn. I'll send my men to fetch you then.' He turned away, doing nothing to hide his triumphant smile.

He'd won, and we both knew it.

Between serving him again and certain death, what choice did I have?

I waited until my tormentor had left, then fell back against the wall, sliding down until I was sitting on the rough stone. I didn't fight back the tears. No one could see me anyway, so I cried, maybe for the first time since I'd signed my contract with the Dark Brotherhood. The illusion of freedom I'd had here was utterly shattered. I'd bought myself out, but now I understood that the only way to leave Jagon Vir's service would be in a coffin.

'*No*. As long as I live, I won't give up. He will regret forcing my hand.'

I curled up in the corner, swearing to the gods above and below that I would find a way to destroy Jagon before his malice killed what good was left in me.

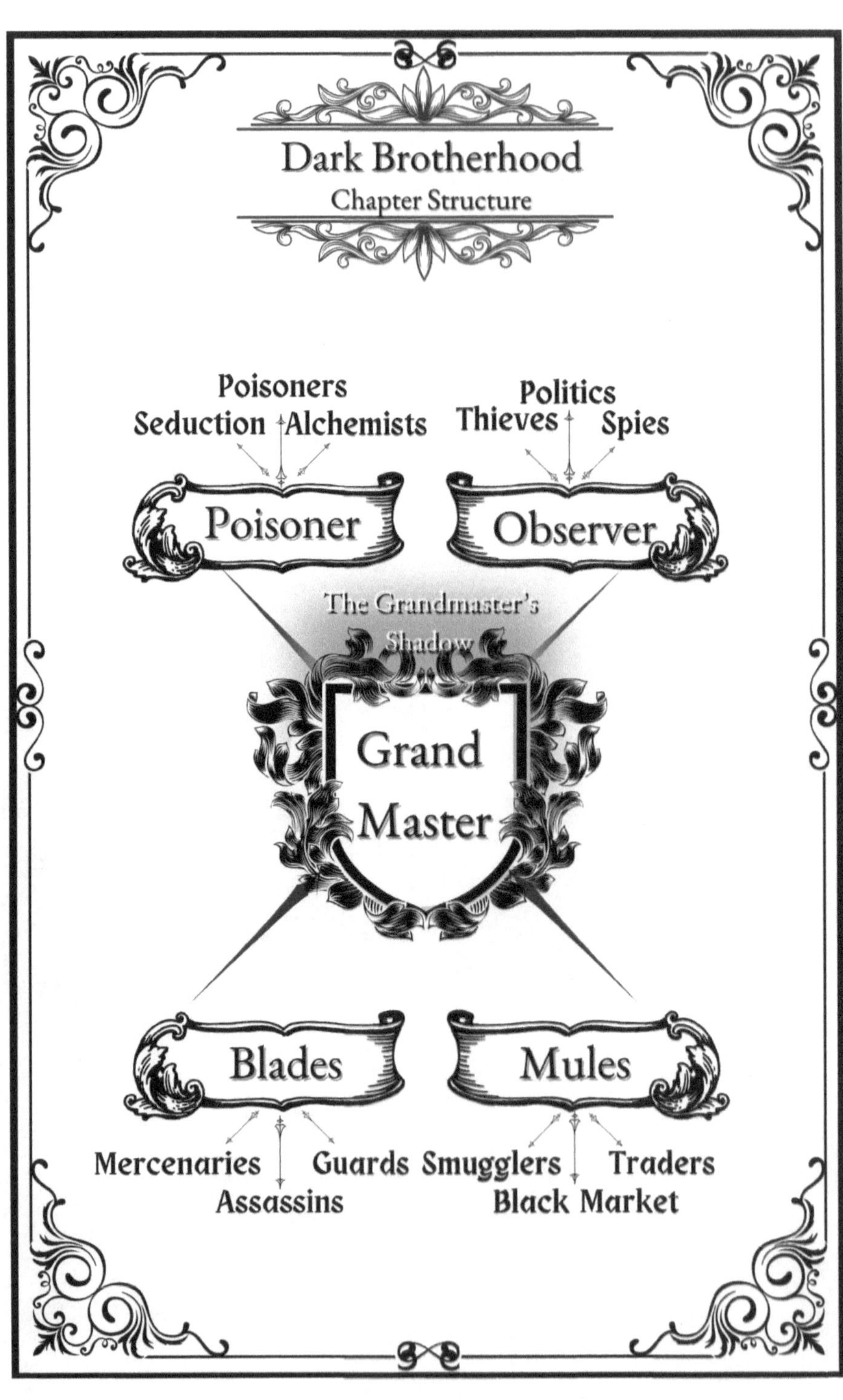

Dark Brotherhood
Chapter Structure
Poisoners
Seduction Alchemists
Politics
Thieves Spies
Poisoner
Observer
The Grandmaster's Shadow
Grand Master
Blades
Mules
Mercenaries Guards
Assassins
Smugglers Traders
Black Market

Chapter 3

Roksana

I wasn't sure how long I sat there, tears falling silently, until a rustle in the darkness startled me.

'Drah'sa?'

I gasped, scrambling to the iron bars. 'Here,' I answered. A moment later, I saw a pair of familiar bright blue eyes staring at me with concern. 'How . . .? Why? I thought you'd left me,' I babbled, grasping the rusty metal so hard my knuckles were white.

'Tch, I'd never leave you in danger. But if I'd defended you, Młot would've locked me up too. I danced to his beat, and it paid off. I am, however, mad as hell that you didn't tell me. I don't care about your past, woman. We've all made mistakes, but fuck, finding out that way? It hurt,' he grumbled as he reached down into his bag.

'The life I left behind wasn't something I wanted to brag about . . . Wait, how did you get here?' I asked, watching him reveal a shiny and very sturdy-looking set of lockpicks. 'It's no use; I broke mine on this damn lock. Whoever made it was a bloody genius.'

'Pfft, I'd be insulted if you weren't right. You're lucky that "genius" is happy to help. Now let's see what I can do.' He grinned, releasing my hand before carefully snaking his tools into the lock. 'Oh, by the way, while I was sitting in the tavern wondering how to get you out, I learned that your friend bribed the guards to look the other way. Most of them are patrolling the other side of the mine right now.'

The speed at which Tova had the lock clicking open was amazing. 'You mad tinkerer. I will sing your praises till my last breath!' He looked at me in triumph before I lunged forward and hugged him.

I wasn't tall; Tova was only a head shorter, but kneeling on the ground, I was the perfect height to lay my head on his chest as he awkwardly patted me on the back.

'It was only a few hours. I didn't realise it would frighten you that much,' he whispered in my ear. 'Come on, we need to get you out before your other rescuers arrive.'

'Thank you. Go, now! I'll find my own way out. It's too dangerous to be around me right now.'

Jagon was ready to use Lily to force my compliance. If he knew about Tova, he wouldn't hesitate to hurt another friend.

'Dangerous, my arse. Besides, you couldn't find your way through the mines even if I chiselled a map on your arm. Stop fussing, and let's go.'

He was right. The route we took meandered like a drunken miner, each corridor darker than the next. I knew Tova was choosing paths no one used to avoid capture, but as I had no idea where we were, I had to rely on him to lead the way.

It took far too long, but eventually, I felt a chill breeze on my cheek and saw a faint light at the end of the tunnel.

'We're almost there. It won't be easy, but it's the only way out of the city,' Tova said.

The warning in his voice gave me pause. 'I can manage,' I said, regretting my words as soon as we exited the tunnel to stand on a narrow shelf high above the forest floor.

I could see the entire valley of Wiosna stretched out before me—a patchwork of lush forest and scattered fields cradling a handful of human settlements. It was a peculiar kingdom, with one great city hidden beneath the earth and a vast wilderness above, dotted with nameless outposts. It begun with the dwarves, who had carved out a trading town at the mouth of an ore-rich mountain. But as the money started flowing, the other races had come to share the wealth, creating the prosperous kingdom.

'We just need to head for the river, then walk downstream until we reach the Kingdom of Dagome. Unless you have a different idea,' Tova said, placing a hand on the small of my back.

'You can't go, at least not now. The man who betrayed my secret to Młot . . . if we get caught together, he'll use you to force my hand.'

'Do you think I can be so easily used?' Tova asked softly, but he didn't know Jagon as well as I did.

'Yes, that's what Jagon does. He breaks people, uses them and discards them as he pleases. I can't let him hurt you because he wants to control me. You need to stay and live as if I were your enemy. Tell everyone how that bitch deceived you, curse my name in every language you know, and stay safe.'

Tova placed his hands on his hips, challenging me. 'What the fuck's happening, Sana? And don't lie to me. Since my parents died, you're the only family I have left. If you want me to let you go alone, you'd best give me a bloody good reason.'

'When I left Truso all those years ago, I abandoned those I loved, hoping my absence would keep them safe. Now that Jagon knows where I am, they are once again in danger. However, returning to Truso will . . . well, it's complicated, but I'm not welcome there, and my return will cause a few ripples. Give me a month, then come to The House of Lillies. They'll know where I am. Before you leave, see if anyone knows why Jagon's here. That bastard has to be involved in the illegal srebrec trade. Given his abilities, I wouldn't bet against him feeding Młot's paranoia.'

'Fuck! Fine, but you're taking this.' I looked at the coin pouch in his hand and shook my head. 'Once you get to a village, buy yourself a comfortable journey.'

'I can't take your money . . .'

'Yes, you can. I'll sell your possessions and tell everyone you owe me. I won't lose out. Come on, take it.'

This time, Tova let me embrace him, patting me gently on the back when my breath shuddered with unshed tears. 'I'll see you in a month, drah'sa. I swear it. With Svarog's[1] blessing, we'll drain all the ale in Truso and bash some heads together soon. Don't cry, sweetheart. I promise I'll be safe and come with news.' Just then, the sound of raised voices echoed down the corridor. 'Dam it, they shouldn't have discovered the empty cell this soon.'

'Fuck, it's Jagon's goons. How do I get down?' I asked.

He pulled a dainty rope ladder from behind a rock, attaching it to a worryingly worn ring next to the cliff's edge as I tried to mentally prepare myself to climb down it.

'Come on now, Sana, you can do it, you can fucking do it,' I muttered, grasping the first rung with shaking hands.

'Of course you can fucking do it. You are the only person in the world who can drink this dwarf under the table—a ladder is nothing compared to that,' Tova said as I threw my leg over the edge of a huge vertical drop that ended in rubble at the bottom of the mountain. 'Good luck, drah'sa, and . . . see you soon.'

I kept my gaze on his face, slowly climbing down as the wind lashed the ladder against the granite wall. I prayed to every single god I could remember for the safety of my tinkerer, for the strength to keep going, and for the time to warn my friends about Jagon's plans.

---

1. **Svarog** /pron S-va-roog/ — god of fire, patron of blacksmiths and metalworkers.

I had to stop him. The only way he could control the Brotherhood and break the covenant was by removing two people close to my heart. Boyan, the current grand master, was like a father to me, and Irsha, my Blade, had saved me so many times we'd stopped counting.

I was still swinging above the forest floor when I ran out of rope. With a heavy sigh, I pondered my options before releasing my grip on the ladder. It wasn't far from the ground, but the impact took my breath away as I tumbled down, my dress ripping on the sharp rocks until I rolled to a stop. Everything in me shook as I descended the steep mountain, clinging to every nook and cranny, feeling more like a mountain goat than a person.

When I finally reached a rolling meadow, I was a quivering mess of aching muscles, and the sun had fully risen above the horizon. An overwhelming sense of relief washed over me. I was alive. I had bounced back from danger like a cat with nine lives, but luck could only take me so far. Tears streamed silently from my eyes as I hugged myself, rushing under the cover of the trees.

I was going back to Truso—but as who? A failed healer? A remorseful dark sister who had turned her back on the Brotherhood? As a mage who couldn't cast? Or perhaps as someone entirely new?

The wind whipped my skirt around my ankles, and I almost tripped. I caught myself on a low-hanging branch, steadying my breath along with my steps. Those questions would have to wait. I couldn't afford injury, not now. I might not know which way to go, but I knew where I wanted to be.

Even if going home was the hardest thing of all.

It took me two days to reach the river. The trek proved to be more challenging than I'd expected. Tova, bless his heart, had thought of money but had overlooked simple necessities such as a cloak or food, and the nights were a harsh lesson in survival. My dress, ripped by the rough tumble, offered little warmth as I curled up between tree roots, hoping night predators would overlook my makeshift shelter.

On the third day, I could barely keep my eyes open as the sun rose over the horizon. Dirt clung to me like a second skin as I hid, shivering in the night's cold. Worse, the weather, starvation, and an array of cuts and bruises had given me a fever. The world spun around me as I tried to stand from my improvised bed, the colours blurring in a delirious haze.

I burst into bitter laughter. 'Healer, heal thyself,' I muttered as I stumbled towards a willow and placed my forehead on the trunk. 'I'm sorry,' I whispered, picking up a flat, sharp rock from the ground before hacking the rough bark away to get to the softer layer beneath. I chewed on the bitter strands, but the raw bark could only help so much.

This will have to do. I've bought myself a day . . . maybe less.

I pondered my dire situation as I waited for my fever to decrease. 'It can't be far now; somewhere, there's a village with an inn and a big, hot bath. Oh gods, there'll be a warm bed and food . . . I'll bet they even have fish stew and apple pie.'

Sheer tenacity and a focus on the simple pleasures of life kept me walking along the riverbank for hours after that. My daydreams felt so real, I could smell the food cooking—not fish, surprisingly, but a rabbit stew, like hunters make from the animals they snare.

I licked my lips and followed the delicious scent, uncaring if it was real or my wishful thinking. Whether it was a woodcutter's hut or a hunting lodge, I was ready to beg, borrow, or steal for a moment of respite and hot food on a plate.

'You could never be a hero, Sana. Three days in a forest and you'd sell your soul to Veles for a mouthful of food.'

My chuckle turned into a nasty curse when a twig smacked me in the face. The undergrowth was so dense here that it felt like the forest wanted to stop me from advancing. I grasped the low-hanging branch and pushed through, hugging my face to the uneven bark as I struggled.

Just a little farther. Gods, I should have spent more time outside, I thought, feeling my heart pound in my chest after such simple exercise.

Once I pushed through, there was nothing but the rush of blood in my ears. When it subsided, laughter and masculine voices dragged my attention to the clearing ahead of me. I hesitated, my steps faltering, but I didn't know how to live in the forest and asking for help was my only chance of finding some food. I licked my lips again, gathering my courage as I wiped the pine sap on my hands off on my dress.

I wished I could see through the undergrowth, but the tangled branches only revealed glimpses of a flickering fire. A root snapped under my foot, and I stilled, holding my breath before slowly continuing, careful not to make too much noise.

I approached what looked like a rough campsite, with an open fire and bedrolls becoming visible as I drew closer. I checked the position of my hairpin, ensuring it was within easy reach. Drawing a breath, I stepped into the clearing, only for the heat to assault me. Harsh, unfiltered sunlight pierced my eyes, bringing with it an instant sting of tears. I froze, squinting against the glare, waiting motionlessly until my vision adjusted to the unforgiving brightness. As the blur began to fade, a shape took form.

'Fuck,' I breathed, moving back. My luck had been bad lately, but this was beyond ridiculous. I'd followed the scent of a hot meal and landed myself squarely in trouble, like a cat fleeing the rain only to leap straight into a flooded gutter.

'They haven't seen me,' I muttered, looking around, my gaze briefly landing on the trees growing at the top of a small hill. Something was there, and I instinctively took another step back.

Out of all the danger I could have encountered during my escape, I had to stumble upon a hunting party. Three men sprawled near the fire, roasting rabbits, and I recognised one of them from the Dark Brotherhood.

'It's been two days. How long will he make us wait?' asked a tall, bearded man, probing the meat with a dagger.

'As long as it takes. You heard Jagon. He was furious she escaped. Our illustrious master paid a pretty penny for the guards to avert their eyes, but when he came for her, she'd already gone. What a fucking mess. You should have seen him foaming from the mouth as he issued our orders. So, sit on your arse and be happy you're here and not searching the deepest recesses of a dwarven mine instead,' answered another, and I swallowed hard as I tried to retreat.

'She's his little chit, isn't she? I swear the bastard was smiling when he returned from the dungeon,' the third rogue said before standing. 'I just don't get it. He could have any dark sister—why does he want this one?'

Because he's obsessed with me, you moron, I thought.

I was almost out of sight. A few more steps, and I could turn and run for safety, but the cold edge of a blade was suddenly pressed against my neck.

'Leaving the party so soon, sweetheart? I'm afraid I can't allow that. Jagon will have my balls if I don't bring you in.'

Before I could overthink, I shifted to the side, ramming my elbow into the man's stomach. Then, when he gasped and dropped the knife, I shot forward.

'Get her! Nightshade's here!' he grunted, raising the alarm.

Fear bolstered my strength, and I shrugged off my exhaustion, ignoring the sorry state of my boots as I ran as fast as my legs would carry me. My chest burned, and twigs smacked my face, but no matter where I went, my enemies drew closer. Maybe if I'd been rested, I might've stood a chance, but as I stumbled over another root, losing my footing, I felt hands grasping my arm and tackling me to the ground.

As we tumbled, I hammered my fist into a leering face, but neither the sickening crunch of his nose nor the blood gushing from it deterred him.

'Oh, you like it rough? Fine, princess, Jagon can have you once I've taken my turn and you've paid for my broken nose.' My captor spat blood in my eyes before capturing my hands and pinning them above my head.

'Let me go, let me fucking go!' I screamed, attempting to headbutt my assailant, but the other men rushed in, and before I knew it, they had me pinned to the ground, unable to do anything while their hands roamed over my body.

'Look at this, what a pretty bird. Now I know why Jagon wants her. She's got the face of an alkonost,[2] not to mention a good pair of tits to go with it,' said one, grasping the collar of my dress and yanking hard to expose me.

'Well, he only said to capture her alive. Jagon never said we couldn't have a bit of fun, and I think we deserve a little something for waiting in the cold,' answered his companion.

Cold understanding flooded my veins with rage. There was nothing I could do, not without my poisons, and not against four Brotherhood

---

2. **Alkonost** — a legendary woman-headed bird that has a healing touch, an otherworldly beautiful face, and a mesmerizingly alluring voice capable of making anyone who hears her forget all their sorrows and worries.

killers. But Jagon wanted me to live, and even these bastards wouldn't cross the poison master. I stopped thrashing.

'I won't forget this,' I said, deathly calm. 'One day soon, I'm going to kill you and then dance on your rotting corpses. Your flesh will burn, your bones will melt, your breath will freeze, and you'll beg me to end your pitiful existence, but I'll just savour your screams.' I spat the words out like a curse. The aether shifted around me, power I could barely touch now shocking me with its strength, filling my blood with venom. Vicious green strands curled around my body, lashing like vipers.

My attackers stopped, momentarily glancing at one another in panic. They couldn't see it, but the most primitive part of their soul sensed the danger.

'You pathetic pieces of shit,' I hissed. 'You think you've won? I'll carve your faces into my memory, and if you so much as touch me, know this—you'll be fucking your own death.'

'Shut up! Shut the fuck up!' shouted the one whose hand rested on my throat. He grabbed a rock and hit my temple, once, twice . . . His hand squeezed harder, black spots dancing in front of my eyes. My vision blurred as I fought to breathe, writhing against his grip.

So, this is how it ends.

Regret dulled my senses, heavier than pain. I'd never feared death—only a life left unfinished. I still had so much to learn, so much to live for, and my power had finally responded. Even if it was nothing like I'd expected, it was enough. I was more than the Deadly Nightshade . . . except now no one would ever know, and even those I loved would remember me only as a poisoner who had abandoned them.

Veles, God of the Underworld, if I'm to die here, let me return as a wraith. Let me take my vengeance.

Something splashed across my face, hot and sticky, the familiar taste filling my mouth with its metallic tang. A battle roiled around me as darkness pulled at the edges of my mind. The pain vanished, and so did the regret. My killers were killing each other. The dark god had listened to my plea.

Accept my soul, Veles, I prayed as a voice, deep and wrathful, chased me into the void.

'You'll take your turn in death.'

Chapter 4

Reynard

I sat on a tree stump, closing my eyes while my men busied them-selves setting up the camp in a forest clearing.

'Careful with that!' someone shouted, followed by a loud snap. When I glanced over, I saw a soldier unfolding my private coat of arms. It was like the idiot *wanted* everyone to know that 'Reynard Erenhart, War King of Dagome,' was travelling with a small troop through a foreign kingdom.

I sighed. 'Oh, for fuck's sake, why not add "shoot here?"' I mumbled to myself.

The soldiers saluted the moment they saw me stalk towards them. 'Take that down. Unless there's a reason you're announcing to everyone who we are?' I asked with a tight smile, not wishing to face another assassination attempt. My captain rushed in, dressing them down without mercy, and I walked off to find a quiet spot to think.

Młot's letter was burning a hole in my pocket. It wasn't even an official request, just a simple note bearing his private seal, now broken, the paper worn soft from being clenched in my fist too many times. When I first read it, I was sure it was a forgery; there was no sane reason behind such an outrageous command otherwise. Why would he have ordered me to shut down the University of Magic and dissolve both the Court of Aether and the Council of Mages? And his final words . . .

'They are dangerous to us all. Follow my advice, or I'll be forced to take action.'

'What bloody action? What's gotten into him?'

I wasn't sure if travelling to Młot's kingdom was the smartest idea, but he wouldn't come to Dagome, and after his men had turned away my ambassadors, I didn't have a choice.

One thing was certain: being outside felt good. Far from the palace, without the endless yapping of the Royal Council snapping their requests at me, the constant buzz in my head had quietened to a manageable level. Not that I had any trouble controlling my temper, but it was . . . tiring. We'd been travelling for two days already, but I felt more rested than I had in months.

'Where are you going?' Riordan asked when I approached my horse.

'To the river. I'll wash Kary down and enjoy some peace. I have to plan how to deal with Młot.'

He rolled his eyes. 'Then at least take a bloody squire and your sword. Don't go too far, either. We still haven't traced the fae who tried to shoot you last week.'

His concerned outrage made me chuckle, but I dutifully took my sword from a squire's hands and, for good measure, added a dagger to my belt.

'Yes, mother. What else do you want me to take, a crossbow? Or maybe a mage who keeps forgetting his place and ordering me around? You know, I think your worry would ease if you did some manual labour,' I said, chuckling as I gestured to the pile of logs my men had started chopping in preparation for the evening.

'No, thank you, Your Majesty. I have plenty of work already, but have you spared a thought for the people who might see a king washing his horse like an ordinary warrior? What would they think?'

'That I look good in a wet shirt? I don't know, Ri, you tell me—but first, could you point those people out? Because we haven't seen a single traveller the entire day,' I said with a grin. I turned to a young man, still in training, who was serving us during our journey. 'Come on, boy, you've been volunteered. Protect your king before our soon-to-be royal mage pops a vein scolding us both.'

'I'm not . . .' Riordan sighed, approaching me. 'I'm serious, Rey. You're not invincible, no matter what you may believe, and if you want time to think, then think about Duke Tivala's proposal. His representative consistently opposes you at every council meeting, and the southern province is barely contributing any taxes or resources. We both know what that means.'

'That they're hoarding them, likely planning to rebel. I know, but it's not that simple. Having a queen from the south would only strengthen Tivala's position, but I promise I'll give it some thought,' I said, jumping on Kary and waving for the squire to follow.

The river was close by. It wound between hills, sometimes spreading out into occasional floodplains to create slower, shallower waters. We stopped by a bend where the water swirled and slowed, giving the sun time to take the harsh mountain chill away. My stallion rushed into the river as soon as his saddle and tackle hit the ground, and I soon followed, much to the horror of my squire.

'Sir, maybe I should do that?' he asked, standing on the riverbank, watching as we enjoyed the currents.

'And take away my pleasure? No, thank you. It'll be our little secret. Go take a nap while I work,' I said, grinning at the blush that crawled up his cheek.

'I would never . . .' he started, but I waved him off.

'Yes, you would. I was a squire once, and I still remember how to sleep with eyes open while at attention.'

He blushed harder, fumbling with the collar of his shirt, but I'd already turned to my horse. I scrubbed his dark coat until it shone in the soft summer light. The freedom of the simple task was invigorating, but it soon became chilly as clouds covered the sun.

I led my mount out of the water and dressed hastily.

'I'm going for a walk. Stay here and guard the horses,' I said, walking towards a small hill nearby. The boy's eyes widened.

'You mustn't go alone, sire . . . the mage will be furious if I don't go along.'

'And how do you intend to stop your king?' I asked with amusement, taking pity on him and patting his shoulder. 'We won't tell Riordan but mind your words and never presume to give me commands.'

The sounds of the river faded away, replaced by those of birds and other wildlife the farther I walked. The hill was small but quite steep, distracting me enough to forget Riordan's request.

Despite my friend's concerns, I'd already considered the marriage contract Tivala had proposed. I had a duty to Dagome, and a queen from the south *would* be best suited for the role. In fact, I had signed the document Tivala sent, thinking it would be easier to accept a loveless marriage once the ink had sunk into the vellum . . . But looking at the Erenhart name on the page, I hadn't been able to put the royal seal on it, let alone send it.

So, I hid it, stalling for time, keeping my decision secret even from my friend. Marriage contracts, once made public, were almost unbreakable, and I didn't want to marry a woman I hadn't even seen yet. My objections were based almost entirely on my dislike of Duke Tivala and his scheming. I doubted it would improve if his daughter became my queen.

'I don't want an enemy in my bed,' I muttered, stroking a bear's claw marks gouged deeply into the rough bark of an old oak tree.

Soon, I stopped at the brow of the hill, where a small copse of young trees provided convenient shade and a panorama of Wiosna. A few wisps of smoke caught my attention, and I looked down at a small clearing where some hunters had set up camp.

Maybe Riordan was right in warning me about travellers, I mused, assessing the men below. They didn't look like typical hunters, and the camp appeared freshly made.

A flash of gold caught my attention.

It was hard to make out many details, but a woman was standing just at the edge of the clearing, as still as a statue. She raised her head, looking up in my direction, and it felt like our gazes met, though I was sure she couldn't see me in the shadows. She took a step back then, disappearing into the forest like a vila[1], a nature spirit as beautiful and capricious as life itself. I held my breath, unable to look away.

Suddenly, male voices cut through the sounds of nature, shouting angrily, followed by her scream. Before I knew it, I had my sword in hand, charging in their direction. I strained my ears, trying to identify the sounds I was hearing, hoping they weren't what they seemed to be.

Deadwood and tree branches snapped and fell as I leapt into the clearing, changing direction when I heard the woman shouting curses. My heart was in my throat as I sprinted, but the moment I saw the hunters, the world slowed.

Four men had her pinned to the ground. One was sitting on top of her, hand on her throat. Two others were tearing at her shirt, while the

---

1. **Vila** /vi-wa/ — a beautiful female nature spirit who dwells in pristine corners of the natural world, from forests and meadows to rivers and lakes. They possess supernatural healing abilities and the power of shapeshifting. Their eyes and dance can bewitch men who often perish from unrequited love.

last man kept hitting her head, shouting for his turn. My vision turned red.

'You'll take your turn in death.'

My voice carried, but they didn't pay attention. One woman against four men—yet she fought like a mountain lion, thrashing and cursing her attackers until one last strike ended her struggles, her head lolling to the side.

Rage surged through my veins, white hot and blinding. My battle cry drowned out the men's shouts as my first swing cut the nearest attacker nearly in half. He stumbled, his legs failing, hands clutching futilely at his sword as he collapsed.

The next cur put up more of a fight. He was good, but I was better. Years of training and fighting had honed my body, making the parry child's play. However, his style gave me a pause; the way he twisted, moving instantly from defence to attack, reminded me of the Dark Brotherhood. I didn't have time to think about it as the third man joined in, and after a brief exchange, I cleaved the head from his shoulders and maimed the other, sinking the blade in his chest as he scrambled away, whimpering in defeat.

I turned, catching sight of the final hunter running away. My instincts screamed at me to chase him, but one look at the female's greying skin and I was kneeling, gently lifting her from the forest floor.

'I'm sorry, I should have arrived earlier,' I whispered, propping her up as I searched for signs of life. She sucked in a breath, and my racing heart calmed a little.

She's alive, thank the gods. Riordan will know what to do.

Still holding her limp body, I unhooked my cloak and wrapped it around her, covering everything those bastards had exposed. A number of cuts and bruises marred her skin, yet she was still so breathtaking. Strands of honey-gold hair had slipped free from her braid, loosened during the struggle. My fingers traced the soft curve of her cheek, following the delicate slope of her small, pointed nose. Long lashes cast gossamer shadows against her pale skin, and for a moment, I simply marvelled.

My hands seemed so large against her body, the blood on them smearing as I kept her warm.

'I would kill them again for you, and I would make sure they suffered,' I said, realising that the ripped rags still hanging on her were a healer's kirtle. 'What were you doing alone in the forest? How long were you lost, little healer?' I muttered, frowning at her injuries. Some marks were fresh, others days old, their deep purple hues fading into a sickly green.

She stirred in my arms but didn't open her eyes.

'Never mind, Riordan will find out.' I stood, holding her carefully as I walked towards the top of the hill to get to where I'd left my horse near the river.

I felt centred, helping this woman. The southern uprising, the stress of marriage and politics—it could all vanish up Veles' arse and stay there for all I cared. Meeting her, fighting for her, had stirred something in me I thought I'd lost. It reminded me of who I used to be—a man with purpose, with a clear path and a single goal: to protect those who relied on my strength.

It wasn't long before I spotted the squire resting under the tree, my horse nodding off beside him.

'We're almost there,' I whispered to her, batting away the insects attracted to her blood-matted hair when something caught my eye. I brushed the strands aside, hoping I was mistaken, but the truth was before me, tattooed just beneath her hairline.

A rune—scarcely visible; small, but unmistakable. My breath hitched.

The mark of the Dark Brotherhood.

She wasn't a lost wanderer, a healer missing in the woods—but one of them. A dark sister.

'No, there must be another explanation for this.' I rubbed the rune, but it was firmly etched into her skin, only reddening under my rough handling.

Her body jerked in my hold, and I bent over to put her down, hoping to prevent further injury. She swore, twisting and fighting. I instinctively put my hand on her chest, pressing her down. 'Stop fighting,'

Her eyes snapped open—glassy, unfocused, yet arresting in their hazel brilliance. She was conscious, but not fully *there*. Still, I couldn't look away. My body stilled, caught by the luminous fire flickering in those depths. Hazel deepened into a verdant green, alive with lightning that seemed to crackle from within, and something inside me shifted. A low growl rumbled in my throat, my heart pounding in time with the strange pull of her presence, of the intoxicating scent—all lilac and honey—overwhelming my senses.

Unable to resist, I reached out to stroke her cheek as the sensation in my core expanded, stretching like an awakened giant. But as I moved, a twig snapped under my shifting weight, and she screamed, lashing out at my questing hands.

Confusion, shock, and pain flooded back into her eyes, utter panic fuelling her strength. I raised my palms to calm her when the flash of metal caught my attention. My instincts screamed for me to move, but my body failed me. I reared back too late, and a sharp blade sliced through my cheek.

Agony exploded in my face. I fell back, ripping the blade away, clutching at my burning flesh while she bolted without a second look, leaving me roaring in the mud.

The wound burned like aethereal fire, but worse was the creeping weakness that drained my limbs. I could barely stay upright, staggering towards my horse—only to collapse after two steps as my stomach re-belled and I fell helplessly to the ground.

Whether it was magic or poison, it didn't matter. I'd been tricked. My enemies had finally found a way to kill me.

But as my strength bled away, the power that had awakened when I had drowned in my assassin's gaze surged in defiance. The legacy of the Erenhart line—the berserker's rage—filled my blood, refusing to let me die, forcing me to live so that I could take my vengeance.

Chapter 5

Reynard

Whether it was my lineage or pure, bloody-minded stubbornness, I refused to lie down and die. My collapse was rapid and painful, but the sting of bruised flesh was nothing compared to the inferno engulfing my face. I crawled blindly, howling for my squire, until I heard him running, shouting my name in a panicked, breathless voice.

It had to be poison . . . *She* was poison—a perfect honey trap for an idiot desperate to be a hero. I wasn't afraid of death, but I was not ready for it. Certainly not one such as this, crawling like a worm in the mud, wishing I could tear the skin off my face to escape the torment.

'Fuck!' I roared, shaking my head as the world spun on its axis. 'You fucking fool, bewitched by a pretty face!'

Nausea shredded my guts, and a sour taste filled my mouth. I heaved as the squire knelt beside me, holding my shoulders. My body shook, sweat pouring from my skin, but I was finally able to take a breath.

'My liege! What happened?' he mumbled as he panicked. 'Are you . . .? We need help . . . The mage! I'll take you to the mage!'

'My horse,' I groaned.

He brought Kary over, and following my gesture, my stallion lay down, letting me crawl onto his back. I realised that my long-dead father's insistence on training horses to pick up injured warriors was saving my life now.

Life, yes, but not my dignity, I thought humourlessly.

Kary stood up, his movements sending another wave of nausea through my limp body.

'Tell Riordan it's poison,' I wheezed as the squire urged my horse into a steady canter, rushing back to camp as fast as the terrain allowed.

Sharp commands broke through my delirium, but I had barely the strength to raise my head when we suddenly stopped. Calloused hands grabbed my arms, and I slid off my mount, hitting the ground like a sack of turnips.

The faces of my men blurred before my eyes, my mind drifting in and out of the void, when a cold, soothing hand landed on my cheek, poking and prodding the bleeding flesh.

'Reynard, stay with me,' Riordan commanded, and coldness spread through the wound before my friend turned to speak to someone. 'Captain! The situation is dire. We need a healer. Take my signet and send someone on the fastest horse we have to fetch Master Ciesko. Let the arch healer know that his king commands it—and tell him to ride a bloody dragon if he must, but he has to be here no later than tomorrow!'

His words rang with the authority of the royal mage of Dagome, and hope died in my chest. If my wound required the services of a dragon and the arch healer, I was as good as dead.

'Tell me the truth,' I groaned, focusing on Riordan's voice.

'The truth is you have a choice.'

Ri's hand trembled while he drew something in front of my face, frost spreading over my cheek, numbing it further. I could see the toll this magic was having on him. He was a psychic mage. Healing was so far from his class and domain that attempting the spell was draining him, bleeding his aether, and I hoped he wouldn't be stupid enough to reach the point where he had to use his life essence to sustain mine.

There was no need for both of us to die.

'What is it?' I rasped.

'The poison is spreading. I'm holding it in place, freezing the tissue, but without an antidote, we . . . There's no time. This is beyond me, but I know it's killing you,' he stuttered, wiping sweat from his forehead before inhaling sharply. 'It's in your eye, a pool of death and tangled aether spreading into your bloodstream. If I can expel it, you might survive . . . but it's your eye, Rey. I don't know how to do it without blinding you.'

I couldn't make sense of Riordan's words, but I latched onto the words 'expel,' 'eye,' and 'blind.' At this point, I almost didn't care what happened next, but I trusted Ri with my life.

'You can do it?' I gasped. He nodded, and as the gravity of the situation settled in, I made my choice.

'Then do it! I can't see through it anyway, but if I die, tell my brother to find out who sent her. She's a dark sister; I found out too late.'

That was all I could think of in the moment—revenge, and the woman who had brought me to my knees. If she was innocent, why would she have attacked me? It had to be a trap. It had to be . . .

I didn't care how little sense it made. I needed something to focus on to help me survive, and revenge mixed with hatred was an excellent reason to carry on living.

'She? Rey, that can wait.'

Riordan gestured to my men, and two of them grabbed my arms firmly. His hands shook as he drew his dagger, and I bit back the command to hold his nerve. When my friend still held back, his eyes wild, I grabbed the blade and thrust it into my eye socket myself.

The world dissolved into agony, but I didn't stop. I clenched my teeth, cutting through my flesh and praying to Perun for the strength to endure. The thunder god of war and berserkers answered my prayers in a flash of gold and fury, keeping me conscious.

My heart threatened to burst from my ribcage as I worked, blood and sweat flowing endlessly, washing away the poison and what little awareness I had left.

With one last twist of the knife, I screamed my defiance to the heavens and collapsed, barely feeling my body bounce off the hard ground. Whether I lived or died, it was out of my hands now.

'Gods, you're the toughest bastard I've ever met,' Riordan muttered, kneeling next to me and pulling my head onto his lap. With another sharp curse, he started chanting, attempting to stem the bleeding. I raised my hand, focusing on my trembling fingers.

'Send . . . find her . . . dagger . . . squire knows . . .' I mumbled before the void swallowed me whole.

'I've withdrawn the stasis spell. He'll awaken soon,' came a voice from the darkness. My consciousness latched on to those words, along with the thumps and squeaks of a moving wagon.

'Let's hope so. Just pray we still have a king when he opens his eyes. The wild magic saved his life, but if the berserker controls him . . .' answered another voice, more mature and obviously exhausted.

'It's Reynard you're talking about. Nothing controls him but himself.'

Lucidity dawned and I realised it was Riordan defending me, but I knew the other man was right. The berserker's rage usually manifested when one was a child. As old as I was, I wasn't sure what it meant for me. If I lost control, who could stop me from killing everyone?

'It's been three days. Rey needs to be conscious before we arrive in Truso. The next session of the Royal Council is three days from now.

With your help, I can hold them off, but the old guards must at least see him walking into the palace.' Riordan was adamant, but all that was on my mind was the realisation that my nightmare hadn't been in my imagination. It had really happened.

The woman's face filled my mind. I searched through my memories, wondering if I'd missed something. The scene looked so real. The men, the chase, and her bruises weren't fake. Yet the men had fought like assassins, and I wouldn't be surprised if they were marked by the Brotherhood just like her.

Was she there to lure me in, or had I just interrupted their leisure? But her screams . . . those were real. *Ugh, but if they* were *real, why would she attack me? Fuck, nothing makes sense.*

Logic failed me, and the more I analysed the situation, the more my thoughts spiralled until a cold, wrinkled hand landed on my cheek, soothing the pit of hell that used to be my face.

'Welcome back, Your Majesty,' Ciesko said, and I opened my remaining eye, blinking until the face before me became recognisable.

'How bad is it?' My question was barely a groan, the words mangled by pain when he removed his hand.

'You'll live, but . . . there were complications,' the healer said, propping up the pillow behind me when I tried to rise.

'Of course,' I said, muttering a curse. 'What kind? And can you do something about this pain? It's hard to focus when it feels like there's a spike being hammered into my skull.'

'I've had some difficulty healing you. Whoever made this poison was a mage—or working with a mage. I cleansed the toxins, but certain components that have saturated your flesh have an anchor that has resisted my magic, so I've isolated them with a lattice of aether. Once we're in Truso, I'll send for someone skilled in purging. Maybe they can help.'

Ciesko glanced to the side, and I followed his gaze to see an exhausted Riordan slumped on the bench wearing a concerned frown.

'Maybe?' I grunted, considering the implications of what had happened. 'And if they can't?'

'The lattice won't hold forever, sire. When it fails, the consequences will be severe, but we have several specialists in Dagome with an affinity for poisons, and there's always the light-fae healers.'

I shook my head. With several open border disputes, informing the light fae that the king of Dagome was injured and barely able to rule was out of the question, at least for now. 'How much time do I have?'

'Months, more likely years. No need to worry, sire.'

Ciesko's answer didn't frighten me. If anything, it brought me peace knowing that I had time to secure my country.

'Did our men at least find any clues about who she was?' I asked, trying to find something I could control.

'The bodies you left behind were Brotherhood members. We also found this,' Riordan said, passing me an object wrapped in cloth, 'next to your cloak.' The bundle was shaped like a dagger, but when I unwrapped it, a small, bloody hairpin with a viper's head fell onto the wagon floor. Its tip was broken, revealing a hollow blade.

Are dwarves in on this, too? I wondered. The item was a prime example of dwarven craftsmanship, similar to the fang blade favoured by alchemists.

A viper-shaped hairpin. Such a little thing to have brought me to my knees. How fitting. The woman herself was a viper, a beautiful creature from the forest and equally deadly. She would pay for this, even if her actions had earned her my reluctant respect. She'd gotten closer than anyone to ending my life, and for that alone, I would grant her the rare courtesy of letting her explain *why* before I drew my blade.

You'll rue not finishing the job, Viper. There's nowhere in Dagome you can hide, and not even the mightiest of noble houses will shield you from me.

'Fuck.' I grasped Riordan's arm as I realised something. 'The council will want an explanation for my missing eye. Find me an excuse for it, before those idiots use it to harry me like a pack of wolves facing a wounded stag,' I said, gesturing to my face.

My return to the capital half-blind and incapacitated would be the perfect opportunity for those who loathed the changes I had made to retaliate. And there was another issue: Who was the traitor in my ranks? Had rolling out my banner been an honest mistake, or a deliberate message letting my enemies know where to find me? Anything seemed possible now.

Anger contorted my features further when I noticed Riordan's fingers dancing through the air. Without the second sight, I couldn't see the aether, but judging by my fury—and his reaction—I'd bet he was drawing a sigil to contain me.

'I'm fine,' I snapped, inhaling deeply. 'Find me an eyepatch to wear so that people don't retch when they see my face. And call the captain of the guard over,' I said, sitting up and trying to get used to my new, altered vision. Everything looked so different, and whenever I moved my head, a wave of nausea left me gasping.

A moment later, a veteran with a brutish face lifted the tent flap and climbed into the slow-moving wagon.

'You wanted to see me, sire?'

'Yes, whatever is whispered by the fire, not a word to anyone about what happened. I was hunting and was injured by—' I paused, trying to find a convenient excuse for the injury. 'By a wild boar, and it was a bloody huge cur. Send one or two hunters out to kill one and throw the carcass on a wagon in case anyone questions it,' I said. When he nodded,

I exhaled, focusing on the here and now. 'When we arrive at the capital, send for the garrison commanders. I want them to send a contingent of scouts to the northern borders.'

'Yes, sire. Anything else?' the captain asked, and all three men looked at me with interest.

'No, you may go,' I replied. When he left, I turned to Riordan. 'How long was I unconscious?'

'Five days,' he answered. When I shot him a questioning look, he explained, 'Two days to bring the healer, and another two days for Master Ciesko to stabilise you. Today is the fifth day since the attack.'

I ground my teeth, exhaling slowly. After five days, even a contingent of scouts might not be able to find her, but I had one more option: the Brotherhood she belonged to.

'That's . . . unfortunate. Let's hope the grand master doesn't try protecting her, or I'll have his head on a spike,' I said with such venom that my mage gave me a quizzical look.

'Are you planning to interrogate him? What about the covenant?' Riordan's frown made me smirk, which only sent a wave of pain across my face.

'The covenant is a worthless scrap of paper if they've deceived me. I will find the truth, Ri . . . and I'll find *her*, whatever the cost.'

I had to face her again—because no matter how much I fought it, my mind dragged me back to that moment, replaying it on a loop until all I could see were her eyes, wide with terror, green lightning sparking in their hazel depths.

What pit of despair did you crawl out from, Viper?

I needed a name for her, and that one fit. She was a warning disguised as beauty—one I had noticed far too late.

We arrived in Truso the next afternoon. Master Ciesko had spent that time working his magic, quite literally, and had performed what Riordan described as a miracle, modifying and enhancing the spell he'd cast on my face. The lattice he'd created to control the poison now also eased a significant amount of the pain. It was a temporary measure, but it helped me appear normal even if I struggled with my depth perception.

The healer, however, looked like he'd been dragged through the Veil kicking and screaming before fighting his way back. I promised him he'd be well rewarded for his help, directing him to rest and replenish his aether reserves before I dismissed him.

Once he'd gone, I addressed Riordan. 'Give me an hour to clean myself up, then call for the grand master—and send the description I gave you to the scouts. I want her found and brought to me unharmed.'

'Are you sure? It can wait until tomorrow.'

'Can it? You want me to rest knowing there's an assassin with magic-resistant poison out there?' I snapped as I entered my quarters, wincing at my servant's sudden gasp when they saw my face.

'Get the bath ready and lay out some casual clothes for me,' I instructed the man. I turned back to Riordan, who was still standing there, his eyes fixed on me, thick with concern.

'Please, don't question me,' I said quietly, offering a faint, apologetic smile that tugged at the edges of my healing scar.

'As you wish,' he answered, leaving me alone. I stripped quickly and stepped into the bath chamber, head bowed, trying not to glance at the mirror. But in the end, curiosity won.

My body was unchanged. Large and well-muscled, a thick layer of hair covered my chest, narrowing into a vertical band down my abdomen. My face, though . . . I ran a hand through my thick black hair. I usually kept it short, as the unruly waves were difficult to contain, but maybe that would change now.

I loosened the eyepatch Riordan had fashioned for me. Beneath it, the empty socket and ugly red scar stood in stark contrast to my lone grey eye. The scar began at my cheek, where the blade had first torn into my skin, and carved its way up to just above my brow. I'd never been the most handsome of men—too sharp-featured, too heavily built, and no crown could soften that. But now, I looked downright terrifying.

'There go my chances of luring pretty maidens to my bed,' I muttered, easing into the large tub of hot water.

'It's not that bad, my liege. Some women like . . . ahh . . . danger.'

My servant's words made me laugh. The poor man was trying to console me, but I knew the truth.

'Yes, people are strange, and some find it thrilling to deal with monsters, but I won't be some pity fuck or a deviant's desire. Hurry and help me wash. I have a meeting in an hour.'

He did what I asked, and half an hour later, my hair still wet and plastered to the nape of my neck, I headed to the audience chamber.

Riordan was already there. Boyan, the grand master of the Dark Brotherhood, stood next to him. He was looking even sicker and thinner than the last time I'd seen him. I frowned when his body shook with a wracking cough.

'Good to see you, Grand Master,' I said, pointing to a chair before sitting.

'Your Majesty, I heard about the accident . . .' he started.

'We both know it wasn't an accident. Your assassins did this to me. I killed the men, but the woman escaped. I want to know her name and who paid her.'

The confusion in his eyes made me feel uneasy.

'I wasn't told of any assassination attempt on your person. Besides, the covenant strictly forbids it. If anyone took such a contract, I'd kill them myself.'

'Would you tell me if you knew? Maybe the money was enough for your people to break the covenant,' I said, gesturing to Riordan, and my mage's hand instantly sketched out a familiar sigil.

When he was ready, I unwrapped the viper hairpin and passed it to Boyan. 'Does this look familiar to you?'

He paled, and his back snapped straight as he looked me dead in the eye.

'Your mage can interrogate me, but I assure you I know nothing of any contracts.' His hand clenched the pin as Riordan's spell wormed its way into his mind. I'd learned to recognise the signs—the slightly glassy eyes, the twitching—as Ri riffled through someone's thoughts.

'Then find out who knows. *Who* went behind your back and paid your men to attack me?' I questioned.

His jaw tightened. 'It would help me if you could describe your attacker. Who should I look for?'

I clamped my lips down on the words that came to mind—*a woman as beautiful as the blush of dawn*—before slowly exhaling.

I tried again. 'She was blonde, quite short and . . . voluptuous.' I nearly groaned when that last word slipped out. My inability to give a better description made me curse under my breath, but as I closed my eye, the memory of her mesmerising gaze tightened something in my chest. 'She has hazel eyes, and she's bloody good with poison. Even the arch healer had trouble with it.'

It could have been a trick of light, but I was sure Boyan stiffened even further, his nostrils flaring. *So, you do know something,* I thought, frowning, when he suddenly declared, 'My king, I swear on my life that there is no one in the Brotherhood who matches your description.'

He was lying to me, right to my face, his thumb stroking the pin's head. My chair creaked ominously as I stood, my large body towering over the frail man. He knew I'd caught him, that I was going to pin his lying tongue to the wall and force his confession.

'He's telling the truth,' Riordan said, making me freeze mid-step.

'*What?* Are you sure?' I asked, staring at my friend in disbelief. 'I know he recognised her description. Rip it from his mind if you have to, I want her name.'

Boyan exhaled, calm and composed despite Riordan's spell holding him enthralled. 'There's no need, sire, but your mage is welcome to check. However, it won't change the fact that no one fitting your description is a member of the Dark Brotherhood. You're welcome to send your men to check the Chapter House's records, but please be discreet for both our sakes.'

'He's telling the truth. There is no such woman in his ranks. I'm sorry, Rey,' Riordan reiterated, and I fell back into my chair, squeezing the armrests so hard the wood cracked.

'Fine, send out your Observers. I want her found. You can name your price,' I said, rubbing my temple as my earlier headache returned.

Was the mark on her temple fake? Another trick to sow discontent between the Crown and the Brotherhood? . . . Is someone trying to strip me of my allies, or was there another reason for her attack?

'I'll find out what happened free of charge as long as Your Majesty lets me do it my way,' Boyan said.

I nodded. 'Fine. Go, and return with results.'

I watched him leave. He walked slowly, his once powerful figure shaking from bouts of coughing. The grand master looked frail, but it was I who felt cornered, each lead falling apart as I reached for them.

The hope of finding her today had kept me going. But now, I had nothing. My Viper remained a mystery, and I was left with no choice but to bargain with fate.

Arachne, Goddess of Fate, bring her to me. Reveal to me who she is . . . who she truly is, and maybe I'll let her live.

But mercy didn't mean forgiveness. And letting her live didn't mean that she wouldn't wish I *had* killed her instead.

Chapter 6

Roksana

T he familiar scent of straw and dried wildflowers teased my senses, reminding me of my childhood. I dreaded this dream, yet I could not resist sinking into the simple pleasure of running barefoot through the Orcish Steppe. Of hiding in the tall, dry grass, and breathing in the scent of daisies as they opened beneath my touch. In my dreams, my mother taught me how to make flowers bloom, how to paint their petals with all the colours of the rainbow . . . They were happy childhood fantasies, my escape from the harsh world I lived in.

The pleasant dream never lasted, though. Fire always crept in, turning a fond memory into a nightmare. This time, however, it felt different. The stench of burning invaded my senses, flames engulfing my ancestral home, but the screams of my family trapped inside became mine. I struggled against the men who assaulted my body with the savagery of wild beasts until they stopped, and the scent of musk and lemongrass chased away the pain.

But I knew better than to give in. I'd trusted Jagon when he first came to take me, and where had it led me? These men were his thugs, and I couldn't let them win.

I fought back, but my enemy didn't let go. His grey eyes bore into mine with a hunger so terrifyingly real that I lashed out with all I had, my poison-filled pin and magic hitting him as I ran for freedom.

My eyes flew open, focusing on my hand as it stabbed upwards, my throat so tight my breath hardly filled my lungs, making me dizzy. The bed I laid on creaked as I sat up, heart racing, drenched in cold sweat from the night terror. It didn't help that I didn't recognise the house I was in.

What's going on?

'Ah, you're finally awake. I thought I'd have to throw you back into the river.' The sharp voice startled me. I blinked, trying to focus on the woman standing in front of me.

'Who are you? Where am I?' I asked, shaking my head until the reality that I was in a strange cottage, its peasant origins clear in the dawn's faint light, finally sank in.

'In my bed, and you've overstayed your welcome. Now move, you need to leave,' said the old woman, pulling off the covers.

'Call me Sana. I thank you for your help, and I'll go, but could you at least tell me who you are, where I am, and how I got here? Oh, and may I ask for my clothes and the purse that came with them? Travelling in a thin chemise will certainly attract too much attention,' I said, standing up. I grasped the edge of the bed; I was as weak as a newborn kitten, and the rapid movement made me giddy.

Despite my meagre height, I towered over the woman in front of me, her back bent by the passing years. And although her skin had weathered over time, her eyes shone with intelligence and strength. Her disdainful huff at my questions nearly made me smile.

'My name tells you nothing, but you may call me Vera. You're in Dagome, or at least that's what most people would say. We're so close to the border that we could even be in Wiosna. As for your arrival, I found you in the river nearly two weeks ago. Since then, you've been in bed, delirious from fever,' she said. 'I called for the healer, but he didn't want to come. Nobody did. They say you're a rusalka[1] and that I should have thrown you back into the water.' She huffed with a shrug, 'Like any rusalka would ever look like a drowned rat.'

Two weeks? I've been here for two weeks? Fever?

I sat back, trying to make sense of my predicament. 'My clothes, please.'

'Please . . . thank you . . . You speak like a lady, yet you wear the mark of the Brotherhood. You're lucky I'm too old to fear an assassin under my roof,' she said, eyeing me suspiciously before pointing to a pile of clothing on the wobbly table. 'I burned your rags; the hands that ripped them weren't kind to the fabric or your flesh. Pick something from there—they're clothes left in payment for my services. I'll feed you, then you can leave.'

I stepped back, eyeing her sharply, but Vera just shrugged.

'Don't even think of killing me, girl. It wouldn't benefit you. I won't say a word to your masters, so just do as you're told.'

With my senses on high alert, I rummaged through the old clothes, trying to pick out the cleanest and least damaged. Finally, I was dressed, and even though the mismatched items made me look like a ruffian ready for a tavern brawl, at least they were warm.

My mouth watered while I waited for her to put the food on the table, but my host was in no rush, apparently. She hobbled to the fireplace, pulling Tova's pouch from a pot and pouring a few coins on the table. 'There. I'm taking these for the food, clothes, and the days I spent watching over you.' She pushed the pouch in my direction. 'You can keep the rest.'

---

1. **Rusalka** — a water spirit; a fair maiden with blond or green hair that protects the waters and sometimes lures men into dancing with her until they die from exhaustion.

Well, that was unexpected. People rarely parted with money they thought they deserved, and I'd already mentally bid goodbye to Tova's coins. She must have noticed my surprise, because she just shrugged.

'I'm an honest woman, and assassin or not, I can see someone hurt you. I won't add to your troubles, Sana of the River,' she said casually. 'Eat, take your money, and leave. The wool merchant should be heading to Truso today. If you hurry, you can catch a ride.'

An hour later, the sun barely above the horizon, I stood on the threshold of her cottage, sweating under the collar from the sheer exhaustion of moving around. I could barely stand. Nevertheless, I bowed to my saviour.

'Makosh[2] bless your heart, Vera. I won't forget your kindness,' I said. She only shrugged once again in response before disappearing inside the cottage. My back creaked as I straightened, and I braced myself before strolling to the village centre to find the merchant.

***

He was exactly where Vera said he'd be, ready to set off. The merchant eyed me warily, his wagon packed to the brim, yet his reluctance to transport me disappeared when I held out several silver coins. The money, however, did not earn me a seat. Instead, he threw a rancid sheepskin in the back with his goods, instructing me to keep my grubby hands to myself.

What would have taken two days to travel by horse stretched to three, but even that was better than walking, and spending most of my time lying on the sheepskin was helping me recover. 'We'll be at the capital by noon,' the merchant shouted, his voice breaking through my thoughts as we stopped near the riverbank. 'Get yourself ready.'

---

2. **Makosh** — goddess of family and females, sometimes called the mother of gods.

I jumped off the wagon to go wash myself, pausing briefly to look at my reflection in the moving water. I smelled like a shepherd's daughter and looked even worse. My hair hung in oily strands, falling on the mismatched clothes stained from the natural oils in the sheepswool. I certainly wouldn't be returning to Truso in a blaze of glory—more like a dog with its tail tucked between its legs. Still, I couldn't arrive unprepared.

The small knife that I'd swiped with the clothing was worthless as a means of defence. However, with my talents, I could create something potent enough to make any Brotherhood lackey pause over forcing me to do their bidding.

The merchant looked at me strangely when I wrapped scraps of fabric around my hands and dived into a nearby ditch. Little did he know that what others thought of as common weeds was a cornucopia of ingredients for someone who knew what to look for.

I returned with a bundle of hemlock, and my companion's eyes widened. 'That stuff's poisonous! Don't let the oxen near it,' he hastily called out. When ingested, hemlock could cause weakness, vomiting, confusion, and an inability to see straight. Introduced directly into the bloodstream, however, it could lead to paralysis within minutes.

I nodded, taking a seat near the small fire he'd lit. Using the knife and a stone, I crushed the stems and leaves, allowing the juice to coat the blade before drying it over the fire. Then, I repeated the process until the entire blade was covered in an oily, black coating. Even though it was all I could muster, it would have to do.

The familiar routine had also given me time to think, and a plan slowly formed in my mind. It might not have been the *best* plan, but with its hint of viciousness, it was one I was proud of.

Without an invitation from the grand master, my return to Truso would be seen as a betrayal of the Brotherhood's rules. The risk of stumbling upon some overeager dark brother and ending up dead in a ditch was real. But even if I couldn't get the old man's permission *beforehand*, I had no doubt he would back me up. Years of serving as his shadow, a position that marked me as his right hand, had taught me a lot about the kind of man he was behind closed doors.

'I can't wait to see you again, Boyan,' I whispered, smiling at my thoughts as I tried to think of a way to alert him to my arrival while giving him time to issue me a formal invitation to return.

Then what? Who can I count on to help me with Jagon?

I quickly catalogued potential allies. Jagon controlled the chapter of poisoners and alchemists, so they'd follow wherever he led. I was sure the Blades—the Brotherhood's chapter of undercover assassins and blades for hire—were entirely under Irsha's command. And my childhood friend would sooner fall on his dagger than betray Boyan.

That left the Mules and the Observers.

The Mules liked their money. Knowing them, those smugglers and traders were most likely helping Jagon with the srebrec ore, which left the Observers as my only unknown.

'Bloody perfect,' I grunted.

The Observers were a difficult bunch—spies and troublemakers. Their intelligence and cunning often led them down individual paths, and their master, Bolko, controlled his chapter in name only.

'So, we're at an impasse . . .' I mused, looking at my weapon, 'or maybe not?'

I smiled at my thoughts. If I could persuade the mages to investigate the illegal srebrec trade, the Mules would have enough troubles to deal with to continue to support Jagon . . . The Observers, on the other hand, always followed power, and I knew exactly who could change the tide. If the king of Dagome learned he had an enemy in the Brotherhood trying to break the covenant, he would surely support the person who brought the news.

My chaotic scheme was beginning to shape itself into a plan that made my chest ache with bittersweet sadness when I realised how easily I had slipped back into my old ways, my old life. A life in which I was always scheming, always keeping people at arm's length—the grand master's shadow once again.

Well, I thought. *Welcome back, Nightshade. It's like you never left,* I thought to myself.

Chapter 7

Roksana

I left the merchant as soon as we passed the guard post at the entrance, sighing in relief when I wasn't stopped.

The city was just as I remembered. Loud, constantly busy, and filled with people trying to turn their luck into gold. I swallowed hard, nostalgia tightening my throat at the sight of market stalls blocking the street.

Here, in the poor quarter, the merchandise was mainly household goods, not-too-fresh food, and trade supplies. But as I walked towards the city centre, colourful wood replaced cloth, delicious aromas filled the air, and small but inviting shops could be found between the haggling merchants, showcasing treasures from all over the Tir ha Mor continent, not just the Lowland Kingdoms.

'Come on, make your move,' I whispered, waiting for someone to make contact. I knew they were watching, and uneasiness crawled down my spine like an army of ants, but no one greeted me.

'You look tired, traveller,' came a voice from behind as a hand brushed over mine. 'If you need a place to stay, I know the perfect inn.'

I turned. The man facing me was a common thug who likely thought he'd spotted a poor, naïve peasant girl he could snatch off the street. As beautiful as Truso was, the city had two souls. The first was hardworking and mostly honest. But the second? It was ancient and as dark as death itself. That was where the Brotherhood thrived.

Brushing my hair in what could be considered an alluring gesture, I uncovered the small tattoo just above my temple. 'What are you offering?'

The man paled, disappearing in the crowd faster than I could blink, and I smiled at how much power the small mark carried.

I passed by an old tavern, pushing my way through the crowd gathered to listen to a bard, when, this time, the tip of a blade pressed against my kidney. A slim male arm wrapped around my neck as if a lover was playfully gathering me into his embrace, and I was dragged into a dark alley.

'Welcome back, Nightshade, we missed you. But announcing your affiliation like that . . . tsk. I was forced to kill the poor bastard. And for what? The woman I remember wasn't this reckless—and certainly didn't smell like she'd crawled out a ram's arse,' he murmured, voice distorted by the mask he was wearing. 'Now, if you could be so kind, come with me before I have to cut that mark off your skin.'

I slipped my blade from its hiding place and laid its edge against the throbbing artery in my assailant's groin. 'Thank you, but no,' I replied, pressing the tip forward. 'Though perhaps you could relay a message for me?'

'Sweetheart, I'm too old for posturing. I'll make it hurt if you insist on playing with that toy. What can your little letter opener do? Shave my balls?'

'Men have always told me size doesn't matter. Oh well . . .' I chuckled, my throaty laughter giving him pause. 'Should we test to see how fast you'll be serenading Veles on your trip across the Veil when my poison fills your blood?' As if by magic, the bard in the tavern chose that moment to warble a long, earsplittingly high note. I winced. 'I wonder . . . will you sound as talented as that crooning fool?'

He stilled, and the knife pressed to my back trembled ever so slightly. 'Still as brazen as a cocksure sailor, I see. Jagon's men are looking for you, and Boyan has ordered you to leave Truso, so let's go. I'll escort you out of the city walls.'

'Is Jagon in the city?'

'No, he's rarely here. Last I heard, he went to Wiosna.' The man's throaty huff made me smile. 'It looks like both he and the king lost something there. Anyway, if I've learned anything about his habits, he'll be back within the week. Now, enough questions. You need to come with me.'

I exhaled slowly. That gave me a week to prepare.

'While I appreciate the warning, I can't leave. Tell the old man that I'm back and still loyal to him. Please request an invitation on my behalf and inform him that I'll pay my respects during the Mabon Feast.' I stepped away then, hiding my relief when he released me.

My assailant removed his mask to rub the bridge of his nose, and I recognised him as a high-ranking Observer.

'Fine, Nightshade, but know this: the old man's influence is waning. I'll bet news of your arrival is already on its way to Jagon, and you know he'll use it against Boyan. You've already broken the law by entering the city without permission. The old man will try to help you, but if you don't show up and word gets out, he's done for, and I won't forgive that,' he said.

I nodded. 'I'll be there. Just make it known that I was invited, and I'll take care of the rest.' I didn't trust him, but I had no other choice. Still, I couldn't resist indulging my curiosity. 'Do you always interpret your orders so freely?'

Amusement crinkled the corners of his eyes. 'Orders are for soldiers. I'm his shadow now, and I make my own decisions. Your presence will slow Jagon down. In fact, it already has. The bastard is currently combing the dwarven mountains looking for his lost little lamb. Boyan might value your life more than the future of the Brotherhood, but I do not. Make no mistake, I am releasing you because you are useful—for now, at least.'

'Happy to hear it. I've always dreamed of having such an ally.' The sarcasm slipped out as I looked him dead in the eye, but the man shrugged, unfazed by my tone.

'I'm your replacement, not your ally. I'll relay your request, and if Boyan still wants you out of the city, he has plenty of Blades to enforce it. My regards, Nightshade,' he said, disappearing into the crowd. My knees buckled. The biggest obstacle was out of my way. Boyan's invitation would remove the target from my back as long as I fulfilled my promise and came to see him during the feast.

I counted the days. I'd left the dwarven kingdom in the heat of summer, and—with my near drowning and the fever afterwards—my journey had taken maybe three weeks, which gave me some time. I had two, possibly three, more weeks before I had to face the Brotherhood. It wasn't enough time to enact a solid plan, but I already had a few ideas, and Jagon's absence presented the perfect opportunity to execute them undisturbed.

I started walking again, passing several shops as I skirted the affluent district, until finally arriving at an opulent building. Its artfully carved latticework announced its owner's wealth as shadowy figures moved sensuously behind darkened crystal windows, hinting at the carnal pleasures hidden inside.

My destination, the infamous House of Lilies, was a banqueting house and a theatre. However, behind its facade of lavish balls and parties, it was a brothel where the cream of Truso's society gathered to enjoy the finest and most perverse desires. Liliana prided herself on catering to her clientele without prejudice. The only rule? No one harmed her entertainers. Those who dared paid in blood, often never to be heard from again.

The sun was setting, but it was still too early for the doors to be open to the public, so I didn't expect a quick answer when I knocked.

'We're closed. Come back in two hours,' came a voice from behind the small, half-open window set just above the knocker, which, despite being shaped like a tree branch, was remarkably similar to a certain part of the male anatomy.

'Not for me, friend,' I said, slipping into the old rhythm. 'Tell the madam Nightshade is back in business.'

I reached into the sad remains of Tova's purse. The owner of Lilies' wasn't fond of being awakened before sundown, so being here this early would likely cost me a pretty penny.

'Madam's in bed,' the voice replied—but the hand that appeared through the window curled into a fist the moment a gold coin landed in its palm. 'But for such a generous patron, I'll see what I can do.'

The window shut, and I leant against the wall and started counting. I hadn't even made it to fifty when the door was yanked open.

Even with tussled hair and a dishevelled negligee, Liliana Ordon was stunning. Her signature white hair, slightly pointed ears, and eyes as blue as a cloudless summer's sky betrayed her fae roots, and although she'd never known her father, his heritage was hard to miss. She studied me for several moments, blinking and shaking her head while the doorman twiddled his thumbs.

'May I come in?' I asked, acutely aware of the protracted silence. My voice seemed to focus Lily's gaze, and she rushed towards me.

'Roksana!' she exclaimed, grabbing my collar and pulling me into a tight hug, tears flowing down her pale cheeks. 'I thought . . . they said . . . Irsha told me you'd left, but I was sure those bastards killed you.'

I stumbled forward, and we would've landed on the corridor floor if not for the helpful doorman catching us.

'Well, I'm alive, but can we talk in private?' I asked, cautiously hiding my emotions.

Liliana and I had forged our bond through shared hardship, though she was never one for overt displays of affection. After coming to a hard-won understanding, I had agreed to craft certain oils for her girls—subtle weapons to use when clients became too bold. Nothing cooled a man's ardour more than a limp dick, and if that didn't work? Well, those occasions ended with oblivion and an empty purse to go with a burning sensation that lasted well past the long walk home to their wives.

But to say Lily never showed affection wouldn't be fair. We had spent countless hours trading stories of misadventures, and in those quiet moments, she came the closest to feeling like family during my time in the Brotherhood. Well—her, and Irsha, master of the Blades and my former lover. Seeing her today was the happiest and most worrisome moment I'd ever had.

'Of course, come in,' she said before turning to the doorman. 'You there, go upstairs and tell the girls to ready the guest room.' She scrunched her nose, only now noticing the stench that surrounded me like a heavy cloud. 'And a bath. Ensure there's plenty of hot water.' To me she said, 'Why do you smell so bad?'

I chuckled, feeling something inside me ease. She seemed healthy and untroubled by Duke Tivala's thugs. 'This lost sheep found her way home in a shepherd's wagon. How else would I smell?'

It looks like Jagon was too busy chasing after my ghost to follow through with his threats, I thought.

'Are you hungry?' Lily's voice broke through my musing.

'Huh?'

'Are you hungry?' she repeated the question, and I nodded with a smile.

'Ravenous, and . . . Thank you. I was going to ask to stay for a night or two,' I said, hesitating. I didn't know how much I could share, but some things she had to know. 'I've come back with trouble on my tail. Jagon found me, and he's already tried blackmailing me with your life.'

She rolled her eyes and shrugged. 'And here I was, thinking my life had become a little too boring and predictable—no one to poison, no one to scandalise with gossip . . .' She laughed. 'So, eat, and then we'll talk. And don't you dare think about leaving. My home is yours. Stay as long as you need.'

My throat tightened. I'd just told her taking me in was dangerous, but she'd brushed it off as if it didn't matter. I followed Lily to the kitchen, fighting the overwhelming urge to turn and run away, leaving her to her comfortable life.

Her kindness, even after all these years, unravelled me, and I was terrified she'd pay the steep price for being my friend.

Chapter 8

Reynard

I knew I should wake up, but a part of me didn't want to, not yet. Her scent filled my soul, and I inhaled deeply, trailing my nose over the soft skin of her neck. Gods, she was my enemy, yet I could not resist her allure.

'Rey,' she breathed, leaning towards me.

Hair, cool and soft like golden silk, flowed through my fingers when I wrapped her thick braid around my hand to pull her closer. My Viper didn't resist. Her lips parted when I kissed them, and I wished I could freeze time. Freeze it right here in this moment, where my desire was still innocent, when I'd thought she was a healer and pondered what could have been. Now, lurking under my visceral need for her, was a fury that ruined everything.

The woman who had made me feel so alive had left me to die, and whatever spell she'd cast on me, I refused to submit to her will.

My hand tightened on her braid, yanking her away. She gasped, her hazel eyes opening wide, the green wildfire dancing in their depths captivating my soul.

'Who are you?' I demanded, rejecting her warmth.

The landscape of my dream transformed into a blizzard. Shock and disbelief flashed in her eyes, like they had in the forest, but I wasn't wrong to demand answers. I wasn't—

'Fuck!' I roared, jerking awake as pain exploded in my face.

My body arched, tangled in the sheets as I screamed, clawing at my scar, the spasms twisting my face into a rictus of pain, until I forced myself to stay still. To calm my erratic heartbeat, knowing this was the only way to stop the pain.

'Haven't you done enough, Viper? When will you stop tormenting me?' I groaned, taking slow, deep breaths. I *hated* this weakness, the pain so harsh that a tear slipped from my remaining eye. It had to be her doing—the same nightmare repeating night after night, robbing me of my sleep.

A sheen of sweat covered my skin, sticky and unpleasant, but I couldn't care less as I stared into the darkness. Ciesko's concoction, a sleeping draught he'd promised would help, was still beside my bed, tempting me. But taking it would be admitting that I no longer controlled my body or mind.

'*No.* I won't drug myself into oblivion. Once I find her, these dreams will stop,' I insisted as the pain finally settled into a familiar, manageable level.

Another promise, another lie, but I needed that shred of hope before the hopelessness of my situation drove me mad. Three weeks I'd searched, but the damn woman had disappeared without a trace. I'd sent soldiers to the borders and had Brotherhood Observers searching the city, but she'd vanished so thoroughly I half believed she was a vila sent to lead me to my doom.

The only place I had found her was in my dreams.

'Were you real, or did I offend the gods?' I whispered into the dark. Was there even a point in asking?

With one final exhale, I completed the breathing exercise Ciesko had taught me; a simple thing, but the only one that helped. No one, not even the mages or the Brotherhood poisoners, could purge the toxin from my scar. The poison, strengthened by some sort of magic, was leaking into my flesh despite the magical lattice.

Even worse, after we tried several things to ease my painful spasms, Ciesko discovered that the containment spell he'd created weakened when my emotions peaked. He taught me to slow down my heart, but with each dream encounter, I felt my control slip.

Sleep was beyond my reach, so I dragged myself out of bed, pulling on a shirt. It was too early to don my formal attire for the day, and it wouldn't be the first time my servants saw their king dressed casually. Not that it mattered what I wore here.

The entire wing was my private apartment. Several rooms linked by a long corridor granted me freedom from the court's stiff protocols. Thick carpet cushioned my footsteps, and I felt like a wandering ghost as I walked down the empty hall. I pushed on the door to my study, and it opened without a sound, revealing a hunched shadow.

A knife appeared in my hand, instinct taking over. *If it's another assassin . . .*

Sharp awareness seized me as I stalked my way over to the desk, ready to strike, until the dim fae lantern revealed the face of my visitor.

I could barely contain my laughter. My 'assassin' was drooling on the desk, ink smeared across his cheek as he snored.

Has he been here all night?

'Riordan, what in Veles' pit are you doing here?' I said, taking a rolled manuscript and swatting him on the head.

The mage looked up, giving me a myopic stare before propping himself up on his fist. 'I could ask the same.' He yawned. 'Were you dreaming of her again?'

'No. Yes. I don't want to talk about it,' I said, realising that lying to a truthseeker made no sense. 'You'd better answer my question, or I'll revoke your access to my private quarters.'

'I will as soon as you explain this.' He pulled out my new tax proposal. 'Rey,'—he sighed—'you can't lower taxes for the merchants. It will affect the income of the southern province and our trade with the orcish tribes. The council will never accept it.'

I pulled the vellum from his hands. 'And what will they do? They already call me a tyrant.' I huffed a humourless laugh. 'It was easy for them to love their king when I led our men to victory in the Second Necromancer's War, when they didn't expect me to return alive—but implement tax reforms and suddenly I'm worse than the Lich King,' I said, turning my face away from the compassion I saw in Riordan's eyes.

What I hadn't told him was that every time I faced the disgruntled nobles on the Royal Council, every time I heard them complain about the laws I passed, muttering all the while about my berserker-tainted bloodline, I thought that maybe I should have died as a hero rather than survive to become the villain.

'Stop worrying and shift your arse from my chair,' I said instead, looking at the smudged ink. 'And the next time you decide to take a nap, please refrain from slobbering all over the tax records.'

Riordan rolled his eyes and walked over to the drinks cabinet, reaching for the wine.

'The war's over, Rey. You don't have to rush; change is good, but you need to ease the nobles into it, not push them so quickly. I know your ideas will benefit Dagome, but these people are accustomed to doing as they please, not being led—and they're certainly not an army that follows orders. You'd have less trouble if you let them talk themselves into agreeing instead of employing heavy-handed military tactics to deal with the issues.'

He was right, but not only had the war ended, but our old alliances were falling apart. I knew the only way to protect my kingdom now was to make Dagome unassailable to any enemy.

'I don't have time for the soft approach, Ri. Not now. The spasms are occurring more frequently, and after the last one, Ciesko told me there's nothing more he can do. If my days are numbered, I *must* ensure that Dagome is strong enough to survive after my death.'

'We'll find her before that, Rey. She'll have the antidote,' my friend answered quietly. He picked up another document from the pile, and a portrait—a miniature of a woman with curly brown hair—fell onto my desk. He raised it to the light. 'A new distraction?"

'No, just another cornerstone of the nobility offering me his daughter,' I said, taking it, and the letter, from his hands and putting them in a drawer. 'One of the burdens I bear,' I grumbled, knowing I had no right to complain about the heavy weight of the crown.

Proposals had flooded in when the other nobles learned that Duke Tivala had taken the initiative. Now, every one of them hoped their daughter would be the next queen of Dagome. It felt like an auction, and I was the stallion they wanted to breed their future winners from.

'Rey, you'll have to take a wife eventually. Does it matter which you pick if it's just to be a transaction?' Riordan asked, and my jaw instinctively clenched.

'The problem is that I don't want it to be a "transaction." I'm not so naïve to believe she'll love me, but I want the woman I take to my bed to at least like me. And if she bears my child, I want someone strong enough to be a good regent. Is that too much to ask?' My words sounded harsh, even to my ears, and I felt a tinge of guilt when his eyebrows drew closer. Still, I'd had enough of this subject.

I grabbed the scout reports, hoping to distract him. 'We need to focus on this.' I gave him several files, ignoring his raised eyebrows.

'You want me to read them right now?'

'No. I want you to take them and read them in your *own* office. It's the middle of the night, so maybe you should go home before the servants start thinking you're my lover?'

The bastard's laughter annoyed me almost as much as his eye roll. 'Forgive me, Your Majesty, for working tirelessly to find the woman of your dreams. And no offence, but I prefer my partners to be soft and feminine.' He quirked an eyebrow. 'Though I'm sure I could find you a dark fae if you want to follow your brother's example and divide your affection.'

'I see you've grown brazen. You must be ready to accept the position of royal mage, then. The paperwork is still in my drawer—all you have to do is sign it. In fact, I'm sure it'll make your grandfather quite happy,' I said with a lazy smile, knowing he dreaded taking on his official duties.

'I'm not ready . . .'

'Yes, you are. Besides, aren't you already behaving like it's official? Walking into my private quarters like they were your stables, advising me to take a male lover . . .' I quipped, feigning displeasure, but we both knew I welcomed his visits and boldness that made being the king feel less . . . lonely.

'You know, thinking about it, I suddenly feel a powerful urge to return home,' Riordan said with a smirk. 'Don't stay up too long—you'll need a clear head if you want to pass this decree tomorrow.'

He left, and I took the opportunity to read through more paperwork once I was alone. The latest intelligence from my spies revealed nothing new. Młot was still sending shipments somewhere south. I didn't know who was helping him, but the route he used couldn't be more dangerous, passing through the swamplands on our border, where even my most skilled trackers lost the trail.

Piran's Swamp sprawled between the Care'etavos Empire, the Kingdom of Lumivitae, and the Dukedom of Tivalaran—a festering no-man's-land crawling with creatures too ancient and deadly to name. Entire patrols vanished there before they even sensed danger.

What frustrated me most was not knowing which of those realms the srebrec was destined for. The dark fae of Care'etavos and the light fae of Lumivitae both relied heavily on magic, making them less likely to want large quantities of the ore—yet their extensive knowledge of its uses meant they surely understood its potential. And then there was Tivalaran and its ever-irritating duke, a constant political thorn in my side.

The uncertainty gnawed at me, but unless the trade route passed through Dagome, I couldn't use force to intercept the shipments without giving my neighbours reason to start a war. Tivalaran was the only place I could enter. Well, I *could* have if the old duke hadn't refused me. An old law passed by some idiot years ago had granted the dukedom vassal status rather than integrating it fully into Dagome, effectively tying my hands. *I need a reason, one the duke can't refuse,* I thought, pulling out the contract he'd sent.

Marrying Tivala's only living child would end the vassal state conundrum, giving me full control over the fertile region, with its easy access to the sea and trade with the rest of Tir ha Mor. It was a perfect political choice—except I felt nothing but disdain for the woman who allowed herself to become a pawn in the political games between her father and the Crown.

I strode over to the window and forced it open. My breath misted the air, but the wind from the river and the night's chill calmed my senses, bringing with it the longing I'd spent too long trying to hide.

'Orm, you bloody bastard, if you only knew how I envy you,' I muttered, closing my eye as I recalled a memory from five years ago. It had been late autumn when Annika, my brother's mate, had stood in Dagome's throne room and challenged the world for her Anchors. It was at that moment that I realised the brother I'd pitied had found something I craved—a woman with integrity and courage. She'd stood by her men to the bitter end, even facing down a goddess to save their lives.

The moon shone on my face with its cold, unfeeling light, deepening the shadows lurking in every corner, but my attention was caught by the shooting star that cut across the sky, disappearing over the horizon. As futile as it was to wish upon a star, deep down, I hoped that maybe it was a sign that Inga Tivala was the woman who could stand by my side. Perhaps I was just fighting fate.

'Fine, let's give it a chance,' I muttered to myself.

I wrote a quick note asking my secretary to go ahead and invite all the noble families to the Winter Solstice Ball, something I'd been holding off on. It was still almost four months away, giving me a chance to stall the nobles and see my potential bride before deciding on my future queen.

Shuffling through the rest of my correspondence, the last letter made me smile. It was from my brother, and the gods knew I needed good news. They'd finally convinced Annika to bear their child, and though no one knew whether it was my brother's or Alaric's—the third in their relationship and one of Annika's other Anchors—the love was evident in every word.

I was happy for him, even if it meant I wouldn't see him as often. Orm already complained that Vahin, his dragon, refused to take Annika into the sky or leave her side for longer than the few hours it took to patrol the Ozar Kingdom.

'And that's how you finally get grounded.' I chuckled, feeling a warmth slowly spread throughout my chest, chasing the bad mood away.

I signed a few more documents, placing them in a neat stack for my assistant before deciding to go back to bed. I didn't want to answer any questions if, once again, they found me working through the night. As I stood to leave, one final issue came to mind.

'*Arrange a meeting with Boyan*,' I wrote at the bottom of my notes. It was time the grand master of the Dark Brotherhood updated me on his search for my mystery woman.

If I were ever going to be wed, I couldn't be dreaming of kissing another. I had to kill this yearning, because my heart wasn't as big as my brother's. It could only fit one person, and it had better be the woman I married.

Chapter 9

Roksana

G *ods, it feels so good to be clean.*

Lily had insisted I wash up in her room with its private bath chamber, and I'd spent the entire afternoon here. After a hearty lunch and soaking for hours in the lilac-scented water, I was now curled up on a wide, plush sofa with a glass of the sweetest autumn wine I'd ever tasted. My skin was soft, almost glowing from all the oils the maid had used. Only my hands still betrayed my work as an herbalist and healer for the dwarven king. The stains from crushing herbs had refused to leave my fingertips, no matter how hard the poor woman had scrubbed.

'Feeling better?' Liliana entered the room, the subtle scent of her lily of the valley perfume trailing after her.

'Much better, thank you. There's even some skin left.' I laughed, presenting my pink complexion. 'The dwarves are good people, but their idea of luxury is a communal bath in frigid water. Only Tova understood that women need to soak every now and again . . .' I stuttered into silence when her eyebrow raised in quiet judgment.

'Someone . . . special?' she asked.

I nodded. 'Yes, but not in the way you're thinking. Tova is . . . I don't know, he's like a cross between a grumpy older brother and a guardian spirit. And he can fix anything,' I said, the conversation with Lily flowing as if I'd never left. 'He may join me at some point—at least, I hope so. But don't worry, I'll find a place for us to stay so that I'm not abusing your hospitality for too long.'

I took a sip of my drink, letting the blissful sweetness dissolve on my tongue.

'You're always welcome, and if this Tova made an impression on you, he's more than welcome to stay as well. We have plenty of things to fix,' she quipped, moving closer and placing her hand on my knee. 'Now, tell me what troubles you, and I'll do my best to help.'

I blew out a breath. 'Jagon knows I killed Ignac Tivala—and how. He's using that to blackmail me. I'm the ace up his sleeve for a repeat performance, but this time . . . it's a bigger fish.' I tightened my grip on the glass. 'You're his bargaining chip. He plans on making you the scapegoat and is threatening to tell the old duke you orchestrated his son's death. I'll find a way to silence the bastard, but we need to be ready for anything. You need more guards and . . . an escape route.'

'So, you returned because of me.' She sighed before giving me a smile. 'I won't run away, Roksana. Jagon is a piece of shit, and we'll deal with him together. Now, calm down and promise me you won't follow his orders. Since the new king took over, life has changed, and Duke Tivala has faded into obscurity. He's not the same man who'd silenced the kingdom while his son went on a killing spree.'

'It still won't stop the old bastard from hiring someone to knife you in a dark alley or poison your wine.'

'And who would he hire? One of Irsha's Blades? He would never . . .' She bristled, stuttering a bit before resuming her usual tone. 'I mean, all you have to do is to tell Irsha. He wouldn't let any of his men harm your friend.'

'That's true, but I still had to return to Truso so I could tell him, no?' I quipped. She looked at me sharply, a flash of uncertainty in her gaze. 'Lily, don't worry. I'm not going to fall into Jagon's hands or give him another card to use against me. I have a plan that will hopefully distract him from his little game. And you won't be put in harm's way.'

'Oh, now *that* sounds like fun. Does Boyan know? I can send him a message to let him know his favourite shadow is back to cause mischief,' she teased.

'Oh, he knows. I'm just laying low until I receive an official invitation. It won't take long, so like I said, there's nothing to worry about,' I said, hoping I hadn't overestimated the old man's affection for me.

'Thank the gods, then. Let's drink to that.' She poured some wine and raised her glass. 'To the good old times. To revenge, blushing maidens, their poisonous kisses, and beating the bastards down.'

'No more poisonous kisses or virgin dances, please . . . Gods, that was humiliating.' I chuckled, remembering my clumsy performance meant to lure Duke Tivala's heir into taking me to his secret lair. His death had marked the beginning of my friendship with Lily, the only person in the entire city willing to stop the man responsible for the disappearance of several young women.

Ignac Tivala had been a deviant of the worst kind—someone who had loved his solitude, and using women as a canvas for his carving knife. While Liliana had devised a scheme to lure him to her establishment, I had come up with the poison that had become the crown jewel of my collection—a lip rouge I named *Wrath of Lilies*, so toxic that only my magic could neutralise it. When he kissed me, I let him ravage my lips, then smiled as he suffered, feeling nothing but satisfaction at the perverse justice of it all.

Lost in the reminiscence, I barely heard Lily's next words.

'I know you needed to leave, but I'm still mad that you just disappeared. That bloody note you left me—"*I'm fine and will contact you when I'm settled*"—did absolutely nothing to help. Did your arms drop off? Because we never heard from you again.' Lily's voice had slowly risen until she was almost shouting by the last word. 'When I went to the Brotherhood to ask about what happened, Irsha told me that you'd just thrown your bondage price on the grand master's table and left. Gods, Sana! He had such a haunted look on his face, I thought the Brotherhood had had you killed and covered it up!'

Lily turned away abruptly, then opened her wardrobe and pulled out an exquisite shimmering gown that highlighted her natural beauty.

I just stared, open-mouthed, wondering what to say. I couldn't share everything, but I knew I had to provide an explanation for my silence. 'I was afraid Jagon would hurt you if he knew we'd spoken, and . . . I was afraid you'd talk me out of leaving. I'd had enough of a life where I had to kill for every moron and his donkey who paid me. Then that bastard . . . he was so *intense*. Jagon behaved like I belonged to him, not as a poisoner or apprentice, but as his woman,' I spat.

She whirled back around, frowning at me, and I instantly regretted telling her. I'd intended to take that secret to the grave, but I couldn't hold it in any longer. 'I fended him off, but Irsha would have noticed and challenged him eventually, then Boyan would have intervened . . .' I said before adding quietly, 'You know I never wanted that life in the first place. But then I left, and I realised the grass wasn't any greener on the other side, and that I missed you and this city.'

Liliana looked at me for a long moment, sadness deepening the bright blue of her eyes. She understood. Her career wasn't exactly what young girls dreamed of either.

'So, you ran away. Now you're back, and you've landed in the middle of a vicious battle for the Brotherhood. The grand master is ill—some say it's the graveyard cough, others that he's been poisoned, but the dogs are fighting over the bones, so to speak.'

'That explains why Jagon's behaving like he already owns the place and insisted on my return to Truso without Boyan's invitation,' I said.

For Lily's benefit, I explained what had happened in Wiosna, skipping over the name of the target Jagon wanted me to kill.

'Don't tell me he wants you to kill Irsha. I can't imagine Boyan would let that happen without an official challenge,' she commented while I helped lace her bodice.

'No, but the position of grand master has to be his primary focus, and if Irsha still harbours feelings for me, I could be used as leverage against him.'

'Well, one way or another, you're here. Okay, tell me the perfect plan I'm sure you've come up with, and we'll get it done,' Lily said, sitting next to me.

'Not perfect—half-baked at best. I need to weaken Jagon's position. He has deals that he knows can't see the light of day or fall under the scrutiny of the mages. That's where I'll start. Do they still hold Petitioners' Day at the Court of Aether?'

'Yes, every Wednesday, but what does the Court of Aether have to do with any of this?' Lily asked, confusion marring her features.

I had a one-word answer: 'Srebrec.'

'Veles' pit. Yes, you mentioned that.' She sat on the edge of the sofa, clearly invested in my story, and I couldn't help but smile.

'Młot is trading it. Jagon is the middleman, but I bet he's getting a big slice of the cake. So imagine how happy the mages will be knowing someone in our kingdom is helping sell ore that could put magical collars on their necks. If they disrupt his plans, Jagon will have to find another way to move his merchandise, and that should take him out of Truso for a while.'

'Well then, you'll need some decent clothes. Those mages are snobbish bastards and won't allow beggars into their public areas. We'll find you something appropriate to wear tomorrow,' she said, pausing at the sound of the gong announcing the start of the business day. Lily stood with the elegance of a dancer, turning back towards me. 'Would you like to join us downstairs? Who knows, maybe someone will catch your eye and warm your bed tonight.' She winked.

I burst out laughing. I was in no shape or mood to enjoy the pleasures her business was famous for.

'No, thank you,' I said, rising slowly.

Liliana gave a small nod. 'If you change your mind, simply come downstairs. Our people will be happy to see you.'

She left the room, and I stood alone, the weight of exhaustion settling over me. There was no point in lingering in her chamber, so I made my way to my own.

Drawn to the window, I looked out at the city. The nightlife in Truso blossomed with the lighting of its pleasure district's myriad torches. Some opportunistic soul had added a line of fae lanterns to the noble quarter, for obvious reasons, even extending it to the illustrious heights of the king's palace. At this early hour, people were still rushing around, determined to finish their business before seeking entertainment. I saw masked men and women in rich clothing heading to The House of Lilies, while soft music and the sounds of laughter filled the street each time the doorman answered their knocks.

The noise faded into the distance as I turned away.

Sleep claimed me quickly once I hit the bed, deep and dreamless, and I welcomed its sweet embrace.

***

A hand pressed against my mouth, waking me from my slumber, and I lashed out, hammering a fist into the dark figure leaning over me. With a grunt, the man stepped back, and I leapt out of bed, reaching for the knife I'd left under my pillow.

'For fuck's sake, Sana, it's just me,' a deep masculine voice muttered next to my bed, a voice I instantly recognised.

'Are you out of your mind, Irsha? I could have killed you!' I snapped, throwing the knife on the table, only to squeal when he grabbed me and I ended up plastered to the broad chest of the master of the Blades. I couldn't help sighing as his arms locked around me.

I'd missed this massive man with his infectious smile, tanned skin that shone like a polished bronze, and deep brown eyes. He'd stood by me even when I was a fumbling apprentice in Jagon's workshop. After a moment of hesitation, I closed my eyes and let the familiar sense of security seep into me with the peace of his steadfast friendship.

A peace that, unfortunately, didn't last long before he laid into me.

'You came back to Truso, and where did you go? To a wretched brothel—as if you forgot the way to my house. Veles' pit, Sana.' He leant back, but his hands still rested on my shoulders. 'Did I hurt you somehow and you didn't want to see me?'

I opened my mouth to speak, but he put a finger on my lips. 'No, spare me that gutless shit. Whatever your explanation is, we're family, and family doesn't disappear like a fucking ghost and then ignore you when they return. If I hadn't been there when Boyan's shadow reported to him, I still wouldn't know.'

He said it all with such accusation in his voice that I lowered my head in shame. There had been a time when Irsha and I were lovers. Those times were long gone, but returning to Truso was making me realise that in my desperation to escape Jagon's clutches, I'd really hurt those I'd left behind.

'I didn't want to put you in a difficult position,' I said, pulling a loose thread on his shirt to avoid looking him in the eye.

'I'm the master of the Blades. If anyone has a problem with whom I'm seen with, they can discuss it with my daggers. Sana, look at me . . . Please, sweetheart, look at me,' he said, waving his hand in front of my nose, making me squint. He smirked at my pouting expression before grasping my chin and tilting it up. 'I missed you, Nightshade. I missed you so fucking much. Without my troublemaker to cause mischief, the Brotherhood just hasn't felt like home.'

Irsha's grip tightened, a frown appearing on his face before he released me, his fingers trailing over the faint fingerprints still visible on my neck. 'They're dead, I presume?' he asked, smiling when I nodded. 'Good, it'll spare me searching for the bastards,' he said, pushing me onto the bed before jumping onto it next to me.

'You could at least take your boots off,' I said, rolling my eyes.

He shrugged. 'Like that ever bothered you before.'

'Times have changed. I'm a sophisticated woman now, a healer for the dwarven king, and I won't tolerate a dirty bastard in my bed,' I said, doing my utmost to keep a straight face.

Irsha turned to the side, his eyes narrowing as he looked at me. Uncertainty flashed in his gaze, as if he was unsure if I was joking. Seeing the deadly Blade looking so lost, I couldn't help but chuckle.

'You're an arsehole, Roksana. That certainly hasn't changed. Fine, maybe I should visit Lily. She'd ask me *nicely* to remove my clock, boots, and anything else she wanted.' He lay back with his hands under his head and released a deep, relaxed sigh. 'Just like the good old days.'

'Keep Lily out of this,' I said, swatting his shoulder. 'Someone will think you're getting sentimental in your old age, Blade,' I said, mimicking his posture. 'Since you're here, make yourself useful and tell me what's going on in the Brotherhood. I want to know why Jagon feels bold enough to go behind Boyan's back.'

'The usual bullshit. We're getting ready for a change in leadership. Boyan's gotten weak; the graveyard cough's made it hard for him to lead the Brotherhood, so the masters are fighting for his seat. Jagon is leading the race, and my Blades are the only ones resisting.'

'But the old man's not dead yet,' I said, feeling protective of the grand master.

'No, but he can't even finish a sentence without coughing up half his lungs.' Irsha seemed to mull something over before turning towards me. 'Jagon's got a backer with enough money to buy out the Mules, and half of the Observers are tempted by the gold being thrown around. I fear I'll have to bow my head to that bastard soon enough.'

There was a bitterness in his tone that hadn't been there when I left Truso, and I took a moment to study my first true friend. A web of wrinkles marred the corners of his eyes, making him look tired. Irsha had aged, but worse, he just appeared defeated. I reached out and stroked his cheek.

'How bad is it?'

'Bad, Sana. So bad, I wonder whether I made a mistake not following you when you left the Brotherhood,' he murmured, pressing his cheek into my palm.

'Then I'll fix it. I don't know how yet . . . but I know where to start,' I said, smiling before pushing him off the bed. 'Now, shift your arse and go home. Ask the old man to get the Observers off my back. I have places to be, preferably in secret. Oh, and when I officially present myself to the Brotherhood, act as if you're seeing me for the first time.'

Irsha raised his eyebrow before locking me in another of his famous bear hugs.

'You've barely arrived, and things are already looking up. Are you sure you don't want me to stay? I'm better at cuddling now, and you could tell me all about the havoc you've wrought while you were away,' he said, grinning.

I swatted him. 'Go away, you menace—and remember what I said. As for cuddling, you might have gotten better at it, but I bet your snoring's worse. So off you go, Blade. I choose to sleep alone.'

He rolled his eyes and leapt onto the windowsill. 'Spoilsport. See you later, Nightshade. Don't start trouble without me.'

Chapter 10

Roksana

Lily cautioned me not to expect much from the Court of Aether, but after engaging considerable resources to get here, I wasn't going to give up. Three hours of sitting around waiting while they let everyone else in, and I'd had enough.

'I swear, if they brush me off again, I'm going to pour rowan tree tincture in their well. Let's see if they notice me then, between their runs to the privy,' I muttered, closing my eyes and leaning my head against the cold wall.

'That wouldn't be advisable, and would make everyone's life difficult,' answered a voice from above.

My eyes immediately snapped open. I hadn't heard him arrive, but a young man in an ornate kaftan gazed down at me with unbridled amusement. Uneasiness built in my core under his scrutiny, and then I felt it—a gentle hand combing through my memories.

'Stop that this instant. I didn't give permission for you to violate my privacy,' I sneered, realising he was a psychic mage, rudely looking through my mind.

'Interesting. You blocked me. Most ordinary mages can't even detect my presence. Who taught you?'

I opened my mouth to tell him he wasn't the first mage to try it, and that I'd paid a pretty penny to the dark fae to learn to shield my thoughts, but he didn't give me a chance.

'Never mind, you can tell the council when they ask. They'll see you now. What's your name, mage?'

My fists tightened. I'd been made to sit here, flattening my arse against an unforgiving stone because they were too busy to listen to a commoner. But now that they thought I was a mage . . .

'You're mistaken. I'm no mage,' I said, brushing my hair back to uncover the small Brotherhood rune.

The man's brows shot up. 'What kind of fool do you take me for? Come with me,' he said before muttering under his breath, 'An unclassified mage at your age. Gods, this won't end well.' He stopped mid-sentence and grabbed my elbow, turning me to look at him. 'You know about the agreement? The one that states the Brotherhood must surrender any and every mage it finds to the Court of Aether?'

I blinked, surprised by the revelation. That was news to me. I thought Boyan forbade contracting anyone before puberty because he had a conscience, not because he had to wait to see if they manifested gifts. It made perfect sense. Why train a child and introduce it to the Brotherhood's secrets if you had to surrender them to the mages at the first flicker of power?

Again, the mage didn't give me time to answer, hustling me along, and his dismissiveness rubbed me the wrong way. *If I didn't need your help to get in, I'd teach you some manners,* I thought. Still, instead of bristling and posturing, my lips curled into my most enticing smile as I meekly followed him.

'Oh, you think that's interesting?' I asked. 'I have more secrets to spill, and I bet your friends will be delighted.'

'They aren't my friends, or yours, so behave. Consider this a warning. Most council members won't be happy over this revelation, especially when given in such a boastful tone.' He motioned to the guard and whispered in his ear. The man saluted, rushing away, and my new companion gestured me onwards.

'Of course, my lord. I would ask for your name, as I'm sure you already know mine after your . . . *inspection.*'

'Bogdan Rescorla,' he answered shortly, leading me into a meeting room where two men and a woman were packing their quills and parchment with utterly bored expressions. After a moment of confusion, the man sitting at the head of the table frowned, his fingers tapping rhythmically on the polished surface.

'I told you we're done for today. You were supposed to send the applicants away, not bring one here,' he said briskly.

'This isn't just an applicant, Lord Otokar. She's a mage . . . from the Dark Brotherhood,' my guide answered, nodding his head in a slight bow.

'Thank you for seeing me,' I said. 'My name—'

Otokar interrupted me with a raised hand, addressing Bogdan. 'I'm sorry, from the Brotherhood? What nonsense is this? Does this woman claim to be a mage?' His angry glare promised me retribution for the reckless claim.

'No, my lord. But I scanned her thoughts before she shielded herself. She is a mage.'

Bogdan's words made Otokar gasp, and he immediately turned to his compatriots to start a whispered conversation.

I clapped my hands to quickly regain their attention. 'Excuse me! I'm no mage. I can see aether, yes, but that's not the reason I'm here. Now, will you hear me out?'

They paused, looking at me with such bewilderment that I wondered if they heard a word I'd said. *Gods, why do mages have to be such arseholes?*

I forced a smile. 'I don't work for the Brotherhood anymore. For the last five years, I've been working as a healer in Wiosna. I came to petition for their h—'

The man at the head of the table raised his hand, silencing me . . . again. My jaw was painfully tight as I tried to contain my anger, mentally calling them every nasty name under the sun, this time allowing Bogdan to listen.

'The dwarven kingdom isn't under our jurisdiction. Whatever's happening there, we have no hand nor interest in it. How long have you been a mage?' Otokar said as the other two nodded in agreement.

'You'll soon have an interest in it when you find yourself bound in augurec manacles. Młot is mining srebrec, forging it into weapons to use against mages and selling it to anyone who wants it,' I said, pausing to let my words to sink in. They all looked at me like I was an annoying bug. 'For the gods' sakes, I came here to inform you that you're *in danger*, not discuss my abilities.'

'Mind your words . . . and your thoughts. I warned you,' Bogdan hissed from beside me.

I spun towards him. 'Go f . . . find somewhere your opinion is wanted,' I snapped, turning back to the council.

'Listen, it isn't some small amount. He's been mining it for months. In fact, he's dug out so much of it, the aether flux is killing his people,' I said. 'It's a nasty death. My infirmary was full of them—and not just miners, but ordinary people, too. So many have died because of his greed. You have to cut off this trade before any more perish—'

'It is not for us to intervene,' Otokar answered nonchalantly. 'As for the ore, it's probably of inferior quality, anyway.'

I saw red. 'Do you have *any* self-preservation instincts? What inferior quality? Its aether shines so brightly that it puts the beacon fires on

Kupala's Night[1] to shame. He's selling the purest srebrec, and has mined so much of it that it'll turn all the mages in Truso into mumbling idiots drawing symbols in the air! Don't you care?'

All three mages suddenly turned in my direction.

'Srebrec doesn't have its own aether,' Otokar said. 'It absorbs it from mages. The stronger the mage, the stronger the aura . . . and the stronger the srebrec glows. Tell me, have you felt weaker when you were near it?' he asked. When I gaped at him, stunned by what he'd just said, he snapped his fingers. 'Bogdan, check her mind.'

I instantly snapped my mental barriers shut, making Bogdan wince as he rubbed his temple.

'I can't. She's blocked me, my lord. That's why I brought her here. It looks like the Brotherhood failed to declare a mage of the High Order in their ranks.'

Three angry gasps followed my guide's answer.

'Don't you people ever *listen*? I'm not a mage. I've never been trained!' I shouted.

'Training doesn't make you a mage; it only hones your skills,' Otokar said distractedly.

The female mage chimed in, 'She must be tested. What if we've missed another conduit?'

'Tested? I wouldn't trust a Brotherhood mongrel with our mages,' the third one said. 'Bogdan, take her to the prison, and then we'll decide.'

Otokar waved him off. 'Oh, grow a pair. What can she do? Pickpocket your trinkets? I'll assign her as a battle mage if she passes the test.'

I looked at them, completely lost. How could they be missing the point? It all felt so surreal. 'You really don't care, do you?'

---

1. **Kupala's Night** — an ancient holiday celebrating the summer equinox with high fires and fertility rituals.

I stepped back as Otokar approached me, wondering how big a mistake I'd made coming here. *Has the Brotherhood paid them to look the other way?* That would be disastrous. I shook my head, taking another step back when he reached for me. 'Keep your hands off me,' I snapped, avoiding his grasp. 'I'm not going with you!'

I heard the door behind me open, but I focused on the mage weaving a thick web of spells in front of me. I could see the strands of aether glistening between his fingers, and my hand wandered to the pouch next to my belt, ready to throw some *sleeper's ash* in his face.

'There's no need for such unseemly behaviour, Otokar. Go back to your seat,' a gentle, mature voice commanded, and the three mages sagged as if someone had cut their strings.

I turned around. A tall man around my age, with striking auburn hair and eyes as green as a spring meadow, stood behind me, observing my reaction with unbridled curiosity. Noticing that he had my attention, he gestured to the door.

'Come, my lady. It's time we had a proper discussion.'

'Master Riordan, you can't! She's dangerous . . .' the chairman exclaimed, but my saviour only smirked.

'Oh, I know she is. A Brotherhood member candidly coming to the mages' court?' He sounded so pleased with himself that I studied him closely. 'However, she's clearly not stupid. I can't say that for the other people in this room,' he said, pursing his lips. 'Otokar, I outrank all three of you combined. If you try to stop me, I'll ensure the three of you can never again stuff your pockets by selecting only the most . . . *enticing* petitions to grant.'

No one moved an inch, confirming my suspicions that bribery played a role in their selective hearing.

Riordan smirked. 'I thought so,' he said, leading us out. The door slammed shut behind us and I exhaled, a wave of relief washing over me.

'Riordan?' I asked, following the man. 'As in the royal mage, Riordan? I thought you'd be older . . . and greyer,' I blurted out before I could stop myself.

His mouth fell open at my remark. Then I saw his lips twitch in suppressed amusement as a guard snickered behind me.

'You're thinking of Riordan Arendell, my grandfather,' he said.

'I'm sorry, it was a little confusing,' I replied, trying to keep up. My silk dress kept wrapping itself around my knees, slowing me down.

'Yes, my mother wanted to honour her father, thinking he would be long dead before the name could confuse anyone. As you can see, she was gravely mistaken,' he jested, opening a set of heavy doors. 'After you, my lady. I'm dying to hear what you can tell me about the situation in Wiosna.'

For the first time since I'd come here, I felt a glimmer of hope.

'I'll tell you everything you want to know as long as you promise to help,' I said, entering the surprisingly small room.

Riordan gestured to a chair. 'Let's start with your name. I can't promise you anything, but it would help if I knew what we're dealing with. If it's easier for you, I can read it directly from your mind,' he offered, and for a split second, I felt my heart stutter to a halt, hoping he wouldn't do that.

'My name is Roksana Regnav, and no, thank you, I'd appreciate it if you stayed away from my mind. I didn't come here to lie, and telling you all I know about the illegal trade is in my best interests. You don't need to know my motivations.'

He passed me a goblet of wine, and I took it, grateful to have something to hold in my trembling hands.

'Eloquently put, but I feel I must warn you that I'm a high-order truthseeker. Even if inactive, my magic will tell me if you lie, and then I'll be forced to use my spells to find the truth. If you still wish to continue, then I'm all ears.'

I nodded, then took a sip of wine and detailed everything I knew about the mine, the accidents, and the ore. I told him about the wagons leaving Wiosna for the south and the increased patrols that accompanied each departure.

'And why is halting this srebrec trade important to you?' he finally asked.

I raised my eyebrow. 'Let me see . . . what kind of lie would ease your mind, Master Riordan?'

'Fair enough.' He chuckled. 'Okay, you've shared enough for me to investigate the matter. Now, we have one last issue to tackle,' he said, giving me a long, assessing stare. 'How long have you known you can channel aether, and exactly *what* are we going to do with you, Mistress Regnav?'

Chapter 11

Roksana

I returned much later than expected, and all was silent in The House of Lilies. Not wanting to disturb the resting entertainers, I grabbed a quick snack from the kitchen and went straight to my room. There was a lot to think about. Discovering my magic was stronger than I'd ever thought possible was one thing, but being forced to attend the next student intake at the University of Magic was entirely different.

Before sending me home, Riordan had drawn a small rune on my wrist—a harmless beacon that would activate if I didn't enter the university on recruitment day, allowing him to find me. It was that or be dragged away for testing as Otokar had wanted.

Sitting on the small chair in front of the vanity in my room, I played with a hairbrush, uncertainty and a hint of disappointment staring back at me when I looked in the mirror.

Is my magic worth it?

I wanted to learn, but what I'd receive in exchange was another leash, another master to follow. Still, this deep-seated need in my core grew stronger with each passing year, making it almost impossible to resist. If I were truthful with myself, I'd have to admit that behind my desire to help the dwarves was a compulsion to explore the power I'd so long denied. Purging poisons was no longer enough—maybe it never had been.

'I heard you'd returned. Any luck?' Lily glided into the room and took the brush from my hands, looking at my reflection in the mirror.

'Frankly? I have no idea, but it definitely didn't go as planned,' I said, letting her gentle hands calm the turmoil in my mind as she unbraided my hair and deftly brushed it.

She chuckled. 'Care to elaborate, or do I have to squeeze every drop of information out of you?'

I sighed. 'I told them about the ore, and they didn't care—well, all except one. His name is Riordan, and he seemed reasonable. That is, until he forced me into becoming the university's newest mage recruit.'

'What?' Lily nearly dropped the brush, and I realised I'd never told her about my gift.

'I can see aether, and it helps with my poisons. That's my big secret. It's how I could kill Tivala using poison on my lips without dying. I thought that was all I could do, but the council thinks I'm some high-order mage, and now they want me tested . . .' I hid my face in my hands, overwhelmed by the situation.

I waited for more questions, but they never came. Instead, Lily resumed her careful brushing. I raised my head and met her eyes in the mirror.

'Why do I get the feeling you knew?'

Lily's hand stilled for a moment. 'I didn't, but I suspected,' she said. 'We all have our secrets, and I knew you'd tell me when you were ready, but the real question is, did you agree?'

'I wasn't given a choice. Besides, it's what I've always wanted. To learn about my gift. I need to explore and figure out how to harness the power I feel at my fingertips. So maybe it's not that bad?'

She shook her head. 'I don't know. You can't ride two horses, Sana, at least not these horses. The Brotherhood and the mages coexist in a delicate balance. The rules are set in stone to prevent conflicting interests. If you disturb that, it won't just be your life in danger—the repercussions may affect all of Truso if they start to fight over you.'

Lily's concerns echoed my own.

'I can't do much about it now, though I'll fix what I can. But to do that, I need to see the king,' I said, hissing when Lily's hand tightened on my hair.

'What?' She blanched. 'Gods give me strength, why him?'

I turned to face her. 'Because he might be interested in finding out someone's plotting treason and wants him dead?'

'Jagon wanted you to kill the *king*? Oh gods, that's a breach of the covenant. Sana, think this over! This will destroy the Brotherhood.'

'That's why I need to see him in person,' I said, smiling when I saw the confusion in Lily's eyes. 'If he learns through a third party or an anonymous letter, he'll go after the Brotherhood, but if a dark sister came to him with the warning, risking her life . . .'

'You want him to believe Jagon's gone rogue and the Brotherhood is innocent?'

'Yes, and that we'll find out who's behind the threat on his life. I know Jagon's working for someone powerful—Irsha visited me last night and confirmed it. So if I'm going to remove Jagon, I'll have to take care of his employer, too. Preferably before they come after me.'

'You're playing with fire, Sana. You really think the king will listen to you, let alone take your words seriously?'

'Wouldn't you listen to someone skilled enough to enter your bedroom and who *wasn't* trying to kill you?' I tried to grin to cover the unease I felt about my plan. 'I'll offer my services to help him expose his enemies in exchange for his protection from Tivala. Then, once King Reynard eliminates the mastermind behind all this, I'll point to Jagon as the rogue who took money for his life.'

I grasped her hands, feeling guilty about how much my admission had upset her.

'Lily, everything will be fine. I'll tell the king it was Boyan's idea and that he's cleaning house. I know how all of this sounds, but I'm trying to protect us.'

'You're bloody insane and will get yourself killed. Mages, the Brotherhood, and now the king . . . How are you going to juggle them all? Even if this works, what if Boyan dies? Jagon . . . you know he's the likeliest candidate to become the next grand master.' Lily pulled away and paced the room.

'Jagon will never replace Boyan as long as I'm alive. I'll kill him if I have to.'

There were only two ways to remove a chapter or grand master without the entire Brotherhood hunting you down—a vote of no confidence or the challenge of combat. Not that I stood a chance in either.

Lily gave me a sharp look. 'Let's hope it doesn't come to that. Still, for your plan to work, you have to get to the king first. How do you intend to do that? He's increased his guards since his accident.'

'With enough sleeping powder to tranquillise an army?' I chuckled when she frowned. 'Alright, I had planned to ask Irsha if any of his men could sneak me inside.'

Lily looked at me for a long time before she closed her eyes and shook her head. 'I don't know if you're insane or inspired, but if I can't stop you, I may have a way to help you. Don't ask Irsha. If they caught him . . . it's easier to explain a single woman than the Blades' master,' she said, the protectiveness in her voice surprising me. 'I know a man who works in the palace and has a way into the king's quarters, but once you're in his private wing, the rest will be up to you.'

'That's better than I'd hoped for.'

'Good. I'll leave for now. Get yourself ready. I'll have my contact come for you around midnight.'

I watched her go, then set myself to the task of braiding my hair. Lily was right. Most of my plan equated to 'fucking around and finding out,' but what else could I do? I had no money, no influence, and my friends were in danger because of *me*.

But luck was on my side—I'd made it to Truso and escaped the Court of Aether intact. Maybe after my ordeal in the forest, Arachne, the goddess of fate, was finally smiling down at me.

That I remembered little of what happened that day was a blessing. It was almost as if my mind was forcing me to forget the feeling of being helpless under those abusive hands. The more time passed, the more my memories blurred. That is, all except one . . . the memory of the man with grey eyes felt different, but maybe I only remembered him specifically because I'd killed him.

I rolled my shoulders, brushing off the uneasy feeling the thought brought, and focused on the task at hand. I had to present myself not as a threat, but as an *opportunity*. That meant no visible weapons and a simple kirtle instead of what I'd normally worn when I was in the Dark Brotherhood. I needed something modest, practical, and feminine, with many pockets to conceal those nonexistent weapons . . .

'The perfect outfit for an audience with the king.' I smiled at my reflection while I finished pinning my braid into a crown. The rumours were that Reynard was an imposing man but chivalrous to women, and I fully intended to play to this trait for my own safety.

The moon was high in the sky when I looked up at the abandoned warehouse, its façade foreboding, half-hidden by the fog sweeping in from the river. The building sat at the end of the port district, where hardly any passersby could be seen. Lily's contact stood impatiently by the doors and I wondered why we were here in the first place.

'Are you sure this is the entrance?' I asked as he fumbled with a key.

'Yes. You didn't think I'd lead you through the front gates, did you?' His voice fused with the screeching of the lock, but his strong southern accent still caught my attention. 'This is the only way to get to the king's private quarters,' he said as we approached a trapdoor hidden behind some broken crates.

He passed me a small piece of paper and a torch. 'A map. In case you need to escape through a different way. That's all I can do for you,' he told me before promptly disappearing into the shadows.

The tight entrance gave me pause. It was a difficult route, but a small pouch of sleeping powder weighed down my belt, ready to silence any unfortunate souls that got in my way.

You can do it, Sana.

I exhaled, fingers tightening on the torch. It barely provided any light, intensifying the feeling of claustrophobia as I pushed into the seemingly endless corridor. It didn't take long for the flame to flicker and die, but I'd already seen the beginning of a set of stairs and was soon heading towards the faint light above.

Finally, I stood in front of a small door secured with a latch.

'All right, Sana, time to meet the king,' I muttered, opening the door and jumping when it snapped shut behind me, catching the edge of my cloak. The small gap was just enough to keep the door open, so, shrugging the cloak off, I stepped deeper into what looked like a study.

The soft glow of the full moon illuminated the space. The shadows of furniture scattered around the room and the piles of paper threatening to fall off a desk told me the owner was comfortable living in chaos . . . or had a profound aversion to cleaning.

Needing to find the king's bedroom, I checked the map before peeking into the corridor. Voices drifted through the silence—low murmurs from behind two ornate doors the map had marked as the wing's entrance. Ironically, the king's decision to keep the entire wing private was now working in my favour.

I frowned, trying to decipher the map's writing in the faint light. If I'd read it right, King Reynard's bedroom was the third door on the left.

My hands trembled as I eased the study door shut behind me. Then I ran—quiet, quick—towards the room labelled as his private sanctuary. I froze as the handle turned easily beneath my fingers.

No lock. No barrier. Just a threshold between me and whatever waited for me on the other side. I hesitated, imagining all the ways this could go wrong, but all I could hope for now was to leave with my body and mind intact.

In fact, I was challenging fate. And fate knew it.

Chapter 12

Roksana

The moment I opened the door, the warm, masculine scent of musk and lemongrass wrapped around me like a whispered promise. I paused, one hand still on the handle, eyes falling shut as I breathed it in and let it steady me.

'He should bottle this,' I murmured, a small smile tugging at my lips as the fragrance stirred something deep and strangely comforting. My pulse eased.

A shape stirred on the bed at the soft creak beneath my foot as I walked farther into the room. I went still, breath caught in my throat, until he settled again.

This was the challenging part.

I had to wake the king and convince him I *wasn't* there to end his life before he ended *mine* by mistake.

My hand gripped the sleeping powder, just in case he wasn't receptive, before I touched the fae lantern beside the bed to gradually brighten it. Men of the sword were dangerous beasts to wake, so I did my best to avoid startling him. The plan had seemed perfect in my head, but he continued sleeping, the muscles in his neck tensing as he whispered something in his dreams. I waited, but relying on the light to wake him didn't seem to be working, so I reluctantly bent down and softly placed a hand on his arm, turning him to face me.

'Wake up, Your Majesty,' I whispered in a gentle tone, holding the powder ready.

At that, the king finally jerked awake, grabbing me by the neck and throwing me onto the bed. Startled, the sleeping dust fell forgotten from my hand as I caught sight of his face.

'Gods . . . It's you!' I gasped, the words tumbling from my mouth as my eyes locked onto a face contorted into a dazed, hungry expression.

His mouth crashed against mine in a kiss so fierce it stole my ability to think, and I moaned helplessly as his lips devoured me. The possessiveness of the kiss, the single-minded focus with which he took me, was . . . deliciously insane. No one had ever kissed me like this.

No one had dared.

His beard tickled my skin while his tongue pressed insistently against my lips, and I let him in. The War King was a man who took what he wanted, and he caged me under his body while still protecting me from being crushed. My pulse thundered in my ears, fear dissolving into a forbidden ache I had no business feeling. My hips rose instinctively, and through the thin barrier of our clothes, I felt the friction of his hard length pressing against me.

The sensation sobered me up.

No, this is wrong!

Acting on that single thought, I bit his lip as hard as I could, grabbing an empty potion bottle from beside his bed and smashing it on his temple. He reared back just enough for me to scramble away and bolt for the door.

But gods, was he fast.

Before I knew it, he'd grasped my shoulder and spun me around, slamming my back into the wall. Whether it was the play of light or my imagination, his eye seemed to blaze with a golden glow as he towered above me, cutting off my escape.

'You aren't a dream.'

Bewildered, his gaze darted over every inch of my face, searching for . . . something.

Had he been dreaming of me? I hadn't finished the thought when he shook me like a rag doll.

'You aren't a fucking dream!'

The golden halo around his iris shone brighter, its glow hypnotising me as it grew, filling his eye with pure, unbridled rage.

'How are you alive?' I whispered, shocked.

He smirked, licking his bloody lip, hissing as he probed it. 'So eager to make me bleed again?' he asked, wiping the blood and smearing it on my lips. 'Here, have a taste, Viper. Is that why you came here? To finish the job?'

My heart hammered against my ribs as I stood there gaping, unable to believe my eyes.

The man I'd killed was standing before me, dressed only in silk trousers. Tall and imposing, his massive body strained against some unseen force, while the wolf-like focus in his eye turned him into a savage predator.

And I was his prey.

'Answer me!' he snarled. 'Did you come here to finish the job?'

I bolted, instinct taking over, but he lunged after me, his movements a blur. I didn't stand a chance—not even Irsha was as fast as him. He wedged his knee between my thighs while he locked his hand around my throat as I struggled in his grasp. He leant down to whisper in my ear, the rough scar on his cheek rubbing across my skin.

'Do you know how many nights you've haunted my dreams? To have you in my grasp, helpless, knowing all it would take is a one firm squeeze and I would end this torment . . .' He trailed his nose over my skin as his hand flexed on my neck. 'And yet it doesn't feel like enough. Your death is not enough for the pain you've caused me.'

He pushed his leg forward, forcing my legs further apart while he observed my efforts to free myself with that satisfied smirk.

'I searched my entire kingdom for you, and here you are, uninvited. Do you think you have any hope of escape?' The look in his eye made me shiver. 'If you want to live, then you'll answer my questions,' he said, tilting my chin high. 'Every. Single. One of them.'

Like I believe his offer when all I see is death lurking in his gaze.

I cursed the fear threatening to overwhelm me.

He shifted, his muscled thigh rubbing between my legs, causing an unexpected jolt of pleasure, adding embarrassment to the mix. A whimper escaped me.

Gods, why the fuck am I even aroused by this?

'Stop it,' he growled, his hand tightening on my throat.

'Stop what?' I wanted to ask but couldn't.

The pressure of his grasp increased, and I clawed at his fingers, desperate to breathe. I got in one lucky kick and his hand relaxed. With a pained gulp, I dragged in enough air to speak.

'Please . . .' I wheezed, reaching for his face. He caught my hand, but the glow in his eye dimmed a little, and I could breathe again.

'Already begging for mercy? Yet what mercy did you show me? Look at *my face*.'

The pain in his voice was so visceral that my gaze drifted to the injury I had caused.

He laughed humourlessly. 'Are you pleased with your handiwork, Viper? Tell me—give me a reason I shouldn't kill you right now.'

Pushing words through my tight throat was painful, but I didn't have a choice. 'I'm not . . . your enemy,' I said.

'Really? Then I'd hate to see what you do to your friends.' He huffed in disdain, his hand again tightening on my neck, but he seemed to be more in control of himself. The vicious snarl abated, replaced by steel in his voice when he asked, 'Do you fear death, little Viper? Because I still remember how it felt, teetering on the edge of madness, praying for the strength to endure as I carved out my eye.'

He . . . did that to himself?

That explained why he was still alive, but I'd never known a man capable of such an act.

'I know . . . who wants . . . you dead . . .' I managed to force out, my throat throbbing within his grasp. The king's frown grew deeper as he studied me with suspicion.

'Fine. Talk. Tell me, then, assassin, who wants me dead? No. First, tell me your name.'

He released my throat then, only to catch my wrists. My relief was short-lived as he pulled both arms above my head. One large hand easily held them down, while his other forced my head up. He was so close that I could smell the blood drying on his lips.

'I want the truth, Viper. If you lie . . . your death won't be swift or merciful, and I'll personally enjoy your suffering.'

But are you ready for the truth? I thought. *I'm dead, anyway, if you can't accept it.* The uncertainty of my fate, my reaction to his touch, and most of all, his arrogance, awakened a spark of defiance within me.

'I'm Roksana Regnav,' I croaked. 'Let me go, and we can talk.'

The giant stretched my arms up farther, making me whimper again, and his low, foreboding laugh sent a shiver down my spine.

'How about . . . no?' he said, his eye narrowing as he watched me struggle, the muscles beneath his skin twitching. 'Don't think for a second you can make demands. Now, *tell me*. Who sent you to kill me in the forest?'

I hated how my body trembled in his grasp, betraying my weakness, but because of that, I felt the anger at his constant accusations get the better of me.

'Nobody, but I wish I'd killed you! Should I ask *you* what you were doing in that forest, forcing yourself onto a helpless woman? What is it—you like hunting peasant girls for sport? Do you like taking them kicking and screaming?' I asked. 'You're supposed to be a fucking war hero?'—I laughed—'You're no different to a beast, fighting over the right to *rape* me first.' The memory I'd buried deep in my mind resurfaced, and a sneer twisted my features. 'Go on, King Reynard. Show me the kind of man you really are.'

His eye narrowed to a slit, but the words had tumbled out before I could stop them.

I was done. I knew it.

A vein pulsed in his neck as he drew back his free hand, fingers balling into a fist. I turned away, squeezing my eyes shut, waiting for the blow to land. I almost laughed at the utter mess my life had become, but I promised myself that whatever happened next, I wouldn't cry or beg.

Only—the blow never came, and I slowly turned my head forward again, cracking an eye open. He stood there, legs spread, panting like a wild animal, a deep frown marring his features. His fist tightened and opened rhythmically. Noticing my gaze, he exhaled, and something shifted in his expression. As if whatever monster lurked beneath his skin hid behind the ironclad façade.

'I didn't force myself on you . . . Is that why you disfigured my face?'

His words, or rather, the broken tone of his voice, gave me pause. This massive man was holding himself back despite my outburst. My anger flickered and died.

Had I misjudged him?

A sliver of hope blossomed within me, and I forced my body to relax in his grasp.

'Did you, even for a moment, consider that our first meeting was an accident and what happened next was a tragic misunderstanding?' I whispered, trying to keep my voice calm.

'Finding a Dark Brotherhood spawn with her thugs at the dwarven border just as I arrived was a misunderstanding? Don't insult my intelligence.' The anger still burned in his eye, but the mindless rage had bled away, and I sensed my chance.

'I wasn't with them. The man who sent them after me also wants your head. I thought you were one of them.' I sucked in a breath. 'I thought you were wanting to take your turn . . .' My voice broke, tapering off while his brows drew closer. The king shook his head, searching for something in my eyes, his expression strangely vulnerable. However, moments later, his features hardened.

'Spare me your lies. You're like a fox trapped in a snare, willing to do anything to get away,' he said, though there was a flicker of uncertainty there that maintained my hope.

'Then spare my life until you find the truth. I was running from Wiosna. Send a messenger to Młot's court to confirm, if you'd like. I worked there as a healer before I was imprisoned under false pretences,' I said. 'As soon as I arrived in Truso, I tried to warn people, to warn the mages.'

I didn't know how much I could disclose without revealing all my cards and losing my bargaining power, but his gaze softened the longer I spoke.

'I swear I didn't plan this. Please . . . release my wrists.' I hated begging, but my shoulders felt like they were coming out of their sockets, and tears fell unwillingly from my eyes. 'You're hurting me.'

'Do you think I'm someone who'll break at the sight of a woman's tears?' he asked, but he eased back on the pressure

I sighed in relief.

'Guards!' he yelled.

'No, wait, please. Listen to me—'

My words were cut short when he placed a hand on my mouth, his thumb brushing a stray tear from my cheek. My eyes widened, surprised by his actions, and I pressed myself back against the wall, but he pushed in closer.

'Stop.' He blew out a breath. 'Just stop. You can't soften me with your tears. The man who'd fall for such tricks died in the forest. You fooled me once . . . I won't let it happen again,' he said calmly.

Closing his eye, he inhaled deeply. 'Enjoy your petty victory, little Viper. You'll live until I confirm your story.'

I turned my head to the side as I needed my mouth free to speak. If he didn't listen to me, next time, he might encounter a more proficient killer. But he tightened his grip, not allowing me to move.

'Stop fighting me. You damaged more than my eye that day, so for your own sake, don't make me lose my temper again,' he said, his hand shifting only for a moment as he crowded his body so close to mine that my breath hitched.

'I'm not . . . please stop,' I whispered, tensing when his forehead touched mine.

'Fuck . . . for Perun's sake, be quiet.'

He said it so softly, almost pleadingly, that I exhaled slowly and complied.

He confused me. His eye was so dilated I could barely see the iris, and beads of sweat trailed down his face, mixing with the blood from the cut on his lip. Reynard looked like a man fighting an internal struggle as he breathed in and out, his expanding chest touching mine without him even noticing.

I relaxed in his grip once again, forcing my eyes closed. I remained still until, with a quiet grunt, he pulled away. When I was brave enough to look at him again, he appeared to be in control.

'I think I'll keep you for a very long time, Viper,' he said, placing a hand on my cheek. His touch was gentle this time, but a sense of dread washed over me. I couldn't be trapped here. Boyan's position was at stake. If I didn't show up at the Mabon feast, Jagon would surely use it as an excuse to issue a formal challenge.

'No.'

'No? Oh, you thought if we talked, I'd let you go?' He laughed. 'I may not want to kill you, but that doesn't mean you'll gain your freedom. Whatever the truth may be, you maimed the king. You committed an offence punishable by death, and your life is now *mine*.'

I flinched, panting with panic. More tears came as he tightened his grip again. Fighting him was futile. Without my poisons, I was just a woman, half his size, barely trained in stealth and combat, and with no illusions about what my chances were.

Think, Sana. You have until the feast. He's already changed his mind about killing you.

The thought eased my fears.

Reynard smiled. 'I see you understand now. I'm not a man to be trifled with.'

He dropped his hand, leaving me unrestrained.

'Call your truthseeker,' I said. 'They'll confirm my story. But please, once they finish with my mind, let me go. My friends will be in danger if I remain here . . . I've risked my family's lives to come warn you.'

'And why should I care?'

'Because you are supposed to be a decent man!'

The stubborn oaf heard me but refused to listen. I had no way of convincing him, though if I gave him a reason to trust me, I was sure he'd let me go.

'Fine!' I said, exasperated. 'I'll take a blood oath. I'll return to you once I ensure my family is safe, but please, you *have* to let me go.'

He gasped, taking a step back. A blood oath bound a person's life to their promise, only death freeing them from its shackles. My proposal was a reckless one, but I was hoping to phrase my oath cleverly enough to avoid the direst consequences. I reached for the short dagger on my belt to seal the deal.

His reaction was intuitive, and before I knew it, the blade was flying across the room. The movement brought him close again, so close I could feel the heat of his body against my skin.

'Never draw a blade in my presence,' he snarled.

His words were deathly cold, but before I could answer, armed men entered the room. I swallowed hard, almost sagging to the floor, when the king suddenly released me.

'Take her to the cells—the ones in the old castle with functioning wards. No one is to visit her until I allow it.'

He turned towards me then, his gaze hardening.

'Strip.'

'No!' I answered, my gaze shifting between the three men. They had me trapped like a cornered rabbit. I glanced toward the window.

If I could survive the fall . . .

The king followed my gaze and moved, blocking my path.

'You three, turn around,' he commanded his men before stepping into my space. 'No one will touch you, but I won't let you keep any blades or poisons on you. Now, strip. Unless you want me to do it for you?' he asked, picking up the dagger I'd dropped.

'If I do, could I at least send a message to my friend—'

'And warn my enemies? Not a chance.'

'You're a fucking arsehole,' I said, swallowing back tears. I'd achieved nothing by coming here. The only plan I'd had had just fallen apart because this stubborn man refused to listen.

He smirked, crossing his arms over his chest. His muscles tensed, highlighting his warrior's frame, but all I could see was the brute forcing my submission.

'Arsehole?' he mused. 'I don't know about that. You're still alive. Some gratitude's in order, don't you think? Let's see if a few days in a cell will improve your manners.'

Moments later, my dress lay in a pile on the floor. I took off my blouse, dreading the moment I'd have to remove the simple linen chemise that barely touched the top of my thighs.

'Stop.'

His order caught me mid-movement, and I raised my eyes, meeting his gaze.

'What? Suddenly afraid to see some tits?' I sneered, raising my chin high and reaching for the lace of my final covering. I was done begging, determined not to give him the satisfaction of seeing me beaten down and afraid.

'Why would I spoil a moment I could enjoy later?' He grabbed my hand, preventing me from disrobing, unfazed as I stared at him in challenge. 'You can't hide a weapon under this scrap of fabric,' he said, calling for the guard.' You there, check her boots, then take her to the cells.'

The guard slid his hands along my calves, pushing his fingers inside my boots while I held the king's gaze. His jaw bunched, tightening rhythmically before he snarled, 'That's enough. Take her.'

I was grabbed and led out of the room. Before the door closed, I turned around to look at the man whose intense gaze seemed to burn a hole in my soul. The corner of his mouth tilted up and he placed a hand on his chest as he delivered a mocking bow.

'Sleep well, little Viper, and get used to your new home. I feel we'll be spending a lot of time together . . .'

He grated on me so much in that moment that before I could stop myself, I shouted back, 'Eat shit and die, bastard!'

Only to hear my curse answered with a burst of laughter.

Chapter 13

Reynard

I watched the woman as she was escorted away. Once the door finally closed, I dropped heavily onto the nearest seat and hid my face in my hands.

'What the fuck just happened?' I muttered, attempting to control my breathing to avoid triggering the spasms.

My mind was spinning.

Nothing made sense, but even with everything that had just happened, it was her eyes that haunted me. My tongue darted out and probed my swollen lip again, the damaged skin pulsing dully. A stark reminder that my dream had almost turned me into the beast she had accused me of being, that my body had betrayed me at the worst possible moment.

I shifted, adjusting myself, and pressed on the seam of my trousers. Uneasiness built in my chest. I was a ruthless man, but not a violent one, and not one easily aroused by a pretty face.

Even in that blasted forest, there was no wrongness in my touch, and my only concern was her safety. I was fascinated by her, yes. Her delicate features and unbending spirit as she fought off her attackers were captivating, but more than anything, I wanted to protect her. I hadn't reacted well after seeing her tattoo, but I'd . . .

No. I am not the villain in this story, and I won't let you paint me as one, Viper.

I grabbed a quill and paper and wrote a quick note to the northern garrison requesting that the commander send a man to Wiosna to confirm her story.

This mess could not be allowed to continue. I needed to get to the bottom of this, whatever the cost. Her accusation burned a hole in my mind, but more than clearing my name, I needed proof she could be trusted before I disclosed that her poison still burned in my veins.

I should have called Riordan and ended the issue here and now, but after we'd interrogated Boyan, I realised that even a psychic mage could be deceived. I *knew* the grand master had lied about the hairpin . . . I just didn't know how he did it.

I would still use my truthseeker, but this time I wouldn't trust my life entirely to magic, not where Roksana was concerned.

I had to give it to her. She'd stood her ground. Warriors much stronger than her had cowered in fear when facing my anger, yet the woman had looked me in the eye as I held her dainty neck and had demanded to be let go.

My hand flexed. I could still feel her pulse fluttering under my fingertips, as fragile as a sparrow's, even when she had confronted me as if I weren't the king but some village idiot refusing to see reason.

Maybe I was an idiot, as I hadn't learnt my lesson. The fascination that had awakened when I first saw her was still there, brought back by her touch and dubious story, fighting with my need for justice.

'Gods, what the fuck is wrong with me?' I groaned, annoyed that I found her courage so appealing. Loneliness might be messing with my head, but this was seriously out of control.

I wasn't a chaste man, but whom I chose to bed, and when, had always been rational. The ladies of the court, with their fake smiles and low curtsies, were well aware of it. They were intent on using me for money or power, so I let them mount me like a fucking stallion without remorse in exchange for whatever benefit they wanted.

My would-be assassin had at least earned my respect for not begging or trying to seduce her way out of the situation. Gaining access to the king's chambers was no simple job—

Wait, how did she get in here? I thought, walking back towards my nightstand.

The room was still dark. The single fae lantern illuminated very little, so I spoke the command to activate the main lights, and my chambers were flooded with radiance. I consciously looked around, checking for anything amiss.

My bedroom was spacious, and although it seemed cluttered, I knew where everything was, so it was easy to see that nothing had been touched. It looked like she had gone straight to my bed, stopping only to trigger the lantern. Now, adding to the general chaos, there was a pile of female clothes, unmistakable evidence that tonight's escapade wasn't a dream.

I looked at the clothes and huffed humourlessly. She must have thought so low of me when I ordered her to strip. It hadn't been about humiliating her, but I'd enjoyed the defiance in her eyes before she yielded, her response delighting me in its simplicity. *Eat shit and die*—when had anyone spoken to me so brazenly as that?

Sitting on the edge of my bed, I reached for a bottle of mead. I didn't bother with a glass, gulping the contents straight from the source before leaning back, replaying everything, hoping to see something I'd missed.

My gaze drifted back over to her clothes, and I bent over, picking up the simple white shirt. It smelled faintly of flowers, and when I brought it to my nose, I recognised the scents of lilac and honey, along with something else—an intoxicating, feminine fragrance that made my head spin. I made the mistake of burying my face into the fabric and inhaling deeply.

'What the . . .' I groaned, dropping to my knees, fighting the urge to rush after her.

'No!' I slammed my hand on the stone floor. The pain of the impact brought me clarity, but the memory of her eyes, luminescent in the fae light and brimming with tears, wouldn't fade. I could still feel her silky skin under my hands, the rapid thump of her heartbeat as she tried to speak.

'Fuck, woman,' I muttered, throwing the fabric away as if it had burned me. It was a humiliating spectacle, but it explained my odd behaviour. She was an expert poisoner who'd not only crafted the poison that was slowly killing me but an aphrodisiac that muddled my senses, stripping me of reason.

'Congratulations, Viper. You've bested me in ways I didn't expect,' I muttered, blowing my nose to remove the rest of her scent.

I should have felt reassured that I'd caught her little trick, but my lack of control irritated me. I adjusted myself again, wondering if slapping the damn thing would make it lie down before briefly considering releasing my pent-up tension in the easiest way a man can.

A grim laugh escaped me at that thought. It would be the lowest of lows, but if a hint of an aphrodisiac and a pretty face had made me so hard, maybe it was time to satisfy my needs before abstinence left me falling prey to this honey trap.

I needed something, or rather someone, to distract me from such intrusive thoughts. I pulled the bell cord, and moments later, a sleepy servant opened the door to my bedroom.

'You called, sire?'

'Send for Riordan. Tell him it's an emergency and to attend immediately. I've had a visitor.'

At the words 'emergency' and 'visitor,' the servant's spine snapped as straight as a rod. He glanced around, noticing the clothes on the floor, and panic flashed through his visage.

'And their body?' he stuttered, his breath quickening with each passing minute.

'You can stop looking. There are no bodies nor blood to clean up,' I snapped, and he had the decency to look embarrassed.

'I will call for Master Riordan immediately. Anything else you need, sire?'

'Tell the captain of the guard to search my private quarters and interrogate the men on duty tonight. I want his report on what he discovers immediately, no matter how insignificant it may be. That's all.' I waved him off, focusing my gaze on the pile of clothing before leaning forward and searching through it—this time avoiding the lilac scent.

That damn woman gained entrance into my room with a blade and the gods know what else, I thought, frowning at the strange-looking vials, leaving them for Riordan to inspect.

'Well, I'll find out tomorrow when Riordan interrogates her . . .' I said just as the door opened and the tussled head of the mage himself appeared through the gap.

'Pray tell, what interrogation do I have to perform, and why can't whatever you're planning wait until I return from the Care'etavos Empire? Where, mind you, I should be going *tomorrow morning*,' he asked, covering his mouth to stifle a yawn. 'Why am I awake in the middle of the night?'

The air around Ri's body shimmered before the aether settled. I knew mages could always see the magical energy that filled our world and manipulate it to their needs, but those born to the sword and honest work only ever noticed the slightest hints of its existence. The only time mundane men like me had ever seen the aether completely was when

Annika, my brother's mate, had decimated an undead army in a display of terrifying conduit power.

'I just wanted to see you and needed someone to share my mead.'

'Gods, I'm going to hex you one day,' he muttered under his breath. 'It's well past midnight, and I have a long journey ahead.'

'I heard that, mage.' I couldn't help but smile. 'You can sleep in the carriage, but if my skin turns green or my cock falls off, I'll know who to blame.'

Riordan sighed as if realising he'd spoken out loud, and he bowed. 'Blame me for whatever you want, just let me sleep. I'll serve you with my counsel when I return.'

'I'm sorry, did you think I was giving you a choice?' I smirked, pointing to a chair. 'Now, where were you when an assassin tried to kill me again just moments ago?'

His eyebrows rose but he simply shrugged. 'In bed, sleeping like a baby. As you are still alive and sitting there wearing a smug grin, I'm assuming you dealt with the fool?' He gestured to the pile of clothes. 'Why did you really call for me? I'm no necromancer to be interrogating bodies or a maid who'll take out your laundry.'

'You know, you're quite the grumpy bastard when woken from your beauty sleep,' I said, pouring a generous measure of mead into a goblet and pushing it his direction. 'Drink. You'll need it to swallow the news I have.'

Riordan reached for the drink, and I waited until his mouth was full before unveiling my news.

'The woman from the forest came to pay me a visit,' I said, grinning as his eyes widened. 'I caught my Viper, and I've locked her in a cage.'

Riordan gasped, spilling the mead as he stared at me in disbelief. 'How? Why . . .? Are those *hers*?' He moved towards the clothing on the floor and grabbed the shirt I'd held before.

'Don't! It's soaked in an aphrodisiac . . .' I tried to warn him, but it was too late, and he sniffed it before looking at me curiously.

'How drunk are you? It's just lilac perfume. You can find it in any brothel . . . although this one *is* of good quality,' he said, throwing the shirt aside and rummaging through the rest of her clothes while I gaped at his crotch like an idiot.

'Is she so good that it only works on me?' I speculated under my breath, but even to myself, that sounded far-fetched.

'What? Never mind. Look at this! It's a proper alchemist's belt. This woman knows her trade.' Riordan stood up with the leather strip in hand. The vials attached to it glistened, filled with unknown liquids and powders. He placed them on the table before adding two knives to the bizarre collection—one a simple dagger and the other a small paring knife coated in an oily black substance.

'So, she came armed with poison,' I said, pushing the belt aside, my doubts about her story solidifying under the weight of the evidence. 'I want you to examine them. And her. After a night in a cell, she should be sufficiently motivated to talk. I want to know who paid her.'

'Motivated?' he responded. 'If you want her motivated, find a torturer, not a truthseeker.'

Riordan raised the knife, twisting it slowly, letting the oily substance catch the light before he licked his finger and rubbed it on the blade. Some of the coating wore off on his fingertip, and he brought it to his lips.

'What in Veles' pit are you doing?' I reached out to grab his hand, but he stopped me.

'Hemlock, but . . . Why is the aether doing that . . .? Interesting.' Riordan studied me, his gaze inscrutable, before he once again picked up my attacker's shirt off the floor. 'Rey, the woman who attacked you .

. . she might be a mage or, at least, a hedge witch. Did you feel anything strange? Did she try to bewitch you?'

'No.' I glanced at the shirt. 'Maybe? The Brotherhood doesn't work with mages, though,' I said, watching him draw a symbol over the fabric. 'Please don't tell me there's another faction out for my blood. Truly, if there were anyone I could trust to lead this country, I'd hand it over faster than I could grab my coat on the way out.'

My comment expressed the emotions that had been building inside me since Annika had proclaimed me king years ago. I couldn't trust anyone with these sentiments, except here I was letting them out. One look at Ri's concerned frown, and I was wishing I could take the words back.

'Rey? What aren't you telling me?' he asked softly.

'I'm just tired. No, exhausted. Every day is a constant struggle, and Duke Tivala is only the latest of my annoyances. Did I tell you that the old bastard sent our entire garrison back? Despite all of the pirate raids decimating the coastline towns, he insists that he has enough men in his service to deal with it. He said, and I quote, that a garrison would only "overburden the locals."' I scoffed, shaking my head. 'And of course, that bloody principality law granted by my predecessor forbids me from entering his lands forcefully. I summoned him to explain, but all of a sudden, he is "too old," and the death of his son has supposedly made leaving the duchy difficult.'

'His son's death? That was five years ago, and even then, they'd been estranged for ages after the duchess passed. I'm sure his heir being a nasty piece of work didn't help matters either,' Riordan said.

'Yes, well. He was still his heir.' I shook my head. 'Besides, it's only an excuse. In the same letter as he told me that, he confirmed his attendance for the Winter Solstice Ball, so that he may introduce his daughter to me,' I said, pouring myself more mead. 'The duke's either senile and doesn't know what he's doing or so calculating that he's running laps around us. Either way, we no longer have any soldiers in the Tivalaran province. So, I have a decision to make: wait and see how this plays out or disregard the law and take the province by force.'

'And?' Ri prompted.

'I don't want to be a king who starts a civil war. It would be easier if his heir were alive. Then I could simply declare the old duke incapable of ruling and push the responsibility onto his son.'

Asking Riordan to join me had been an impulsive decision, but I was glad he'd come. Discussing this was helping me focus on the issues instead of dwelling on my visitor. We sat in a comfortable silence, and I looked at the man sitting opposite me as he stretched out on his chair, already half asleep. His long auburn hair trailed over the edge of the seat as he settled into a more relaxed position, and my thoughts drifted to Orm, my brother.

Orm had found his happiness not only with a woman who had bound their hearts, but also with the dark fae who'd been his friend for years—a friendship that had grown into a love I envied.

After Orm's departure, Riordan had helped me, stepping into his shoes, and it hadn't been a small role to fill. However, I knew it would never evolve into the type of relationship my brother had with his mate, Alaric. I liked female company, probably a little too much, but none of the women that had caught my eye ever became anything more than a fling.

Sometimes, I wondered if I was incapable of love.

'Why do I have the feeling you're ogling me?' Riordan's amused tone cut through my musings, and I shook my head.

'As if.' I covered the unscarred side of my face. 'I'm just wallowing in self-pity. With my face as it is now, it'll be a miracle if any woman chooses to warm my bed . . . Maybe the royal mage position should come with a few extra duties,' I quipped, watching his eyebrows shoot up before he started laughing.

'Good luck with getting me to help in that area. Stop worrying. I bet there'll be more than a few maidens willing to polish the king's sceptre,' Ri said, still laughing before his face turned serious. 'But shifting focus from your *beauty* and Ignac Tivala's untimely overdose, have you considered asking the light fae kingdom about how they deal with pirates? They have a fleet,' he pointed out, propping himself up. 'If we can convince Prince Iasno'ta to patrol our waters, you could thwart those on Tivala's coasts without causing a civil war. After all, the light fae are still our allies.'

'They *were* our allies. Now, they treat us like a poor cousin hoping for a handout. With the defeat of the Lich King, the coalition fell apart like last year's socks. No one feels the need to honour the old treaty if there's no threat to their homes.'

I sighed, leaning back and closing my eyes. 'That's why I'm sending you to Care'etavos to renegotiate the trade agreement with the dark fae. Somehow, they've learned about my condition, and I want to ensure that the empress doesn't get any interesting ideas. I'm afraid our only ally now is Ozar, and that's only because my brother sits on the throne.'

Riordan winced, a deep frown replacing his carefree attitude. 'That complicates things. Too many coincidences in such a short time.'

'Yes, and my night visitor might hold some answers. That's why I need you to interrogate her as soon as you return,' I said, rubbing the scar on my cheek. *When did life become so complicated that I can't even tell my friend that I don't fully trust his magic?* 'She gave me her story. I want to ensure we're asking the right questions.'

'Fine, of course. You'll have your truthseeker,' Riordan said. He looked to the side, his gaze sliding over the clothes as he frowned. 'That reminds me . . . I also had an interesting encounter recently. A woman came to the Court of Aether yesterday—a refugee from Wiosna.'

The bastard smiled as I sat up, wondering if I had heard him right.

'I see that got your attention, and I must admit, she grabbed mine. A pretty little thing that somehow managed to bring three council members *this* close to apoplexy,' he said, pressing his thumb and forefinger together before reaching for his drink, but I grasped his hand, stalling it.

'And?'

'And she confirmed what we suspected. Młot is mining and trading srebrec. If what she said is true, the buyer already has more than enough ore to cause trouble for Dagome's mages.'

I sighed heavily, unsure of what to do now. Suspecting our former ally was one thing, but knowing it for sure? That was a blow. Even if I'd expected it, I was still taken aback by the sheer audacity.

'Did she tell you who he's trading with?'

'No, she only found out because she was working as a healer and had to treat miners injured by a cave-in and aether flux from the ore,' he said, lifting the goblet to his mouth when I finally released his hand.

I could barely breathe.

'You checked her story, yes? I want you to question her again,' I said, leaning towards him as my mind raced.

Riordan shook his head. 'I checked as much as I could, but that's the thing. The reason our council lit up like Svarog's fire was the fact that our healer can see aether yet isn't registered as a mage. And . . .' He paused dramatically and I rolled my eyes at his theatrics. 'She's a former member of the Dark Brotherhood.'

All the gears in my head suddenly clicked into place, forming a coherent story. I choked on my mead, wheezing out one last question between my coughs.

'What's her name?'

Chapter 14

Roksana

I couldn't stop shaking, but I didn't know whether it was the cold or my fury at being ignored. Not that it mattered. Sat on the floor, nearly naked, I knew the cold would be the end of me.

The meagre straw pile I'd curled up on didn't stop the chill from seeping into my bones, making my teeth chatter as I realised how much trouble I was in.

'I maimed the king of Dagome . . . Gods, what a shit show,' I muttered, rocking back and forth. He hadn't killed me, and I thanked every deity I could think of for that, but what was I going to do now?

Reynard's scarred face flashed across my mind. Messy raven hair, cut in a high and tight on one side and grown out to a medium length on the other, fell over the empty eye socket, as if he'd tried to hide the scar my hairpin had left behind. His beautiful grey eye, framed by long eyelashes, burned with anger even after his kiss had left me breathless, and I marvelled at his ruthless allure. I sucked in my lower lip, groaning with embarrassment as I remembered how eagerly I had yielded to his touch.

'That's never happening again,' I promised myself. I'd be a fool not to be afraid of him, yet when he had brushed away my tears, there was a gentleness in him . . . as if he was looking for a reason not to be harsh with me.

'Just like I'm trying to find some redeeming qualities in him.' I sighed, rubbing my arms when a draft swept through my cell.

Pushing thoughts of Reynard aside, I counted the days left until Mabon. I had close to two weeks to convince him to release me before the Brotherhood fell apart.

If, of course, I don't freeze to death in the meantime, I thought, tapping the wall. The cell was old, its stone construction having survived for five centuries, and it looked as though it would last another five. To make matters worse, the cell was located next to the river, and its tiny window was open to the brisk wind, causing me to shudder every time I left my legs exposed.

Worry had me biting my lip, but it didn't hurt as much as I expected, and I felt a shiver of fear run down my spine. *If my body is going numb, how much time do I have left?*

'Fuck you and the horse you rode in on—could've at least given me my kirtle back,' I muttered, promising retribution to the arrogant bastard who locked me in here.

I sighed. I knew I was really just angry at my own lack of planning. 'Think with your head, Sana. Never let the heart guide the knife.' Jagon had beaten that mantra into my flesh, and it never rang truer than now.

It had been an impulsive decision to kill the Tivala family's heir, and thanks to my former master, it had come back to bite me in the arse. Another impulsive decision, and I was breaking into the king's bedchamber, thinking I could convince him that his life was in danger.

I groaned.

Well, he definitely agrees with that. Unfortunately, he also thought *I* was that danger.

Now, I was locked in an impenetrable cell, and the king was my only chance at freedom.

While I pondered over strategy, the darkness fled, and I noticed two figures on the staircase outside my cell. One of them was hiding a fae lantern beneath his cloak.

'Is that her? The master won't be happy that she came to kill Reynard. You should have left her in Wiosna. Now your little pet is a problem. Are you sure she hasn't betrayed us? We've already changed the srebrec's route . . . don't want any more obstacles, Jagon.'

They huddled together, and the whispers became difficult to hear. I tried to make sense of the broken sentences, but as they drew closer, the corridor's acoustics made it easier to hear fragments of their conversation once more.

'—we had to change the route anyway, with so many patrols on the roads. Tell your . . . I need her as insurance against the king's behaviour. Not to mention her . . . keep the old man in check. Boyan will hesitate before acting if it harms his precious shadow . . .' Jagon's voice trailed off, and I wished I could pour molten iron down his conniving throat.

'—what use . . . against a strategist like him? . . . construction will start soon. My man was able to secure the seal on the contract today. If the king decides to withdraw, we'll be ready.' The man coughed, and his voice gained a rasp but grew stronger, and I could finally hear him clearly.

'You have long arms to have someone so close to the king,' Jagon said, apparently fishing for more information.

'Not anymore. Because of your pet's antics, the captain of the guard has brought in truthseekers. My man had to abandon his post, so you'd better ensure he has safe passage south, and I'll let you keep her alive in return. I'll even convince my master that she's useful to our plans. Oh, and keep an eye on the dwarves. Młot is getting more paranoid, and I'm sure Master would like to keep Truso intact.'

The man turned towards my cell, a dark shadow hiding his face, giving him the appearance of a wraith. Under the cloak, he wore the colours of the palace guard, and when he raised his head, I glimpsed pasty white skin. He huffed with disdain at my inspection before wordlessly turning on his heel and disappearing into the shadows. I was listening to his retreating steps so intently that Jagon's voice startled me when he spoke.

'Roksana . . . Roksana, look at what that brute did to you.' Jagon came closer, shaking his head. 'You should have accepted my offer. Now there is little I can do to help,' he said as I moved away from him. A lazy smirk stretched across his lips as his gaze trailed over my body. 'Although I have to admit this outfit looks good on you in the moonlight, especially since the chill makes everything so . . . tight,' he added, his gaze lingering on my breasts.

I felt an innate need to cover up but refused to give him the satisfaction.

'How did you know I was here? Did you bribe that guard?' I asked, placing my hands on my hips, playing to his lowest instincts.

If Jagon believed he had power over me, I could spin it in my favour. I'd always preferred working for stupid men with loose tongues, and although Jagon wasn't stupid, his ego was so large I was amazed he could carry it. The chapter master believed everyone danced to his tune, and that was something I could exploit.

'He's none of your concern. As to how I knew, I have eyes every-where. Did you think your stunt with the Court of Aether would go unnoticed just because I was away? Or that you could sneak out of the whorehouse, and no one would know where you went?'

His expression grew colder. 'There is only one thing that baffles me . . . Reynard kept you alive. He's killed every assassin the disgruntled nobles have sent his way, yet here you are. Why, Roksana? What did you promise him? Did you offer him your body to save your life?' His hands tightened on the bars of my prison, knuckles creaking in the near silence.

When I looked up at his face, Jagon's lips were set in a thin line, and I knew the expression all too well from the years we spent together.

'Please.' I scoffed. 'Don't tell me you're jealous?'

I was fifteen when Jagon saved me from some mercenaries and gave me the means of revenge. For years, I'd believed he was a harsh but fair master. I had followed in his footsteps, learning everything about poisons and antidotes, about how a simple herb or substance could affect a person. Then, I grew into my body and started noticing certain things—the way he looked at me, how close he stood, and how all the men around me quickly lost interest.

When I turned twenty, in a drunken stupor, Jagon told me he'd been promoted to chapter master of the poisoners and how, together, we would take control of the Dark Brotherhood. Then he'd kissed me before passing out on the floor.

That was the moment I realised I had to buy my freedom or accept the fact that I'd unwillingly end up in his bed.

Refocusing on the present, I saw Jagon's eyes narrow. His stare bore into mine until he suddenly smiled, relaxing.

'I'm not jealous. There's no point. You belong to me, Roksana. I created you, nurtured your talent. Everything you are is because of me.'

'Oh yes, all the bullying you ignored, the poison you put in my meals to study their effects, making me work without rest because you had another order to fill. All of that certainly made me into the woman I am now.'

'I made you into the most feared poisoner in the Brotherhood. You were so good that Boyan chose you to be his shadow. I even let you leave and have your fun with the dwarves, but your folly ends now. You *will* return to my service and be grateful for it.'

'And if I refuse?'

'Then you will live a long and miserable life while I kill everyone you love and every man who has ever touched you,' he said.

When I didn't respond, anger flashed across his features. Pure malice tinged his voice when he spoke again.

'But first, I'll let you rot here until you learn your lesson. Your misguided attempts to harm me have produced some interesting effects. It would seem that the king and the Court of Aether are more interested in *you* than the srebrec trade. Tell me, are you the mysterious woman he's been searching through all of Dagome for?'

I snorted with bitter amusement. 'Oh, he did that for me? So, if he worked so hard to find me, do you really think he'll just let me go now? That he'll just let me serve as a lackey to a second-rate chapter master?'

Goading Jagon wasn't the best idea, but I couldn't help myself. His delusion of having me by his side, working with him in any shape or form, was so ridiculous I almost laughed out loud.

'You still think you have the upper hand?' he asked. 'Okay. Let's talk about Liliana, then. About the testimony from a disgruntled worker that paints an interesting picture of the death of Tivala's heir. How our sweet little courtesan had arranged a meeting between him and a renowned poisoner in her House of Lilies . . .' He smirked. 'Even if no one believes the ramblings of a discarded whore, I have a sample of a remarkable lip gloss in my workshop that would provide enough evidence. What did you name it, *Wrath of Lilies*? Imagine what Duke Tivala would say if I were to present him with that . . . How long would it be before her head is on display over the city gates?'

I clenched my fists, fighting to control my anger. 'You wouldn't dare,' I whispered, but Jagon laughed.

'Oh yes, I would. To have you, I'd destroy her, take her apart piece by piece, as you watch her lose everything before I kill her. Fight me, and I'll be wiping away your tears as you bury your friend's bloated corpse.'

I gasped, falling backwards until I hit the wall.

'You're a fucking monster,' I spat.

'I am, and you are the gem *I* found amongst the ashes of your family.' He grinned, clearly enjoying the moment. 'You will stand beside me, Roksana. The sooner you understand that, the better for you and those around you. It is your fate.'

I slowly raised my head and looked at him—at the narrow, hawkish face with its sharp nose and thin lips. He was barely forty years old, but I saw the wrinkles in the corner of his eyes and the grey tint of his pale skin from years of working with toxic fumes.

I wanted to study him, to learn the map of his life force, because I was going to dismantle his very existence. Jagon had won today, and I had to yield. However, the bastard didn't realise that his hunger for power, his obsession to own me, and his twisted lust had awakened a monster that was going to devour him.

I wrapped my fingers around Jagon's hand, noticing his surprise when I lowered my head submissively to hide the hatred in my eyes.

'Fine, but leave Lily alone, and you'll have me . . . just as you always wanted. But Jagon—if she dies, *so will you*. I'll make sure of it.'

Jagon's breath hitched, and his free hand eagerly covered mine. I felt it tremble as he caressed my skin.

'My beautiful Nightshade. You may hate me now, but you'll soon realise I'm doing this for your own good.' The feeling of his thumb stroking my knuckles made me nauseous, but I didn't move.

'And you're leaving me here for my own good?' I asked.

He smirked. 'Yes, that will be best, I think. The king sent soldiers to every shithole in Dagome trying to find you. I can't let them accidentally disrupt my plans in their fervour to find his precious prisoner once again, so you'll have to endure for now.' He reached into his coat and pulled a tiny vial from his pocket. 'Just in case that ugly bastard tries touching you,' he said. 'A dab behind the ears and the scent will cool any man's ardour.'

'I thought you wanted me to keep him busy?'

'Chasing you, yes, but not touching you. Don't forget who you belong to, Roksana.'

I took the vial and smiled gratefully, knowing that I'd fuck Reynard in the cold, wet dungeon just to spite this bastard.

'Of course, Master,' I said, inclining my head, hating the gesture that always seemed to please him.

Quick as a snake, Jagon reached through the bars and grabbed my chin, tilting my head up. 'I know you hate me. Don't think, even for a second, that you can deceive me with your fake compliance. This coy pose means nothing,' he said. 'I never aspired to have your love. Your skills'—he slowly looked me up and down—'and your body, are more than sufficient.'

He released me, stepping away before placing a hand on his chest and bowing slightly.

'Until we meet again, my dear. Don't forget to use my gift if he tries touching you.'

I stood motionless, clutching the vial as he left until all I could hear was silence. Only then did I throw it at the wall with such force that the glass shattered. I didn't cry. If anything, I felt numb, my forced submission leaving a sour taste in my mouth. If this was the gods' way of telling me I'd pissed them off by injuring the king, I'd certainly received the message.

My body grew colder with each passing moment, and my thoughts turned sluggish and disorganised. Not that thinking clearly would help. There was nothing I could do against the cold.

Fuck my life, I thought, hours later, as the first blush of dawn peeked through the narrow window. I told myself the warmth from the sun finally coming up was why I'd stopped shivering, why the ache in my fingers and toes had dulled into nothing. But I knew that wasn't right. I forced myself upright, swaying slightly as I stepped into the pale beam of morning light.

'Roksana, what are you doing here?'

I turned my head towards the cell door, huffing a dry laugh when I saw Riordan peering through the bars with a shocked expression.

'Me? Oh, I don't know, trying to stay alive after some bastard locked me in here?' I said with a shrug, curling up under the sun's warm rays.

'A pity the cold didn't freeze your tongue, Viper,' Reynard said as he came up behind Riordan, his posture surprisingly relaxed for someone who'd been woken in the middle of the night.

Another chuckle slipped out.

Of course he's relaxed. He *didn't spend most of the night in a cell, freezing his butt off after being threatened.*

'How can I help you, Your Majesty? More questions to answer? Or did you come to gloat? Maybe you want the last scrap of my clothing?' I asked, executing a lopsided curtsy.

'Roksana, don't make things worse,' Riordan tried to intervene, but I only stared at Reynard, who, with a smug expression, raised two fingers, gesturing to someone behind him to open the door.

The king stepped in and wrapped his cloak around me. His gesture caught me off guard, and I instinctively grasped its edges, wrapping them tighter while enjoying the heat of his body still trapped in the heavy fabric. When I held my silence, looking at him curiously, he shrugged.

'Don't flatter yourself, Viper. I'm not interested in your body any more than I'd want to fuck a snowman.'

I wished I were strong enough to rip off his cloak and throw it at his feet, but it was very warm, and I was a pragmatic woman.

'I hate you,' I said simply, imagining my fist breaking his strong, chiselled jaw.

'I knew there was something connecting us,' he answered, the corner of his lips curling up ever so slightly before he gestured to some servants. 'Take the lady to the bathhouse. Scrub her until her skin is red and raw, then scrub her again. Burn whatever she's wearing and dress her in . . . something different.'

Immediately, two serving women wearing unyielding expressions entered the cell.

'What? Why?' I asked, baffled, shifting back when one of the women reached for my elbow. 'Keep your hands off me!'

'Go with them, Viper. And if you even think of escaping, think again, because next time, I'll send male guards with you.' At his words, both women approached again, and I took a deep breath as every muscle in my body tightened.

'No, don't touch me. I'll go by myself,' I said through clenched teeth, but instead of looking at me, they looked at Reynard.

'I don't care, as long as she cooperates,' he said with a shrug.

We walked along the barely-lit dank corridors until we reached a small, unobtrusive door. One of the maids opened it and led me out into a tiny courtyard filled with herbs and vegetables.

I restrained myself when I noticed how tense the women had become.

Do they think I'd make a run for it? I snorted as I looked down at my bare legs. *Yeah, I don't think so.*

I bit my lip, worrying about Lily, hoping she wouldn't get caught in between the king and Jagon any more than she already was.

We passed through two more doors until we entered a room that surrounded us with steam, the heat a blessing to my ice-cold body. Unfortunately, it also triggered a weakness that sent me sprawling to the floor, terrifying my guardians. I was dragged to a large wooden tub filled with water, where one of them helped me get in while the other disappeared to the gods knew where.

As Reynard had ordered, I was scrubbed and then scrubbed again, shivering so hard that water splashed from the tub while my teeth clattered like a marching army. Finally, I was left alone and allowed to immerse myself in the hot water.

'This wasn't too stupid an idea—for a man,' I muttered with a smirk, sinking down and letting the water close over my head. The tub was big enough for three people and must have been used as a communal bath for the servants.

The heat worked its magic as I stretched out and lay on the bottom. Bubbles escaped my lips, but I held on, unwilling to emerge into the chill air. All of a sudden, a muffled female scream surprised me right before an enormous shadow fell over me and a hand yanked me to the surface.

The movement was so rapid and unexpected that I gasped, inhaling the fluid as I was dragged up. I coughed and spluttered like a drowned rat.

'You think to escape me by drowning, Viper? I won't let you hurt yourself, not in my fucking palace. Your life is *mine*, and only I can take it.' Reynard held me dangling by the neck, his quiet anger more chilling than the draft from the wide-open doors. He spared me a single glance before dropping me back into the tub, splashing water on the stone floor.

'See to her. Ensure she is healthy, and don't leave her alone until I question her.' Reynard snapped the commands, barely looking at me.

'I wasn't trying . . .' I protested, but he'd already left, slamming the door, leaving me with the serving women and an old man in a healer's robes. I pulled my knees to my chest, hiding myself from their judgemental stares before asking as calmly as I could, 'Can someone please explain what just happened?'

While the serving women helped me dress in a simple chemise and kirtle, I discovered that, seeing me collapse, and how violently I had shivered in the water, a healer had been sent for. Unfortunately for me, the healer had been with the king, and as soon as my condition was mentioned, both men stormed in here to find me at the bottom of the tub.

'Someone just kill me, because if you don't, embarrassment certainly will,' I groaned, sitting on a bench while I let the servants dry my hair.

'My lady, our king would never hurt an innocent woman,' the old healer chimed in. 'His manners might be brisk, but he is a righteous man. Maybe . . . try not to anger him?'

I rolled my eyes and sighed deeply. 'How? Every time he sees me, I swear I can see steam coming out of his ears.'

My remark provoked a few sniggers, which gave me hope that the servants were more than obedient tools following orders. I waited until the healer finished his examinations, and when he left, I turned towards them.

'I won't give you any trouble. Not to you, and not to the king, but I'd like to ask one favour. Could you please deliver a message to The House of Lilies?' I asked, and their faces instantly turned cold and unfriendly. 'It's nothing terrible, and I'm happy for you to share its contents with the king. Can someone please just visit the madam and let her know that I'm fine and will be staying with a friend for a few days? I don't want her to worry or cause trouble.'

There was very little chance that they would fulfil my request, but I had to try.

'I will ask His Majesty, but I wouldn't count on his agreement,' the older woman answered, and my hope drained into the gutter.

Chapter 15

Roksana

The sun hung high above the horizon as I was led back through the palace. Contrary to my expectations, the serving women didn't return me to my cell, instead heading towards one of the palace's wings high above the ground overlooking the river.

'Where are you taking me?' I asked, squinting as the sun's rays fell on my face.

'As per His Majesty's orders, you will be held under house arrest. He has assigned you a room in the visitor's quarters,' the guard accompanying us answered.

I stopped, turning towards him. 'Why?'

'How should I know? The king doesn't ask my opinion,' he snapped. 'Now move, woman, unless you want to be taken back to your cell.'

A few moments later, he opened an ornate door and gestured for me to enter. I took a step in and had to grasp the doorframe, completely surprised by my new prison.

Even a high-born lady wouldn't turn her nose up at such luxury.

A grand four-poster bed anchored the room, its presence commanding yet elegant. Sunlight spilled through a west-facing window overlooking the river, casting a golden glow over the entire space as I gaped. I took in the view of water birds flitting down to the river's shallows, their cheerful calls as they enjoyed the morning sun drawing a smile from me.

Nearby, a small table stood topped with a sewing basket, basic toiletries, and a modest vanity mirror, and I noticed a neat stack of well-thumbed books on one side of the bed. Nothing was amiss, and though the colour palette leaned towards bland pastels, the room was stunning. With its soft rugs, cosy throws, and gentle quiet, it exuded a warm, welcoming atmosphere.

'And what will I be doing here?' I asked, turning to face the servants as they prepared to leave.

'Resting? Eating? How should I know? I wasn't given specific instructions. Just be grateful the king allowed your message to be delivered,' one of them answered.

'But don't try anything stupid,' the guard warned. 'My orders are clear. If you hurt anyone or attempt to escape, you will end up in the old castle again. And I'd love nothing more than to throw you back into the dungeon.' He smiled cruelly. 'In fact . . . I know the perfect cell for you—one that is often flooded. Now get inside,' he said before brutally pushing me forward.

I stumbled, hissing when my hip painfully connected with the edge of the table. 'You *mother*—oh, pleased to see you again, Your Majesty.'

Reynard didn't even look at me as he held the guard by the scruff of his neck. The man's feet dangled above the ground, but the king seemingly hadn't broken a sweat. His stormy expression was bad news for my assailant.

'I gave a command for the lady to be treated as a *guest*. If you struggle to understand that, you aren't good enough to be in my service.'

The tone of his voice could freeze the river below, so detached and devoid of emotion that it was difficult to reconcile it with the angry, passionate man from last night. As soon as he let go of the guard's neck, my assailant bowed deeply.

'Forgive me, sire, but we all know why she was arrested. She doesn't deserve such quarters. Someone like her should be put to death, not provided with luxuries.'

'Did I *ask* your opinion?' Reynard said, his eye narrowing as he lifted an eyebrow at the man who dared question him. *There* was the War King—pure, ruthless danger. The guard visibly shrank, mumbling his apologies, but the king wasn't done yet. 'Tell everyone that anyone who lays a hand on this woman will be my next sparring partner, and that I won't hold back.'

The man paled, his mouth opening with such a shocked expression that I sniggered. Reynard looked at me, the corner of his lips lifting slightly in a covert smile as he walked inside and closed the door behind him.

'How do you feel?'

'Better than him. I'm glad to see you terrorise everyone equally,' I said, unable to resist the little jibe. 'Should I ask what you do to them during this *sparring*, or is that a royal secret?'

His gaze was so focused on me that I felt naked beneath his scrutiny despite being fully clothed.

'It's just sword practice, where I stretch my muscles and teach them a lesson or two. Sometimes it gets a little . . . boisterous,' he said. 'Is it warm enough in here?'

'What?' My genuine confusion at the sudden change of subject made him huff before he leaned against the doorframe, keeping his distance from me.

'The healer told me you were suffering from the cold sickness. I should have left you with something to cover yourself with.' His fingers drummed on the wood before he made a fist. 'Well, you have blankets aplenty now.'

Indeed I did. The bed was buried under furs and quilts, some of which had fallen on the floor.

Is he trying to apologise?

That was the last thing I'd expected after his previously arrogant display.

Another shard of anger melted inside me.

'Thank you, and I'm fine.' I gestured for him to sit. 'It's not my first time sleeping on a stone-cold floor.'

There was only one chair, and even as he shook his head, I walked to the bed, leaving him with the option. It took a moment to clear a space to sit, but as I did, I wrapped a soft wool shawl over my shoulders. 'Thank you for letting me send my friend a message, and for the accommodation.'

He laughed. '"Staying with a friend?" How could I refuse such a nicely phrased request?' he said, licking his slightly swollen lower lip. 'Riordan confirmed your story about warning the mages.'

So, this is my reward.

I didn't push the subject. Growing up in the Brotherhood had taught me that there was only so much grovelling or arguing a man could take in one day, and he had done a lot already.

Despite the abundance of space, Reynard still stood at the door, observing my battle with the throws with an amused expression.

'You know you can sit down. The door won't fall off its hinges if you stop leaning on it,' I said.

His lips twitched, and he coughed, looking away as if being amused by me was a crime. 'Thank you, Viper. I'll stay where I am. I have a few questions, though.'

'Ah, now we discover the price for all this luxury. Of course, Your Majesty. I'll answer all your queries. Every. Single. One of them,' I said, throwing his words from last night in his face. 'So, what do you want to know? Do you want to hear about Wiosna or about who wants you dead?'

'Those can wait for Riordan. He'll be back in two days, maybe a little longer. I . . .' He paused as if holding himself back before his posture relaxed again. 'Tell me, little Viper, why did you join the Brotherhood? What were you looking for? Money? Power?'

'Revenge, but why are you assuming I had a choice?' I answered, placing my hand on my stomach as it rumbled.

Reynard frowned before opening the door and calling for food. This time, when he closed it, he sat on the chair near the door.

I rolled my eyes. 'Sitting so far away is bizarre. You can come closer, I won't bite.'

I don't know what had made me say that, but he looked me dead in the eye and licked the small wound on his lower lip, as if reminding me that I *had*, in fact, bit him. My cheeks heated with embarrassment and his smile grew bigger.

'First lie . . . but I'll let it slide,' he said, stretching out on the chair. 'Why did you want revenge?'

'My parents. They were killed when I was young. And before you ask, my father was no saint, just a horse trader who thought swindling a local chieftain was the height of cleverness. His triumph only lasted a few days before a group of mercenaries turned up asking for money . . . I'm sure you can guess how that went,' I said, unwilling to share the painful memories.

'I still want to hear it,' he answered calmly.

'Only if you promise to leave me alone after I tell you. I'm tired and want to rest.'

His brows shot up before he scoffed. 'You still think you can tell me what to do? Just answer me, Viper. How did you become a dark sister?'

'After the mercenaries burned my family alive as . . . an example, keeping me for . . . a bit of fun, a man turned up and offered them money to be my first,' I stuttered, the memory of that day still difficult to talk about.

Reynard stood from the chair and moved towards me, halting mid-step. 'Did he hurt you?'

'No. Although I almost hurt *him*. I promised to rip his neck open with my teeth if he came any closer,' I said. 'Seeing that I was serious, my willingness to kill earned me a contract and the means to avenge my family. The price for my soul was a small bag of herbs and the instructions on how to poison those bastards with it. And before you pity me—I enjoyed every moment that I stood there, watching them die in agony next to the ashes of my mother and sister.'

I turned my head towards the window, hiding my unwanted tears. 'That was my first kill,' I whispered, seeking comfort in the shawl as I wrapped it tighter around me. 'Now you can leave. I'm too tired to listen to your judgement.'

My story wasn't a secret. Jagon bragged about it often, letting everyone know that *he* was the one who had found the 'gem amongst the ashes.'

Still, even after all these years, it was difficult to talk about it. My father was a naïve fool who had earned his fate, but my mother had possessed a childlike innocence that made her death even more horrible. It often felt like her spirit was elsewhere as she looked at me with those verdant green eyes, her smile making the flowers bloom.

My mother lived simply, happily. She loved her garden and the orchard, her kindness and laughter burning brightest when we cavorted between the trees, fireflies dancing around us. What those bastards did to her . . . what they wanted to do to *me* . . .

I took a deep, calming breath, blinking away the tears while I pushed my bittersweet memories back into the deep recesses of my soul. 'Please leave, Your Majesty. It wasn't a lie, and I'm tired.'

My words caught him off guard. Reynard frowned, but before he could argue, a soft knock announced the arrival of the food he'd ordered. Still, he looked indecisive, silently watching the maidservant as she placed the tray on the table.

'You know I'll check this story,' he said finally.

I nodded. 'I expect no less. The grand master has a record of it. Just ask him to send you a copy from the archives. As for the contract, I burned it when I bought my freedom,' I said, turning my attention to the food.

I didn't want to look at Reynard, not right now. I didn't need his pity or his understanding or his disbelief, just . . . his absence.

He got the message.

I waited until the door closed behind him before I sat to eat my breakfast. Sun, sweet pastries, and herbal tea slowly erased the traces of sadness, allowing me to focus on my surroundings.

What am I caught up in now? I wondered, falling back onto the bed, pleasantly sated after my meal.

Well, whatever it is, at least it has gilded bars.

I allowed myself a small smile, testing the deliciously soft mattress while stroking the finest silk bedding.

Reynard was an enigma I couldn't decipher. His rage at seeing me made perfect sense, but his kindness? The bath, this room, and the strange apology felt like a trap or some twisted game. I didn't like the uncertainty or gratitude I felt because of it, and I certainly shouldn't like the broody, brutal bastard himself.

My bones creaked as I stretched out, yawning so hard my jaw popped. I fought my exhaustion, knowing I should find a means of escape. A valiant hero would rip up the bedding and sneak away through the window, but I was no hero. The window overlooked a massive drop that ended in jumbled, sharp rocks, and I was too bloody tired to swing on the end of a makeshift rope like some deranged squirrel.

Half asleep, my thoughts again drifted to Reynard. It was no surprise I hadn't recognised him in the forest. On Dagome's coins, his profile looked chiselled and unforgiving, but up close, he was handsome, with an intriguing softness to his lips, especially when he kissed.

I moaned, pushing my face into a pillow, annoyed and embarrassed by my reaction to him. But gods, did the man know how to kiss.

If we weren't enemies . . . I thought, trailing a finger over my lips.

His harshness matched the defined lines and sculpted muscles beneath his tanned skin. His short black beard and eyepatch that now covered his scar only added to the illusion, making him look more like a villain or an ancient warlord from tales of old, the kind whispered to blushing daughters to warn them of the world's dangers. And unfortunately, as much as I wished to deny it, I'd really liked that kiss.

'Get those stupid thoughts out of your head, Sana,' I muttered. 'It'll never happen again.'

It didn't matter if he had his moments.

Reynard was still the king. And I was still his prisoner.

'Sana. Wake up, troublemaker, we need to go,' a gentle voice whispered next to my ear.

When I opened my eyes, shadows danced in the fading light of twi-light, and a large, looming shape knelt next to my bed. The scent of burnt caramel, the signature of Irsha's favourite mead, instantly calmed my senses.

'What are you doing here?' I whispered, reaching up to stroke his face.

'I came to rescue my princess from her ivory tower,' he said, and I rolled my eyes when I felt his smile widen. 'Now come on, we don't have much time.'

He tried to pull me out of bed, but I shook my head. 'No, wait. Let me think.'

'We don't have time. The guards are about to change, so we need to go,' he urged. 'Sana, Jagon's back, and the Brotherhood's in uproar. Boyan issued your invitation, but Jagon challenged him, claiming it was just a cover-up and that Boyan no longer had control over the city. I need to take you to a safe house before he learns where you are.'

'He already knows, and he threatened Lily to keep me in check,' I said.

Irsha cursed, standing up. 'I'll kill that motherfucker. What did he say? Is she in danger now?'

'No, you know the rules. If you kill him now, the rest of the Brotherhood will hunt you down as a traitor. The only way to kill Jagon and stay alive is to challenge him during the grand master's trial when Boyan dies.'

Irsha muttered another curse. 'I hate to see you in danger . . . or Lily, for that matter. She's so delicate,' he said, his last remark surprising me. Lily might look like a porcelain doll, but beneath her fragile exterior lay a core of steel and a will that often scared me.

'I know, but Jagon is only part of the problem. There was a man with him—' I paused, wondering how to voice my concerns. 'The way he spoke . . . he's bad news, Irsha. I fear something much bigger than your, my, or even the Brotherhood's plans is in play.'

'Alright, but that changes nothing in the moment. We need to get you out of here, and our time is running out. Get dressed. *Now,*' he said.

'No. Trust me. I need to stay,' I responded, expecting Irsha's pained groan. 'But please do something for me. Remember that lip rouge I made? It's somewhere in Jagon's workshop, and there are probably some letters incriminating Lily there as well. We need them. Without that evidence, Jagon has nothing to submit to the court.' I paused. 'And should Tivala find out and try to circumnavigate the court by hiring a Blade to end her . . . Well, the request must go through you.'

He smiled. 'You sound like you're still Boyan's shadow.'

'I sound like a woman who won't lose another family to vengeful arseholes,' I said, pushing him off the bed. 'Now, go and bribe Jagon's current apprentice. I'm sure my former master makes their life just as miserable as he did mine. They'll likely be willing to provide a little information for some money—and Irsha? Wait for me. I'll be back, I promise.'

'Or I could just throw you over my shoulder and leave with you now,' he said, visibly irritated once more.

'Come on, Blade, you can always return and play hero tomorrow if need be. Trust my judgement and keep an eye out for any strangers with southern accents and pasty white skin hanging around Jagon.'

'You saw his backer?' Irsha asked, playing with his dagger.

'Only a servant, unfortunately, and only his chin,' I said, smirking. 'The little shit wasn't too happy that Jagon kept me alive. So just keep an eye out while I try begging forgiveness for stabbing the king in the face.'

'That was *you*? The woman he's been searching for like a madman? Fuuuuck Roksana, you really know how to make life interesting, don't you?'

'Yeah, tell me about it.' I rolled my eyes, not mentioning that I'd spent the last few hours dreaming of the king. My poor Blade might have thought I'd completely lost my mind.

'Fine, I'll come back soon—unless you manage to convince our illustrious monarch to release you,' Irsha said before bending and kissing my forehead. 'Be careful, Nightshade, and don't worry about Lily. I'll stay with her.' He was pulling away when we heard the heavy footsteps of the returning guards, and we both jerked back.

Irsha shook his head and unwrapped a thin but durable cord from his waist. 'This is all your fault,' he said with a smile, tying the cord to the bedpost. 'Let's hope no one sees my sorry arse dangling from the window. Untie the cord once I'm down and I'll collect it later.'

He climbed through the window, barely visible in the darkness that had replaced the twilight, while I sat on the windowsill thinking over the concern and fondness in his voice when he had mentioned Lily's name. I remembered that tone from when he was courting me, and I could only hope he hadn't fallen for the courtesan whose moniker was the 'Ice Queen.'

One way or another, he'd protect her. However, I had little hope that Irsha would find the rouge. My Blade was a skilled assassin, and he'd proven it by sneaking in here despite all the guards, but asking him to search Jagon's workshop was like expecting him to find a needle in a haystack, especially with its many hidden areas. We still had time, but a niggling doubt irked me.

Am I making a mistake by staying here?

No. I owed the king a sliver of trust, if only as a way to repay his defence of me in the forest. Rested, fed, and out of direct danger, I could no longer avoid thinking about how everything between us had started. Despite my excuses, maiming the man whose only crime was that of trying to help me weighed heavily on my conscience.

'I wish I could turn back time,' I whispered, staring at the starry sky until a noise dragged my attention to another balcony where a solitary figure stood motionlessly looking at my window.

I easily recognised the shape. Only one man could be so tall, so imposing, even from this distance.

I doubted Reynard could see me, but had he seen Irsha? As if in answer to my question, he spun around and disappeared inside.

'Well, this will be interesting,' I mused, untying the cord and letting it fall before closing the window. With no better option, I went back to bed and waited for him to arrive.

If I'd learnt anything about the king, it was that he wouldn't come and ask questions politely but charge in with the power of a blizzard.

And I needed to find a way to calm the storm.

Chapter 16

Roksana

The large pillow pressed to my chest was a childish defensive gesture, but I needed a barrier. Something to hold on to as I faced the king's wrath. Long, decisive footsteps sounded in the corridor before a few curt words outside informed me he had arrived.

'Just stay calm,' I whispered, preparing to be dangled from his grasp while he snarled questions at me.

A polite knock, followed by a pause, was the last thing I expected.

'Enter?' I answered, unsure why the door wasn't flying off its hinges, but as soon as Reynard came into the room, I understood. It felt like the temperature instantly dropped, and I shivered when I saw his rigid posture.

'Good evening, Viper,' he said through gritted teeth, perfectly enunciating every word. 'I'm pleased that you've found the room suitable enough for receiving guests but before I bolt the window, would you care to tell me who was visiting and why?'

Reynard wouldn't look at me as he addressed me. His gaze was fixed somewhere above my head, icy grey eye studying the tapestries with a cold, unblinking stare that did nothing to ease my tension. I knew I was looking death in the face. The scourge of the battlefield, whose ruthlessness had won the war, was now directing his glacial anger at *me*.

My knees buckled when I stood, and the pillow fell from my hands, forgotten.

'He's a friend and no threat to you.'

'I will be the judge of that,' he said, his tone clipped. 'This *friend* . . . does he have a name?'

'Not for you, sire,' I replied as calmly as I could. My heart hammered in my chest. As much as I wanted to placate the king, I wouldn't betray Irsha.

'Not . . . for me,' he echoed, his body stiffening before he exhaled slowly. 'Did it not occur to you that I should be made *aware* of any visitors?' he questioned, waving a hand over the fae lamp, the soft light brightening the room as he looked around.

'He's already gone, but I'm sure you saw that,' I said quietly, watching the conflicting emotions flash across the king's face before he shook his head.

'I'm trying, Viper. I'm trying to be understanding, to be kind, but you make it so fucking difficult.'

He stepped closer, dominating the space. Reynard hadn't fully dressed before coming to my room, and the casual dark brown trousers and white shirt he wore did nothing to hide his muscular chest, especially with the poorly tied laces falling loose.

'Why was he here?' he asked. 'What are you planning?'

He lifted his hand to my face, and I swallowed hard, waiting as it hovered near my throat before he grabbed the bedpost behind me.

'You will tell me, Viper, or I'll call the truthseeker and order him to eviscerate your mind.'

Instinctively, I took a step back. The edge of the bed collided with my legs, forcing me to sit, and my muscles tensed as I lifted my head. The sensation of being utterly at his mercy was difficult to ignore, but when I met his gaze, Reynard's expression shifted from one of anger to confusion. He ran his hand through his messy hair in a gesture I'd observed earlier, a little tick when he seemed uncertain that made him appear so much more human.

Than his hand dropped and his pupil dilated as he ran his thumb over my lips, parting them ever so slightly. The gentleness of the simple gesture made me gasp, the soft sound shattering the stillness.

'I meant no harm, Your Majesty,' I blurted out, finding my position so vulnerable that I struggled to breathe. 'My friend was concerned and came to check on me. If I were planning something, I would've left with him like he asked.'

His eyebrow shot up before he huffed a humourless laugh.

'You want me to believe that the woman who told me to "eat shit and die," who claims to hate me, *chose* to stay in the palace when she could escape?'

Is he even aware that he's touching me? I thought, heat crawling up my neck when his fingers trailed gently over my jawline, and for the first time since he'd come, I didn't hear ice in his voice when he asked, 'Why?'

'To prove I'm not your enemy,' I answered. I placed my hand on his abdomen, pushing him away. It was like trying to move a marble statue, each muscle, each rigid line chiselled to perfection, barely flexing as I touched them. 'And if you wouldn't mind, my name is Sana. Not Viper or Nightshade, just Sana.'

My voice sounded small, even to my ears. He didn't move at first, his gaze drifting to my hand, as if he only just noticed how close we were and that he was still caressing my face. Reynard reminded me of the orcish chieftains—brutal men with unparalleled strength, yet unexpectedly gentle when they wanted to be.

His brows drew closer before he stepped away.

'Nightshade? The Deadly Nightshade?' he asked, and I cursed myself for carelessly revealing my Brotherhood name. 'You were Boyan's shadow. I knew that old bastard lied to me.'

His triumphant smile made me wonder if he was congratulating himself on discovering another piece of the puzzle.

How he knew about it baffled me. The position of shadow was one of trust: The grand master's spy and enforcer—a person with the deepest insight into Brotherhood business, their skills and loyalty used to control and discipline the others.

'I always wondered who it was executing Boyan's enemies at the twitch of his finger . . .' The corner of his lip lifted, the soft baritone of his voice like molasses flowing down my spine. 'The princess of rogues. My choice of rooms, it seems, was perfect.'

Reynard walked to the table and poured himself some wine, still with that same lopsided, knowing smile.

'Oh, for fuck's sake, I'm no princess,' I muttered. His eyebrow rose before he took another sip of his drink, annoying me with his arrogance. 'You are so confusing,' I said after a moment of silence.

'So are you, little Viper. A woman capable of violence, yet you risk my wrath to protect your friend. You're someone whom Boyan found worthy of knowing his secrets, yet here you are, offering up your own so freely I wonder if I need a truthseeker at all, especially after his blunder.' The king placed his empty glass on the table and walked towards the window, turning off the fae light as he passed. 'I don't know if you're a trap or an opportunity, but we are going to find out.'

Reynard stood there for a long moment, his reflection obscuring the dark panorama barely visible in the moonlight, before he pointed to the space in front of him.

'Come here.'

'Why?'

'Because I said to?'

'If you want to throw me out of the window, shouldn't you open it first?'

He tilted his head, watching me in silence, and I would have sold my soul to know what plans were forming in that thick skull of his.

'I won't force you, but there is a question I want answered before I decide what to do with you.'

I wanted to refuse, but something in his gaze made me realise he was testing me again. Fabric rustled as I stepped towards him, enjoying the disbelief that flashed across his features, so briefly that I thought I'd imagined it.

'Closer,' he said when I stopped just out of arm's reach. It was more than close enough for me, but I took another step until we were almost touching.

'I can see the hesitation in your eyes, my brave Viper. So many questions you want to ask, yet here you are,' he said, a small smile ghosting his lips. 'Stay still, no matter what I do. I won't hurt you. You have my word.'

I nodded tentatively at the bizarre request, lowering my head. His scent—as fresh as the steppe in spring, lemongrass and musk mixed with a powerful masculine aroma that made my heart beat faster—overwhelmed me . . . I dreaded him seeing the blush that coloured my cheeks.

Reynard seemed just as affected by my proximity. A bead of perspiration trailed down his collarbone, another drop of sweat forming above the throbbing pulse in his neck.

'Good, now turn around and put your hands on the windowsill,' he said in a husky tone.

It was too much for me. The heat glowing on my face crawled over my chest.

'Sire, whatever the question is, I don't want to fight you again. But I will if you try forcing me . . .' I said, pulling away, but he caught my hand and guided it to the stone windowsill.

'I told you I wouldn't hurt you, Viper, but I'm angry and I can't even explain why. If you ever let a man enter your room without my knowledge again, I'll show you exactly the kind of brute I can be,' he whispered, the threat in his voice mixed with a lower, more guttural sound. I pulled away, eyes wide in shock.

He exhaled slowly, releasing his hold and letting me escape. 'Show me you trust me, Roksana. Let me find my answers.'

He waited for my decision, but I didn't know what to do, especially with him standing so close, observing my reactions.

Ignoring my instincts, I placed my shaking hands back on the windowsill, holding onto it so hard that my knuckles turned white. My mind protested but my body's response confused me. I was trembling, pulse thrumming in my throat as my nipples peaked, much too visible under my chemise for my comfort, but the tension wasn't unpleasant. If anything, I was curious about what he wanted and why asking me questions required him to stand so close that the heat of his body enveloped me like a blanket.

In the end, it wasn't Reynard's request that frightened me, but the pleasure I felt at seeing the hunger in his gaze . . . the pleasure I mustn't explore.

The tension built until I came close to whimpering. Then he tilted my head to the side, the gesture so primal my internal voice screamed at me to escape this predator before he ripped open my throat.

I stared at his reflection in the dark window, waiting. Determination crept into his gaze before he took my hair, twisting it away from my neck. His fingertips grazed over my skin, as gently as the stroke of a feather, but it was enough for heat to awaken in my core. Time slowed, and my breath misted the window as I watched, fascinated by our reflection. His head dipped. His nose touched the side of my neck, and I inhaled sharply, letting him pull me closer until our bodies touched.

'Do you like that, little Viper?' His husky voice vibrated against my skin, his thick beard teasing me.

I wanted to say no, but that would've been a lie. Instead, my pleading gaze traced his movements as the king's muscles flexed, his body tense behind me. His free hand grabbed the windowsill next to mine, thumb caressing my knuckles, while he breathed in again. A long, pained groan reverberated in his throat while the glass reflected the golden glow that flashed dangerously in his eye.

'Your Majesty, what's . . .' I asked breathlessly, desperate to put some barrier between us, even if they were just words. My body softened in his hands, surrendering the moment his hand tightened in my hair. A low rumbling sound escaped him while I fought to stay still, to resist the dangerous allure of his pure, absolute control. I could see his need, his desire, yet his touch remained gentle. When our eyes met in the window, goosebumps prickled over my skin.

'Call me Rey,' he whispered in my ear, his breath caressing my sensitive skin. I felt like prey staring into the golden gaze of a wolf, unable to avert my eyes, hypnotised by the danger. 'Call me Rey, Sanika,' he commanded, his fingers shifting to encircle my throat.

I shivered at the raw emotion in the endearment. Sanika was the name for the first blush of dawn while night still reigned in the sky. A hope that darkness would pass and Zorya, the heavenly maiden, would open the sky and allow the sun to rise.

My mind raced as I prayed he wouldn't notice how much he was affecting me.

'Rey, please . . .' I muttered.

He released the windowsill and wrapped his arm around me, crushing me to his chest.

'I like my name on your lips, and I fucking hate myself for it,' he said. A tremor ran through his body as if he were battling a monster for control.

Despite being trapped against Reynard's chest, my instincts told me he would never succumb, that I was safe in his embrace. For the longest time, we stood like statues until he eventually closed his eyes.

A knock on the door startled us both.

'Fuck,' he grumbled, finally pulling away while I called for the visitor to enter, happy to not be alone. A servant walked in with a tray, her face draining of colour when she noticed Reynard by the window.

'I'm so sorry, sire. The guard told me the lady was awake, but he didn't mention a visitor. She hasn't eaten since morning, so I thought . . .' she stuttered.

'Good. Make sure you look after her,' he said, not even looking at the poor girl. 'But right now, leave us.'

The nightstand wobbled when he knocked against it, the infuriating man turning his back on me as he grabbed the wine bottle and drained it dry in a few deep gulps.

'Will you at least tell me why you were sniffing me?' I asked cautiously, still shaken by the entire experience.

'I had my reasons,' came the curt, controlled answer. Reynard gestured to the tray. 'Eat and rest. Tomorrow, my healer will examine you.'

'Why? What now?' I stepped towards him, but he put his hand out, stopping me. 'Is this another hoop to jump through before you let me go? How many times must I prove I'm on your side?'

The bastard looked me dead in the eye and laughed as if my question was a joke.

'As many times as needed,' he said, and I realised the horrible truth.

Reynard Erenhart had no plans to let me go.

'You can't keep me here forever—'

'I can do whatever I want, Viper, but I'm not a cruel man, just . . . cautious. I'll have Riordan interrogate you as soon as he's back. Until then, indulge me. The Brotherhood's records confirm your childhood story, and Boyan was ready to swear a blood oath that you haven't come here to end me. However, there's still many questions that need answering.'

'What questions? Whether I prefer death by blade or poison?' I snapped, annoyed by the obstacles he kept placing before me, the pleasure his touch had awakened now replaced by righteous anger.

'You assume I'm giving you a choice. I am no longer seeking your death . . . Maybe I never was,' he said, a hint of wistfulness in his voice.

'So, you'd rather let the Brotherhood fall than take a risk and let me go? I need to go back before the situation worsens. Could you please just *listen* to what I'm saying for a change?' I said through clenched teeth, doing my best not to shout.

'I'm listening, but there is too much at stake to take your word at face value, no matter how pretty it is.' His tone was so bitter that I frowned. 'Since the end of the war, there have been five assassination attempts on me, and countless schemes to remove me from the throne. One attempt was by a guard I had trained and trusted with my life. Do you know what it taught me?'

'That everyone has a price?' I asked, resigned. He wasn't wrong. Everyone had a price, though often, it wasn't money but the life of someone they cherished that forced people to perform despicable deeds. 'Did you ever ask him why he did it?'

'No. He was dead the moment he drew a blade on me,' Reynard answered. 'But I learned that danger rarely comes with a warning, that even the most trusted friend can betray you for the right price.'

'Then maybe he didn't have a choice? Maybe he traded your life for someone he loved?'

'Everybody has a choice, Sana. Just like I chose to spare your life after you tried to murder me.' He turned towards me. 'It takes more than a day to earn my trust, and you're facing the consequences of your actions, so stop complaining that the world isn't catering to your wishes.'

'Gods, how could you have won a war when you are so blind to what's in front of you?'

'I wasn't half-blind during the war . . . that's entirely on you,' he said, his demeanour growing colder the longer I argued. 'Now, that's enough, Roksana. This isn't a negotiation. Just do as I say.'

It took all my patience not to grab the pitcher of water and smash it over his head. I was beside myself. I'd thought we were making progress, but now it felt like he'd cheated in a game with rules I didn't understand.

'Fine, I'll see your healer, the truthseeker, let you sniff me like a bloodhound—if you promise to let me go.'

He smirked, reaching for the door. 'I would never make promises I can't keep.'

'You bloody bastard, I trusted you!'

He paused, turning his head just enough to meet my gaze, his expression hardening. 'Yes, but that doesn't mean I trust *you*.'

That was the final straw. I grabbed the pitcher and hurled it at him with every ounce of strength I had. The damn man ducked, and my poorly aimed missile smashed against the guard's breastplate. My victim looked at me with such hostility that I shrank back.

Reynard's eyes flicked between the soaked guard and me, a wicked grin tugging at his lips. His voice was smooth and perfectly calm when he said, 'Please don't demolish your room, Roksana. Unless you want to move into my bedroom? I'm sure you remember the way.'

My mouth fell open, confounded by his words.

Reynard bowed and slowly closed the door—while I wondered why the man who claimed he hated me was acting like he wanted me between his sheets.

Chapter 17

Reynard

I swore under my breath for the hundredth time. How long had I been sitting here, unable to think of anything except the scent of that woman's hair? The stack of unread paperwork on my desk was a testament to my distraction, and that was just this morning's reports and petitions. The pile my assistant had slammed down threatened to bury me as it teetered on the edge, but I found it impossible to care. I wished I were more like Orm. My brother could do this with a smile on his face, the bureaucracy calming to his savage heart.

I could still feel her, her scent lingering on my fingertips driving me insane, but I couldn't let it affect me. That Viper could be my salvation if I trusted her enough to reveal that her poison was slowly killing me.

'Don't give yourself false hope,' I muttered once again, but the hope awakened this morning refused to die. Once Riordan had confirmed she was the same woman who had come to warn the mages, I went to talk to her, only to see my fucking guard manhandling her.

Maybe I should go to the garrison?

A few rounds sparring with that arsehole might bring me peace of mind.

My grip tightened on my quill and the delicate tool snapped, staining my hand with ink. This loss of control wasn't helpful, so with a deep breath, I wiped the stain, pushing aside the ruined document, and grabbed another file.

The page in front of me was a merchant's petition, the Dwarven League asking for reduced taxes on their precious metals. I'd rejected it already, but the stubborn bastards wouldn't give up and sent me at least one petition a week.

Do they think I'll sign one by mistake, or are they trying to wear me down?

Just as I'd expected, since I'd returned half-blind, many took it as a sign of weakness. Meetings with the Royal Council had become an endless battle, the old families fiercely opposing my reforms, and various factions had flooded me with demands, as if I were more susceptible to falling for their nonsense now that I'd been injured.

I lost an eye, for fuck's sake, not half my brain.

Only my army remained loyal, showing me steadfast support, but they long ago learned that a man's value was more than the sum of his body parts.

I glanced briefly at the stained-glass window overlooking the river, my guest once again occupying my mind, confounding me with her attitude.

Why did she do that? I wondered. Roksana's promise to fight me if I overstepped had impressed me, but she'd done more than trust me. I'd felt her reaction, seen the blush of desire.

And I almost gave in, forgetting who she was and what she had done. Calling her Sanika was a mistake, but her reflection, a ray of light surrounded by the darkness of my presence threatening to consume her, was just that—the hope before dawn.

Gods, what am I thinking?

Would it have been different if we'd met in better circumstances? Would we still be denying this maddeningly irresistible desire that filled the air with the tension of an approaching storm?

'Will I be able to let you go?' I muttered, knowing this couldn't carry on.

Fascinating as she was, and despite her reasons, Roksana had caused the unthinkable and paved the way for Dagome's enemies to ramp up their demands. After the war, I'd promised myself I'd not use brute force to rule my country, but because of her, I might not be able to keep that vow.

But today . . . Today was madness.

I'd only wanted to test if the scent that drove me crazy the other night was still there. The servants had done a good job bathing her, but it hadn't changed a thing, and as soon as my nose touched her skin, I'd lost myself in her.

The documents stacked in front of me chose that moment to wobble, spilling over my desk and bringing me back to reality. I had more important issues to deal with than the woman sleeping under my roof.

I grabbed the morning papers, determined to read through them even if it took all night.

Annoyingly, the next reports weren't critical either. They were about quarrelling nobles that the chancellor could deal with, and two related to the mages that I put aside for Riordan. Then I came across an unmarked envelope slipped between the official letters.

Your Majesty,

The Observers you stationed on the border have noticed increased movement between our kingdom and the Care'etavos Empire. Two days ago, a wagon became bogged down on a muddy road. Its axles were so deep that it took several horses to pull it out. The mage working with us became ill upon getting close and confirmed it was srebrec. We will track this shipment wherever it goes and keep you informed.

Additionally, a month ago, our spies noticed bulwark construction on the Tivalaran border. I'll update you as soon as we receive more information.

The letter was unsigned, but I easily recognised Arto's style of writing. If anyone could gather intel on Tivala, it was my sergeant-turned-spy, even if his disguise was one of a disgruntled former soldier who drank and fornicated his way around Dagome. Roksana thought she'd disclosed new information by telling the mages about the illegal srebrec trade, but I already knew about Młot's little side business. I just hadn't known he was so callously sacrificing his people for it.

However, the bulwarks on the border of Tivalaran were a surprise. I'd have to investigate those sooner rather than later.

'I hope that old fool isn't building a wall,' I muttered, reaching for a new quill and drafting orders to send more sentinels to the region to observe their movements.

As soon as I was done, my mind drifted again, and I caught myself staring through the window, wondering if she was asleep.

'I give up.' I sighed, banging my head on the desk before calling the guards.

'Bring the arch healer,' I said, waiting impatiently, even as guilt crept in. It was almost midnight, but I needed an answer, or at least a theory.

An hour later, Ciesko walked in, concern etched in the weathered lines of his face.

'Is the poison troubling you again, sire?'

He came closer, but when he tried to place a hand on my injured face, I stopped him.

'Not the poison—a Viper. I have the assassin in my custody, but the situation is complicated.'

'Oh?' Eagerness flashed in his eyes. 'Did she talk? If not, I'll coax the antidote out of her. If that doesn't help, I'm sure Riordan has his ways.'

'No,' I said, my answer startling him. 'I want Riordan interrogating her, but only when I'm certain she won't cause further damage will I take any potion of her design.'

Ciesko pulled up a chair and sat next to me with the professional, benevolent patience that many healers adopted in conversations with lost causes or total idiots.

'If that's your decision, then what is it that is troubling you now, sire?' he asked, taking my hand, and for the first time in my life, I felt utterly defeated.

'I can't get her out of my head. I react unnaturally . . .' I paused, struggling to admit my feelings. 'I can't control myself around her.'

'And how can I help with that? Do you need a calming draught?'

'No, I want you to examine her. Something happened between us in the forest, right before she struck me . . . I need to know if it's her magic or something in her body that's making a fool of me. I'll take any explanation, whatever it is.'

'I can examine her, sire, but you likely know the answer already. I'm not sure, however, if you're ready to admit it.'

'Stop talking in riddles, Ciesko.'

Like it or not, I had to know. I couldn't be tethered to the whims of a woman, especially a shadow of the Brotherhood. My determination must have been apparent on my face, because Ciesko sighed before continuing.

'I treated your wounds during the Battle of the Rift, and I can recognise your aether signature in a room full of people,' he said, confusing me because I thought we were talking about Roksana. He smiled. 'But since the accident, your signature has changed. The pattern has become more chaotic and much stronger, closely resembling your brother's.'

'Oh, please don't tell me that at the ripe old age of thirty-five I'm destined to become a dragon rider?'

I laughed it off, but he remained serious.

'I don't think you'll be able to bond with a dragon, no, but the wild magic within you has grown stronger. If not for the stasis spell Riordan put you in, I'm afraid you would have lost your sanity to the power that kept you alive.'

'How the fuck did that happen?' I shot up from the chair and walked to the window where I'd previously stood watching a man escape from Sana's balcony.

'Hard to say. Wild magic is called that for a reason. No one can predict what it will do. All we know is that your bloodline has a strong affinity for its chaos, creating at least one dragon rider a generation, while those who do not become riders are seeded with the berserker's rage. There have even been cases where near-death experiences have awakened the power.'

'So you don't think she hexed me . . . but how does that explain this obsession? Especially with her scent. Why do I feel like this? I should despise her for what she did,' I said, drumming my fingers on the desk's surface with such force that Ciesko shifted in his chair, fear flashing in his eyes.

I was afraid of losing control. I saw what wild magic had done to my brother. He was barely eight years old when he almost killed a man and I'd had to witness him being dragged away to the Cave of Choosing. My mother wailed, clawing at my father's arm when they took him, and I promised I would never let that happen ever again.

'Sire, if I may? I heard the young lady is attractive. Wild magic can react strangely when emotions are enflamed . . . I can promise you one thing, though—if you'd despise her as you claim you should, with the wild magic in control . . .' He paused, muttering, 'How to put this gently?' to himself. 'Your guest wouldn't be sleeping peacefully in her room, and I would be by her side, healing what was left of her.'

'You mean I'd have violated her.' I stated it emotionlessly, but my entire soul recoiled at such a thought. The wave of protectiveness that washed over me left me confused, but despite the violence of our first meeting, I couldn't hate my bewitching Viper.

'Is there any way I can weaken these feelings?' I asked. If there was the slightest chance I could be cured of this peculiar affliction, I'd take it.

'Time and distance, possibly? Right now, your senses are heightened and every reaction exaggerated. You could ask your brother. I heard he had a similar reaction to his mate. Or if you know someone you're drawn to in a similar way, try spending more time with them?' Ciesko smiled, patting my shoulder. 'Wild magic works in mysterious ways, but we are not animals, sire. Our actions are our own.'

I nodded, unconvinced by the old healer's words. He hadn't felt the maelstrom in my soul when I held her in my arms.

'I still want you to examine her at your earliest convenience. Something feels odd about her, and I can't neglect any avenue when it comes to her.'

Ciesko nodded, and I inclined my head, signalling his dismissal.

Alone, I stood by the window, gazing into the darkness. This conversation would have amused Roksana. Despite what I'd said to her earlier, if Ciesko confirmed she'd done nothing to me, I would let her go.

I could not be under the same roof with a woman whose touch threatened to unravel my sanity.

Chapter 18

Roksana

I stretched out, savouring the warm sun, unwilling to open my eyes. If I was to have another day like the last two, I had no reason to. Despite Reynard's insistence, I had seen no healer; no one had come to visit me, not even the king. I spent my time locked in the room, watching the birds, reading, and eating elaborate meals while waiting for the healer, the truthseeker—anybody, really. I wanted to jump through whichever hoop Reynard wanted me to jump through next and escape this gilded cage he'd put me in.

This will end today, even if I have to fake an illness, I thought, smirking. Judging by his reaction when he thought I'd tried to drown myself, I could expect the king to storm in as soon as the healer informed him I'd sneezed.

I had been more than ready to cooperate, but I hadn't prepared to be bored.

As the plan settled in my head, I stretched again, inhaling deeply. The scent of herbs overwhelmed my senses, and I focused, trying to identify them. 'Lavender, rosemary, with a hint of lily of the valley, and something else . . . pine honey?'

It was my favourite pastime. One had to learn how to recognise the scent of herbs and other ingredients in Jagon's service. Failure to do so led to his next level of 'teaching,' in which the poison master would force his apprentices to drink whichever potion they'd failed to identify.

'Very good, Mistress Regnav, but you missed the ash and lime.'

The mature voice startled me. I scrambled backwards, grabbing the bedsheet as I looked around, my eyes struggling to adjust to the brightness.

'Will you people learn to knock and wait for an answer?' I snapped, squinting at the figure beside the bed.

The man chuckled, moving closer. 'The king told me you were feisty. Calm down, child, I mean no harm.' He smelled like healing balm, the composition suggesting a blend used to increase blood flow and heal burns.

'I suppose you're the healer? Did our illustrious monarch send you?' I asked cautiously.

The elderly man nodded, his face breaking into an honest, welcoming smile.

'I am indeed. Master Ciesko, at your service. I'm sorry for the delay, but we had an incident in the city, a small fire whose victims needed my attention.' He approached until I had to lift my head to look at him. 'I was asked to test your blood for poisons and magical properties.'

I huffed in annoyance. 'Of course, why not? Just in case he wants to know, I'm not a virgin, either,' I quipped before I could stop myself. 'Wait . . . Ciesko? The arch healer, Ciesko?'

So, Reynard smelled something, freaked out, and now we're right back to no trust. Does he think I'm secreting poison or carrying the plague? Why else would he send for the arch healer if not to ensure I didn't pose a serious threat?

Ciesko's chuckle broke through my stream of thoughts. 'The king didn't ask for such an . . . unusual investigation. Though it wouldn't surprise me if he were interested in the result.' He reached for my hand. 'Will you cooperate, my lady?'

'Do I have a choice?'

It was a rhetorical question; I was already stretching out my arm. I placed my wrist in his warm, wrinkled hand, my eyes following his movements, observing as he drew a sigil before aligning it with another tattooed on his palm. Warmth flooded me, removing my lingering tiredness, and I sighed, briefly closing my eyes until a sharp pain made me hiss.

A translucent symbol shimmered over my skin, slowly turning crimson, becoming saturated with my blood. Ciesko frowned when the colour changed from shades of deep crimson to a vivid green with golden strands swirling within its depths.

'And what does that mean? Am I turning into a lizard?' I asked, pointing at the tumultuous emerald, curiosity getting the better of me. He didn't answer. Instead, Ciesko's gaze shifted from professional kindness to one of cold assessment.

'You don't know? Hmm. Riordan mentioned you can see aether, but this . . .' His hand tightened on mine, and instead of a pleasant, reassuring warmth, something else washed through me, the sensation followed by a burning pain that made me hiss. He was probing my body, and not gently. Pressure built in my core before Ciesko's eyebrows grew closer.

'Yes, and not weak either . . .' he muttered to himself, tightening his grasp even further when I tried to pull away.

'That's enough, thank you,' I said firmly, yanking my arm from his grasp.

'I was surprised when Reynard ordered me to do this, but . . . hmm . . . our king is more perceptive than I thought,' he said, his smile widening with each passing moment. 'What a discovery, my dear Roksana, what potential!'

Ciesko mumbled something else, his eyes darting from side to side, but whatever discussion he was having in his head, his excitement sent an icy shiver running down my spine.

'Your enthusiasm is unsettling. Will you tell me what you found, or is it a secret only the Court of Aether can know?'

'Secret . . . no, you have the right to know who you are. But gods—a vivamancer? Oh my, my bright, untrained gem, you will be a sensation at the university,' he said as he stood. My remark about the lizard was becoming less amusing with each passing moment.

'Sensation? Like a stuffed striga[1] or the corpse of a basilisk?' I asked, fear turning into sarcasm while I tried to unravel his ramblings.

'No, my dear. Like a mage of the High Order, which you are about to be. You need training, and lots of it, but that will come after the geas.[2] The king cannot refuse me.'

Ciesko's agitation was becoming worrisome.

'What are you talking about? Geas? Am I a threat?' I asked, wondering if I should slap him to get some sense out of him.

'There's nothing to worry about, my dear. And the danger can be contained. I will arrange everything for you. Please excuse me. I must look into it before the Court of Aether does something stupid. Your situation is . . . precarious, but it's no bother. I'll cut your ties with the Brotherhood and train you myself. That's for the best.'

'What if I don't agree?' I asked cautiously.

'Dear child, did I ask for your agreement? A vivamancer's power is too volatile for you to be allowed free rein,' he said with a benevolent smile. I coughed, my throat constricting.

---

1. **Striga** — a female demon born of a violent death who hunts those who have wronged her; appears as a skinny female with two rows of teeth, large claws, and leather-like hair.

2. **Geas (s.)/geasa (pl.)** — a form of magical compulsion, curse, or obligation. Those under a geas are required to follow certain conditions or orders, risking death for disobedience.

'What . . .? Wait! What's a damn vivamancer?' I reached out, trying to grasp the older man's hand, but he was already rushing away. Still, my words made him pause.

'A rare magic, unseen, erased from this part of the world . . . until now. And I'm the one who discovered you! We'll need to confirm it, of course, but I know I'm right. Gods, everybody believes your kind is extinct. Where does your family live?'

'We lived on the Orcish Steppe. My father raised horses there . . .' I said, still utterly confused. The arch healer, however, looked like a dragon had dropped a treasure in his lap.

'That would explain it. Wild magic is strong there, especially around the Grey Peaks Mountains.' He rubbed his chin, wearing a thousand-yard stare. 'How could we have missed you? Never mind, don't say a word to anyone. It is paramount to your safety. Not even Riordan or the king must know until it's safe. I will let you know.'

I gritted my teeth, trying to remain calm despite my heart hammering so hard I could feel my pulse in my throat. Was this why I couldn't light a single flame despite being able to see aether? A word he'd used in his jumbled speech had also stood out and concerned me the most—*erased*.

He'd said my type of magic had been *erased* from Tir ha Mor, and I was afraid to ask who'd done that and why. If my ability were as rare as he claimed, would the same thing happen to me? Or would I be prodded and probed until I wished for death?

I'd wanted to learn, to find a mentor, but in gaining both, my life had taken another turn on fate's twisting road.

'Master Ciesko. I haven't decided if I wish to pursue magic, but if I do, I promise you'll be the first to know,' I said, bowing my head respectfully, hoping that would be enough to curb the old healer's enthusiasm.

It wasn't.

He was still talking to himself in a distracted, self-absorbed manner, as if I wasn't a person but an object to be studied.

I found it hard to breathe.

Ciesko must have noticed because he was suddenly by my side, a
hand on my back, coaxing me to inhale. I felt the strands of his magic
shifting around my body while he spoke softly, as if to a child.

'You're overwhelmed. I'm sorry, it's a lot to take in. Rest, and
don't worry. Vivamancy is a gift that must be nurtured. The king
might be holding you here now, but the force of creation will always
find a way. Fate brought you to me for a reason . . .' He paused,
placing his hand on my cheek in a fatherly gesture I hadn't expected
from a stranger. 'You were born a mage, raised to be a killer, but in
the end, only you can determine who you become. All I ask is that
you give me a chance to show you the way.'

I swallowed hard, but my panic subsided.

Ask? You are not asking but pushing me where you want me to be, I
thought, forcing a smile. I wasn't a young apprentice who could be
moulded to his expectations, and I wouldn't discard half of my life
on his whims.

Ciesko waited patiently for my response, his expression filled with
empathy. I knew he expected my enthusiasm, but all I could manage
to do was play for time. I pulled away, letting the mage's hand drop
to his side.

'Master Ciesko, thank you for everything, but I cannot give you
an answer right now. There's my current situation to deal with first.'

'Yes, but—'

A loud knock interrupted our conversation, the door opening to
reveal Riordan.

'Master Ciesko, are you finished? The king is losing patience, and if I have to hold him back any longer, I'll end up in an early grave,' he said without looking at me.

'Riordan, does that mean I can see the king?' I asked.

My hope rose at seeing the mage, but it didn't last.

'His Majesty is busy with other things,' he replied, making me sigh.

'Then please do me a favour. Tell him that keeping me under lock and key isn't benefiting anyone. I'm calm and compliant, but that will change if he insists on playing games,' I said, pointing to Ciesko's sigil still glowing on my forearm. 'If he wants answers, he can ask me now—or the next time he sends someone, they'll find an empty room.'

Riordan sighed heavily, shaking his head.

'My hair will turn grey dealing with you two. Fine, I'll ask him, but you can't go dressed like that. Reynard would have my head if I paraded you around wearing only a nightgown like some second-class virgin.'

The remark cracked my carefully crafted façade. 'What the crud is a second-class virgin?' I asked before looking around. 'And what can I wear? My clothes have vanished.' I frowned, noticing that not only had my kirtle disappeared, but my boots were gone too.

'I'm surprised you've never heard of . . . Well, I doubt women in the Brotherhood ever need to see a healer to ask to be returned to . . . their natural state,' he said, and my mouth dropped open. I didn't even notice when he clapped his hands and the door opened again, revealing a maid with a handful of fabric. 'Come in and help the lady.'

'Someone would ask for that?'

Riordan sniggered. 'Many, especially after a failed engagement. Get dressed, Roksana. If you're lucky, I'll come and get you in an hour.'

I nodded, suddenly tired despite having woken up late, unsure what would happen if, despite the interrogation, Reynard still wouldn't let me go. Interrogation by truthseeker was always a tricky business. As much as I wanted to tell him the truth about Jagon's affairs and our encounter in the forest, there were Brotherhood secrets no one should be privy to. How would he react if I refused to answer?

My sudden stillness must have caught the psychic mage's attention because he sighed again. 'Do not be afraid, Roksana. I can't believe I'm saying this, but I'm on your side. The king's not a monster, whatever you may think of him.'

I felt a sarcastic comment straining to escape, but I didn't want to antagonise my one ally, at least for now.

'He might not be a monster, but he is a stubborn and infuriately arrogant oaf who doesn't listen to reason. Now, could you please leave so I can dress?' I asked, kicking myself as I watched the maid set out some clothes.

Riordan fought valiantly to keep a straight face at my characterisation of the king before both men left the room. I didn't miss Ciesko whispering in his ear while gesturing in my direction. Whatever the revelation was, Riordan paused, glancing at me strangely as the door closed.

A short while later, a beautiful royal blue gown was artfully draped over my body in the softest of embraces. Unfortunately, as pretty as it was, the dress was too tight across my chest, even if it swept nicely over the curve of my hips, accentuating my waist. It was clear the gown was made for someone less encumbered than I, and it didn't help that age had added a little extra padding to my body. Every time I took a deep breath, the laces holding the velvet bodice together creaked, stretching the fabric at the seams.

I looked at the maid who was biting her lips to restrain her laughter.

'I'm sorry, my lady,' she said. 'It was the king's choice, and he wasn't in the mood to discuss sizes.'

I blinked, looking at her. 'The king . . . picked the dress?'

If I'd thought nothing could surprise me, I was wrong. The image of that muscled giant inspecting frilly dresses and picking one out for me was my undoing. I bent over, laughing so hard that the dress creaked even more, sending me into a complete meltdown.

It was official. I was going insane.

Riordan must have thought the same when he entered the room, frowning as I tried to breathe, tears streaming down my face.

'Roksana? He'll see you . . . What's going on?'

'The king picked the dress . . . and it creaks,' I explained, gasping for breath.

The mage frowned, but as I spread my arms, reproducing the sound, his lips twitched as he controlled his laughter.

'That's not all. Look at this.' Out of pure mischief, I took a deep breath. The bodice groaned before a pinging snap announced the top eyelet holding it together had broken under the strain, revealing much more of my cleavage. 'Oof. There, I can breathe now.'

'I can't . . . So that's why he visited the chancellor's daughter earlier,' Riordan muttered, desperately trying to keep his composure. Only the maid looked distraught.

'My lady, please stop, we don't have anything else for you . . .'

'Fine . . . fine, let's go,' I said, gesturing to Riordan. 'Lead the way, Mage, and just so you know, I won't be curtsying.'

'I wouldn't expect it. Not after that display,' he answered, giving me his arm. 'I wish we'd met earlier, Roksana. You are truly interesting—and more entertaining than I'd ever have thought,' he said carelessly. I realised Riordan and I were similar in age, even if he acted more mature than I did.

'I live to serve. Poisons, laughter . . . I'm a singing, dancing, year-round peasant's fair,' I said with a polite bow, and this time, his laughter filled the corridor.

The mage led us through endless halls, and I sighed in relief when we passed the doors to the dungeon and the grand throne room before heading to a much smaller audience chamber. Before we entered, Riordan stopped.

'A word of warning,' he cautioned. 'Despite what you did to him, Rey rose above it, and instead of revenge, he wants to understand. A lesser man would've killed you, but he has more compassion than I, so don't waste this chance and make him regret trusting you.'

I pulled away from him, his words catching me off guard. It was more than a warning; it was advice.

The guards before us opened the doors, and I stepped forward.

'Thank you, but I assure you I never wanted to hurt the king,' I said with a tense smile, adding for good measure, 'And that won't change.'

I raised my head high and strode confidently into the room, leaving him to catch up with me.

Riordan's words burned because they were true. A lesser man would have killed me, though Reynard—confusing and arrogant as he was—hadn't truly hurt me. In the grand scheme of things, fingerprint bruises and a night spent on cold stones were nothing compared to what I did to him.

I'm trying to atone. I hope you can see that, my broody king, I thought, approaching the figure on the throne as he sat there with a stone-cold expression.

Except I no longer believed in his coldness, even if I didn't understand him.

The man who had held me by the window hadn't feel cold in the least as he'd pressed his body to mine. Now, I wanted to know what else was hidden within the heart of the king who appeared as lonely as the stars in the night sky.

Chapter 19

Roksana

The modest surroundings chosen for my interrogation surprised me. Instead of a cold interior dripping with opulence, the room had a cosiness that felt comforting. The only sign a king used this room was a slightly larger chair sitting on a small dais, tastefully accented with gold leaf. Everything else was . . . homely. Wooden benches were covered in throws and furs, providing comfortable seats; tapestries softened the plain stone walls, depicting hunting scenes and court life; while a thick rug underfoot silenced the sound of footsteps.

I felt the tension melt from my shoulders, and I involuntarily smiled at Reynard. He watched our entrance with an intense focus, documents piled on his lap and the table beside him.

'You wanted to see me, Viper,' he said in a casual tone, gesturing for me to sit. 'What's so important that I had to dismiss the Privy Council early?'

'You know my name, sire. I would be grateful if you used it,' I answered dryly, mildly annoyed by his use of the strange moniker in front of Riordan. 'Roksana or Mistress Regnav will do.'

His eyebrow lifted ever so slightly at my retort, and he leaned back, supporting his chin on his fist. Reynard's lips lifted in a smile that didn't reach his eyes.

'Not "Sana" anymore? Well, the name is a little gentle for such a sharp-tongued woman, I suppose.'

I grimaced at his teasing, but shrugged it off, trying to stay calm.

'Sana is for friends, and I don't think friendship is any way to describe our relationship,' I answered.

A corner of the king's mouth twisted into a lopsided smile.

'Foolish me. I thought we'd reached an understanding. Right, Viper, it is then,' he said, gesturing to Riordan, his gaze never leaving mine. The mage walked over and stood beside the king. 'Riordan told me you chose this interrogation over my hospitality. Does that mean I can expect the truth?'

'Have I lied to you even *once* since you imprisoned me?' I snapped, the tension between my shoulder blades returning. 'I have enjoyed your hospitality, but not the delay or being locked in this admittedly very comfortable prison.'

'I haven't asked any questions worthy of your lies. As for the delay, Riordan only returned this morning, and Ciesko was busy in the city. Please forgive me for prioritising Dagome over my private business,' Reynard answered, his jaw set in a hard line, as if he were scolding a spoiled brat demanding attention. I bit my lip, wishing the earth would swallow me whole.

'I'm sorry. I didn't know . . .' I stuttered, taking a step back when he stood up and approached me, his towering presence forcing me to look up.

'If you want me to interrogate you now, I'll do it. But it's a path of no return, and for some unknown reason, the thought of executing you has lost its appeal . . .'

'Well, thank fuck for small mercies,' I said before I could stop myself, but instead of anger, mirth lit the king's features.

'Fuck? What an interesting choice of words. Is that on your mind, Viper?'

'Nooo . . . for some unexplained reason, the thought of fucking a complete stranger doesn't hold much appeal,' I quipped.

'Because of your "friend" who likes to come over uninvited?' he said, jaw tightening, but despite the sharpness in his voice, he didn't lash out. However, when he looked away, his smile was gone.

'*No* . . . Because you told me you hate my guts, and I won't let anyone trying to teach me a lesson touch me,' I said, shrugging. My body stiffened when he studied my face, searching for a hint of mockery, but I held his challenging gaze.

'Hmm . . . That's a good rule to have, but rest assured, you would enjoy *any* lessons I chose to give.'

'I guess we'll never find out,' I said, hoping he missed the hitch in my breath when his gaze drifted to my lips. I was suddenly aware of how close he stood. Reynard continued to search for something in my face while the tension grew between us, forcing me to look away. Slowly, his smile returned, and before I knew it, he shook his head, stepping away.

'I guess we won't. Let's return to the reason you're here,' he said, glancing back as he returned to his chair. 'Remember, Viper, even if it implicates you, I want the pure, unvarnished truth, so choose your words wisely.'

I certainly will, I thought, wishing I could look half as in control as he. Unfortunately, my dress was losing the fight to protect my modesty whenever I moved, and I had to hunch my shoulders to keep it laced.

'I hope you're ready to listen, Your Majesty. My neck's still sore from the last time I was honest with you,' I said nonchalantly, enjoying the sight of Reynard shifting uncomfortably as his hands tightened on the armrests.

Riordan turned, giving me such a glare that I felt like a thief caught red handed before he hammered the nail into my proverbial coffin.

'A lie. Her neck does not hurt, and she liked your touch.'

Reynard's eye narrowed. 'Are you testing me, Viper?'

'More like testing your mage, and he's proved himself an accomplished ars . . . person.'

A forced smile tightened my lips, and with a truly insufferable eye roll, Riordan shrugged. But I wasn't done yet.

'Besides, you shouldn't be too upset. It was just a little teasing—similar to yours when you came to visit me that night,' I said, looking the mage in the eye, wondering if he knew what Reynard had done in my bedroom.

'I was testing you; teasing is reserved for lovers,' the king answered with a stone-cold expression. His eyebrows drew together and he gestured for the mage to continue.

An inquisition sigil appeared in the air, awakened to life with a few flickers of the hand. I braced myself when I saw the shimmering, magical strands settle over me, the tendrils so icy that my skin prickled with goosebumps. While a strong truthseeker didn't need a sigil to sense a lie, the inquisition sigil forced the truth and punished resistance. I'd endured one as a test before Boyan had made me his shadow, and I dreaded repeating the experience.

I was still marvelling at the ephemeral yet detailed structure of the spell when Reynard asked his first question.

'Were you going to kill me when you came to my bedroom?'

'No,' I answered as pressure built in my head.

Riordan was doing more than just listening to my words. The spell's tendrils latched onto my mind and examined the thoughts and images associated with them. I relaxed, looked him in the eye, and smirked before focusing on the Orcish Steppe, full of flowers and horses prancing around.

He snorted before his expression returned to the perfect indifference of an inquisitor mage.

'Were you trying to kill me in the forest?' Reynard asked, frowning at the change in Riordan's attitude

'Not exactly.'

'What the fuck does that mean?' The king grasped his armrests so hard that the wood bent, disappointment and disbelief saturating his voice. 'Why did you do it, Viper?' He pointed to his empty eye socket.

'Because I didn't know any better. I was dazed. They'd knocked me out, and the last thing I remembered was a man forcing himself on me. When I regained consciousness, another massive brute was holding me against my will. So, no, I didn't want to kill the king of Dagome, but I *did* want to kill the man I thought was attacking me,' I snapped, grinding my teeth when the pressure built to the point of pain. I realised Riordan was wanting to see the memory for himself, so I let him in.

The truthseeker staggered, grasping the back of a chair. His gaze turned glassy as he sifted through my memories, drowning in my terror.

'She's telling the truth. She was terrified . . . The blood, the pain, the feeling of violation . . . fuck, the stench of death.' His voice became hoarse, desolate, all because I had let him feel everything.

We both flinched when Reynard smashed his fist on the armrest, his other hand rubbing the rapidly reddening scar on his face.

'Godsdamn it, I was trying to help! I survived an uprising, war, and assassins, but lost my eye because I stank of those bastards' blood?'

'You wanted the truth,' I said, swallowing hard. 'I'm sorry . . . I really am.'

I watched the king warily, noticing how his hand trembled as he dragged it through his hair, his tick betraying how agitated he was. Then Reynard's breathing became erratic, his injured face contorting in a spasm, but he closed his eyes and exhaled slowly, forcing himself to stay calm.

He's in pain . . . but why?

I wanted to console him, but didn't know how, so I offered another apology, wincing at how flat it sounded. 'For what it's worth, thank you for saving me that day. If I could undo the harm I've done, I would, no matter the cost.' My voice was barely a whisper, but it was enough to make him look at me.

'For what it's worth . . .' He huffed a dry laugh, shaking his head. 'For what it's worth? The gods must be laughing at me after placing you in my path.'

His gaze lingered on my face, his lips thinning. I could almost see the battle being waged behind those tortured features and wished I could offer more than an apology.

'I think I preferred believing you planned it . . .' he said, sounding so defeated. 'Now everything feels like it was fate's idea of a sick joke.'

I stayed silent, understanding how he felt. It had been easier to justify my actions when I'd thought it was my rapist I'd killed with my poison. Knowing I'd hurt the man who had *saved* me instead weighed heavily on my conscience.

'Would you do it?' he asked.

I looked up, confused.

'Would you have tried to kill me if you'd been asked, if . . . if someone had paid or . . . forced you?' he clarified.

I studied the man before me, ignoring his station. The anger had disappeared, and Reynard sounded almost . . . vulnerable.

It nearly broke me, but I had to answer the question despite knowing Jagon might actually force my hand. My response had to be truthful; otherwise, Riordan would know. Worse, if I didn't answer, the inquisition spell would eviscerate my mind.

I prayed my words wouldn't break this shallow truce between us.

'They already did, and I refused.'

'Why?' Reynard asked coldly. 'Wasn't the money good enough?'

'They didn't offer money, but even if they had, I wouldn't break the covenant between the Dark Brotherhood and the Crown.' The words came easily, as there was no lie in them, no half-truth. I may have been forced into the Brotherhood, but what little integrity I had left drew a line no money could erase.

'She's telling the truth,' Riordan said, but the king didn't look at him.

'I know,' Reynard snapped before his expression softened. 'Why did you really come to me that night? Forgive me, but I don't believe you crept in just to warn the king.'

'I knew someone of my standing wouldn't get an audience with you. After the disaster at the Court of Aether, I had to try something. Your enemies are my enemies. Helping you was the only way to get rid of the man who's after me.'

'Who is he?' Whether or not Reynard intended it, his question came out as a menacing growl, and I instinctively flinched. I didn't want to reveal Brotherhood secrets, but looking at the king, I knew he wouldn't let this go.

'Jagon, the poison chapter master—but before you lead your proverbial cavalry onto an empty field, hear me out. He's just an opportunistic fuck being bankrolled by someone powerful. That's your true enemy, just as Jagon is mine.'

'So, you wanted to use me. Fine, Viper, I can understand that, but why come in person? Why not tell Riordan?'

'Oh, perhaps because I didn't know who to trust? In warning you, I'm not only going against the strongest chapter master in the Brotherhood but putting my dearest friend in danger. Now, here I am, a prisoner, unable to do anything. If I'm lucky enough to be released, I'll have to think of a lie to explain why I'm still alive,' I responded, swallowing hard because saying it out loud was forcing me to face the hopelessness of my situation. 'You've backed me into a corner, so please, give me a way out.'

Reynard and Riordan exchanged glances, but whatever the result of their silent communication, I wasn't privy to it.

'So the Brotherhood wants to kill me?' Reynard asked resignedly.

'The Brotherhood?' I sighed. 'No. But there's an ongoing power struggle, and everyone's looking out for themselves, with the less scrupulous members working against the grand master's wishes. My friend considers you a worthy king, so even if it's hard to believe, I thought maybe you'd be interested in a good opportunity.'

For the first time during the interrogation, Reynard smiled—genuinely smiled—and the sight was devastating.

I looked at the floor, trying to hide the heat crawling up my cheeks, a surprising reaction to the man who'd captured me. It was ridiculous, but I had to admit that when he wasn't choking me, imprisoning me, or letting his mage dig around in my mind—so, in essence, when he wasn't a total bastard—Reynard was a man who radiated danger in such a scorching manner that I wanted to dip my fingers in the fire just to see if it burned.

'Alright, little Viper, tell me how we can help each other,' he said in an almost playful tone before controlling it once more. 'Starting with the man who's paying Jagon. I'll protect you, but I need their name. If you don't know that, I need to know what they look like, or anything else that will help us identify them.'

I shook my head. 'I don't know their name. I only saw his proxy. He spoke with a southern accent and wore a palace guard's uniform. You have enemies in your court.'

Reynard muttered a curse. 'Godsdamn it. We'll interrogate them all, but it would be easier if you could re—' Reynard paused, frowning. That was when I noticed the commotion outside the chamber. 'What in the pit's going on out there?'

He gestured to the guard by the door, who opened it to reveal a steward standing with his back to the entrance, waving his arms around erratically. Once he realised the door was open, he turned around, relief written all over his face.

'Your Majesty, these people insist on seeing you. It's about the prisoner no one's supposed to know about,' he said cautiously. 'I refused, but the dwarf started to fight.'

'Tova,' I whispered, my heart stuttering when I recognised him struggling with a guard.

Reynard frowned, his gaze switching between the steward and me. Finally, he gestured.

'Bring them forth.'

I stood frozen as two guards escorted Tova and Lily in, shaking my head when Lily looked at me in confusion.

Tova frowned when I signalled for him to be quiet. I hoped their presence wouldn't make the situation worse, but I knew the chances were slim with my impulsive tinkerer around.

Lily had gone all out on her outfit. Her long gown accentuated her curves whilst still modestly covering her body. It rustled quietly as she stepped forward, sinking to her knees, the pale blue dress pooling around her like water.

'Your Majesty, may we speak in private?' she asked, pulling Tova's sleeve, but he stood tall, glaring at Reynard so intently that I half expected the king to erupt in flames. 'Master Orenson and I have information that may be essential to Dagome's safety, but it is for your ears only.'

Reynard straightened in his chair, and, following an unspoken command, the guards stepped closer to Tova.

'I see you've noticed my captive, Master Orenson. I'm guessing you came here to demand her freedom rather than help the Crown?'

'Sire, we—' Lily started, but Tova didn't let her finish.

'Damn right. First, Młot—the last dimwit who imprisoned her—refused to listen in Wiosna. Now I find my drah'sa a captive here too? Care to explain yourself, *Your Majesty*?' Tova said. I felt the blood drain from my face when the blunt end of the guard's spear hit the back of the dwarf's knees, forcing him to the floor.

'No!' I threw myself towards Tova when another soldier swung to strike, but I didn't even get close.

'Enough!'

Reynard had moved so fast that before I'd taken a single step, he'd grabbed my collar and pulled me into his arms.

The dress's straining seams couldn't handle the force, and with a loud ripping sound, my bodice tore apart. I gasped, trying to grab the fabric, when I was spun around and, before fully realising what was going on, pressed against Reynard's chest. My modesty had been preserved, but at what cost? The scent of musk and lemongrass enveloped me while muscular arms held me so tight I couldn't move.

'Let me go!' I hissed, pushing against his chest but he didn't budge.

'The front of your dress has split open, so stay where you are unless you want to give my guards something to ogle at,' he chastised me before looking at Lily. 'How are you called, Mistress?'

'I don't bloody care if they see my tits as long as they stop hurting my friend,' I said, pushing harder as I tried to free myself, my worry for Tova much stronger than my fear of the king. 'Let me go. I'm not your dog to be pulled around on a leash.'

'But *I* care!' Reynard only tightened his grip. His nostrils flared as he bent to my ear. 'Roksana, let me handle the situation,' he hissed, lips so close that his breath stirred my hair.

'But they—'

'They reacted because your knight in not-so-shining armour grabbed his axe. Their job is to defend their king, and that's exactly what they did.'

The insult I'd had ready died on my lips; I hadn't seen Tova's hands move. In the sudden silence, I felt Reynard's heart thumping beneath my hand, but he wasn't paying attention to me. Instead, he looked up at a very pale Lily and asked, 'Your name, my lady . . . please.'

'Liliana Ordon, sire,' Lily answered instantly, sitting back on her heels with a dazed look on her face.

'I assume you are also Roksana's friend?'

'Yes, my lord. I received a message saying she was here, so I came to enquire as to her status.'

'Interesting . . . but we can talk about that later. Please surrender your shawl, my lady,' Reynard reached over, expecting her compliance.

Lily carefully unwrapped the silk wrap around her shoulders and held it out. 'My lord, please unhand Sana,' she said quietly, her hands trembling as she avoided touching him.

'And if I choose not to?'

Lily bit her lip but couldn't come up with an answer. Still, judgement burned in her eyes, so heavy that the king flinched when she raised her head and locked gazes with him.

'Everybody out,' Reynard commanded, the muscles under my hand tensing. I pulled away, but his fingers dug into my flesh, preventing my escape. 'Not you, Viper. We need to talk.'

'Don't you dare hurt her!' Tova shouted from where the guards held him.

'Oh, for fuck's sake, someone take him to a cell,' Reynard said.

I shook my head at Lily when she opened her mouth to speak.

'Sire, I don't think this is a good idea,' Riordan said, but Reynard waved him off.

'Go with them. Ensure the dwarf is secure and that Mistress Ordon is comfortable. I want to talk with Roksana alone.'

Hesitation lingered in Riordan's eyes, but in the end, he complied.

'Yes, Your Majesty.'

The sound of a door closing had never felt so final.

Chapter 20

Roksana

Reynard held me to his chest until the snap of the lock announced everyone's exit. His muscles tensed, resisting my efforts to pull away, and when I looked up, a contented smirk tilted the corner of his lips.

Finally, when Lily's shawl covered my exposed cleavage, he released me with a flourish.

'There, now you won't cause any trouble,' he said in a lighthearted tone, but my mind was in a different place.

'Please don't hurt them, sire,' I whispered, dropping to my knees. I wasn't beyond begging. For Tova and Lily, I would sell my soul to Veles; prostrating myself before the king was nothing in comparison.

'What . . .?' Reynard's confusion was obvious as he caught hold of my shoulders, lifting me up. 'There's no need for that, Sana.'

'There's every need. I meant no disrespect—*they* meant no disrespect . . . Even if Tova reached for his weapon, you can't kill him . . . please,' I begged, ignoring the spasming of the injured part of his face.

The king's hand dropped off my shoulder as if I'd scalded him. I watched with growing concern as Reynard fought to control his breath, coming in laboured pants as he tried to slow it down.

I recognised the signs. He was using a technique taught by healers to manage pain, but what was hurting? The swiftness with which he applied the method could only be explained by extensive practice.

'Roksana, you need to leave—' he started, and I gasped in horror when the twitching scar contorted, his neck creaking as his muscles pulled so tight I could almost see their cords flexing under his skin.

'No! What is going on? How can I help?' I turned around, looking for something, anything, I might use, but Reynard grabbed my wrist.

'No one can see me like this . . . the Royal Council . . . they think I'm . . . a monster,' he hissed, and I bit my lip, ignoring the pain his tight grip was causing. Calloused fingers encircled my wrist like a vice, but Reynard seemed oblivious to the fact he was hurting me. 'If they learn of it—'

His breath caught, but I'd heard enough. The Brotherhood weren't the only ones in the midst of a power struggle.

'Fine, then sit the fuck down and tell me what's going on,' I said, pushing him back.

He stumbled, falling onto his massive chair, grasping my hand as he fell and dragging me with him. With one arm immobilised in his grip and the other flailing around, I ended up straddling his legs.

'Your poison.' His voice was hoarse, as if the pain had rubbed off the veneer of humanity from him. 'These spasms are your doing, Viper. And no one in all Truso can remove your venom.'

'Wha—' My mouth fell open. 'Gods, are you telling me it is still inside you?'

As soon as I said it, a terrified realisation made my legs buckle, and I landed on his lap. I was alone with the king, who looked like he was dying from my poison.

Who'll believe I'm not using the opportunity to finish the job?

'It's under the skin, in my eye socket. Ciesko isolated it, but whatever magic he used, it's failing.' He groaned, still fighting the spasms. 'You killed me, Viper, even if I have a long and painful way to go.'

'And none of you idiots thought to ask the source?' I asked, reaching for his face. 'I'll purge it, but you must stay still.'

Reynard swatted my hand away before pressing his fingers to the large, angry scar. 'You want me to trust you with something not even the arch healer could cure? I've only just discovered you did this by accident, and I still don't know how far you'll go to gain your freedom.'

'Damn you and your stubbornness. You prefer suffering to letting me do the one thing I'm good at?!'

'Please, Viper, just go. Tell the guards to call Riordan,' he said, leaning forward, his breath shallow and fast. I knew arguing with him wasn't helping, but he was sorely mistaken if he thought I'd leave him to suffer.

I couldn't.

Seeing this powerful man on the verge of breaking changed something within me. Reynard didn't deserve this after trying to help me, and I wouldn't let him stop me from doing what was right.

'Listen to me, you obstinate arse. I'm going to purge the poison, and you're going to *let me* do it,' I said when he finally looked at me. 'If you won't do it for yourself, then do it for me. You're the reason those men didn't . . . Like it or not, I refuse to let you die.'

A moment passed before he answered.

'Blood oath . . . swear . . . a blood oath first,' Reynard ground out, his body sagging in the chair. I began to worry that Ciesko's magic had failed and time was running out. Still, it was a lot to ask. Binding myself to the king with an unbreakable oath was the last thing I wanted.

But what if he dies because I hesitated?

The challenge in Reynard's eye lit a fire in my chest.

He doesn't expect me to do it.

'Fine, as long as you swear no harm will come to Tova and Liliana—not now or ever, as long as it's in your power to prevent it. Swear you'll protect their lives, and you'll have your oath.'

'Setting terms even now, Viper?' A bitter laugh escaped him, even as he struggled to speak. 'You first. Say . . . that you'll never use your abilities against me. And that you'll never willingly leave me without me releasing you from your oath.'

'Or I could wait until you lose consciousness and do what I want, you frustrating, annoying . . .' I countered, shuddering when a quiet, agonised moan escaped his lips, and a golden ring appeared in his grey eye. I'd read enough books about magic to know what it meant. Reynard had wild magic in his blood, and it manifested under duress . . .

The question was, what kind of monster lurked under his skin?

'Leave, godsdamn it.'

His words were more of a growl, and I felt the aether surrounding him shift, changing its form. It would be so easy to walk away and call a healer. They could contain the poison, maybe even neutralise it before it affected him again. That was what Jagon would do—save his own sorry arse and leave a good man to suffer.

They think I'm a monster.

His words, a haunting truth to them, wouldn't let me walk away. *I* was the one who had hurt the king, the reason people saw him as a 'monster.' It was my responsibility to fix whatever I could—and it was breaking my heart to see him in such agony. Besides, if Reynard swore the oath, he would be bound to protect my friends, not just from himself, but from anyone that threatened their safety.

Fate's web tightened around me, demanding I bind myself to the king. Without hesitation, I took a small letter opener from the table and scored my palm.

'I, Roksana Regnav, swear on the gods above and below with conscious intent to never harm Reynard Erenhart, the War King of Dagome . . . and to never leave him as long as I control my destiny or he releases me from this oath.'

Reynard nodded. His large, calloused swordsman's hand trembled when he extended it towards me. I drew a bloody line across his palm and clasped it with my own.

'I, Reynard Erenhart, swear on the gods above and below with conscious intent to protect Tova Orenson and Liliana Ordon and not punish them for current or future deeds as long as it is in my power to do so.'

Our blood sizzled as it mixed. The aether wrapped itself around our hands, green and golden threads entwined in perfect harmony, sealing the bond. That was all that mattered. Lily and Tova were safe, and I could help this royal idiot before the pain drove him insane.

'So can I touch you now?' I asked, and he nodded. I leant forward, placing a hand on the injured part of his face. 'Please trust me. It won't be easy, but I know what I'm doing.'

I'd never purged poison while sitting on a patient's lap before, but the awkward position allowed me to cup his face in both hands while I inspected the damaged flesh under his scar with my magic. The poison lay deep in the muscle, obscured by the healer's intricate lattice, but I could still recognise my handiwork.

Reynard was panting hard, perspiration beading on his forehead as I probed the scar. It would be so much easier if whomever had helped him hadn't isolate the toxin with such an impressive spell, but as long as I could reach it, my magic would do its job.

'It won't take long, I promise,' I muttered, adjusting my hand to his cheek exploring the aethereal mesh trapping the poison. Reynard groaned, but didn't move. Instead, his hands drifted to my hips, holding me in place. The artery in his neck thumped rapidly, his muscles straining, and I used my sleeve to wipe the sweat off his forehead.

'I'm sorry. It will be better soon,' I said, cradling his face in both of my hands.

'Just do it, Roksana. I can take it,' he said, the golden glow completely overtaking his eye.

His body shuddered under my questing touch. The enhanced contact helped me locate a flaw in the countless threads of aether interwoven to contain the caustic liquid.

That's it! This is why Reynard is suffering.

It appeared the deadly mixture of nightshade, rosary pea, water hemlock, and wintergreen oil was seeping into his bloodstream, slowly killing him.

'Gods, you're a tough bastard. This would kill a bull,' I muttered, pulling at a strand, trying to unravel the magic. His hands jerked, fingers digging painfully into my flesh, but if he could endure the pain, so could I.

'I'm difficult to kill, but not immune to pain.'

His voice was barely a whisper, but I was astonished at the remarkable virility this man possessed. Every part of him was powerful. The life force I saw in others were mere wisps in comparison. Reynard's body pulsated so strongly with life that I suspected it was destroying the delicate mesh that contained the poison.

Reynard Erenhart was something else, something I didn't truly understand, but I was awestruck. I used his aether and my instincts as a guide, flowing with the primal force as it scoured the unnatural spell.

'Yes!' I exclaimed when I finally found it—the spell's anchor, a loose strand I could pull to unravel the healer's entire mesh. Praying I wasn't making a mistake, I tugged on the glistening thread.

'Embrace me,' I said, pressing my forehead to his, and when his arms locked around me, I yanked it loose. The lattice that protected the king from the horrors of my creation unravelled, Reynard's guttural cry filling the room.

'Roksana . . . please.'

The words, gentle and pleading after such an echoing shout, pulled at my heart.

Reynard fought against the agony, his face forced into a rictus of spasming muscle as the poison flooded his bloodstream, but I had no time for hesitation or mercy.

'Come to me,' I whispered, focusing on my aether in the poison. The familiar energy swirled and changed direction, flowing towards me, pulling the liquid with it. It seeped through the king's skin, and I gathered it on my fingers—a thin translucent layer of death, coating them like a strange paint. I continued until I was sure there was nothing left. Only then did I tear its bonds apart, the residue dissolving on my fingertips.

Reynard's head dropped to my shoulder, exhaustion in every panting, shuddering breath. I embraced him, gently stroking his back, laughing like a maniac.

'We did it. You'll live, Rey. I told you I could do it.'

My triumph was filled with an unhealthy dose of relief. A quiet voice in my head admitted that I'd acted rashly, but it was easy to ignore it. I'd corrected at least one of my mistakes and could feel a small sense of achievement.

As my laughter quietened, I noticed Reynard's silence . . . and his arms as he pulled me closer, inhaling sharply.

Then I remembered where, and how, I was sitting.

'It's done, Your Majesty. You can let me go.' His title slipped from my lips, a desperate attempt to place a barrier between us. Without a task to perform, this closeness felt like too much, felt too intimate.

My breath hitched when he raised his head and fixed me with the glowing golden gaze of a berserker.

'No,' he growled, arms flexing around me, pressing me closer.

Fear slid down my spine like a trickle of freezing water. I stilled, knowing enough about predators not to trigger him further with my fight. After a moment, the gold bled from his eye, and he exhaled slowly.

'What am I going to do with you?' he asked, reaching for a lock of my hair and twisting it around his fingers.

'You can unhand me. That would be a good start,' I said, determined to hide how his touch and the hunger in his gaze were affecting me.

'I could, but I don't want to. You are a surprising creature, my little Viper. What you did was . . . nothing short of a miracle,' he said in an eerily calm voice. I exhaled with relief. This time, when I pulled back, he let me go.

'I did what needed doing. Now, will you keep your oath? Tova and Lily—you promised to release them with no retribution.'

Reynard smirked, stretching out in the chair. 'You know, I know someone just like you. She faced a goddess to save her lover . . . Tell me, are you in love with the dwarf? Was that why you tried to shield him with your body and gave your oath to protect him?'

What? Is he bloody serious?

I huffed in disbelief, the question taking me aback.

'I have no lover. Tova is . . . I'm his drah'sa—his sister, someone he'll challenge a king for. Please . . . when will you free him?'

With each word from my lips, Reynard visibly relaxed. My bloody handprint marked his face, making him look like some ancient war chief, but he looked calm, almost happy.

'Later,' he promised. 'His stay in a cell is simply a lesson in manners. You can see him tomorrow, you have my word. But only after he's had a polite conversation with Riordan, of course. Then Orenson can crawl back up Veles' arse if he so chooses.'

'What about me? Am I free to leave?' I asked.

He stared at me with an unreadable expression.

'Free? Are you trying to trick me out of your oath, little Viper? I'm not freeing you—not now, maybe never,' he said, stroking his scar as if he couldn't believe it no longer hurt. 'However, I will allow you to leave the palace, but not Truso, and you'll work for *me*, Roksana.'

'So, my leash just got longer?'

'For now, yes, but we can revisit this discussion once you've fulfilled my request. Be my spy. Return to the Brotherhood and find out who's behind Jagon and where the srebrec's going,' he said.

I frowned.

'That wasn't a part of the oath!' I snapped, walking to the large window to give myself some time to think. 'What happens if I refuse?'

'Then you'll leave me no choice. If you won't help me end this threat, I'll have to do it myself. And as I don't know who to trust, I'll have to wipe the Brotherhood from the face of the earth,' he responded, smiling bitterly. 'That is the harsh truth. So, what will it be, Viper? Will you work for me?'

It was no choice at all. As happy as I was at the prospect of Jagon's and his cronies' deaths, there was Boyan and Irsha to think about . . . They were the heart and soul of the Brotherhood, as were many others who had found structure and shelter within the Chapter House's walls.

'Congratulations, Your Majesty. You have your assassin,' I snapped, feeling the cage of this voluntary trap locking around me. 'How should I contact you? I can't keep sneaking into your bedroom,' I said, focusing on the practicalities of my hopeless situation.

'You will meet with Riordan. You just proved Ciesko was right and that you can manipulate aether. I will ensure my mage is part of your training regimen.'

'You've got it all planned out, don't you?'

'I didn't plan to have an attack in front of you. Even I'm not that cunning,' he said with a smirk that made me want to choke him. 'But the rest? I don't like taking chances. I was open with my plans, and I will honour my vow, just not in the way either of us expected,' he concluded, coming closer and wrapping the shawl tighter around my shoulders. He paused for a moment, hesitation written all over his face before gentleness softened his features.

'Thank you, Sanika. Your help has returned my life to me . . . and given me the hope I'd long since lost,' he said, fingers lingering on my shoulders. A bird's cry outside broke through the moment, and Reynard stepped away. 'Now go. Liliana should be waiting for you in a carriage. Rest and await my orders.'

'You are such a manipulative bastard,' I whispered, unsure what to think.

His cheek muscle twitched before he released a humourless laugh.

'No, my beautiful poison, I'm much worse. I'm the king.'

Chapter 21

Regnard

The wound on my palm stung, but the blood was already congealing, a darkening scab slowly forming. The slight pain felt strange, a pale shadow of the agony that had plagued me for weeks. I couldn't stop staring at it, at the mark that bound me to my Viper. Each flex of my fingers sent a jolt of possessiveness straight into my heart.

Perun's arse, I need to send her away.

This strange healing only exacerbated the yearning that continued to grow after that nighttime visit. I wasn't sure how long I could stay away from her bedroom, but Roksana was set on leaving, making it clear my attention wasn't welcome.

And yet, she had healed me. Her insistence; her brazen words; and her gentle, caring touch had given me back the life I'd thought lost forever, the time needed to sort out the mess my kingdom had become. I would live because she had chosen *me* before freedom.

Roksana Regnav was more than just an assassin, but I didn't know what to make of her yet.

'What do you intend to do with the dwarf?' Riordan asked, entering the room. He hadn't taken two steps before he stopped, staring at me in shock. 'What happened? Why are you covered in blood? Did she . . . Why are you smiling?'

His questions made my grin even wider. I'd completely forgotten Sana had placed her freshly cut palm on my face, and judging by Riordan's expression, the mark she left behind must have been striking. I couldn't help but tease him a little.

'We had a little accident. It's just blood. It will wash off.'

'Rey.' The warning in Riordan's voice matched the anxiousness in his step as he strode forward. 'I don't know what that woman did this time, but you'll tell me, and you'll do it right now, or I'll dive so deep into your mind you'll recall the day you came out of your father's bollocks!' Riordan rarely used obscenities, and that, along with a familiar pressure building in my head, made me stop teasing him.

'Ri, cut it out and make yourself useful,' I snapped. I knew why he was worried, so I forgave his intrusion into my thoughts. 'Grab us a drink! It's time to celebrate.'

He went to fulfil my request while I thought about how to explain the situation and avoid the barrage of questions that would certainly follow. In the end, I chose the simple truth.

'Roksana witnessed the spasms, and . . . she purged the poison.'

The sound of shattering glass made me sigh. Wine flowed like a red stream on the polished stone floor, saturating the room with the scent of fermented grapes and alcohol. Riordan stared at it, empty-handed, shaking as he blinked, his eyes surprisingly glossy, as if he was holding back tears. That wasn't a good sign, and his questioning hadn't even started. After a moment, he exhaled, grabbed a bottle of moonshine and poured two generous measures, stepping over the shards before passing me a drink.

'Talk. And after we're done, let Ciesko examine you. If she truly did it—' He stopped, emptying his cup in one gulp while I enjoyed the burning sensation flowing down my throat and observed my friend. Riordan masked his worry well, and only now did the cracks in his mask show me how much he cared.

'Alright. I will. But I know she did it. The pain is gone, completely gone,' I said, smiling as he regained his composure.

'How did that happen? And was that why our poisoner walked out scowling hard enough to frighten a striga?' he asked, his inquisitorial tone so formal I chuckled, rolling my eyes.

My thoughts drifted to the moment her dress ripped and the mortifying certainty I'd felt that if any guard leered at her, I wouldn't be able to stop myself from ensuring they never did so again. What had happened next was a blur of rage and pain while her presence, her touch, anchored me, even if her magic had tried to rip my face off.

'I don't know how it started, Ri, but I know how it ended.'

With a clink of the glass, he put his goblet aside and leaned towards me. 'As happy as I am she helped, it was reckless of you to let her do that without a healer by your side.'

'I insisted she swear a blood oath first. That was my condition for letting her purge the poison.' I stretched out my hand, letting him see the scar before adding, 'And she was scowling because I ordered her to work for me and find the man behind Jagon. I wasn't reckless, but I *was* desperate.'

That reminded me of another task.

I walked to the desk to draft a short order, calling for a servant. 'Take this to the captain of the guard.' I felt Riordan's questioning look as the man took the letter, bowed, and left. 'I want her under observation. I want someone watching her at all times, day and night . . . and another set of eyes following that poisonous prick, Jagon—her ex-master.'

'Why? I've confirmed her words.' The offence in his tone was clear but misplaced. 'Do you still suspect her?'

'No, I just want her safe. My gut tells me she's neck-deep in this mess. Boyan's shadow returns to the city just as the mystery of the srebrec and a faceless enemy who wants me dead comes to light?' I sighed, gesturing for him to pour another drink. 'You know, it was so much easier dealing with this situation when I thought she was just an assassin than now with all this . . . chaos. Roksana is different than what I expected,' I said quietly.

Riordan looked at me, a frown creasing his face as his magic filled in the gaps I had purposefully left out.

'Rey, please don't tell me that out of all the women in the country, you fancy the low-born rogue who almost killed you. Was that why you visited her at night?'

'No, that was a mistake. I went to her room to test a theory. Remember me asking about aphrodisiacs?' I said. He nodded. 'I had her bathed and thought I'd check . . .'

'And?' he probed.

'And there's no aphrodisiac, no enhancements, *nothing* that could explain why her scent is irresistible to me.'

'You like her?' Riordan asked, moving closer, but I shook my head.

'I don't even know her. It's just . . . a visceral reaction. Ciesko believes that it's connected to my family's wild magic and the injury, but that's ridiculous . . . right?'

'Yet you pulled her away from the dwarf when she jumped in to protect him.'

I knew what Riordan was doing. Since he'd become my advisor, he'd also become a mirror for my thoughts. With his magic, I couldn't lie to him, and it forced me to face the truth, uncomfortable as it was.

'She was willing to be hurt to protect another man. I didn't like it.'

Riordan narrowed his eyes, the air around him shimmering. He was working with the aether, and I raised my hand to stop him.

'No. Don't peek into my mind. That's the raw truth. I didn't like it, and if I understood why, I'd tell you,' I said, angry and confused because it felt like someone had flipped my world upside down and set it on fire.

'Fine, but that brings us back to my original question. What are you going to do with the dwarf?'

'I don't know. I didn't have any special plans when I sent the annoying prick to the cells.'

'Do you find him "annoying" simply because Roksana rushed to defend him?' Riordan quipped, and I had to close my eye, fighting the urge to smack him.

'Don't sass me, mage,' I answered, hearing him chuckle. 'You have until tomorrow to question this Tova Orenson. Find out what he knows about the srebrec and compare his answers with Sana's. If there are any disparities or new information, let me know,' I said, feeling the oath tightening like a noose around my neck, my heart picking up the pace at the invisible strangulation. 'Just . . . don't hurt him. When you're done, kick him and his shitty attitude out of my palace.'

'You swore you'd protect him, didn't you? Why? And don't try to deny it—I saw your aether react as soon as you mentioned his name,' he said before sighing.

I shrugged apologetically. 'I was in no position to discuss the terms in depth. Fuck, it was a miracle I could speak at all.'

'What's done is done, I suppose,' Riordan said. 'I'll speak with Ciesko. He might also be able to help with the Roksana situation. You know, your brother had similar issues after meeting his wife . . .'

I shook my head. 'I trust your counsel, but don't bring my brother into this. I'll handle it myself,' I said, remembering one other thing. 'Oh, and tell Ciesko that I have signed the document. Roksana can go through her geas ceremony with the other mages during the winter solstice.'

Riordan's mouth fell open and he stared at me in shock, making me wonder what I'd missed. Ciesko was the arch healer of Dagome, a Court of Aether High Council member. The document he'd asked me to sign was a standard form for mages recommended to undergo a geas. It didn't cross my mind to question his request.

'He said nothing to me,' my friend said finally. 'Let me talk to him first. It's not a decision made unilaterally and certainly not our regular practice.'

'The arch healer of Dagome requested it after examining her. It appeared perfectly reasonable,' I said defensively.

Ri's jaw tightened. 'With Roksana's unusual position, he should have discussed it with me since everybody knows I'm the proxy for the royal mage, my grandfather.' He huffed angrily. 'The old fool is overstepping his bounds. Besides, what kind of message does this send? That the Brotherhood's in possession of a mage so strong we need a geas to control her?'

Riordan's anger made little sense. Geasa were designed to protect the kingdom and ordinary people from mages who wanted to usurp power. If Ciesko thought one was needed, who was I to question an experienced member of the council?

I mirrored Riordan's thoughts to find out what was troubling him.

'What if she *is* powerful enough to need a geas? I'm sure I won't need to use it, and the only person who would have the key to her soul is the mute custodian of the geas vault. Ri, it's just an additional protection in case someone tries to use her against me.'

'There will be repercussions,' he said. 'Hiding an ordinary mage with Brotherhood ties is one thing. But a titled mage, ennobled by geas, is not something you can sweep under the rug. Neither the Brotherhood nor the mages will take it lightly—especially the Brotherhood. They'll see her power growing and want her under their thumb.'

'Maybe that's what we need,' I said. 'Something to make a splash and see what floats to the surface.'

He hesitated. 'Yes, but—'

'No buts. You've seen the reports. Marauders are ravaging the South unchallenged. The noble houses aren't just blocking my attempts to send our army—they're backing Duke Tivala while he feeds them empty assurances. And now they're using my injury to chip away at my authority. Whether Tivala is behind it or someone else stands to gain from our kingdom's unravelling, I need to know. We need to find out who we're fighting against.'

I approached my friend and grasped him by the shoulder. 'I'm not reckless, but Sana saw a Southerner with Jagon. Someone from the palace. If she finds out who he is, I can follow the breadcrumbs to his master without alerting our enemies. If I have evidence that Tivala's plotting against me—against Dagome—the noble houses can kiss my royal arse. I will be free to depose the old bastard and send our army without risking civil war.'

'You are the king; your word is law,' Riordan said. 'They can shout as much as they want, but the army will follow you.'

I shook my head.

'Don't be like one of those fools who thinks the king has absolute power. Many monarchs have lost their kingdoms and their heads because they thought their backsides were forever nailed to the throne.'

'And you think that woman will give you all the answers?' he asked.

I took a moment to control my anger before answering.

'You have a better idea? Be my guest. Tell me, how else can I fix this when all our leads end with Roksana and the Brotherhood?' I ran a hand through my hair, a habit of mine whenever I failed to control my irritation. My jaw tightened when the string of my eyepatch caught on my finger. 'I'm clutching at straws here. I just need one fucking person to believe I'm doing all of this for a good reason.'

'Reynard . . .' Riordan sighed, shaking his head. 'I know you'd do anything for this kingdom.' He looked older, and his resigned expression

didn't fit his usually carefree demeanour. 'It's just . . . the geas ritual . . .
it almost broke me.'

'Then ensure that doesn't happen to her,' I said. At his confusion, I
realised I had no idea what I was talking about.

'Rey, once she enters the geas hall, there's no way back, and no one can
help her,' he said gently.

'Then find another way to ensure her magic can't be used against
Dagome. Talk to Ciesko. You two can work it out between you.' It wasn't
the most convincing evasion, but I'd just seen firsthand that she could
outperform the arch healer in purging poisons at least, and even if that
was the only thing she could do, it was no small thing.

'Fine, but you'll listen to your friend and get some rest. I'll tell the
steward to postpone the garrison visit until this afternoon. The last
several weeks have been taxing, and frankly, you look like shit, Rey. The
soldiers shouldn't see their king looking as if he were a step away from
the grave.'

Riordan's gall betrayed his distress. If it would make him happier, I
was ready to let him have the last word.

'If it'll cease your nagging, mage, I'll take a nap. But don't tell anyone
you have the power to send your king to bed,' I jested to lighten the
mood, and was rewarded with a fleeting smile.

'No, not king. *Friend*. I'm on your side, Rey. Please remember
that—even if we argue, I'm always on your side.'

As I walked to my bedroom, a young man dressed in a scribe's livery
accosted me in the corridor, requesting my time. I was going to ask where
my usual assistant was but remembered he'd asked to be dismissed as he

had to look after a family member. Of course, I could not deny him, even if training a new aide was unpalatable.

'My lord, one of your spies is here to report about the event in the city,' he said, glancing nervously behind him.

'Bring him in,' I responded, inhaling the familiar scent of books, ink, and wax as I entered my office.

The door creaked open again as I fell into my chair, and a merchant walked in, led by the guard. His fearful glances made him look like he wanted to drop to his knees and cry. I gestured him closer, but he only took one step before standing still and fumbling with his hat.

'What do you have to report?' I asked when he raised his head.

'I'm not sure if it's important, but the Brotherhood has contracted several food vendors. They're having a Mabon feast at the end of next week. Rumour says this one is special; all the chapter masters and their successors are going.'

'And that is . . . unusual?' I was uncertain as to why a party should be my concern.

'Nothing good comes from these meetings. Every time all of the chapter masters are under one roof, bad things happen . . . The merchants are getting worried, sire,' he replied before mumbling to himself. I waved him off, noting the visible relief on his face as he retreated.

'What are your orders, my lord?' my scribe asked when we were alone in the room.

'No orders. I'll take a look myself. Ensure I have nothing planned for the day of the feast,' I said, feeling a rush of excitement at the thought of an excursion. I hadn't been in the city for a while. My spasms had prevented me from taking solitary trips, confining me to the palace and a few trusted locations, but now I could once again go out into the dark underbelly of my kingdom and gain a better perspective.

'My lord, if I may . . .' The steward's shocked face made me smile. 'It's too dangerous, especially with your injury.'

'That's no longer a problem,' I said, and suddenly, the idea of a midday rest wasn't so irksome. I could relax before dealing with the new recruitment proposal the lord marshal had submitted earlier—and not just visit the garrison, but stay the night in the fields and train with my soldiers.

The realisation that I was once again free hit me like a hammer.

With renewed energy, I completed some more work, and half an hour later, I was in my bedroom, kicking off my shoes and lying on the bed. However, despite my weariness, sleep refused to come. My thoughts kept drifting to my feisty Viper, no matter how much I tried to dispel them. The woman's mere existence was a challenge, and her boldness? Nobody had ever called me an 'obstinate arse,' especially not to my face.

Gods, she is pure chaos. Dangerous, unpredictable, and so fucking alluring . . .

'Not this again,' I groaned, sitting up, unwilling to give in to temptation.

My gaze drifted to the map I had found in Roksana's belongings, still lying on the table. That was something that could occupy my mind—finding the traitor in my ranks, peering in from the shadows. I called for a servant and ordered them to bring me the captain of the guard.

I was already pacing when there was a knock on my door.

'Come,' I said. I was in no mood for pleasantries, and the moment the captain walked in, I asked, 'Did you find the traitor who created this map straight to my room?'

The warrior snapped to attention, his spine so rigid it looked like someone had shoved a spear through it. A deep crimson spread up from his neck, coating his face in embarrassment.

'No, sire. I've been questioning the men under a truthseeker's magic since your guest surrendered the map. All I know is that she entered through the tunnel that leads to your study, and guards have already secured it. However, I take full responsibility for my lapse in judgement.'

'I'm not assigning blame, Captain, but looking for solutions. An enemy spy is within our ranks, and I want them found,' I said coldly, my mind working on the situation. 'For now, change it all. Study that map and adjust the guard posts to cover the gaps, then revise the patrols accordingly. Make them as unpredictable as possible, with different times and different routes . . . and make a fake copy of the guard's schedule. Hide it but ensure it can be found.' A cruel smile ghosted my lips. 'Let's set a trap for this rat.'

The captain of the guard's grin mirrored my own as he relaxed a fraction. 'Yes, sire. Of course, Your Majesty.'

I couldn't help rolling my eyes at the flurry of honorifics, but as soon as he stopped prostrating himself, we spent an hour discussing the changes until I dismissed him. When the door closed behind his retreating back, I sighed in relief, happy at finally having accomplished something.

I stretched out on the bed and placed an arm behind my head, calculating my forces and planning a series of manoeuvres to bring them closer to the southern borders without alerting the nobles. I hoped that once I removed Tivala, I could secure his province in one fell swoop. However, the numbers kept mixing in my head replaced by the feeling of Sana's legs pressed to my thighs.

I thought about the moment before she had cleansed the poison—her body leaning so hard against me, the swell of her breasts rubbing my chest, alluring even through the haze of pain.

I shook my head. I wanted a woman I could not have.

Not now, not when the country was in uproar, and not a dark sister. Not if I wanted to stay on the throne.

'This is beyond ridiculous,' I groaned, my hand drifting down. If I was ever going to fall asleep, I needed to ease this tension. My cock throbbed as I grasped it while I pulled out her shirt that had somehow ended up under my pillow.

'You're a sick bastard,' I muttered to myself, inhaling deeply as I recalled the memory of her straddling me on the throne, but it felt so good to give in to this craving. Roksana's eyes, their hazel depths illuminated by the green lightning of her power, dominated my thoughts as I stroked myself to completion, her name slipping from my lips as I came.

I might have scolded myself for yearning for a woman who thought nothing of me, but it was her image that finally brought me peace.

Chapter 22

Roksana

The carriage taking us back to the House of Lilies bounced over the uneven cobblestones, making pretending to sleep impossible. I was curled up in the corner, Lily's gaze from the seat across from me drilling a hole into my head. I ignored her, needing to gather my thoughts before our inevitable conversation.

'What an utter mess,' I snorted as I stared at the thin red line on my palm that tied me to the king. If I'd thought that healing Reynard would make him more lenient, he'd proved me wrong before the blood had even congealed.

'Will you talk to me instead of muttering and huffing like a lunatic?' Lily snapped, and I finally looked at her. 'What happened? What went wrong?'

'Everything. Oh Lily, I messed up so bad . . .' I sighed, hiding my face in my hands.

Lily's eyes kept widening as I regaled her with the story of Jagon's visit to my cell, but it was my dealings with the king, from blinding him to that misbegotten blood oath, that made her clasp her hands to her chest and shake her head.

'Sweet Makosh, Mother of Gods! Sana, what did you do to offend fate? That's . . . I mean . . .' Lily stuttered, gaping at me.

'Utterly insane, impossible, and unworkable? Yes, but somehow, despite the drawbacks, I got what I wanted. Reynard will help me with

Jagon, and Ciesko will teach me magic.' I bit my tongue before I told her about the vivamancy. 'It's just, the price . . . I don't know if I can handle it.'

'At least you're free.'

'Free? It's simply a longer leash.' It was difficult to hide the bitterness in my voice as I showed her the cut on my palm. 'I can only go as far as he allows. He's watching me, too. Didn't you notice the guard nearly breaking his neck to follow us when we left?' I smirked when Lily leaned out the window to look back. 'Oh, and Tova's in prison, though that's the least of my worries. Maybe a night in a cell will cool his temper. Bloody dolt almost got himself killed.'

Lily's eyebrows drew together in a deep frown. I knew she was about to lose her temper and give me a piece of her mind, but I was willing to listen and apologise for worrying her. I had Reynard's oath that he'd protect them both from harm. That was all that mattered.

'Anyway,' I said, 'if my impulsive friend doesn't turn up by tomorrow, I'll go back to the palace and make a fuss. Now, please tell me, how the fuck did you two get in there in the first place?'

'Impulsive? That *crazy* dwarf turned up on my doorstep this morning, demanding to see you, and threatened my bouncer with an axe! My idiot guard told him you were in the palace, and that was it. There was no stopping him. Tova stormed off, and I followed, hoping to keep him from getting killed.'

I smiled involuntarily. 'Tova is stubborn, hotheaded . . . and as loyal as a dragon. Give it time and you'll end up liking him as much as I do.'

Lily smirked. 'I doubt it. I prefer men who bring flowers. I'll leave the ones swinging their big weapons to you. So, what now? We wait until the Mabon feast?'

'I need to arrange some things before making my grand entrance at the Brotherhood,' I said, biting my lip, wondering if I should tell her.

'When Jagon visited me in my cell he told me that he has evidence that implicates you as the murderer of Tivala's son, despite me doing the deed. So tonight, I'm going to retrieve it.'

Lily sat motionless, her face turning pale—a remarkable feat given her almost translucent complexion—before a determined expression crossed her features.

'Sana, Jagon's a manipulative liar. There's a good chance he has nothing, and even if he does, I don't want you to risk it. He might want you alive, but there are plenty of others who would be happy to see you dead rather than returning to Boyan's service.' She pursed her lips in a huff. 'Besides, half of the City Council moan their pleasure in my basement. I also have something to trade with if it comes to buying their favour.'

I recognised that tone. Lily was all business. She was a woman who had dragged herself up from the gutters of Truso with nothing but a shrewd mind and ethereal beauty. She might play coy for her patrons, but the Lily I knew tackled problems head-on. Still, I wouldn't let her become collateral damage in my war.

'I'll be fine. Don't forget—I know the Chapter House like the back of my hand. Plus, I'm good friends with Dagome's best assassin. With Irsha guarding my back, it'll be child's play.'

'Oh, the same friend who sat by my side these last days like a bloody gargoyle, scaring my customers away?' Lily said, rolling her eyes in such an exaggerated way that I chuckled, and she soon joined me.

'Be kind to him, Ice Queen. He likes you, and it is nice to have your own personal gargoyle with twin daggers in hand,' I said, and her gaze softened before a faint blush tinted her cheeks.

'He hasn't even touched me.'

'And he won't. His mother was a courtesan, and he learned early on that even if she allowed something to happen, it didn't mean she wanted it. He'll flirt, but if you want something more, you'll need to make the first move.'

It was more than I should have said, but I didn't feel like it betrayed Irsha's trust. My heart had broken for him every time he'd been pushed aside thanks to women misunderstanding his intentions.

'That explains so many things . . .' Lily said with a small smile, and I wondered whether there was more to her cryptic statement.

True to my word, as soon as we were back, I changed into some practical clothing, then sent Lily's errand boy to shops around the city. I didn't have the time, money, or a workshop to create anything elaborate for my planned heist, so I just made a few simple potions and powders that would increase my chances of escape from the Chapter House should something go wrong.

The youngster returned with everything I had asked for, as well as some interesting gossip from the market square.

'It looks like Jagon's going to make his grand move, thinking I'm stuck in the palace dungeons. The Mabon feast this year is going to be epic,' I said to Lily, who had entered my room and instantly started fanning herself. 'Oh, sorry about the fumes.'

'Sana, if I knew you were going to turn your room into a poisoner's workshop, I would've locked you in the basement,' she said, coughing into her sleeve. 'I came to tell you a friend in the palace has informed me that your dwarf will be released sooner rather than later because, to quote her, "even the truthseeker thinks he's a belligerent bastard."'

I burst out laughing, spilling a few drops of my potion on the table. The wood blackened instantly, and my eyebrows shot up at the effect.

'Was that supposed to happen?' Lily asked, and I shook my head.

'No, but since the arch healer told me I had some rare type of ability, I thought I'd experiment a little. I was trying to make it stronger by manipulating the aether. It was supposed to be a skin irritant for your girls to use to deal with unwanted admirers, but I think it's a little too strong for that.'

'Teaching them a lesson probably shouldn't end with burning their prick off.' Lily chuckled as we both observed the fizzling until it stopped.

'It was just a little clover oil; it shouldn't fizzle,' I said, trying to remember what I had done with the energy contained within the fluid.

Lily bent over the table and inhaled before looking at me with a broad smile. 'It smells divine. If it can somehow be stored, I can ask the artisans to create something to fragrance a room with it. The men will love it—especially those who like to play with their swords.'

'Why sword . . .' I frowned because it made little sense. 'Ohh.' I understood when she wriggled her pinkies and crossed them.

'So, Mabon's feast. What do you want to do?' she asked after we stopped laughing, and I realised she must have heard the gossip.

I pulled out the letter she had given me earlier, showing her the broken seal. Despite the cracks, a wax crow figure was still visible, marking it as an official invitation from the grand master.

'I have a free pass to make my grand entrance,' I said. 'I intend to make it so spectacular that no one will dare think I ignored Boyan or came for his position by using my status as his former shadow.'

'Now that, I can help with!' Lily smiled before gesturing to my little workshop. 'Finish whatever you're doing and come downstairs. We'll need to take your measurements. If the Deadly Nightshade is returning home, we must make her entrance one they'll never forget.'

'Are you sure I'll survive your ladies dolling me up? And please remember, I need something functional. Things could get ugly in there, so I need to be able to fight.'

She just smirked before leaving the room, and a mild feeling of panic settled in. Now that Lily was involved, I'd better get ready for fireworks . . . and expenses.

Chapter 23

Roksana

'Sana, may I come in?' Irsha's voice came through the door—polite, but uncertain.

I quickly opened it, but he didn't step inside.

His eyes scanned me, sharp with suspicion. 'Why do you look like a dark sister of the Blades? You have an invitation. Why the masquerade?'

'Because I need to sneak into the Chapter House before I officially proclaim my return,' I said, pulling him into my room before walking back to the table and attaching an alchemist belt to my skirt.

'I couldn't find anything in Jagon's workshop. The place was so neat, I was afraid to touch anything . . . I don't even know what was in half the bottles. I tried bribing his apprentice, but the poor sod feared his master too much to take my money,' he said, sitting heavily on a chair. 'Though I'm guessing you knew that would happen.'

I smiled at his reflection in the mirror. 'Stop looking like a beaten puppy. I know you did your best, but some things can only be spotted if you know what you're looking for. Tell me if anything's changed in the Chapter House, or can I safely assume Jagon's workshop is still on the first floor?'

Irsha groaned, closing his eyes for a moment. 'So you've lost the last of your marbles. If Jagon catches you sneaking in and stealing his stuff, he'll use it against Boyan, and the old man's already hanging onto his position by a thread.'

'I have to do this. I'm going to bow to Boyan and disclose my involvement with the mages. You know that will cause Jagon to lose his shit and take it as a declaration of war so I need to ensure Lily's safety,' I said, wrapping my braid around my head in a peasant crown before pulling up my hood. 'Can you create a little distraction so I can slip in?'

'No,' he said, and I turned towards him, frowning as he adjusted my hood. 'I'll get you in, but if you get into trouble, you withdraw. I don't want to lose my friend because she's too stubborn to retreat. As for Lily's safety, leave it to me.'

'Fine,' I said when he reached for the mask lying on the table. I was itching to ask how he was going to protect her, but in the end, I let it slide. 'So, shall we?'

'Of course. Now, be a good assassin, keep your head down, and walk behind your master,' he replied with a smirk, placing the mask on my face, making me almost indistinguishable from any other dark sister.

As soon as he'd fastened the ties, Irsha's demeanour changed completely. As we left my room, I walked beside him out of habit but his barked command to 'Step back' made me falter, and I muttered an apology. When we were outside, I stayed back, keeping my hood low whilst looking around for danger. If any observer had spotted me then, I would have looked like a clumsy apprentice, which was exactly what I was aiming for.

'Master Vilkor, a pleasure to see you, sir. Who's your companion?'

I heard the guard's challenge and hunched my shoulders into a position that allowed me to drop my hand to my dagger.

Irsha smacked me upside the head. 'Behave, child.' I released my weapon and cowered. 'Just an idiot who can't follow simple orders,' he said to the guard.

The guards fell over themselves laughing, wishing Irsha good luck on training 'stupid' as they opened the doors and let us into the Chapter House.

Irsha grabbed me by the scruff of the neck, forcing me to stumble ahead. My friend played the annoyed mentor to perfection, but he was a large man, and his fake discipline left real bruises. It didn't take long to arrive at the corridor near Jagon's workshop, but my body was aching by the time we got there.

'Wait here,' Irsha said. 'I'll check if Jagon's inside. As soon as you hear raised voices, wait a slow count of thirty, then slip into the room.' I nodded, finding a hiding spot in a shadowy nook. I waited with a handful of sleeper's ash, ready for anyone who may have discovered me.

Irsha marched inside the workshop, and a moment later, shattering glass and raised male voices echoed down the corridor right before the door snapped open.

'How dare you suggest any poison I supply is substandard! If Boyan doesn't reprimand you for this, Blade, I will.'

Irsha's reply was smooth as ever. 'I have the poison in my quarters. It couldn't even make a frog bleed. Maybe talk to your apprentices—because my assassins can't be gambling their lives on something that weak.'

I couldn't help smirking. If there was one sure way to draw Jagon out of his den, it was to insult his craftsmanship. Irsha knew that—and plucked at my former master's ego like a well-tuned lute.

Footsteps faded down the corridor, Jagon's furious voice trailing behind them, still demanding Irsha retract his 'slander' or face the consequences.

I slid out from my little nook and walked towards the door, only hesitating for a moment before I turned the handle.

It was like travelling back in time to a place I still saw in my nightmares.

I promptly glanced around the shelves where various ingredients were stored, neatly organised. They had clearly been set out by an apprentice who knew that if they made the slightest mistake, Jagon would force them to test his newest poison.

'The old bastard hasn't changed,' I muttered, quickly scanning the notes left on his desk, careful not to make a mess. Unfortunately, all the schemata and notes were just old recipes used for teaching the basics. I hadn't expected much, but I still peeked at Jagon's journals. Again, there was nothing out of the ordinary, although one thing caught my attention: There were far too many orders from the South, and one of the poisons requested affected a mage's ability to use aether. Frankly, it was the largest order of lanara poison I'd seen in my life, and I took a mental note of the date and quantity.

In the hidden compartments of his desk, I found a second ledger, full of names I didn't recognise, so I used a quill to record those which sounded vaguely familiar or important on my arm. Still, there was no signed confession or any trace of the small box with the lip gloss I had made several years ago.

When I'd finished with the desk, I moved on to Jagon's favourite picture, a gloomy landscape of his homeland. I was rummaging through the potent concoctions hidden behind it when I heard noises outside.

My former master was returning, and I was elbow-deep in his precious inventions.

'Fuck,' I muttered, rushing towards a hidden partition I vaguely remembered.

The hidden passage opened when I pressed the last petal of a rose carved into the wall, and I slipped inside, stifling my relieved sigh. Jagon had never revealed this space to me, but after he'd forced me to drink a particularly lethal poison, I'd awakened on the floor earlier than he expected and played dead. He must have forgotten about me, but I'd watched him, noticing the catch he used to access the secret room.

'Check everything. That bonehead wouldn't have dragged me out of here if he weren't planning something. Ensure all the orders are coded and secured.'

My breath hitched at hearing Jagon's words until I reminded myself that Irsha and Jagon had equal power in the Brotherhood.

'The orders are untouched, my lord. Are you sure it was a ploy?' a much younger voice answered.

'Of course it was, and I'm betting Roksana's behind it. That idiot Blade hasn't communicated with his chapter since she reappeared in Truso, and I'm betting he's spending his nights with her.' Jagon released such a theatrical sigh, I could almost see him rolling his eyes. 'My Nightshade used to love to use him against me, and I can't even blame her for taking advantage of the sentimental fool,' Jagon said with such disdain that I wanted to throw something caustic in his face.

'Nothing seems to be touched or moved. I've even checked the shelves of rare ingredients and poisons,' the apprentice said, and I congratulated myself for carefully placing every bottle back in its place.

'Good, fine. You're free to go,' Jagon said.

After a moment, I heard a door close, followed by footsteps approaching my hideout. I was in a narrow corridor that led to a cluttered room with no windows—at least, that's what I remembered from my one and only visit. I started to panic when I heard the clicking of the carved petal and grabbed a handful of sleeper's ash, ready to blow it into the poison master's face when a voice rang out.

'Master Jagon, there's a message from the dwarven kingdom.'

'Later,' Jagon snapped.

'But . . . they halved the last delivery and brought nothing this time. The messenger's threatening to leave,' the voice insisted.

'What's that paranoid bastard up to now?' Jagon muttered before his footsteps moved away.

I didn't recognise the speaker from their voice but blessed them with all my heart. After several moments of silence, a door slammed in the distance. Whether it was Irsha's ploy or a fortunate coincidence, I didn't have time to spare thinking about it. I patted the surrounding space until my hand landed on the familiar shape of a fae light, and a soft glow soon illuminated the room.

I took a glance around and nearly laughed. Jagon had always left the cleaning to his apprentices, and in a place where only he could enter, the layers of dust were so thick they felt like cat fur. However, his disdain for cleaning had left a small space cleared of dust, giving away where he'd most recently worked.

A small chest sat in the roughly cleaned area, inviting me to open it, and when I did, I smiled at the familiar metal box I found inside. My best poison, *Wrath of Lilies*, which I'd used to kill Ignac Tivala, still smelled like lilacs. I took a pinch, rubbing it between my fingers, and my aether instantly recognised and neutralised the familiar pattern. 'I shouldn't have left you here,' I muttered, switching the box out with one I'd brought with me—if Jagon ever tried using it as evidence, he'd simply be presenting the court with a costly beauty product.

I was about to leave when my gaze landed on a bookshelf with another clean space in front of a book's spine, indicating the poison master had withdrawn it often. Out of curiosity, I took the book and let it fall open naturally. It opened to a very stained page detailing an old recipe, and the more I read, the more my eyes widened.

I was holding possibly the only copy of *The Poisons of Ozar*, a book lost centuries ago, before the First Necromancer's War. Leaving it in Jagon's possession felt like a crime, but, grinding my teeth, I put it back in its place, rushing out of the workshop.

I returned to the nook I'd used earlier and was immediately accosted by Irsha.

'Sana, fuck, I thought that bastard caught you. Boyan almost ripped my tongue out for accusing Jagon of incompetence, so I hope you found what you were looking for.'

'Partially,' I said, fighting my nervous laughter, 'though I did find something very interesting. Come on, let's go back to the House of Lilies. I'll buy you a beer and tell you all about it.'

'I can't,' he said. 'But I'll escort you out of the building. Some of my men were injured today and I need to see them. I've been neglecting my duties, and that won't do, especially with Jagon's meddling.'

'Okay, then I'll see you when I make my official return. Thank you for helping,' I responded, pulling my hood up and following him back out onto the street.

'I'll be ready for the chaos, but in the meantime, be careful,' Irsha cautioned me as he pulled me into a hug. 'I'll be too busy to pull you from the king's or Jagon's clutches.'

'Always,' I said.

I disappeared into the crowd, unable to stop smiling under the mask. Outsmarting Jagon was a reward in and of itself, but my plans had expanded. One look at the poisons and I'd realised that leaving had been a mistake. I hadn't found freedom by serving Młot, or knowledge by attempting to train myself in the art of magic.

I couldn't be just a mage, or just a poisoner . . . I was both.

If the rules governing our world prevented me from becoming what I was always meant to be, it was time to change them.

Because I refused to choose, and I wouldn't allow anyone to force me to run away again.

Chapter 24

Reynard

The swell of her hips, the fire in her eyes, her intoxicating scent . . . I hid my face in my hands and groaned in frustration.

Gods, why can't I free myself of these thoughts?

Even the movement of the curtains in the breeze reminded me of her dress as it had exposed her legs.

I'd had Roksana followed, not that I doubted she'd hold to her oath, but the woman was reckless enough to have gone to the mages and sneak into my bedchamber. In a city like Truso, such impulsiveness could easily end in the icy waters of the river—all it would take was a stealthy knife in a dark alley. Yet, even having my guards track her didn't assuage the uneasiness I felt. Knowing that she was somewhere in the city, beyond my reach, made me nervous.

Protecting her has become pivotal to my plans. That's the only reason I feel like this, I reasoned with myself. The voice in the back of my mind scoffed at the thought.

'What are you doing now, Viper? Getting ready for bed or mixing another concoction to turn someone else's life upside down?' I mused. Then, as if on command, an insistent knocking rattled the door.

'Enter.'

'Your Majesty.' The guard bowed, barely coming into the room. 'We lost her.'

It took a moment for his words to sink in. I stood up, the old leather chair I had been sitting in crashing into the wall as I approached the bowing guard.

'How?' I asked through gritted teeth. 'She's barely left the palace, and you've *already* lost her? What happened? Did someone take her?'

Did the oath fail? Has she escaped? Fuck, if she's fooled me . . . I wondered.

That possibility was easier to bear. If she escaped, she was safe.

But if she'd been taken . . .

The guard broke through my train of thought before it spiralled into foolish action. 'Sire, we don't know exactly what happened. But we lost her after she arrived at The House of Lilies.'

My brows drew closer. 'You're bothering me because she's staying at her friend's?'

I had to train my men better if they became alarmed simply because the woman was resting.

'The thing is, sire, she isn't. We have people inside. A guard and a maid who report on the guests. Both swore on their lives that your prisoner arrived, but that after someone visited her room, she vanished, though she wasn't seen leaving the building. They searched the place and found no trace of her. No one, save the owner, perhaps, knows what happened,' he said, and I bit back a curse.

'Did they check the basement?'

'The basement, the rooms, everywhere. I posted one of our younger recruits there a month ago. The maid's been there since we'd noticed how many nobles frequent the business. They know the House of Lilies inside out, and I trust them when they say Roksana Regnav is not in the building.'

I wasn't surprised he had taken the initiative. When I became king, I had ordered my spies to infiltrate prominent public establishments, guesthouses, taverns, brothels, and even shops popular with the nobility. I wanted to know who was doing what, where, and with how much money. If they happened to mention their plans, so much the better. I didn't know how Roksana had avoided my spies, but I would find out.

'Tell your contact that someone in a wolf mask will soon visit. He should ensure the man gains entry without any questions,' I said, a plan forming in my head.

The only person who might know where my Viper was would be Liliana, the owner of the brothel, though I doubted she'd volunteer the information. Still, few stay tight-lipped when standing before the king. I thought about the dwarf in my cells, and I smirked, knowing how useful he was about to be if Roksana had tricked me.

'Go to the cells and tell the overseer to post two guards on the dwarf. He must not be harmed, but if he disappears, I'll have their heads.'

The man bowed, retreating, and I exhaled softly, returning to my desk and drafting a message to Riordan. After I'd signed it, I went to the window, jerking it open to look at the city below. A chill wind filled with the promise of rain blew past, giving me goosebumps and scattering my letters to the floor, but I ignored them.

A shiver of excitement ran down my spine as I turned and pulled a custom-made wolf mask from a drawer. It covered the upper half of my face and its enchanted red glass eyes allowed me to see the world; however, any who'd look back at me would only see their own reflection.

Masks were popular in Truso, and I'd bet my life that every noble cheating on his wife in the middle of the night had one, but this one was unique. I'd paid well for it to be enchanted to help me blend into the crowd, even with my imposing figure. I'd had it made a long time ago, before the war, when I used to sneak into the capital for meetings with the nobles conspiring to depose the old king.

'The man with a wolf's face and the woman with a viper's touch . . . What a pair we are,' I whispered, looking at the wolf's muzzle in the mirror as I fastened a short sword onto my belt and a blackened vambrace on my wrist. 'Time to hunt.'

The House of Lilies was bustling by the time I arrived. Fae lights and flickering candles created dark shadows, obscuring those who came seeking illicit pleasure. Music and chatter spilled out every time the doors opened, flooding the street with light and laughter.

From the outside, it was a theatre house and restaurant, but once inside, there was more entertainment than could be found on any menu. Lilies' offered shows and good food, but in its alcoves and private rooms, the rich could also indulge in pleasures of the flesh and mind. Beneath its glamour, there was even a basement with a stylised dungeon for those desiring pain or submission. I didn't care for such practices, but as long as no one's consent was violated, I forbade the authorities from intervening. It was better to have a controlled outlet for certain needs than to have bodies on the street.

The bouncer, a well-built man, nodded as I entered, no questions asked, despite the murmurs of those still waiting their turn. Still, they quickly quieted when I turned to look at them, posturing as the type of guest whose position granted them priority in such an establishment. No one challenged me.

I instinctively searched for the scent of lilac and honey among the luxury perfumes and delicious roasted meats and desserts, as if I had any chance of finding her in this crowd.

'Welcome, kind sir. May I offer you refreshment?' a hostess asked as she balanced a heavy tray with a variety of drinks on one hand.

I took the closest goblet, not looking at its contents, stepping to the side to avoid a drunk couple that stumbled in after me.

'Absinthe? A rare but excellent choice, my lord. Would you like to meet Madam Liliana to discuss your . . . interests?' the hostess said as I glanced at the green liquid sparkling in the candlelight. *Does one's choice of drink have a hidden meaning?* Whatever it meant, it suited my needs, so I nodded, letting her lead me into a bustling room.

Liliana sat in a secluded alcove, fanning herself as she observed the mingling guests. From what I'd been told about her, the Ice Queen of Truso was never seen with a lover or took an interest in the pleasures her House was famous for. The woman had more of a regal air about her than any of the noble ladies of my court, and I couldn't help smiling when she turned to greet me.

'Welcome to The House of Lilies, Sir . . .?'

'My name is of no consequence, but I'd be grateful if we could speak in private.'

A crease marred her otherwise perfect features, but after a moment's hesitation, Liliana nodded, sending away both the hostess and the servant waiting on her.

'What topic of conversation prevents you from sharing your name . . . or face? A word of warning, before we talk,' she said, pointing at the armed man observing us from a distance, 'we may be alone, but I am not unguarded.'

I got to the point. 'I'm looking for my Viper. If you've helped her escape, this House, and all of its pleasures, will be erased from the city while you watch from my dungeons.'

My words were followed by the sharp snap of her closing fan. Liliana stood up, the colour draining from her face, though that was the only sign of her fear.

'What do you want from her, Your Majesty?'

'Find some other name to address me by when I'm wearing this mask. If I'd wanted my presence known, I would have arrived surrounded by guards. Roksana—I want her whereabouts, that's all.'

'Sana is resting, Wolf,' she said. 'If you wish to see her, I can ask her to visit you tomorrow.'

Our standoff was attracting some attention, with several entertainers exchanging glances and making a flurry of unusual gestures. I recognised the language of those born without hearing; using it in this place was a touch of genius. None of the clients seemed to notice, but I saw several people moving closer.

'Please sit down, Madam. Neither of us wants to see your staff get hurt over such a minor issue. Perhaps you could reassure them as well? Surely, in this profession, you've learned how to handle difficult clients.'

Liliana gave the staff one of her famous smiles, her free hand moving in a similar way to the entertainers'.

I need to use this in the army, I thought, impressed by how effective their silent communication was.

Once she was sitting comfortably, I pressed for the truth.

'Now tell me why you're lying and surrender Roksana's location.'

Liliana's hands tightened on the armchair, her knuckles turning white. She looked away, focusing on the stage where two acrobats were performing a complicated balancing act.

'I know you think the worst of her, but Roksana is a good person. She came back to keep me safe, and you want me to betray her?' she said without looking at me, but a disdainful smirk tilted the corner of her lips. 'If you feel the need to intimidate a whore with your power, so be it. I can establish another brothel, but a friendship like hers is more precious than any money I could earn. All I'm willing to do for you is deliver a message to Roksana that you want to talk.'

I nodded, admiring the quiet courage of a woman willing to put loyalty above her safety. However, her passive resistance and the absence of a certain poisoner after I'd just threatened her friend confirmed that Sana wasn't in the building. Luckily, Liliana's covert glances towards the entrance told me she expected my Viper to return soon.

'I'd prefer speaking with her today, so we'll wait, and hope Roksana's friendship is as strong as you insist,' I said, picking up the absinthe and swirling the green liquid before emptying it, grimacing at the bitter burning in my throat. 'Know this, Madam: If she doesn't turn up by midnight, I'll see if locking up another of her friends will hasten her return.'

'Of course, my lord. I expect no less. I can even lend you a dungeon. It is always available to my discerning clients.'

Lily's reaction to my threat made it difficult to maintain a menacing presence, and after a moment of silence, I asked, 'What does this mean . . . my choice of drink?'

'It means you want to experience the touch of green fae. It leaves you helpless, unable to move or speak, while pleasure is taken from you. Some like to be used that way, but I rarely approve the request, and you were brought here to hear my refusal.'

'Oh . . .'

My fumbled response brought a smirk to her face, and we both fell silent. Studying her regal poise, I noticed the moment she spotted Roksana, her eyes widening ever so slightly. It was her hands, however, that really gave it away.

At Liliana's small, covert gesture, a woman slipped away, rushing up the stairs to whisper in the poisoner's ear before gesturing for her to go upstairs. I half expected Roksana to flee, but she snapped her head up, her face thunderous, and strode down the stairs towards us.

'I believe I've found what I was looking for,' I said.

Liliana followed my gaze, muttering a curse when she saw Sana marching towards us.

The courtesan moved to intercept her friend, but I wanted to see what Roksana would do next.

'Please return to your seat, Madam,' I said, placing my hand on her shoulder just as the heavy curtains moved and Sana walked in.

My Viper's pupils dilated at my gesture, causing me to snap my hand away and snatch Roxana's fist just before she could throw something at me.

'What the fuck you think you're doing?' she asked, pulling free from my grasp and pushing between me and Liliana.

'Sana, no—'

'Lily, leave. You've entertained this patron long enough,' Roksana said, and I wholeheartedly agreed with the sentiment.

'You don't know who he is,' the courtesan whispered, but my Viper was determined to remove her friend from my presence. 'Fine, but Sana, please remember where you are during your discussion,' she said, turning to me. 'Wolf.' She inclined her head and slipped away.

I stood, silently observing their interaction, paying particular attention to Roksana. Traces of tonight's escapade clung to her, the dark sister's dress unable to hide them. There was a smudge of dirt on her cheek, and her honey-gold hair was dusted with the remains of cobwebs.

My curiosity was piqued.

'You kept me waiting,' I said, reaching out to pluck the silvery thread draped over her temple. Before I could touch it, Sana caught my wrist while her free hand struck so fast, I could barely see it. I did, however, feel the unmistakable tip of a blade pressed to my throat.

'I asked you a question... *Wolf.*'

'Oh, we were simply discussing my choice of drink while waiting for you, Viper,' I teased, taking hold of the blade between my fingers, careful not to cut myself. 'Now, will you tell me where you've been, or are you determined to remove something other than my eye?'

A tremor ran through Roksana's body, making the blade tremble in my grasp, and I released it quickly, unwilling to risk another encounter with the Nightshade's poison.

'Why are you here?' she asked. 'I agreed to work for you and took your oath. There's no need to pester my friends.'

'And have you been?'

'Been what?'

'Working for me? Was that why you disappeared and have returned covered in dust and cobwebs?' I questioned, reaching for her once again. This time, she didn't stop me as I ran my fingers through her hair, then showed her the silvery threads.

'You wanted me to find your enemy. Well, I'm working on it. So stop trying to control my every step. I'll contact you the moment I have any information,' she said, frowning when I moved closer, intrigued by the ink on her arm.

I reached for her wrist, but she swatted my hand away and pulled her sleeve down exposing the writing. The ink was so smudged I could barely decipher the names, but they all looked familiar.

'I found those names?' she asked. 'Are they important?'

'Courtiers, a few nobles . . . What is this?'

'Those are the people Jagon pays or receives money from,' she said. 'They were in his ledger.' She paused, seeing my frown. 'I transcribed it hoping it might help you.'

I took her arm, my finger trailing over the soft skin that prickled with goosebumps under my touch.

'You are surprisingly efficient.'

I didn't hide the appreciation in my voice. She'd discovered more in one day than my spies had in months. I leant over, memorising each name I could decipher before turning her hand and brushing my lips over her knuckles.

'What now?' she asked, frowning at my gesture, though she didn't pull her hand from mine. All I could think about was holding her again.

But how?

A sudden change in the music gave me an idea. The lights dimmed and a darker, sultrier rhythm took hold of the room—velvet and danger stitched into every note.

'Dance with me, Roksana.'

I hadn't danced the obraka[1] in years. It was too intimate for court and too intimidating for many men. The dance demanded more than the strength necessary to lift one's partner—it required closeness. Control. The chance to feel what her dress was meant to keep hidden.

'Why? We can continue here if you have more questions. I'm tired and not in the mood to play games,' she said, glancing towards the exit, but I didn't let go, her defiance goading the predator in me.

'I insist,' I said, smiling even though the wolf mask concealed most of my features. 'One dance, and you can rest for the night, I promise.'

'Fine,' she said, rolling her eyes. 'Lead us to the floor, *Wolf*.'

The nickname on her lips sent a quiet thrill through me as we walked through the crowd. When she gave a begrudging curtsy, I laughed, surprised by how much I enjoyed her reluctant acceptance.

The dance floor had quieted, the crowd's attention drifting elsewhere and leaving us in a rare pocket of stillness. In our dark attire, we stood

---

1. **Obraka** — a slow and sensual dance relying on physical touch and showcasing the male's strength to lift their partner.

out against the riot of colour that surrounded us, but I didn't care. My focus was entirely on Roksana.

I turned with a flourish and bowed, offering my hand to her. Her eyes blazed as she accepted it with a sigh edged in annoyance. Her fingers barely touched mine, but the power behind them was unmistakable. The moment our hands met, the connection between us grounded my soul.

I drew her in close, sliding my free hand to her waist, unable to resist a gentle squeeze. Her breath hitched as she rested her hand on my shoulder, and our eyes locked just as the song's opening chords faded.

We moved in perfect sync, each step drawing us deeper into the rhythm as we stared into each other's eyes, unable to look away. Roksana danced like she was born to it, and I couldn't help the smile that tugged at my lips. The moment she noticed, however, she looked away.

'Look at me, Sana,' I said, lifting her into the air before slowly sliding her down my body, feeling her hands slide over the soft fabric of my shirt. I expected her to ignore me, but when I held her at eye level, she met my gaze.

'I thought you'd found a way to escape,' I murmured as I spun her away, then drew her back against me, her spine flush to my chest as we swept into the next movement. 'Or worse, that someone had taken you against your will.'

I hadn't intended to admit I'd come chasing after her, but the words slipped from my lips before I could stop them, and something akin to resignation crossed her features.

'I couldn't even if I wanted to,' she said. 'I'm bound by our oath and a shared enemy. Jagon threatened to expose secrets I couldn't allow to surface, and I had to prevent that. That was all. Nothing that concerns you or Dagome.'

I barely heard her, distracted by the warmth and alluring scent of her body. Still, Sana's words carved out a distance I didn't like.

'Everything you do concerns me, Viper.'

I lifted her again, maybe a bit too high, as she gasped, her hand flying to the side of my neck. Her touch scorched me, but my heart leapt at the feeling, and I missed a step as I held her close.

A litany of curses burned through my mind as I corrected my position, annoyed at a quiet snigger from the crowd. *Focus!* I ordered myself as we moved through another turn, but I was lost in her eyes, in the smile that blossomed on her lips, and the quiet chuckle that followed my clumsiness.

I spun her, realising that I was smiling again. Lilac and honey teased my senses, and I was profoundly grateful for the mask that kept me from pressing my lips to the hollow of her neck.

'Share your worries,' I heard myself say, my voice lower, harsher, as a darkness rose from the depths of my soul. 'Let me make them disappear.'

She shook her head, refusing my help, and I bit my tongue as I tried to tether the sudden heat, the anger, that coursed through my veins.

Had Ciesko been right?

When he'd told me his theory about my reaction to Roksana, I'd almost scoffed. My brother Orm was the one afflicted with wild magic. It had never manifested in me. Yet, the arch healer was sure that my cursed heritage had awakened at Sana's distress in the forest, and that it had saved my life from her poison. As I battled the urge to strangle the person who'd caused her pain, I conceded that he might be right.

The music quickened, approaching its dramatic crescendo, and I spun Roksana so swiftly her long braid loosened, strands unravelling in a golden arc. Time slowed as her hair coiled around my neck like a silken collar, linking us together as the last notes of the song faded into silence.

She laughed, reaching for her unruly braid, the sound light and careless, but I stood motionless.

Was this how it felt to submit to the green fae her friend had mentioned?

My nostrils flared, breathing her in, each inhale eroding my will to release myself from her beautiful snare.

'Your strength is breathtaking, Wolf.' She chuckled, fingers working to untangle her braid. 'I'm glad I didn't choke you. That would have been yet another transgression to add to my infamous record of crimes against the Crown,' she teased. She looked up at me then, stepping away as soon as she was free, her voice shifting. 'I'm sorry. It wasn't on purpose.'

The defensiveness in her tone snapped me out of my trance, though my heart still lagged. I shook my head, trying not to fixate on the faint blush colouring her cheeks.

'I know it wasn't, Sanika,' I murmured, coughing into my hand to mask the softness in my voice. 'I promised to only steal one dance, so I'll leave you to your rest,' I said, turning on my heel and heading for the exit, leaving my partner looking confused in the middle of the dance floor.

I glanced back and saw Liliana approach her with a questioning look, but Roksana simply shrugged before they both returned to the alcove.

Outside, I inhaled deeply, trying to clear my head. The cool air filled my lungs, the familiar smells of hearth smoke and damp stone calming my racing heart as my feet carried me towards the river.

The streets had quieted, only a few late wanderers slipping home this late at night. I stopped at the waterfront and let the quiet murmur of the waves splashing in the harbour calm my soul while the moon turned my shadow into a hulking monster on the ground.

'Why did it have to be you?' I whispered, the words vanishing into the wind as I fought the warmth blossoming in my heart.

No, I'm stronger than this.

I had to be. I couldn't let this infatuation overshadow my duties as king.

I repeated it like a prayer, but it was all for nothing. Something darker and overpowering had already taken hold, tethering me to the woman who had collared me with her braid.

Chapter 25

Roksana

A few days later

The day of the Mabon feast finally arrived, and despite my preparations, I was still daunted by the prospect of facing the chapter masters during the banquet.

Still, it wasn't as stressful as my meeting with Tova had been. Lily's prediction of my friend's release was, of course, correct. In fact, he'd returned to The House of Lilies within hours of my strange encounter with Reynard.

I groaned at the memory of his return.

Gods, he'd been so angry, striding through the empty ballroom just after dawn. I'd rushed towards him, but he stopped me, his palm held out. His nostrils had flared, throat bobbing frantically as if he was trying to tame emotions that threatened to choke him.

Tova rarely displayed feelings other than joviality or anger. Pain, especially sadness, he hid deep in his heart, but this time, he was visibly shaken.

'Did Reynard . . .? Gods, he swore he wouldn't hurt you. I'm going to—' I was fuming, embracing him despite his protests. We both needed it, even if the proud dwarf would never admit it.

'He didn't hurt me. It was the most comfortable dungeon I've ever been in. Yet, the whole time I thought . . . Młot's been searching for you since your escape, but all they found were corpses. I thought I'd lost you.'

He finally enveloped my shoulders with a vice-like strength. 'That's the last time I let you go into danger alone. Last bloody time, drah'sa . . . I can't lose my little sister.'

Tova was true to his word, staying beside me until we settled into a more comfortable routine. One where I could walk out of The House of Lilies without a suspicious dwarf asking where I was going or insisting on escorting me.

I sighed heavily, focusing on the here and now, wondering how to convince Tova he couldn't come to the Chapter House with me tonight as I stared in the mirror.

Thanks to Lily and two of her more mature entertainers, I was armed and ready to face my brethren—well, almost ready. There were still four women fussing around me, and after the third time they caught me sighing, Lily pinched my arm and narrowed her eyes.

'I think I look good enough,' I said, chuckling when one of the girls pulled my belt tighter for the hundredth time. 'It's a bunch of murderers and spies, not a royal ball.'

'You're walking into a den of wolves. Your outfit is your armour. The way you look and how you carry yourself tells them whether you're predator or prey,' Lily said, nodding with appreciation when I attached my weapon of choice, a custom-made poison-infused dagger, to my thigh holster.

I had no idea how she had obtained one in such a short period of time, but I had a feeling Tova was involved. The weapon, an Alchemist's Fang, was famously difficult to make due to its unusual design, and had earned its name due to its slightly curved blade and the unique surprise it contained.

I drew the dagger, a delicate masterpiece forged from two leaves of metal, and slid my finger over the curved edge. I still needed to fill it with poison but wanted to test the needle first.

The woman helping me yelped, pulling away when it shot forward, and I chuckled, twisting it slowly back inside the blade.

'Don't worry, I didn't add the poison yet,' I said, patting her shoulder before turning to Lily. 'My absence wasn't so long that they'd forget the Deadly Nightshade.'

My smile widened as my hand glided over my midnight blue dress.

It was a practical outfit, similar to a battle mage's robe. Its worth was not in the cut or its embellishments, but in the choice of fabric. The southern velvet could withstand fire for several minutes, and its interwoven silver threads worked almost as well as chain mail. The vertical slits in the dress allowed me to hide my dagger whilst providing me freedom of movement, and the alchemist belt—with its loops for small vials and potions—was of the best dwarven design.

To the casual passerby, the dress didn't betray the opulence behind it. To anyone knowledgeable, however, including those in the Dark Brotherhood and Thieves' Guild, it was attire worthy of a queen.

'Oh, I'm sure they remember, but in a good way?' Lily asked as she wrapped a dark fae shadow cloak around me. 'You did the unthinkable and burned your contract, leaving a position many would kill for. It's best to remind them who you are.'

I admired the way the cloak absorbed the light, obscuring my form beneath its fabric. Lily hadn't pulled any punches in her efforts.

Mischief danced in my eyes as I leapt forward and embraced her, whispering my thanks as I kissed her cheek. The blush rapidly spreading across her face made me giggle as we shared a moment until the door suddenly opened with such force that it bounced off the wall.

'You sent me to look for a house because you wanted to sneak away?' Tova pushed inside, huffing like a pissed-off badger, eyeing me suspiciously. 'Tell me where you're going! Right the fuck now!'

The worry on his face made me feel guilty for trying to deceive him. I'd tried to spare him, but it appeared I'd done more harm than good with my attempt.

'I sent you out because we need a home with workshops for both of us. Or would you like me to choose your workspace? Fae style perhaps, with large windows?' I answered, grinning at the tight set of his lips. 'Did you find anything suitable?'

'Maybe? There's an empty townhouse that we can look over tomorrow. Now, tell me where you're going.' He sighed, dragging a hand down his face. 'Please?' he whispered.

His plea twisted something in my chest, making me sigh.

'Don't you dare huff at me, drah'sa,' he said, raising a finger and shaking it at me. 'Trouble follows you like the stench after an army. I have good reason to be concerned.'

'That's a truly colourful comparison.' I chuckled, stroking my dress. 'It's the autumnal equinox. I'm going to the Mabon feast at the Chapter House.'

Tova's eyebrows drew together. I could see that he was counting the days in his head until, with a deep sigh and a much calmer expression, he placed a hand on his axe. 'I forgot that was today. Alright, let's go—but you owe me a beer on the way back.'

'You can't come,' I said. 'Not this time.' Tova opened his mouth to protest, but I shook my head. 'My arrival will cause a dangerous upheaval. If I bring an outsider with me, it will weaken my position, and the weak die in the Brotherhood.'

'So what do you want me to do? Sit here twiddling my thumbs? At least let me escort you to the door.' Tova resisted until Lily's hand on his shoulder forced him to look at her.

'Master Orenson, I need your assistance tonight. A dwarven caravan purchased an entire night here, and the money they paid was . . . well, obscene. You don't get that much from honest trade,' she said.

'And what does that have to do with me?' Tova asked, moving closer to Lily.

'Well, I need a distraction. Someone they can focus on while my entertainers fish for their secrets,' she answered with a mischievous grin, and ever so slightly, Tova's posture relaxed. 'I'm sure you have a story or two to tell, and so interesting that my girls will fall over themselves fighting for your attention. Men rarely appreciate such competition and like to boast about stories of their own, especially after being served dwarven spirits.'

Lily had built her business on coaxing men into submitting to her every whim, and Tova—bless his heart—wasn't immune to her charms. He glanced between us, loyalty fighting with the desire to prove himself to the woman who was currently looking at him as if he were a hero of legend. I was so impressed that I wondered why no one had employed her as a spymaster yet.

'Wonderful,' I said. 'You heard her, tinkerer. Only you can drink an entire tavern under the table. We need your very special talent to find out how these supposedly ordinary dwarven merchants can afford a night at Lily's.'

Tova narrowed his eyes, looking between Lily and me again before shaking his head with a deep huff.

'Why do I feel like this is just to keep me inside? Are you sure you'll be alright alone, drah'sa? You're the only family I have left; tell me the truth.'

'The truth is I was raised there. I'm no innocent lamb waiting for slaughter. Trust me, I can manage,' I said, tugging at the slit of my dress. 'I can fight—you know this—and I'm not going there empty-handed.'

Tova nodded when my gesture revealed not just the dagger at my thigh but the pouches and vials I'd prepared. Each contained a potentially lethal substance, slightly altered by tinkering with my newly discovered abilities.

'Fine, but if you're not back by morning, I'm going there to bash in some heads. I mean it, Sana,' Tova grumbled and turned to Lily, who, in the meantime, had been quietly conversing with one of her maids. 'So, what exactly do you want me to do?'

The sway of Lily's hips as she returned to Tova's side had my poor friend utterly entranced. *We all have our weaknesses,* I thought as I stifled a laugh. Tova's was that he loved beautiful women almost as much as he enjoyed creating his devices—and Lily was nothing short of a work of art.

She raised her hand, offering it for just a moment. Tova, ever the gentleman, wasted no time. He took it with surprising delicacy and kissed her fingers. When he looked up, Lily greeted him with a smile.

'If you would be so kind as to escort me this evening,' she said, 'I'll introduce you to the party. As for your stories, well, I'm sure you've led a most interesting life, Master Inventor. My girls will serve the liquor, and if a drinking competition starts, so much the better. Once they're relaxed, my entertainers will ask for more stories, and we'll let the merchants talk.'

She paused, a flicker of mischief lighting her expression. 'If they are simply men who've had a lucky windfall, they'll have the time of their lives. But if they're some of the ones smuggling srebrec . . . well, perhaps we'll get some answers.'

Tova's eyes lit up, and I was happy to see him so animated. He started preening his kaftan and brushing his beard. Lily noticed and added smoothly, 'That's all I ask. Though I do hope we can enjoy each other's company as well.'

She laughed softly, and Tova, entirely captivated, kissed her hand once more.

'I won't need to pretend to enjoy the company of such an exquisite beauty,' he said with a flourish. 'You, my lady, are the rarest of gems, adorned by the finest setting. If I could capture your radiance in a jewel, it would brighten the entire kingdom.'

I bit my lip to keep my shit-eating grin at bay. Tova's swaggering flattery had earned him many a maiden's blushing smile, and by helping me, Lily had exposed herself to the full force of his dwarven charm.

I wrapped my cloak tighter around me as warmth blossomed in my chest. Tova still held Lily's hand, and she looked genuinely pleased by his compliment. The feeling spread through my chest as I watched them together, easily picturing Irsha joining us. I thanked the gods for my strange, mismatched family and vowed to protect them, whatever it took.

Snapping out of my thoughts, I waved goodbye.

'I'll see you both later,' I said, slipping away with a smile—and praying I came back in one piece.

Chapter 26

Roksana

Truso's nightlife had only just begun to stir when I stepped out of Lily's, the scent of roasted meats and spiced breads curling through the air from nearby street vendors. I hadn't made it far before the crowd thickened; soon, I had to pause as richly dressed individuals pushed past in pursuit of their evening's entertainment.

I stiffened as a group of masked strangers came too close for comfort. None of them were my confusing wolf or Jagon's goons—just men chasing thrills they could indulge in without tarnishing their names. I huffed, half-amused, half-annoyed, and pressed on, silently scolding myself for the foolish flicker of hope that one of them might have been Reynard.

After our last encounter, I expected . . . more. That he'd left me unmolested for five days was strangely disappointing. Those were dangerous sentiments to have, so I pushed them to the back of my mind and merged back into the swirl of colour and noise, heading for the Chapter House.

Above me, stars shimmered in the sky, an early warning of the autumn equinox's bite. The air wasn't freezing yet, but sharp enough to make me pull my cloak close. Fae lanterns swayed between buildings, their glow shining beside torchlight, casting gold across the cobbles where music and laughter had replaced the midday shouts of merchants. Truso never slept and was rarely quiet.

Shadows stirred behind me—figures lingering in dim alcoves or perched on rooftops, watching as I walked. The dagger in my grip offered some comfort, but it was the pinch of sleeper's ash in my other hand that truly steadied me.

Blood thrummed in my ears, a rhythm of warning I refused to ignore. Instead of shoving the fear down, I used it to my advantage. The Brotherhood might be on the verge of conflict, but whoever was tailing me wouldn't strike without provocation.

I paused before a jewellery shop, pretending to admire the delicate trinkets in its window.

'If you think this will intimidate me, you arsehole, you're sadly mistaken,' I muttered under my breath, my thoughts drifting to Jagon while I scanned the reflections behind me. Unfortunately, all I could see was my determined expression.

In a way, I should be grateful to my former master. I'd been feeling suffocated in the dwarven kingdom for some time but had been too stubborn to admit it and leave. Now, the lost daughter had found her way home, mature enough that fear of him no longer controlled my choices.

I was nearly at the Brotherhood's mansion when I realised something was wrong. The unease I'd carried since leaving Lily's had thickened into something heavier and now felt oppressive. The men following me were no longer hiding, sending me a clear warning.

I stopped several metres away from the building's front door. The stone walls towered over me, the pale light of the rising moon creating a stark contrast to the dark granite. But tonight, the usually dark windows were all lit, and there were no guards—almost as if Boyan had left the welcome mat out . . .

I glanced around, listening to the sounds of the night and trying to sense which direction the attack would come from.

And it would come—I felt it in my gut, anticipation building with each breath. The faintest rustling behind me was the only sign of what was to come, but before I could react, someone covered my mouth and pulled me into a dark corner.

'Not so fast, sweetheart. You can't be that stupid. Jagon told us to give you time and plenty of hints to change your mind, but this is taking too long.'

The rough whisper made me flinch, but I refused to go quietly and bit the dirty hand as hard as I could.

'Fucking *bitch*,' the man who'd grabbed me grunted, shaking his hand while I spun, spitting out the foul taste of his blood. 'Last chance,' he said, pulling out a knife and twirling it between his fingers. 'Get the fuck away from here or—'

'Or what?' I scoffed, bringing my fist up to my lips and blowing hard. My attacker gasped as the shimmering white powder coated his face. My grin widened as his breathing turned into a choking cough, and he stumbled to his knees with wide, bulging eyes.

'That's what I thought. Goodnight, dumbass.'

His head collided with the wall before hitting the ground, and I winced. 'Gods, why are the stupid ones always filthy?' I muttered, wiping my mouth.

I turned, about to leave the alley when something landed on my shoulder. My dagger swept up as I turned, only to halt as a hand caught my wrist in a harsh, unforgiving grip. My eyes focused on the familiar mask, and I gulped when I recognised the wolf staring back at me.

'Stop. You're still being followed,' he whispered into my ear as he pressed me to the wall, blocking my view and immobilising me under his body. 'Three more men are about to ambush you.'

I raised my foot and stomped on his instep to get him to move, enjoying the vicious snarl he made before he shifted so that I could breathe again.

'Do you have a death wish, you *idiot*?' I whispered, the fear that I had almost killed the king—again—loosening my tongue. His amused huff made me slam my hand on his chest. 'What if I'd stabbed you? Would you blame me for that, too? You can't keep following me if you want me to be your spy,' I hissed.

He was still close, his chin resting on my head, and despite the fur that covered his mask, I felt him smile before he pulled back, hand resting on the wall behind me.

'Of course, I'd blame you, especially since I wasn't here for you. Still, I just saved you, so the words, "*Thank you, my wonderful protector*," might be in order,' he said with such arrogance that I rolled my eyes.

'You want me to *thank* you? How about, were you born stupid, or did your mother drop you on your head?' I said, empowered by the informality of our discussion. Somehow, hidden behind the mask, Reynard became more of a man and less of a king . . . and I found that I liked it way more than I should.

My bemused expression was reflected in the wolf's red eyes as Reynard's body shook with silent laughter.

'How do you do that, my little Viper? Why am I drawn to the fire in your eyes?' he said eventually, leaning in closer as his finger traced my earlobe.

My confusion turned to shock at his words, and even more so when I pressed back against his caress, my breath catching in my throat.

'What are . . . Look, you need to back away. I have somewhere to be. Maybe you should be more worried about how dangerous I can be. Did that scar not teach you that lesson?' I snapped, but he only laughed harder.

'Ah yes, my eye. You still haven't paid the price for that—and you've grown bolder, maybe a little too bold. I may be forced to lock you away again . . . Though I doubt I'll be able to let you go this time.'

He definitely landed on his head, I thought. His whole attitude baffled me. This wasn't the time or place for . . . whatever this was, even if he'd disguised himself. Observers weren't stupid. He might have worn a mask, but his massive, muscular body and commanding presence were a dead giveaway. Sooner or later, someone would connect the dots, unless . . .

I reached out and touched the mask. Reynard pulled back slightly, startled by my gesture, but I'd already felt it—the traces of aether in the wolf's muzzle tangled into an enchantment.

'Do you follow every assassin you employ, or am I the only one granted this honour?' I asked, pulling his hood farther forward to conceal his dark hair. I didn't know exactly how the enchantment worked, but it was the wrong place to take chances. He stilled, tilting his head down to let me adjust the fabric.

'As I said, I wasn't following you. In fact, I've been trying to avoid you, but it seems fate had other plans. There's a major gathering at the Brotherhood Chapter House today. I wanted to investigate . . . and noticed you heading straight into a trap. Did you know you've been followed since you left the House of Lilies? The man you dispatched was one of many,' he said, tapping my forehead. 'Your life belongs to me. I can't let anyone else take it.'

'How gracious of you,' I responded, 'but my life is my own. I'm only *working* for you—which I could do far more efficiently if you'd let me go.'

The bastard chuckled.

'Oh, I let you go quite some time ago,' he murmured. 'But here you are. Still standing so close I can smell your perfume. Lilac . . . and honey.' His eyes dragged over me. 'You're making me hungry, Viper. It's so tempting, I want to take a bite, right here.' The low rasp of his voice crawled down my spine as his finger traced the curve of my neck, slow and deliberate, before pulling away. I missed his proximity almost instantly.

What is wrong with me?

My mouth opened—probably to argue, to say *something*—but no sound came. His hands weren't anywhere near me, yet mine were still fisted in the fabric of his hood, pulling him back in . . .

Oh, for all the gods, Sana.

I made a weak attempt to push him away, but Reynard was built like a mountain. He didn't move, so I did—stepping aside, head down, trying to hide the burn in my cheeks.

'You should really send your men for errands like this,' I said when I was sure my voice wouldn't betray me.

'And miss all this? Doesn't your king deserve some entertainment? Besides, you seem well-informed, so tell me: Do you know what is happening inside the mansion?' he asked, and I grimaced, wondering how much I could share without risking involvement.

'I have a vague idea . . .' I hedged. 'But I'll know for sure once I'm inside. Let me pass so I can investigate. Who knows'—I shrugged—'I might even have some gossip for you tomorrow.'

He smirked, tilting his head before placing his palm on the wall above my head once more. 'And if I don't step away—what then, Viper? Are you going to put me to sleep like that fool now snoring on the ground? You'll need more than a handful of powder to do that,' he teased, and although I was caged between his body and the wall, the heat radiating from him was comforting rather than threatening.

'It would certainly remove a certain stubborn obstacle in my way.' I sighed, rubbing the bridge of my nose. Reynard seemed to be having the time of his life teasing me, but I was running out of time. 'Look, I really have to go. Should I forget the orders you gave me?'

'No, Viper, you shouldn't forget me . . . or my orders, and I'm stalling for a reason,' he said with a smirk before shifting slightly to let me see the street. 'If you can endure my company for a moment longer, your way in will be much easier. The mask is bespelled to divert onlookers' attention. The two by the door have already lost interest, but I bet more are watching the alley entrance from the rooftop. I'll distract them, but you must tell me what you know. What's so special about this meeting that you're willing to push past me to get inside?'

So, all this teasing and stalling for time was a part of his strategy.

I huffed in annoyance, not because of what he'd done, but because he had deceived me, too. His touch had felt so real. Still, I held back, even when he reached for a lock of hair, wrapping it around a finger.

Oh, no, my wolf. Two can play this game.

I smiled sweetly, sliding my arms around his neck, and drew Reynard close. He didn't resist. When he leaned in—so near I could kiss the curve of his ear—I lowered my voice to a sultry whisper.

'I think someone plans to oust the grand master tonight, using a promise I made after returning to Truso.' Reynard tensed, his muscles straining under my touch. 'I have to enter the Brotherhood house before midnight, or they'll use my absence to remove him.'

'Do you know who will take his place?' Ruthlessness hardened the soft baritone of his voice, and for the first time since meeting him, genuine fear tightened my throat.

'No one . . . if I make my entrance,' I answered quietly, glad his glacial anger wasn't directed at me.

'Then let's go,' he said, already moving. 'I'll get you inside—over their corpses if I have to. Just make sure Boyan keeps his seat.'

With that, he pulled me in close, his broad frame shielding me as we slipped from the alley. Two shadowy figures detached themselves from the wall, their movements flawlessly coordinated as they began to circle to accost me.

'Stop,' I whispered, still hidden behind him. 'Those are trained killers. I can't let them kill the king.'

Reynard turned, and the cheeky, boyish chuckle he released shook his wide shoulders.

'You forget, Viper. I'm a warrior—one who's bloody good with a sword,' he said, reaching for my hood and pulling it over my face, leaving me speechless for the second time tonight. 'Don't worry about me, and keep close to the wall. I'll take care of your little problem.'

He didn't give me time to answer, throwing off his cloak in a dramatic gesture, and I used the distraction to disappear into the shadows while he advanced on the men running towards us.

The clash of steel diverted my attention and when someone leapt from the rooftop, I almost missed his attack. He struck where I'd been standing, but I'd already started running.

Time slowed as I bolted, the man's cudgel whistling past my head. I heard him curse, but it was too late to stop me as I threw myself forward and pushed my way through the heavy bronze doors of the Chapter House. His angry grimace appeared in the gap as I worked to close the doors, my attacker trying to force them open. He reached for me, and I quickly grabbed a handful of sleeping powder and blew it straight into his snarling face.

The thud of his body hitting the floor echoed down the corridor, but I was already striding toward the great hall, shouting at the top of my lungs.

'Sweet wine for the Deadly Nightshade. The prodigal daughter has returned, you swine!'

Chapter 27

Roksana

Brazen and arrogant, my announcement drew out a horde of servants. Now, whatever Jagon had planned, he couldn't deny my presence.

Everything in the Chapter House was just as I remembered. Fae lights still flickered along the hall, casting their glow over walls lined with weapons and trophies. The same worn carpet is stretched out beneath my feet, unable to muffle the groaning floorboards that had always betrayed late-night footsteps.

The building hadn't changed. But I had.

Its grandeur no longer awed me. I felt no urge to prove myself to those within its walls. And yet, I couldn't deny my sentimental feelings. My ever-evolving relationship with Irsha, the uneasy camaraderie with fellow apprentices, the thrill of uncovering forgotten knowledge in the archives—each pulled at me. Even the day I bought out my contract held bittersweet memories for me.

Now, I'd returned, determined and armed with a magic I didn't understand, eager to confront the demons of my past.

I walked past the guards lured in by the commotion, donning the persona of the grand master's shadow. My features settled into cold control, eyes like chips of ice, lips curved in a sneer that reeked of power and indifference.

When I finally stood before the doors to the dining hall, it was like I'd never left, and I began wondering which Sana was the real me. I nodded to the servants, and with a respectful bow, they opened the doors, revealing the arguing, so-called leaders of the Brotherhood.

'How can you say you have everything under control when you can't even bring one woman to heel? She broke the rules by returning to Truso. The invitation was an afterthought because, as always, you're trying to protect her. And what did the wench do? Where did she go? Straight to the king. My men have seen her staying in the royal quarters,' Bolko, the Observers' chapter master, yelled across the table while Boyan daintily dabbed his lips with a pristine linen napkin, his shoulders shaking as he held back a coughing fit.

They're so busy jumping down each other's throats, they haven't even noticed I'm here, I reflected, amused by the situation, but I hadn't come here to watch these ridiculous men tear each other apart.

'So that's where the king placed me. I must admit, it was surprisingly pleasant,' I said, causing the entire room to fall silent.

No one in the large dining chamber moved, everyone focused solely on me. Relief, amusement, but mostly anger flashed across the faces of the men and women gathered at the side tables, but my eyes were on the five imposing figures sitting at the elevated table. Smirking, I approached them with slow, measured steps as heads swivelled to follow my progress.

'I see nothing's changed in my absence. You still can't have a meal without arguing like children,' I taunted, avoiding Jagon's stare, his narrowed eyes exposing his fury as his hand tightened on the table until his knuckles turned white.

'Roksana, you made it.' The relief in the grand master's tone was evident, and my throat constricted.

He looked so frail, older and paler than I remembered. There was resignation in his gaze, the look of an alpha wolf who'd lost control of his pack, surrounded by younger, hungrier wolves waiting for a chance to tear out his throat. He should have stepped down long ago. But I suspected he'd held on, clinging to power not out of pride, but in hopes of finding a successor the warring chapters would accept. I envied the old man's resolve. I only wished he'd found that successor before it had come to this.

I didn't blame him, though. Most of the people seated at the table—barring a few notable exceptions—were either clueless, cruel, or eager to destroy everything he'd tried to build.

'Of course, my lord,' I said, voice smooth. 'It pains me that any here would doubt my word. I would walk on hot coals to dine at your table.'

I bowed deeply, showing my respect. When I looked up, he was smiling. A wet, rattling cough stained his teeth with blood, but the warmth in his expression was so genuine that I did something I'd never done before.

I dropped to my knees.

'I beg your forgiveness for my tardiness. The bodies of my former brethren in the street will attest to the effort I exerted in presenting myself.'

Gasps of surprise and the clatter of cutlery followed my show of submission. If anyone still questioned where my allegiance lay, they had their answer now.

'Welcome home, my beautiful Nightshade. You've been missed. Now, stand up, child, and please join me.'

I smiled at the grand master, rising gracefully, and used the moment to sneak a glance at Jagon.

The poison master was staring at me like a hawk, likely with the same lethal intent as one. His expression was a mixture of anger and reluctant respect, as if he'd only now realised I was no longer his pawn. From the angry chatter surrounding me, it was clear he had Bolko's support, and I'd be surprised if Tymon, the Mules' leader, wasn't in Jagon's pocket as well. So, rather than escalate the situation, I simply gave my former master a respectful nod.

Jagon's brow furrowed, probably calculating the variables and wondering whether I was going to hang him out to dry in front of the entire Brotherhood, but it was too early to confront him. Instead, I stepped towards the grand master.

'Of course, my lord. If you'd like, we could even partake in a relaxing game of chess later. I learned so much playing with you, and I admit I would love to see if I can finally challenge you.'

'Chess?' Bolko interjected. 'Who gave you the right to speak in our presence, Nightshade? You left the Brotherhood. You even left Dagome. You know the rules, and yet you walk into the Chapter House like you fucking own it. Why are you even here?'

I smirked. 'I could say it's none of your business, but if you must know, I met the king during his travels, and his mage discovered something so interesting he requested that I return to Truso. I asked for an invitation, of course, not that the likes of you are entitled to know the grand master's and arch healer's private affairs. But since I'm here, well . . .' I shrugged. 'I'm thinking of staying.' I grinned, enjoying the sight of his thinning lips and gritted teeth before I hammered the nail into the proverbial coffin. 'Especially since the arch healer wants to train me himself, but I guess your spies already told you I can use magic.'

Boyan's head whipped in my direction, joy filling his eyes as if he'd . . . expected this?

'Roksana, is that true? Was that the reason you left?' he asked, leaning forward before he sighed, shaking his head. 'You should have come to me instead of leaving.'

'I'm sorry, but it's been a turbulent time for me. However, the arch healer was so impressed by my healing of Wiosna's miners that he offered to train me under his patronage,' I said, pasting on a bright smile as I lied through my teeth. 'Ask Jagon. He helped dissolve any obligation I had towards King Młot and the Kingdom of Wiosna.'

As expected, Bolko frowned at the mention of Jagon's name, glaring at him with distrust written all over his face. Boyan, on the other hand, sat taller, his shoulders broadening from their usual hunch. Seeing the glee on the old man's face, and his less-than-covert glances at Jagon, he definitely knew it was rubbish.

'You're going to betray us to become a mage?' someone shouted.

'Betray?' I repeated, a smirk curling my lip. 'I'm no longer a dark sister; my scroll was burned to ash. I came only to pay my respects to the grand master. However, seeing as some of you have forgotten the Brotherhood's honour, bickering at the high table like quarrelsome fishwives . . .' I paused, savouring the moment. 'Perhaps I shall renew my contract, this time as a mage, to teach you some manners, you witless cur.'

'You fucking bitch,' came from behind me, the sharp, metallic ring of a sword being drawn cutting through the sudden silence. 'Do you think you can just march back in and we'll take you in?'

'Silence!' I snapped, spinning around as I whipped my hand forward. A small, poisoned needle flew from my fingers, sinking into the shouting man's throat. He swallowed hard, mouth opening wide as he gasped for breath before dropping to his knees. 'Did you forget who I am? Consider that a polite reminder. As for the rest of you—does anyone *else* have a problem with my return?'

The entire room froze, watching while I strolled to my assailant. My smile was cruel as I crouched down to look into the helpless man's eyes, hiding my emotions. I waited until his face turned purple, eyes tearing from the lack of air as he flopped on the floor like a dying fish. Then, I plucked out the needle, allowing him to breathe again.

'I hate fools. Who does this one belong to?' I asked coolly, gripping the man's chin between my fingers.

Irsha rose slowly to his feet. 'He's mine,' he said, approaching with measured grace. 'Apologies for his lack of discipline. He's hot-headed, but skilled. I'd rather not lose a good sword over a bad decision.'

'Since you asked so nicely,' I said, a slow smile curving my lips as he reached for my hand and pressed a kiss to it. Irsha was playing his part perfectly—my long-lost lover and loyal kindred soul, ever willing to stand beside me even if it cost his man his life.

'Ah, my sweet Nightshade,' he murmured, all warmth and charm. 'Always so generous. The Blades have no objection to having mages in our ranks. This misguided soul . . .' he said, watching as I pinched the man's jaw and tipped a vial's contents into his mouth. 'I'll handle his punishment myself.'

I caught Irsha's smirk and responded with a raised brow and a roll of my eyes. Whatever price he'd promised his man for this performance must've been high. My mind raced as I glanced around, gauging everyone's reactions. The room, once silent, was filled with whispers spoken behind my back, but all eyes followed my movements.

'Thank you for your mercy, my lady,' Irsha said, his fingers stroking my forearm. 'Might you also spare a little pity for a man still pining for you after all this time? I have some sweet wine in my chambers.'

'I don't know if I can stay,' I replied, my eyes trained on Jagon. 'Your Blades may have no objection, but what is the opinions of the others?' I leaned into Irsha, playing up my interest, before continuing, 'If I'm forced to leave, visit me at Lilies. I also have sweet wine . . . and a bed that's far more comfortable.'

This little performance wouldn't work if not for our past, but knowing how adamant Jagon had been about the king's touch, I'd played my wild card, hoping he'd believe that only by having me in the Brotherhood would he have access to me.

He was silent, but without his acceptance, the remaining chapter masters would never tolerate a mage.

Irsha frowned, then pulled me into his arms, his voice rumbling through his chest. 'If you're staying, you must join the Blades. The army has battle mages—why not magical assassins in the Brotherhood?

Despite the severity of the situation, the urge to laugh at our charade nearly overtook me.

'No, she won't.' Jagon stepped forward, voice sharp and eyes narrowed in anger. 'Sana was, and is, a poisoner. I don't care if she has magic. She will remain as my poisoner or not at all . . . isn't that right, my dear?'

Irsha didn't move until I gave him a subtle nod. Then, with a shrug and his signature smirk, he raised his hands in surrender and backed off.

'Does that mean you accept my return?' I asked, eyes on Jagon. 'And what of the others?'

After a moment's silence, the two remaining chapter masters—Bolko and Tymon—exchanged a glance with Jagon, then nodded.

'Thank you,' I said, grinning as I turned to the grand master. He raised his glass of wine and dipped his head in silent approval.

'Welcome home, child. I'm afraid that your former position is taken, but if we're to have a mage in our ranks, I shall claim you as my own.'

Jagon looked like he was about to have a stroke. I could practically see the steam rising from his ears, and it took everything in me not to laugh while I waited for him to gather himself.

'My lord,' he said tightly, 'her proximity to you and our secrets under such . . . unusual circumstances could become problematic. I'll admit, I'm curious about Roksana's choice to align with the arch healer. However, ties like that could make her becoming your mage . . . dangerous.'

He reached for my wrist but I stepped back, just out of reach, offering him a demure bow that only barely masked my smirk.

'Dangerous?' I echoed, tilting my head. 'I don't compromise on my principles, and you should know that better than anyone.'

I placed my hand on Jagon's chest, stroking my fingers over his velvet kaftan. His expression tightened, confusion flickering behind his frown. I gave him my most coy smile, as if there were an unspoken agreement between us that no one could ever know.

Jagon's heart quickly sped up beneath my palm, his pupils widening at my tender gesture, but I had already turned towards the others. 'You cannot doubt where my loyalty lies; after all, I'm here, aren't I?' When Bolko and Tymon reluctantly nodded, I knew I'd won.

'Well then,' I said, offering a gracious smile. 'Since the matter is resolved, let's return to dinner. I've caused enough of a disturbance as it is.'

'Roksana!' Jagon hissed, grasping my wrist just as a tremulous hand landed lightly on my shoulder, making me turn my head.

'You won't deny me this last pleasure, I'm sure. If you step into this position, you would also like to have your own mage, Jagon,' Boyan said. I wondered if anyone had noticed that the grand master said 'if,' not 'when.' I did, and I was sure Jagon did, too. 'Come, Roksana, sit beside me and share the tales that earned you the attention of the king's mage.'

Jagon's hand fell away. His jaw clenched, but he bowed and returned to his seat. I stepped forward, offering Boyan my arm and discreetly supporting him as we walked to his place at the table. I made sure my voice rang loud enough to carry.

'Oh, nothing much,' I said lightly. 'He was just surprised I was healing dwarves.'

'I admit, that baffles me, too.' Boyan chuckled, motioning for a servant to pour the wine. 'Those people are built as tough as the rocks they mine. You never fail to surprise me, child. Please tell me more. Caring for our brethren keeps me in Truso, but I enjoy hearing about events from around Tir ha Mor.'

I sat beside him, taking the goblet from his unsteady hand and squeezing it gently when our fingers met. Boyan's patronage had saved me more times than I cared to count. He'd championed me when no one else would, his attention often shielding me from cruelty. But it came at a cost.

Whispers trailed me like smoke—accusations that I shared his bed, that my rise as his shadow was unearned. They only quieted when the first body was found, *Nightshade* scrawled in blood beside it.

Sharing a meal with him again was bittersweet. I recounted my time in Wiosna, and he teased out forgotten memories with the ease of someone who had always known me better than I knew myself. It should have felt like old times. And yet, I couldn't stop noticing the pallor of his skin, the tremble in his limbs.

Whenever I tried to ignore his condition, my gaze landed on the others at the table—their cold stares, the bitter twist of their mouths. None more intense than Jagon's, who only watched me, his food forgotten on his plate.

I may have won this battle, but the war wasn't over, and my former master knew I'd outmanoeuvred him at his own game.

The question was, how would he make me pay?

Chapter 28

Roksana

By the time dinner ended, I had to hide my yawns. Everyone was leaving for their homes, but I postponed my departure as long as I could. A confrontation with Jagon was inevitable, and when even Boyan went to his chambers, ready or not, I had to face him.

As soon as I entered the corridor, a young apprentice accosted me.

'Master Jagon wishes to see you before you leave,' he said nervously, glancing at my hands, obviously expecting me to punish him for talking.

'Oh, for fuck's sake, I won't hurt you. Lead the way,' I answered sharply, making him shrink back. I didn't want to bully the boy, but I was tired, and even retrieving the evidence against Lily hadn't eased my fears that Jagon would harm my friends another way.

I hid my shaking hands when we arrived at the poisoner's lab. Too many times, I'd lain dying on its floor thanks to Jagon's punishments, those experiences leaving me so emotionally scarred that I felt my chest tighten at the mere thought of meeting him here alone.

I'm Roksana Regnav, and I'm no longer his pawn.

I straightened, pushing my shoulders back, and prepared myself. I was done dancing to his tune. I just had to be smart about it.

Jagon was already there, examining the contents of two vials under a fae light. When we entered, my guide turned to leave, but Jagon gestured him closer.

'Please come, both of you. I have something to show you,' he said calmly.

I'd never wanted to run away as much as I did right then. His calm manner meant only one thing: He'd found a way to punish me for ruining his plans—or worse, he'd recouped his losses and wanted to show me I'd achieved nothing.

'What do you think, boy? Blue or purple?' he asked, raising the vials and wiggling them in front of the young man's face.

'No! Let him go,' I said, stepping closer while the boy shook violently beside me.

'P-purple?' His high-pitched stutter was filled with unshed tears. We both knew what was coming.

'Ah, excellent choice. Purple it is,' Jagon said with a bright smile before throwing the liquid at his face.

'You bloody bastard!' I said, throwing my cloak over the apprentice, but Jagon was too fast.

The young man screamed, his voice fading into an agonising rattle as the purple liquid sank into his skin like a thimbleful of water in the desert. I leapt forward, catching him before he hit the floor.

'Antidote!' I yelled, reaching a hand towards Jagon. 'Give me the antidote!' I had to turn the boy onto his side when he convulsed, foaming from the mouth.

'You wanted to remind those stupid pricks who you are,' he said. 'Let me remind you who *I* am, Roksana. You have no grasp of the forces at play or how precarious the Brotherhood's position is.'

He walked closer, watching the dying youngster like it was nothing. If anything, his face projected angry disappointment.

I didn't acknowledge his words.

'I'm doing everything I can to protect our home, to make sure it survives while the world burns around us,' Jagon sneered, smashing the other vial on the floor. 'It should've been a simple takeover, but no, you had to come and ruin everything. A mage, kneeling for that old bastard.' He grasped a handful of my hair, tilting my head back. 'The only man you will kneel for is *me*.'

'Jagon, please! Give me the antidote, he's dying,' I begged.

The boy's face had turned a disturbing shade of blue. His bloodless lips opened, but no air entered his lungs.

'Show me your magic, Nightshade. I finally understand how you survived all those years. Show me your power or the next one will be your whore, and when she dies, I'll choose another and another . . . until everyone you ever knew is dead,' he said, but under the anger and disdain was an unhealthy fascination. 'Show me, Roksana!'

The boy's struggles grew weak, his faint pulse stuttering beneath my questing fingers. Muttering a curse, I ripped his shirt open and placed my hand on his chest. Strands of aether twisted in chaotic patterns, fading one after another as the poison corrupted his body. This concoction, however, wasn't my creation, and it was difficult to control the unknown toxins as they attacked his vital organs. I latched onto the sickly green pollution and let it merge with my magic. The foulness seeped into my body, but I didn't falter until I made it mine, and when my aether saturated the poison, I withdrew it pulling the toxin along with it.

I could barely breathe as fluid filled my lungs while I continued purging the arum extract mixed with distilled heartbreak grass from the apprentice's flesh, letting it coat my skin before expelling it onto the stone floor.

'I hate you,' I croaked as Jagon observed me, his mouth open and pupils dilated in excitement. The transformation was swift, but in suffusing the poison with my magic, I had made a mistake in connecting it to my vital force, and as my patient took a lungful of air, I collapsed on the floor.

'Fascinating . . . I'm glad I waited. You are so much more than she promised,' he muttered, bending to pry the boy's eyes open. I wondered who this mysterious 'she' was, and when I could kill her for giving away my secrets.

'Who . . .?' I tried to ask, but my throat was too constricted to talk.

'Clear. You purged the poison completely within moments; not even my antidote is that fast.' Jagon straightened, and his brows furrowed as his fingers tugged at the lapel of his coat in a rare display of uncertainty.

'Leave us,' he said as soon as his victim's eyes opened. I would have left with him, but I was spent and could only watch helplessly as the boy crawled away, sobbing.

Jagon helped me up, grasping my chin to force me to look at him while I fought overwhelming exhaustion. 'My brightest star. Your heart will always guide your knife, and that's your weakness.' He stroked my cheek, and I froze, staring in shock at the emotion I saw for the first time in his gaze—regret.

'Don't fight me, Roksana. Remember how I helped avenge your parents? . . . You didn't hate me back then,' he said with a strange wistfulness in his voice, sighing when I turned my face away from his touch. 'Fine, study your magic, but remember not to get in my way. I know you love the old man, but he has to go. Times have changed, and we need to as well, but he's still betting on the wrong horse. If you knew what is coming . . .' He paused, and I could swear I saw fear flashing in his eyes before his expression hardened again. 'If the Brotherhood is to survive, he has to go. That's all you need to know.'

I didn't care if he was having second thoughts or if he really believed he was saving the Brotherhood. His indifference to murder made him a dead man, even if he didn't know it yet. An angry tear rolled down my cheek and Jagon wiped it away with his thumb, his face unreadable.

'Don't cry, my beautiful flower. It was just a gentle lesson, unworthy of your tears . . . as long as you understand not to trifle with me again.'

There it was—his unhealthy obsession with me that began the moment he saw me on the Orcish Steppe, its embers fanned to life by my new ability.

He was still holding me, and as much as I hated his touch, I was too weak to escape. Another reason to learn how to use my magic properly—because opposing Jagon when I could barely stand was pointless.

So, I let him pick me up and carry me to a carriage. He was gentle, as if carrying his bride, while I imagined breaking various bones in his body. When I was nestled inside the carriage, he reached for my hand to kiss it goodbye, but I turned away.

He dragged my hand back to him, lifting it to his lips. 'No more defiance or supporting the wrong people. Learn to use your magic and wait until I call you. I may have a soft spot for you, but my leniency has its limits,' he said, gesturing for the coachman to go. 'Take her to the House of Lilies. Ensure she arrives safely.'

To say the journey was uncomfortable was like saying chewing on rocks was awkward. My body was thrown around as the coachman seemingly drove over every bump and into every hole he could, but it encouraged my recovery. By the time we reached the entertainment district and slowed down, I was able to sit up and hold on to the handles.

Finally able to think, I scrubbed the hand Jagon had kissed and ground my teeth.

Still, I'd found his weakness—me. He should have killed me the moment I'd thwarted his plans, yet he let me live, taking his anger out on someone else. That prompted another question: *How far can I push my luck?*

Despite what had happened, the confrontation with Jagon couldn't spoil my sense of victory. I'd managed the impossible by anchoring myself in both worlds, and as much as my body felt like death warmed up, I wanted to share this achievement with someone.

An image of a scarred face with its single steel-grey eye flashed through my mind. Reynard would understand, even if he'd scold me for taking risks.

I don't know why I thought of him, why telling him I'd out-smarted Jagon felt more important than telling Lily or Tova. I shook my head, regretting it when a wave of dizziness swept over me, a reminder that there were more important things to think about than his opinion.

'Keep it together, Sana. He's the king, and you're a commoner with a shady past. No matter how good you smell to him, the most you'll ever be is allies,' I muttered to myself. Our paths couldn't be more different—I was going to help Boyan keep the Brotherhood together and train with Ciesko, while he had a country to rule and enemies far greater than I could imagine to contend with.

Just as I thought I'd finally recovered, my transport pulled up in front of the House of Lilies, and the sudden stop filled my mouth with a sour taste. I fell through the door, latching onto a lawn ornament to steady myself while my stomach emptied itself on the stone pavers. I was still heaving when the door to the house opened.

'Sana? How much did you drink? Now I know why you didn't want to take me to this feast.'

The amusement in Tova's voice grated on my last nerve, but his help was godsent. The dwarf slipped an arm around my waist, hold-ing me upright while he guided me back to my room.

'You look worse than a necromancer after a graveyard shift. If I knew you were going to binge, I would have insisted on joining you,' he said, laying me on the bed and placing an empty basin beside me.

'I'm not drunk,' I croaked when he put a wet cloth on my forehead. I grimaced at the burning in my throat. 'I purged some poison.'

Tova dropped down to look me in the eye, grasping my hand in alarm. 'How can I help? Talk to me, girl. Should I call Lily . . . or the healer?' He squeezed my hand so hard I winced. 'Fuck Sana, you aren't dying, are you? Who did this to you? I'll make lute strings out of his guts.'

'I'll be fine,' I said, pressing the wet, cold cloth to my skin, sighing with relief at how much it helped. 'I forgot how much it hurts. How was your evening?'

'Sana, stop changing the subject. What happened? Who did this?'

'I did it to myself. Jagon was killing his apprentice to teach me a lesson. I just took the hit. But it was worth it, as I learned a few interesting things, and it brought back some sweet, old memories.'

'Of all the stupid, unreasonable things . . .' he said, standing up to jam his fists on his hips and glare at me.

'Tova, remember how much you moaned the day after you won the moonshine drinking competition?' I asked, halting his tirade.

'Yeah, so?'

'So, shut up, you're giving me a headache,' I responded.

Tova sighed, sitting heavily on the bed, stroking my back as I dry heaved.

'Fine, but this conversation isn't over. At least you learned something—we didn't have quite as much luck. The merchants didn't even get drunk, let alone talk to me or Lily's entertainers. They *were* from Wiosna, but one of them remembered buying some of my trinkets, so they clammed up after that. The only thing I learned was that Młot has issued arrest warrants for us, and one of Lily's girls heard they were heading south soon.'

'Would you recognise them if you saw them again?' I asked, unwilling to open my eyes. 'Can you sneak a look at their wagon? It would be helpful to know what goods they're transporting—even better if we could steal a sample, especially since Młot already considers us criminals.'

'I'd recognise them easily. We can have a look tomorrow after viewing the house I told you about. Oh! Two letters came after you left. One, from the arch healer, was more of a note, saying he wanted to see you tomorrow. The other was sealed and stamped with wolf's head, whatever the fuck that means.'

'Read it for me, please,' I said with a sigh, already knowing who'd sent it. Reynard hadn't wasted any time, and as much as I wanted to ignore it, the king's missive might be urgent.

Tova nodded, bringing a fae light closer and cutting off the seal with a swipe of his dagger.

'"You promised me gossip, Viper. Come to see me tomorrow at noon in the palace gardens." There's no signature,' Tova said, inspecting the letter under the light and then heating it over the flame. 'Nope, nothing hidden either.'

He folded the paper and passed it to me.

'He doesn't need one. Only one person calls me Viper and wears a wolf's mask. I guess he seals his letters with a wolf's head, too. It's from the king,' I said, draping an arm over my eyes. 'Tova, call a maid. I need to undress and rest. The world can wait until tomorrow.'

'Well, best recover quickly. We're looking at that house first thing in the morning. I arranged an early viewing.' Tova's lips widened into a wicked grin. 'If you feel anything like you did the day after the drinking contest, it'll be a ghastly day.'

'You're a heartless bastard,' I moaned as I heard him walk towards the door.

'Yeah, but you still love me,' he said with an evil chuckle.

An hour later, I'd washed and changed my clothes with the help of Lily's maid, who promised to come check up on me later. I didn't protest, so tired that my eyelids felt glued together, hoping that the world would leave me to sleep off my encounter with Jagon's poison. Sweet oblivion beckoned, my senses lulled by the music downstairs while a draft made me shiver under the covers.

'I'm fine, just close the window,' I muttered, hearing footsteps approach. I appreciated her care, but this was too much, and irritation made me groan.

'Are you unwell?' a soft baritone asked while a pair of powerful hands wrapped the covers around my body, preventing the inevitable yelp when I jerked awake.

I recognised the voice, but what the fuck was Reynard doing in my room?

'Why are you here?' It was hard to rein in my anger, but I didn't want to raise my voice and risk Tova charging in for another confrontation with the king.

'If I recall correctly, you began this adorable custom of evening visits,' Reynard answered, sitting on my bed. 'Don't blame me for continuing our new tradition.'

'What do you want? I got your letter; can't you wait until tomorrow?'

'Maybe,' he said, 'but seeing my spy vomiting on the pavement, I became a little concerned.'

He finally freed me, so I scrambled back and sat up. 'I'm just drunk. The Brotherhood knows how to party.'

Reynard eyed me suspiciously before grabbing the pitcher on the bedside table and pouring me a cup of water. 'Drink, little Viper,' he said, putting the cup to my lips, but I turned away.

'You know Lily has maids for this? You can go back to your palace.'

I didn't know how to react. He shouldn't be here, and he certainly shouldn't be here to take care of me. I bit my lip, fighting the weakness that came with his gentle touch. Reynard should be the last person I wanted to hold me, but it felt so good, and I was tired of fighting men today.

'Drink, and I'll leave,' he said, still holding the cup. With an exaggerated sigh, I placed my lips on the rim, letting him pull me against his chest. Reynard was massive, warm . . . and perfect. My hand shook a little when I placed it on his, tilting the cup and enjoying the heat of his skin, its rough texture so essentially masculine. The king's smile widened when I snuggled against him, and the corners of those bow-shaped lips pursed a bit when he wiped away the droplets that landed on my chin. The thumping of my heart drowned out every sound as I watched him lick the moisture off his thumb.

'Sanika . . . do you still want me to leave?' His voice was so guttural that I groaned.

No, I don't. But you can't stay . . . I thought, chastising myself for my reluctance to let him go.

Closing my eyes, I pointed to the window. 'Out. Now.' Reynard made me feel things I couldn't afford to feel, and I needed him gone before I changed my mind.

His fleeting disappointment was soon replaced by a mischief that strangely suited him.

'As you wish, little Viper. I'll see you tomorrow when you feel less waspish,' he said, putting his mask back on. With a quick, exaggerated bow, the infuriating man was gone, slipping through the window.

I waited until I heard the dull thud of his feet hitting the ground, then walked to the window and bolted it shut, acutely aware I wasn't cold anymore.

Heat crawled up my cheeks when I realised that I—a commoner, a criminal, a woman struggling to survive—wanted to kiss the king.

But this wasn't a fairytale where the poor orphan could capture the king's heart . . . even if the king did want to kiss her back.

Chapter 29

Roksana

'Rise and shine, sweetheart! I let you sleep as long as I could, but we need to see this house.'

Tova pulled the curtains open, flooding the room with light. I moaned in response and pushed my face into the pillow.

'It's too early,' I grumbled, then squeaked when he pulled the blanket off me, the chill air raising goosebumps on my skin.

'It's not that early, and you've had a good night's sleep. Now, up you get! The maids are waiting,' he said, and I sat up, looking around with swollen eyes.

Something important teased the back of my mind, but I stopped caring the moment my eyes focused on the water sitting by my bedside. My parched throat finally relaxed when I swallowed the cold, sweet liquid, removing last night's bitter aftertaste. Then the memories flooded in.

Drink, little Viper.

Reynard's voice haunted me, and I fell back on the pillows, refusing to even think about it as I tried to rest for a few more minutes. But Tova apparently had a different opinion about what I should be doing. He dipped his fingers in the cup and sprinkled droplets on my face.

'Are you auditioning for the job of torturer in Lily's dungeon?' I snapped, getting out of bed and letting the maids lead me to the steaming water. 'A bath . . . in the morning?'

Tova chuckled behind the privacy screen while the maid barked out her orders and I was suddenly pushed down and scrubbed to within an inch of my life.

'So, where are we going?' I asked.

'First, I need your approval on the house before I can make the proper arrangements. The current owner is somewhat peculiar, so please refrain from arguing, regardless of what I say. Then I'll go buy stuff for my workshop and try to get some information on the dwarven convoy while you play with the mages,' he said, a slight frown creasing his forehead. 'Unless you want me to go with you, but I'm not sure if that would help. I don't know how to deal with those bastards.'

'Hooray for me,' I said, stepping out of the bath so that the maids could dress me and arrange my hair to their satisfaction. I chuckled when I emerged from behind the privacy screen and found Tova half dozing in a chair. 'It didn't take that long. Stop pretending.'

My gentle poke resulted in him stretching, and a short while later, we were marching down the streets towards the artisan quarter.

Truso was full of character, despite—or perhaps because of—being rebuilt over the centuries. It still resembled a merchant town, with the dark castle walls perched atop a small hill guarding both the river and the town below. Although the fortress had now been transformed into a palace with numerous terraces and gardens that extended to the riverbanks, the feel of the place hadn't changed. The noisy streets were filled with languages from all over Tir ha Mor, and the scent of exotic spices hung in the air, a reminder that Truso still retained its merchant's soul.

Tova led me deep into the artisan district, skirting the leatherworkers with a grimace while ignoring the blacksmiths. I enjoyed how the dainty fae facades gave way to sturdy human and dwarven buildings as we walked.

'Master Orenson, I thought you'd changed your mind when I asked if I could meet your wife first. This must be her.' An older man waved us over, turning to walk into a small courtyard. Just as I opened my mouth to correct the gentleman, Tova caught my hand and squeezed it tightly.

'Of course,' he said. 'She is as skilled with herbs as she is beautiful. Your house's two workshops will be perfect for us, and, understandably, you wanted my Sana to see them before deciding. No one wants to deal with an angry woman.'

The man chuckled, gesturing me forward. 'Exactly that. My wife was the same. She always loved having the last word.'

I walked inside, mouthing '*Wife?*' to Tova, but he only shrugged and squeezed my hand again.

When I saw the interior, I soon forgot about having suddenly become 'Mrs Orenson.' The house spoke to my soul. We were definitely going to buy it—even if I had to pretend to be Tova's six-toed grandmother.

The house was warm and welcoming, already fully furnished and ready to be lived in. Its layout was simple: a central corridor split the structure in two, leading to a staircase at the end that rose to three modest bedrooms. On one side, a spacious kitchen flowed naturally into a day room, the transition marked by a wooden beam—likely the last trace of a former partition wall. On the other side was what would be my workshop, its doors perfectly positioned so that when I opened them, I could glance over and see what Tova was cooking on the stove.

It was perfect for our needs. Even better, the detached outdoor workshop came equipped with a small furnace and could be easily converted into a proper tinkerer's manufactory. The décor was simple but cosy, and what truly won me over was the large kitchen hearth and the smaller fireplaces throughout—ideal for curling up beside during long winter nights.

'We'll take it,' I said, after rushing through every room. Tova knew my preferences from our time in Wiosna, and he'd chosen a house so similar to my old home that I instantly felt I belonged here. It just needed a few personal touches. My eagerness made Tova roll his eyes.

'What my wife means is, we'll take it if the price is right and includes the furniture and whatever's currently inside,' he said, stopping briefly when a tolling bell announced midmorning.

'Yes, exactly,' I said, realising the time. 'Can you handle the rest, Tova? I have to go to the university.'

'Of course, my dear. We wouldn't want the arch healer getting upset with you,' he replied with such seriousness that the merchant rubbed his hands together nervously.

'She studies under Master Ciesko . . .?'

I didn't hear the rest, but Tova's contented smile and the way they clasped their hands told me that little nugget of information may have positively influenced negotiations. Turning away, I was sure I'd have a home to return to after a long day of studying with the mages.

The University of Magic looked as intimidating from the inside as it did from the outside. The guards knew my name and let me in, providing instructions for the quickest route to the healer's wing. I marched there with my head high, pretending I wasn't intimidated by the curious and occasionally hostile glares I received. It didn't help that I stood out like a sore thumb in a slit kirtle with my alchemist's belt and daggers while everyone else was dressed in pastels and flowing robes.

'He could have warned me,' I muttered as I made my way through the halls. The covert chuckles of passing students shouldn't have bothered me, but they did. By the time someone finally took mercy on me and pointed me towards Ciesko's office, I was hot under my collar and as angry as a nest of hornets.

'Roksana, I thought you'd decided not to come,' he said when I entered, dodging the precarious stacks of books and whatever was lying on the table. *Please be an animal part...*

'How could I reject your late-night summons, Master Ciesko?' I said when I finally reached the man himself, sitting in a large leather chair. 'It might have helped if you'd told me where your office was, though.'

His eyebrows shot up at my snappy tone.

'Don't be belligerent, child. How could I foresee the infamous Deadly Nightshade having trouble navigating a few corridors?'

My only answer was an annoyed sigh. Trying to tame my hangover, I took a deep, cleansing breath. 'Can we get to the point so I can return home?' I asked as calmly as I could.

Ciesko nodded, coming closer and reaching out a hand.

'Another blood test?' I asked, surrendering my forearm. I'd long ago found that being compliant was easier than arguing with men who insisted on calling me 'child.'

The sigil he sketched with his finger sparked my interest—it was different from the one he'd drawn in the palace. When the last line was finished, I inhaled deeply, feeling a sudden boost of vitality, which removed both my lingering headache and exhaustion.

'Next time,' he said, 'you'll be able to do this yourself rather than coming here with a frown that could darken the sun.'

'As if. Every sigil I've tried comes out wrong or not at all. I don't even know where it is I go wrong,' I answered with a sigh before removing my arm from the arch healer's grasp. 'So why did you call me here?'

'To teach you. I added you to the list for the Solstice Geas Trial, but you should not be idle. We can try simple sigils and practice what you already know before you work on vivamancy.'

'Or I can start learning vivamancy straight away. I told you, none of the sigils I've tried have ever worked.'

'I can't train you in the high arcana without you having undergone the geas trial. That is both common sense and beyond my control,' he said. 'And please remember that no one must know of your unique talent beforehand. I know you want to learn, but others won't be so understanding when they realise an extinct magic has suddenly reappeared. Now, show me what you've been doing with your aether.'

Regardless of his explanation, I wanted more than a vague description of my talent before demonstrating my abilities.

'You can't tell me my power is dangerous without explaining what it is and why I should keep it secret. I deserve to know. Can you tell me what I am? What is a vivamancer, and why are we extinct?'

He sighed, seemingly contemplating something before he responded.

'Vivamancers are mages who can turn aether into life by wielding the power of creation. Your magic is as close to the source of primaeval aether as wild magic itself. When you touch the strands of other living beings, you can enhance their essence or transform them into something completely new.'

A dreamy smile blossomed on his lips, and for a moment, his eyes lost focus.

'Imagine, Roksana, creating new life that can live separate from its master . . . How much I would give to have that ability. A life . . . a being that exists freely, not like golems bound to a mage's will, or the beings animated by necromancy.'

He paused, and after a moment, the wonder and yearning left his features and were replaced by seriousness.

'Your power rivals the gods themselves. Do you see why others might be afraid of you?' he said, picking up a book from the table and opening it to a well-worn page. 'Even before the purge, this trait was rare and only manifested in children born of a certain pairing. However, ever since the Mad Mage, every child exhibiting the trait in Tir ha Mor has been killed. I've heard that some vivamancers still exist across the sea . . . or they did. Now, with Tangra men building up their empire there, who knows? It might just be gossip.'

I was stunned.

Eventually, I lifted my palm into the air, calling for the power inside me—the restless energy I'd sensed in Wiosna. Once it hovered over my skin, I pushed it towards a candle on the table, watching as the flame flickered erratically.

'How can I use it? Show me,' I said to Ciesko, but the healer chuckled and shook his head.

'You'll have to wait until the geas trial, for both your safety and others', but I can teach you how to use other forms of aether. That will make it easier to control your power later.'

'I told you, I can't do other things. Look,' I said, drawing the fire sigil. The energy sizzled and died as soon as I finished the last line.

Thank you, world.

I tried, again and again, reproducing the mark with a dwarven tinker-er's precision, but nothing worked. Ciesko studied me with an amused expression, and when I finally cursed in anger, he chuckled.

'If you've finished trying to prove your point, tell me why you at-tempted a fire sigil.'

'Because it's the easiest, has basic lines, and is simple to draw. I wanted to start easy and work my way up,' I said.

Nodding, Ciesko took a quill and drew a few simple lines on his skin.

'Try to recreate this.'

I studied his sigil. It looked crude, as if he'd drawn it with his eyes closed.

When I was sure I could reproduce the sigil perfectly, I focused on the aether, but as my finger hung in the air, Ciesko said, 'No. Draw it on your skin.'

The energy flowed easily, following my finger, and lines appeared on my forearm. To my surprise, they lingered there, the flow of energy condensing against my skin, numbing it. What I didn't expect was the silver needle the healer sank into my flesh as soon as I finished—nor did I expect to find that it didn't hurt.

'What? It worked, but how?' I gasped, looking at the drop of blood on the small puncture wound.

'You can't use sigils that you have no affinity for. Though, with time, you might be able to learn elemental spells that align with your magic, maybe even create simple illusions if you're lucky. I heard from Riordan that you've already learned how to deflect psychic magic. And the colour of your aether? It means you're a mage of the High Order. Vivamancy is closer to healing than the primal elements. That's why you've found them difficult to create.'

'So where should I start?' I asked, happy to finally have some explanation for the issues I'd been having. I'd purposefully avoided healing spells in Wiosna, unwilling to experiment on the suffering miners until I learned what I was doing. If only I'd known that fear and self-doubt had been preventing me from advancing in what I was most suited for.

Ciesko smiled, observing my reaction before placing a hand on my shoulder.

'At the very beginning. You'll come here daily. Don't look at me like that, child—it will just be for a few hours. Once you learn to heal simple things, you'll come to work with me in the infirmary,' he said, pulling a volume from a shelf. 'Hopefully, in a month, you'll have memorised

The Healer's Manual and *Theory of Aether*,' he added, placing another thick book in my hands. 'And after you've given your geas, I'll find the best teachers available to fill the gaps in my knowledge until you learn to control your power fully.'

'A month? No one can learn all this in a month!' I said. 'Besides, I have other things to do.'

Ciesko smiled before he asked, 'When you tried to learn to use aether, why did you do it? You were already an accomplished poisoner.'

I pondered his question.

Why? Because I felt like there was something more beyond a mundane life—a force that touched my soul, awakening a yearning to immerse myself in it, to feel the world beyond what I could shape with my hands.

'Because it was calling me, and I . . . because I'm not whole without it.'

My answer made him smile even wider. Ciesko placed his hand on my cheek, looking at me with a tenderness I had never seen on my own father's face.

'It calls to all of us, dear child, but you've been denied from answering it for too long. There is an ocean of power raging deep inside you. But before you touch it, you have to learn to control those little strands of aether you can access now.'

He sighed before opening a hidden compartment in his desk.

'Read this,' he said, handing me an old, leatherbound book with gold foil stamping on its cover. 'It's a tale on vivamancy, one of two that still exist. And remember, don't let anyone know who you are—because even most liberal of us will be afraid of a mage who can create living monsters.'

Chapter 30

Reynard

Three weeks. Three godsdamned weeks, and the only contact I'd had from that woman was the crumpled note sitting on my desk.

She always had an excuse for not answering my summons, and now here I was, staring at the bloody thing like it held the answers to all my problems.

I'd received the letter while walking around the gardens like a simpering fool. My fingers were clasped around a hangover draught, hoping she was just unwell and not ignoring my invitation, when a messenger arrived with the note.

I picked it up again, reading the challenging scrawl for what felt like the hundredth time.

King Reynard,

You'll be pleased to hear my plan succeeded, and the war of succession in the Brotherhood has been disrupted. Everyone's scrambling to make new alliances and regroup, so you can thank me later.

Roksana

P.S. Apologies. I was busy with the arch healer and forgot about the meeting. Also, my window is nailed shut.

I crumpled the parchment in my fist again, a reaction I couldn't seem to stop each time I read it. My pride wouldn't let me chase after an unwilling woman. Instead, I took it as a sign that I should follow Ciesko's advice and stay away from her.

All for nothing.

Neither time nor distance cured the burning need to see her. If anything, it'd gotten worse, distracting me from my work.

Did she think her trick at the feast was enough to earn her freedom?

I'd learned more about what occurred during the Mabon feast from Boyan. He'd delivered the information in person, the ailing man so animated when he spoke about Roksana that even if he'd lied when I presented him with her silver hairpin, I didn't have the heart to punish him. From the pride in his voice when he informed me of her new position, to the narrowing of his eyes when asked for updates on her whereabouts, it was clear she held a unique place in the man's heart.

Ciesko held no such qualms. He happily gossiped about every lesson, and in such detail, that something felt off. I could barely get a word in edgewise and was always left wondering if I'd missed something. This, together with the reports from my Observers, gave me a glimpse into her life and insight into her growing skills. And for some time, that was enough.

But what they'd failed to mention was her laughter; the slight narrowing of her eyes when she found my attitude annoying; or her dry wit, which often resulted in the most delicious of insults. Reports were just not enough, and my resolution to stay away was crumbling at its foundations.

'Sire, today's report is here,' my scribe announced as he walked in and placed a folder on my desk.

I squeezed the bridge of my nose, but the simmering anger didn't want to abate. The front page already told me what I could find inside, each blasted page containing the same name. Irsha Vilkor—the man shadowed her wherever she went.

'What do we know about the Blade, Vilkor?' I asked, more to centre my thoughts than because I cared about what my scribe had to say.

'Your Majesty?' he asked, confused, before clearing his throat. 'Well ... he's the youngest chapter master in the Brotherhood's history, unbeatable with daggers, and has never failed a contract. Our intel reports that he and Lady Roksana—' I held up a hand and sighed, unwilling to listen about another man's prowess, especially if it involved my Viper.

I understood that the dangerous aura around the assassin could be attractive to women, but if Sana liked big brutes skilled with weapons, why not choose one who'd won a fucking war?

'Forget it,' I said, returning to my seat. Settled at my desk once more, I noticed a sheet I'd missed in the report with an address and deed of ownership. I knew Sana had bought a house, but the official records took time to arrive. I glanced at it briefly, already aware that she was living with the dwarf, but the title on the deed made me question my eyesight. The property was registered under the names of Mr and Mrs Orenson.

The blood ran cold in my veins. *What's that woman up to now?*

'Veles' pit, what a mess,' I said, opening a bottle of wine while trying to make sense of the situation. My office was my sanctuary, but the dark wood and soft fabrics no longer brought me comfort. I waved a hand over the fae light when the shadows deepened.

What game are you playing, Viper? Is this your way of making me come to you? I wondered, shaking my head. 'You're in for a rude awakening, woman,' I groused, raking a hand through my unruly hair.

I'd let it grow long, shaving only one side, using the thick, wavy strands to veil the worst of my scar—and the empty socket where my eye used to be. My fingers brushed the strap of my eyepatch, and I huffed a bitter laugh. 'Reynard, you bloody idiot. Mooning over a woman who can't even spare time to see you.'

I pushed back from the desk, wincing as the chair scraped across the stone. My eyes drifted towards the tall, arched window that framed the city below. Truso's lights sparkled like a thousand stars, its bustling nightlife thriving under its innocent façade.

The temptation grew in my core. I stood immobile, fighting my instincts, wanting to see her, to find out why the master of the Blades kept her company so often, why she went by Mrs Orenson. Why everyone had her attention . . . except me.

What if someone's stopping her—blackmailing her, perhaps? What if she's in trouble while I'm sitting safely behind a desk, observing the world from above?

'That's a big bag of sweaty bollocks.' I sighed. 'Fuck it, I can't sleep anyway,' I muttered, calling for a servant.

A few moments later, I was dressed in the same outfit as dozens of other revellers that filled the streets at night. If that wasn't enough to conceal my identity, the wolf mask's enchantment would do the rest.

My servant gave me a disapproving stare when I fastened a short sword and duelling shield to my belt, but he'd learned long ago to keep any comments to himself.

'Leave the passage open,' I said. 'And pull the guard. He won't be needed tonight.'

Only a select few knew of the hidden corridor that led from the royal wing, through the old dungeons, and out to the river. I kept it that way, enjoying this gateway to freedom, but since I'd learned how Roksana had used it to sneak into my rooms, I'd kept it guarded—at least while I was in the palace.

'Yes, my lord. Shall I wait up for your return?'

I shook my head. 'No. Come back in the morning.'

Once he'd gone, I pulled a cloak over my shoulders, the hood casting my mask in shadow. Then I slipped into the night and went to find some answers.

It didn't take long to reach the hidden door in the dockside warehouse. The property was owned by the Crown and kept purposefully empty. If I'd had any doubts about blending in, they faded when I was engulfed in the crowd of rowdy sailors, merchants hoping for one last trade, and patrons strolling back and forth between establishments.

I vaguely knew the directions to Sana's house from the address in the report. It was in the artisan's quarter, an area full of houses with private courtyards, arched windows, and cosy gardens.

It wasn't a bad place to live, but the description of green window frames and a tiered red roof were useless in the dark. I needed to ask someone, and the opportunity arose in the form of a street urchin who tried to steal my money. Once I caught his wrist, I pulled the child to the side of the avenue.

'You'll get a coin if you tell me where I can find the dwarf who recently moved into this quarter with his human wife,' I said.

The child whimpered—more in fear than pain, as I was careful not to squeeze too tightly—before he pointed to a small house at the end of the street.

'The dwarf and his mage moved into that one,' he babbled, simultaneously attempting to escape my grasp while holding his free hand out for the coin.

I pulled one out, and it disappeared, the kid running off the moment I released him.

Time to explain yourself, Viper, I thought, striding beneath the carved archway leading to Roksana's house, dropping my hood as soon as I was out of direct view of onlookers.

'Who the fuck are you, and why are you asking about my Sana?' a muffled voice came from the left, followed by the unmistakable touch of cold steel at my throat.

His Sana. The phrase reverberated in my mind, stoking the flames of my ire.

'Lower your weapon or I'll gut you,' I answered in an equally threatening tone, but the man only laughed.

'Oh, I'd like to see you try,' he answered confidently as he shifted behind me, the blade pressing evenly against my skin. It had to be the Blades master. My fists tightened with the need to confront him as I fought my instincts.

'Take that wretched blade away from my neck,' I snarled, my body trembling in anticipation, hoping he wouldn't listen.

'That's all you have to say?' Irsha answered. 'Fine, ask me nicely, and maybe I'll send you back to Jagon in one piece—more or less. Yes, I know that bastard's planning something, so don't bother denying it.'

'I do not serve Jagon, and Roksana is not yours,' I sneered, my body already twisting as I reached for my sword. Its blade flashed in the moonlight, sleek, silent, and deadly, surprising my captor. Blood flowed from where the edge of his dagger had rested, but it was too late. I'd already twisted away from his grip and, with a powerful kick, sent him flying backwards.

'You're signing your own death sentence. Now you'll die like a dog,' Irsha said, lunging at me, his dagger flicking out in a distracting feint, ready to strike at the last moment.

I'd barely slipped my shield on before I used it to knock the thrusting knife to the side, my sword stabbing into the gap I'd created.

I hadn't fought a decent opponent since the war. Five long years of pretending to be civilised, of longing for the thrill of battle, of dancing with death. I couldn't restrain my manic smile when Irsha parried my attack, turning it into a riposte I barely avoided.

'Try harder, Blades master. Do your best, I fucking dare you,' I jeered when he adjusted his stance, attacking again.

Gods, he's fast.

Despite the longer reach of my sword, I still struggled to hold Irsha back, the small round shield covering my hand now decidedly less round.

Stop overthinking, Rey, you can do this.

Another feint. I sneered, ignoring it, only for the dagger to slice through my sleeve, which made me realise I might not win this time.

Fuck!

Light flooded the courtyard as a door opened, and my opponent's eyes flicked to the side. I twisted my wrist, ignoring the pain of the blade scoring my flesh and hit him in the face with my sword's pommel.

'What the pit's going on here?'

Sana's voice drowned out Irsha's grunt, but it didn't stop him from kicking my thigh, and I stumbled, my leg suddenly numb.

I shifted my shoulder as I fell, turning my collapse into a roll, before lifting my sword to parry a long sweeping cut directed at my neck. With a snarl, I pushed back, but something shattered on the floor at our feet. Yellow smoke billowed out, and breathing became impossible. Instinctively, we both fell back, but my foot slipped, forcing me to kneel.

Time slowed as Irsha threw a dagger with such grace that I could only watch in awe as it sped towards my heart. Instinctively, my arm came up, but a blurred shadow jumped between us, shielding me.

'Irsha, no!' Roksana yelled, arms wrapping around me, her body sheltering me from danger. Fire exploded in my chest, filling me with inhuman strength, and I leapt up with a singular thought. *Protect her.*

My weapon was long gone, my arms dragging Sana away from the deadly projectile.

'Are you out of your mind, woman?' I shouted, pushing her to the ground as the dagger sliced through my mask, splitting it in half and grazing my temple as it passed.

'Roksana!' the assassin bellowed, rushing towards us.

I ignored Irsha, focusing on the woman at my feet, still unable to believe she had jumped in to shield me. My fury soon abated when I saw how much she shook.

'Why did you do that, Viper?' I asked quietly, helping her up as gently as I could. Her pupils were blown wide, and her breathing unsteady, so I embraced her, hoping to help by holding her close.

Roksana didn't resist, but Irsha's eyebrows shot up at the sight. He looked like he was about to say something, then wisely thought better of it. Before I could say another word, Roksana shoved me back and punched me—hard—right in the jaw.

'You bloody idiot!' she snapped. 'What kind of stupidity made you challenge Irsha? You could have *died*, you moron. You could have died, and it would've been my fault.' Her voice cracked. 'And now you're fucking bleeding.'

The punch had hit me like a bucket of ice water, clearing my thoughts just in time to see her drawing back for a second swing. I caught her fist midair, pressing it to my chest as my world narrowed to the fire in her eyes.

'There, there,' I teased. 'You don't want to kill the man you just risked your life for.'

She only glared harder, but I didn't care. Whatever had been between her and the master of the Blades, whatever had happened between her and me in the past, this one gesture had erased it all. Roksana had chosen my life above Irsha's, above her own, and I finally didn't feel like a fool for yearning for her.

It was . . . liberating.

'Come inside, Irsha. Sana will join us when she's ready,' Tova called out to the Blade before walking to him and dragging him inside. 'But I have to ask—*why* did you attack the king?'

The assassin groaned, but at Sana's nod, he turned and followed the dwarf through the open door, leaving the two of us alone.

'You protected me, little Viper,' I murmured, tucking an unruly curl behind her ear.

'Couldn't let your rotten corpse stink up my yard. The neighbours would get upset,' she muttered, still fuming, eyes anywhere but on mine.

But I caught the tremor beneath the anger—and my strange sense of triumph only grew.

I lifted her hand and kissed her scraped knuckles.

'Whatever your excuse, I'm grateful. But if you ever do that again, I swear I'll lock you in the palace in a padded room and hire a dragon to guard you.'

I traced a thumb over the reddened skin.

'And next time you want to hit me, get that massive idiot to do it. I'll stand still, I swear. Just don't hurt yourself.' I blew gently across her bruised knuckles.

'You're being ridiculous,' she said, snatching her hand back. But I saw the small, reluctant smile tug at her mouth.

And gods help me—I almost called Irsha back, just to show her I meant every word.

Chapter 31

Roksana

I'm going to kill him. I'm going to look him dead in the eye and force-feed him the nastiest, foulest-smelling poison . . .

I stopped, reining in the storm of revenge fantasies just as Rey kissed my hand, brushing his lips over my scraped knuckles and blowing on them like some gallant idiot. Infuriating as he was, the king had all the predictability of mountain weather. And damn it, I smiled.

I snatched my hand from his and grabbed his elbow instead, dragging him towards the house. My heart had nearly stopped when I saw Irsha draw his knife while this fool had only smiled as if it were the happiest day of his life. I looked back, noticing the blood on his temple, but as Reynard came closer, I caught the unmistakable smell of wine on his breath.

'Next time you want to get drunk and start a fight, tell me so I can pour horse sedative down your throat,' I snapped.

He halted on the steps, forcing me to face him.

'You think I'm drunk, Viper?'

His voice was practically a purr, but all I could see was the damned blood dripping from his wound. The cut was too small to bleed that much unless Irsha had used poison.

'Oh, for fuck's sake, come here,' I muttered, yanking him closer. I leaned in, inspecting the wound. The blood was dark, steady, but not gushing—nothing vital, thank the stars. I moved closer, trying to sniff out poison, but all I could smell was lemongrass and musk.

'If I'd known you cared this much, I would've let your friend cut me a little more,' he murmured, peeling off the remains of his mask and nuzzling my hair. 'Want to lick it, too? I don't mind.'

'One more word,' I said, straightening and shooting him a glare, 'and I'll finish what Irsha started.' I'd instinctively titled my head, giving him access to my neck without realising it.

The grin on Reynard's lips widened. Mask or not, it was a wolf staring back at me, and he knew *exactly* what his words were doing to me. I wished I could forget he was the king and simply enjoy the mischievous man shamelessly flirting with me.

'Come inside. You're bleeding on my stairs,' I said, feeling utterly defeated by this growing attraction.

'My apologies. If you could show me where you'd like me to bleed?' Rey answered, playing with a lock of my hair that had escaped my braid when I fell.

'Gods give me strength,' I muttered, pulling him into the house.

My townhouse was cosy and perfect for a young working couple, but with two hulking men in my kitchen, the space looked uncomfortably small. It didn't help that Tova literally brought his work home with him, the entire table covered with srebrec ore and stolen documents from his latest investigation into the dwarven traders.

Tova's workshop was even worse. It was an outbuilding in our courtyard, at a distance from the house, but ever since he'd fired up the small furnace, you couldn't avoid the smell of smoke in the house. And with srebrec involved, that meant no one was safe.

'Find yourself a chair,' I said, shifting a pile of maps aside. 'And then tell me what in Veles' arse you're doing here.'

'That's an excellent question. I'd like to know that too,' Irsha chimed in, grabbing the pitcher of water and emptying it with a few large gulps. 'Gods, Sana, your creations are getting nastier,' he said, wiping his tongue on my clean tea towel, 'and they taste much worse than I remember.'

'Serves you right for starting a fight,' I shot back. 'And what do you mean you'd like to know too? That's rich. Maybe you should start by explaining why you attacked the king. What if you'd killed him?!'

Irsha opened his mouth, but I cut him off with a hand.

'Just don't. If this was about you two comparing the size of your daggers, I swear . . .'

I shook my head in disappointment, snatching the cloth from Irsha to wet it. Reynard had already claimed a corner of the table, lounging like it was his private salon. That damned smirk of his was firmly in place as he listened to our exchange.

I walked over and pressed the cold cloth to his scalp, trying to stem the bleeding.

He shivered as the water trickled down but said nothing. Instead, he placed his hand over mine, thumb gently stroking my knuckles while he fixed Irsha with a look that could melt steel.

'He started it,' Irsha said, lips tightening, 'turning up armed and wearing a mask. I thought it was one of Jagon's goons!'

'He started it? Oh, brilliant. *How old are you?*' I asked, glancing down to where Reynard's arm now encircled my waist. I ignored it, needing to deal with Irsha first.

'And don't give me that look, Blade,' I said. 'I know about Jagon. Boyan already warned me. Honestly! Do you really think Jagon would send one man for me? What a bloody insult.'

'Don't be so harsh, Sana,' Tova interrupted, appearing with a pair of tankards. He handed one to Irsha and sipped from the other. 'I wasn't expecting the king of Dagome to show up in our courtyard either.' He glanced at Reynard, then added with a smirk, 'Forgive me, Your Majesty, but I can see your hands are too busy to hold a drink.'

That was Tova at his finest, but Rey's smile only grew wider at his jab.

'You are forgiven, Master Orenson. I'd also prefer my hands to stay where they are.'

'Well, I don't prefer it. Now, hold this damn cloth,' I said before turning toward Tova. 'And you—give me that bloody beer.' I pulled away from the king, taking the tankard from the stunned dwarf's hand.

'I was trying to be nice, Sana. That was my beer!' Tova complained.

'Now it's mine. Get yourself another one and pour some for the king since his hands are free.'

Reynard shook with quiet laughter. Even though my body was still tense from the realisation that we had barely avoided serious consequences from his and Irsha's fight, I couldn't help but smile. He looked so . . . relaxed and at home in my humble kitchen. I could easily picture him sitting there, eating breakfast after staying the night.

The mental image shifted—Reynard naked, tousled from sleep—and suddenly, the beer in my hand couldn't touch the dryness in my throat. My pale complexion betrayed my thoughts, and I silently cursed the treacherous blush crawling up my neck. Reynard must have noticed, because the wicked man stretched out on the chair, displaying his impressive physique before reaching up and loosening the laces of his shirt, letting the collar fall open.

I choked as beer flooded my windpipe, causing a coughing fit. Bent in half, I cursed everyone in the room while the three men observed me in silent amusement before Tova patted my back.

'There, there, you don't have to try to kill yourself to prove a point. We're all sorry for upsetting you,' he muttered, marching back into the kitchen. 'Do you want some, Your Majesty?' he called out. 'I know my drah'sa, and trust me, when she's in this mood, it's going to be a long night.'

Cheeky sod.

I grabbed a nearby rolled-up map and smacked him on the back of his head.

'What *mood* exactly?'

'The mood to beat poor innocent men who sacrifice their drink to slake your thirst,' Tova said with a shrug.

Reynard placed the towel on the table and walked over to me. I stepped back when he reached for my hand, but with the table behind me, I couldn't escape. The moment he captured it, he brought my hand to his lips, kissing the inside of my palm while my fingers cradled his cheek.

'Please accept my apologies, Roksana,' he said softly. 'You are right. I shouldn't have visited uninvited, much less have started a fight.'

Then he turned towards Irsha, letting out a resigned sigh.

'Perhaps someday, Blades Master, you'll join me on the training ground. I suspect we could learn a great deal from each other.'

Tova, naturally, snorted in the background, and I braced myself for another jab, but Reynard didn't even turn.

'Not another word, Master Orenson,' he said. 'Our wordplay has come to an end.'

My two closest friends hadn't even realised when my mood had changed from teasing to annoyance, but Reynard had adjusted instantly, as if he were linked to my emotions.

'Are you all right, little Viper? I'm sorry if I took it too far,' he said with such sincerity that a strange sensation blossomed in my stomach. The weight of his words, the apology he didn't have to offer, settled there like the beating wings of a butterfly.

Irsha had enough decency to look embarrassed before he coughed to get my attention.

'Cold water won't stop the bleeding. You'd better look at it, Sana,' he said, and I realised the blood from Rey's wound was still flowing.

It wasn't much, and certainly not anything the massive warrior would notice for several hours, but eventually, with continuous bleeding, even such a small nick could cause problems.

'Alright, let me see it,' I said, touching the edge of the wound, smearing a little blood on my fingertips. A slight opalescent sheen caught my eye, and I turned to look at Irsha with a raised eyebrow.

'Yes, yes, I know. It's just a little herb of grace,' the assassin said, answering my question. 'He'll live.'

'Was it one of mine?' I asked, touching the slightly swollen flesh.

'No, it's a cheap one from Jagon's apprentice. I use it for marks who escape. It's easier to track them if they're bleeding.'

'I don't think I'd survive more of your venom, Viper,' Reynard said, touching the wound. 'It's a small mercy the Blade has a tight purse. Will it stop soon?'

'No, but I can fix it, so shift your rear. We're going to my workshop.' I pointed to the door, grabbing the king's arm. Noticing his frown, I scowled. 'Reynard, it's just on the other side of the corridor. I have the antidote there.'

Once inside my apothecary, he looked around, eyes wide with a curiosity he didn't try to hide.

'Sit and keep your hands to yourself,' I commanded, pretending not to notice his satisfied smirk after I returned with a small bowl of cold water and a set of rags.

'Fighting with Irsha is asking for death. He's a trained killer who isn't trying to win a duel but to kill as quickly as possible. I know he mistook you for Jagon's goon, but you? Why did you fight?' I asked, dipping a rag in the water and bending over to clean the cut of any residual poison. 'Tell me if it becomes too painful. I'll try to be gentle, but herb of grace can make the skin oversensitive.'

Rey closed his eyes and tilted his head backwards, giving me full access to his wound.

'You should trust my abilities, little Viper,' he said, voice low. 'Now, stop worrying about being gentle. You can't hurt me.'

He didn't flinch when I moved between his legs for a better angle.

'Don't tempt me, Kingling,' I muttered. 'I'm still mad at you.'

He chuckled. 'If this is how you express your anger, I have nothing to complain about.'

But the humour faded. His smirk slipped into something quieter, heavier.

'Never, under any circumstances, jump in front of a blade to protect me,' he said, eyes still closed. 'I can't feel afraid when I'm dancing with death—and seeing you in the path of a blade terrified me.'

'What . . . ?'

The word caught in my throat as Rey slipped an arm around my waist and pulled me closer. He looked up at me, gaze burning. Then, without warning, he pressed his face against my midriff and inhaled deeply, as if the scent of me could anchor him.

'I can't stand to see you hurt,' he murmured. 'And I can't seem to stay away from you. Gods know I've tried. What spell have you cast on me, Viper, that I can't stop thinking about you?'

His forehead rested against my stomach for a long moment before he lifted his gaze again.

'Why didn't you come to me after the Brotherhood feast?' he asked.

His words had left me speechless, so I used the moment to dab the antidote powder on a sponge and press it gently to his wound.

'I was busy,' I said quietly. 'But I sent a message.'

It was a weak excuse, and we both knew it. Still, I focused on my task, tilting his chin to the side so I could finish tending the wound. Once the bleeding stopped, however, there was no longer a reason for us to be so close.

'Rey, you have to let me go,' I said softly, waiting for him to move while enjoying the warmth of his large hands touching my body.

He didn't listen.

The soft fae light bathed his dark hair in silver-blue, and in a moment of reckless indulgence, I gave in to temptation, brushing my hand through the silky strands. They slipped through my fingers like water, impossibly soft.

A shuddered breath escaped him, his fingers squeezing my waist tighter as he pulled me to him.

'Do that again,' he breathed, voice rough with need. The sound of it ignited fire across my skin, stunning me with its intensity. 'Sana, please, do it again,' he repeated, nipping at my blouse, teeth pulling at the laces until the knot surrendered, giving him access.

'We can't . . .'

My voice was barely audible, my resistance melting while reason and desire fought inside me. As my breath hitched, I ran my hands over his scalp, playing with his hair while his teeth grazed my skin. The faint sting of his bites was eased by the kisses he trailed down my body.

I was falling—completely and utterly—for a man who could never truly be mine. And I hated how much I wanted him anyway.

Panting, I pulled away with what little willpower I had left.

'Rey . . . no. We can't.'

But the workbench halted my retreat. He followed, relentless, bracing his arms on either side of me.

'Why not? Give me one good reason to step away, Sanika, because I have none.' His hand rose to cradle my head, fingers slipping into my braid, titling my face up to meet his. 'The need to touch you haunts my every thought. I'm a man possessed. I want . . . No, I *need* you.'

His eyes bore into mine, challenging me to object. When I didn't, a slow, wicked smile curved his lips and a heat like molten lava rolled over my body.

'I'm going to lift you onto this bench, little Viper,' he said, voice velvet over steel. 'And then I'm going to get on my knees and savour the scent that's been driving me wild since the moment we met.'

He swept the bench clean with one sharp motion, and I gasped, turning around, startled by his actions—a mistake. His hips pressed against mine, and the hard length pressing through the fabric told me exactly how crazed he felt, how hot and hard I made him.

'Do you know how many nights I've dreamed of holding you like this?' Reynard murmured, fingers encircling my throat as he pulled me closer. His touch was firm, but ever so tender. 'Of hearing those little gasps when your mind resists, but your body yearns to be mine. You invade my nights and my days. I see your eyes, your smile . . . My suffering never ends. Are you so cruel to deny me this respite?'

I whimpered, the traitorous heat between my thighs betraying me. The image of him inside me, taking me right here, was too vivid, too sharp, and my hips tilted instinctively, pressing against him.

I couldn't resist him even if I tried.

'Sanika . . .' he said, pulling my skirt up. 'Don't fight it.'

With a defeated moan, I gave in to the liquid fire he poured into my veins.

A booming crash sounded, and it felt like ice water splashing over me. We both froze. I blinked and my focus snapped back to reality as I recognised the unmistakable clashing of steel.

'Stay behind me,' Reynard snarled, stunning me with his instant transformation from passionate lover to death incarnate as he rushed towards the door, sword and shield in hand.

'In your dreams!' I shouted, hastily straightening my clothes and chasing after him.

The fight might have saved me from making a mistake, but this was my home. The gods have mercy on the idiots who'd invaded it—because I would have none.

And deep down, I wasn't even sure if I'd *wanted* to be saved.

Chapter 32

Roksana

We burst into chaos. Four masked men were swarming Irsha and Tova in the kitchen, using sheer numbers to try and overwhelm them. That edge vanished the moment Reynard surged forward, his short sword driving cleanly through the spine of the one mid-swing at Tova.

The momentum shifted instantly. The remaining attackers retreated, knocking over my new dining table in a clumsy attempt at cover. I nearly cried when Irsha kicked it, cracking the polished surface—before Tova's hammer smashed it to smithereens, forcing me to shield my face from flying debris.

With the renowned master of the Blades and an unmatched war hero pressing the attack, our uninvited guests were hopelessly outmatched. They'd come expecting a helpless woman and a dwarven engineer—not two skilled warriors who made an art form out of killing.

I itched to join the fight, but between Reynard's blade, Irsha's twin daggers, and Tova's axe in play, I was far more likely to be injured by my friends than to contribute. Instead, I observed the spectacle from the corridor until the quiet sound of breaking glass from behind me caught my attention.

Three men were scrambling through my workshop window. They held no weapons—just hessian sacks and coarse rope.

I grinned. Kidnappers.

Sent by whom? Jagon? He'd kept his distance since my performance at the Mabon feast. I'd caught him staring now and then during my visits to the Brotherhood, gaze distant and unreadable, but this wasn't his style. Then again, that haunted look in his eyes hadn't been like him either.

The floor creaked beneath me as I moved deeper into the workshop, casually collecting a few vials from the shelf. The men were too clumsy to be rogue Blades, grunting as they stumbled inside, completely oblivious to the woman with the most poisonous ingredients known to womankind in her hands.

I frowned. The longer I looked at them and thought about it, the more I realised this didn't fit into the Brotherhood's style. These men carried ripped sacks and frayed rope and wore shabby outfits.

Mercenaries—or pirates. Someone hired these idiots to kidnap me. Oh well . . .

The sounds of battle on the other side of the now-closed door drowned out the soft click of the lock. I needed privacy for what came next. Reynard and Tova had never seen this side of me, the ruthless and deadly Nightshade whose reputation was built on the corpses of her enemies. Part of me wanted to keep things that way, but more importantly, I didn't want my men hurt by the poisons I held in my hands.

I exhaled slowly, weighing the vials. Even if these fools had taken this job to avoid starvation, they'd invaded my home.

It was time they learned what happens when you disturb a viper's nest.

'Welcome to my humble abode,' I said, waving my hand over a fae lamp, flooding the room with light.

The man in front hissed, shielding his eyes before drawing a cudgel from his belt.

'Come quietly and you won't get hurt. Master said—'

'Let me guess. Master said I'm just a woman.' I smiled coldly. 'A meek little lamb who'd bleat and do as she's told?'

I laughed, gesturing to the room. 'Take a look around. Do I look trapped to you? Maybe ask yourself—who locked the door?'

'Take her!' The simple command rang out, and all three men rushed towards me.

'Oh, I don't think so.'

I smashed the first vial on the floor in front of them, smoke billowing out and obscuring their vision. This was my only warning, something non-toxic to create fear and make them run.

Sadly, they ignored my generous offer.

A cudgel sliced through the haze, aimed at my head. I didn't move far, just a single step to the side, lifting a second vial to my mouth, dragging out the cork with my teeth and flicking the contents into the face of the weapon's owner. His high-pitched scream made me wince, and I ducked another wild swing before my assailant dropped to his knees, falling silent as his face corroded, staining the floor.

The two who remained were stumbling around, cracking shins and hips on the furniture, giving me time to move.

I need something less caustic, I thought as the floorboards blackened, damaged by the remaining poison.

My fingers found one of my delicate glass orbs filled with white powder—the perfect companion to my Alchemist's Fang. The blade caught the moonlight as I pressed the weak seam of the orb. It fell apart in my hands like spun sugar, glass dissolving into glittering sand. I swept it into the air as they charged, thrusting the shimmering dust into their faces.

The cloud engulfed them, but the man on the right covered his mouth and nose, stumbling to the side as his companion coughed and gagged.

Unluckily for him, the deadly strychnos[1] powder was already in his body.

I wasn't worried about its effect on me. I'd already built an immunity to it and the other poisons in this room, so the lethal substance was doing little more than tickling my nose. I sliced the dying man's throat, giving him the mercy of death before his body started to spasm, and stalked towards my remaining victim.

The realisation of his own mortality settled in the man's eyes, his throat bobbing while he scrambled backwards, frantically trying to wipe the powder from his skin.

I should have felt something—guilt, regret, maybe? However, if Reynard hadn't turned up, I would've been in bed, caught off guard, and my hotheaded dwarf would have sooner died than let someone take me. Whatever their reasons, they'd made their choices, and so had I.

As the thug's back hit the wall, he whimpered, his hands held up to ward off evil, but I didn't stop.

'Who is your master?' I demanded.

His eyes widened. I stepped forward—four steps, three—stalking closer as he scrambled, searching for escape. Just as I raised my dagger, the man screamed in defiance, propelling himself forward, arms reaching out to grab me, howling the words that shocked me into stumbling.

'He knows it was you. If you kill me, he'll just send more—he'll never let you live, bitch!'

The man charged at me, uncaring if he lived or died, but as I moved backwards, my heel snagged on a fallen chair. I fell, still holding my weapon, and my head smacked against the floor, dazing me. A moment later, his full weight crashed down on my chest.

---

1. **Strychnos** — a highly toxic shrub whose bark and berries can cause seizures and imminent death.

All I could see were the man's eyes as his life faded away, my arms trapped beneath his weight as I struggled for breath.

He was dead.

I laid there for what felt like an eternity, unable to look away from my attacker. Someone had sent him, but who and why? What had I done that deserved such force, such fervour? I scrambled out from beneath the body and slowly stood up, looking around at the carnage in my workshop.

The silence was deafening. It was just me, three corpses, and the moonlight shining on my bloodied hands. I wiped them on my ruined blouse before opening the rest of the windows, letting the night breeze disperse the toxins while I searched the bodies. Any doubts I felt about taking their lives faded when I found augurec manacles. If anything, they'd died too quickly, and I wished I'd gotten some answers.

'Maybe the men had better luck,' I muttered, exhaling to ground the buzz still crawling through my limbs.

Why did they come to my home?

Anywhere else, I'd have been limited in which poisons I could have used and would have had to rely on hand-to-hand combat. But here, in my own domain, I could take on a small army. Whoever had ordered the attack had chosen the worst place for it . . . unless they hadn't given instructions and my attackers thought I'd be unprepared.

'Did your master send you to test me?' I wondered, looking at their bloodless faces.

It was a possibility.

I was still turning that thought over when Reynard crashed through the locked door.

Hmm . . . he got more blood on him than I did. The palace maids will be cursing him later.

I looked away to hide my smile, pretending not to notice his heaving chest or the frown on his face as his eyes lingered on the bodies.

'Are you alright . . .? Viper, did they hurt you?'

From one breath to another, he stood beside me, his gaze sweeping over every inch of my body. His hands followed, brushing lightly across my arms and sides, pausing at the bloodstains on my blouse.

With an amused huff, I jerked my chin towards the last corpse.

'It's his, not mine,' I muttered, trying to suppress my smile and the pleased shiver I felt at Rey's concern.

But my smile faded as his eyes roamed the room. Confusion settled over his features as he studied the bloody scene.

He shouldn't be seeing this, came the afterthought, panic tightening my throat the longer he remained quiet.

Irsha strolled in, took one look around, and smirked. His reaction was so casual that I half expected him to offer everyone refreshments.

'You good, sweetheart? Looks like they underestimated the Deadly Nightshade.' He winked. 'I was hoping you'd keep at least one of them alive, but you did always have a bit of a temper.' He turned on his heel, calling towards the kitchen. 'Tova! Can your furnace fit a body, or should I fetch a cart?'

'You did this . . .?' Reynard shook his head as he came closer. His frown deepened, as if he couldn't believe his own eyes. It felt like rejection, and I couldn't even blame him. It was easy to accept I was a dark sister in theory, but seeing the proof of my abilities sprawled on the floor was a completely different story.

My heart twisted bitterly.

Has he ever really seen me, or did he want the carefully crafted vision from his dreams? The sombre realisation awakened a spark of defiance within me. *Three dead bodies and one dead romance—what an outstanding achievement for one night's work*, I thought, stopping in front of him.

'Yes, I did this. It's a part of who I am, and I won't apologise for it.'

I bit my lip, unsure how to deal with the emotions churning inside me. Still, I knew this had to be done. I needed to suppress these feelings and keep him at arm's length. Reynard was so silent that I braced myself for his disgust, then decided to speak first.

'Rey . . . this attraction between us, it doesn't make sense. We live in a world that would never accept the Deadly Nightshade and the War King surrendering to this temptation. You know the rules better than I do, and I don't want to bring more strife into your life.'

He huffed, the corner of his lips twisting as if holding back a comment. Then he laughed, low and dry.

'There you are wrong, little Viper. I make the rules in Dagome, and there's not a single one I wouldn't break to hold you again. If the world has a problem with that . . .' His smile was like drawn steel. 'I pity the world,' he said sharply, marching away and leaving me with the feeling that not even the stench of death would deter the king.

Chapter 33

Reynard

Roksana was many things—fierce, unrelenting, brilliant—but if she thought I'd be shocked by the darkness she'd unleashed to defend her home, she was wrong. I was grateful she'd killed them. So bloody grateful that she had spared me having to show her what *my* darkness looked like. If I'd gotten my hands on the bastards, they'd have been begging to reach the gates of Navia,[1] praying the afterlife would take them just to escape the pain.

My Viper thought I'd recoiled. I was speechless, yes—who wouldn't be, seeing his woman in danger? But she'd mistook silence for judgement. She'd thought I'd condemned her when I was merely holding onto the strings of sanity, the blood pumping through my veins like a raging inferno. My berserker's rage was so close to the surface that her one touch could unravel me.

The autumn breeze curled through her dishevelled hair, while her skin, pale as the moonlight, teased me with glimpses of the mark my teeth had left on her neck. I walked away, unwilling to even look at her until I could control myself. Still, all I could see was the Nightshade standing proud and undefeated, danger coiling in her hazel eyes—a true harbinger of death to her enemies.

---

1. **Navia** — an afterlife where all spirits come to rest after crossing the Veil that divides the spirit world from the living.

Gods, she's magnificent. A deadly queen fit for a war king—my equal. And she thinks I would let her go.

The thought shocked me with its simple truth, and a manic chuckle escaped, bouncing off the kitchen walls as I walked in. I grabbed a tankard from the table, uncaring who it belonged to, and gulped its contents in an attempt to quench my thirst for her.

Irsha and Tova ambled past the doorway, the Blade carrying two men thrown over his shoulders while the dwarf dragged another by the legs. The sound of a head bouncing off the floor interrupted my laughter.

'What's got into him?' Irsha asked.

'I think the king found out our girl's not some wilting flower that needs rescuing,' Tova said with a dismissive shrug, and I couldn't even fault him for his opinion.

'Where are you taking the bodies?' I said, wiping my mouth and setting the tankard aside.

'To the yard's gate,' Irsha replied. 'I'll arrange for someone to dispose of them later. On second thought, incinerating them here wasn't a good idea.'

I nodded and joined them, helping Tova with his burden. Roksana appeared moments later, gripping Irsha's arm with purpose.

'Don't worry about that,' she said. 'Go to the House of Lilies. I have a bad feeling about all of this. Bring Lily here, and if she resists, just throw her over your shoulder. I'll deal with her wrath later.'

The massive assassin nodded, pressing a kiss to her forehead. 'Give me an hour, sweetheart. I can arrange for a wagon on the way back. Best to get rid of the bodies before sunrise,' he responded before turning to me, his assessing stare telling me all I needed to know.

I nodded, offering a wry smile. 'I'll stay and ensure she's safe—*oof*.' I doubled over, scowling at Roksana for elbowing me in the gut. 'What was that for? I'm helping you clean up your corpses, woman, why are you beating me?'

'Exactly. *My* corpses, my house, my rules,' she said. 'And, if anything, I'll ensure *you're* safe, Your Majesty. But—' she softened slightly '—if you help me clean up this mess, I promise to make you some tea.'

She turned then, waving at a departing Irsha. 'Oh, and drag Riordan out of bed, too. His Majesty will need all the support he can get.'

I closed my eyes, adjusting the dead weight in my arms. I shouldn't enjoy being ordered around. Half of the court would have fainted at seeing me covered in blood and cleaning up corpses—but one look at Sana's face, and I readily agreed.

By the time we were done, the moon had crossed its zenith. Though a little more than an hour had passed, the house was mostly in order. I tugged at the damp linen of the shirt clinging to my chest, still soaked from scrubbing bloodstains, when a sudden racket outside made me stiffen.

For a moment, I thought we were under attack again, but it was only Liliana, masterfully draped over Irsha's shoulder, swearing a blue streak while still looking beautiful. Riordan walked in behind them, confusion written all over his face.

'Sana, I know you worry, but would you explain why this brute needed to kidnap me from the middle of the dance floor on my busiest night in months? I was working on a man with enough money to buy out my business!'

Roksana frowned, spearing Irsha with an accusatory glare. 'I'm guessing you haven't told her yet?'

'No,' Riordan chimed in. 'No one told us anything. And judging by Reynard's expression, "come quick, the king needs you" was a gross understatement.'

'We have a problem—and I'm not talking about those nitwits rotting by the gates. So I thought we needed to talk . . . properly talk,' Sana said, gesturing to the seat next to me while the assassin grabbed a chair before pulling Liliana onto his lap despite her protests.

'There aren't enough chairs,' Irsha said, unfazed. 'I carried you over my shoulder. What's the issue with sitting on my knee for a moment?'

I applauded his sound reasoning. I turned to Sana to propose the same, but she shook her head, pulling away.

'No, don't you bloody dare. Riordan can sit on your lap.'

The mage scoffed, rolling his eyes at her proposal. 'So when do I find out what in Veles' pit is going on here?'

'Nothing much,' Tova said, grinning. 'We had a bit of fun with our visitors.'

One look at Sana's serious expression and he didn't continue.

'I needed you all here because I found this,' she said, pulling a set of augurec manacles out of her pocket.

Riordan instinctively pulled away.

'This wasn't a random attack. Someone wanted me, and I think I know who . . . I'm sorry, Lily, but I was worried they'd go after you next.'

Liliana paled, whispering, 'Why?' while Irsha gently stroked her back.

'Because,' Roksana said, avoiding my eyes, 'I think they were sent after me for killing Ignac Tivala.' Interestingly, Irsha didn't seem as surprised by this revelation as the rest of us. 'Jagon knew about it,' Sana added quietly. 'He knew it was Lily who had discovered that the heir of the House of Tivala was murdering women. I guess he wasn't as tight-lipped as he promised.'

A few things clicked into place. I suddenly remembered the way she had questioned me—asking if I was sure the guard who had attacked me had had a choice. The way she had insisted she'd be condemning her family if she told me the full truth when she'd come to warn me.

Anger burned inside me, its fierce heat branding a hatred for Jagon in my heart. He thought to blackmail my Viper? Tivala's son's death was incidental; so, it was she who had cleaned out that trash from the streets of Truso. *Good*.

My eyes shifted to Liliana, perched tensely on Irsha's knee like a terrified dove. The assassin followed my gaze, and without a word, wrapped an arm firmly around her waist, tugging her closer. His challenging glare made my earlier assumption laughable. The Blade may have had a past with my Sana, but it wasn't her he pressed to his chest.

'As soon as we're done here, I'll drag him to my dungeons,' I promised, ready to argue against Sana's protests. Instead, it was Irsha who shook his head.

'That'll be rather difficult. Before our little duel, I was on my way to tell Sana that Jagon had disappeared.'

'What?' Sana asked. 'Are you sure?' Her eyes widened, knuckles whitening when she grabbed the table.

My instinct reacted faster than my logic, and I grasped her belt, pulling her onto my lap before I locked her in my embrace.

'Reynard, I'm all right,' she protested weakly, though she didn't stand.

All eyes turned to us, but rather than permit them to question why Sana was allowing me to hold her, I gestured to Irsha to continue.

'Boyan wanted to see him, but when I went to his workshop, the place was empty. Everything seemed to be in order, but his apprentice looked like a happy little rat, and when I pressed, he said he hadn't seen Jagon for days. It looks like he never returned from one of his journeys.'

'Why did Boyan want to see him?' I asked, brow furrowing as Irsha hesitated—glancing towards Sana as if asking for permission.

'The Brotherhood's been in chaos since Sana's arrival. It looks like Boyan got a second wind. He caught a few troublemakers by the bollocks and started cleaning house. Those who thought he was headed for the grave are now second-guessing themselves and pulling away from Jagon and his clique. I think—though this is my own speculation—that Boyan wanted to call for a challenge.'

Lily looked at Irsha with a baffled expression. 'And who would challenge the master poisoner for his position? Only Sana is at his level— oh gods . . . Boyan wanted her for a chapter master?'

My gaze dropped to the woman in my arms. Her lips twitched into a sad smile just as Irsha gave a slow nod.

She'd known. Maybe it had even been *her* idea.

'I told you I was busy,' she said quietly, not looking at me. 'And that some things would never be possible.'

Dread choked me when I realised the implications.

It was already hard enough—she was a commoner and a dark sister. But this . . .

Even if I forced the nobles of Dagome to accept a Brotherhood chapter mistress as my chosen, there'd be an uproar even I might not be able to contain, especially if Sana wanted to remain in her position.

I wanted her. Gods, I *wanted* her, but I didn't want to see my country bleed again.

'And now you can't do it because without Jagon, there can't be a challenge,' Irsha said with a sigh. 'So you'll have to wait for the Solstice Assembly to get their votes.'

I sucked a breath into my lungs. I still had time to change her mind.

'I . . . maybe it's a coincidence,' Liliana said cautiously, 'but some men from the South were asking my girls odd questions last night.'

'What kind of questions?' I asked, knowing the answer wouldn't be good.

'Mainly about the Winter Solstice Ball at the palace. Such as who was hiring musicians and entertainers, who was catering . . .' she said, smiling when I looked at her sceptically. 'I know that seems normal for someone looking for a job, but right after that, they started asking about sellers of "unusual" herbs and powders. There wasn't any mention of *which* herbs, but one of the men described something made from a flower the girls recognised as nivale.'

Riordan's curse was so colourful that my eyebrows shot up.

'What are you thinking?' I asked.

'That someone is trying to incapacitate mages,' he responded, jaw tight. 'Augurec manacles, nivale—that's got to be lanara poison. Those are only used on those gifted with second sight.'

I nodded. He wasn't wrong.

Sana placed a hand on my forearm. 'That's not the end of it.' She glanced at Tova. 'It's time you tell him about the srebrec.'

'There's not much to tell yet,' Tova said, leaning back in his chair. 'But I'll know more soon. Remember the dwarven merchants Lily wanted me to entertain? Well, they told me next to nothing, but I discovered where they like to stay and with whom they traded. I snuck in one night and grabbed a few scrolls and a sample of their merchandise. They're planning to take it to Wiosna.'

He stretched theatrically, letting silence draw every gaze towards him before finally continuing.

'The scrolls contain schemata for . . . something. I don't know what yet, but I'm working on it. It's designed to trigger . . . something.

He reached for the scroll Sana had hit him with earlier and unrolled it on the table.

It looked like gibberish to me—rows of overlapping squares filled with intricate runes and scattered numbers. But Riordan leaned forward, completely absorbed, his fingers following the symbols as his brows drew tighter and tighter.

'Ri?'

'I'm not sure,' he muttered. 'But this—look here—this set loops around . . . yes, right there. That's the trigger. Master Orenson is right. It's an aethereal loop designed to pull in magic, and . . .' He paused, jaw tightening again. 'Well, I'm not sure what happens then, but any mage caught near this when it's activated would be in real trouble.'

'Make a copy and take it to the university immediately,' I said. 'We need to know what it is.'

Tova looked like he might argue, but I cut him off. 'Please ensure the mages work with Master Orenson. His expertise may be needed to solve this problem, and his insight could be critical.'

Tova hesitated, then nodded. 'Fine. But we should go after the merchants first. And I think I've got something that could help.'

He unrolled a large map of the Lowland Kingdoms across the table.

'Look at this. I've spoken with the oxen handlers, and they all mentioned visiting these backwater villages. Every recent transport from Wiosna has taken a similar route south, bypassing Truso and travelling through the swamp along the border with the Care'etavos Empire. On the way back, they take the usual trade roads.' He looked at Liliana with a smirk. 'And often stop at your establishment to spend what they've earned.'

'It's difficult to control those bloody swamps,' I admitted, eyeing the map. 'Especially since the dark fae are claiming we've been encroaching on their land. However, if you mark the places on the map, I'll send some patrols there to investigate.'

Tova's grin widened.

'I'm guessing there's more to it?' I asked.

'Oh yes, there is. You know what scrooges dwarven merchants are. They turn every gold coin twice before spending it—yet these lot have been making a show of throwing gold around like it's river gravel. They're flashy, deliberate. And while everyone's watching *them*, there's always one who disappears as soon as they head to the entertainment quarter, only to return in the morning.'

'I'll speak to the grand master,' Irsha offered. 'We'll send Observers.'

Tova shook his head. 'No, you can't trust them. Sana told me several of them still support Jagon, and he's neck-deep in the srebrec trade. If we send the wrong men, we'll tip our hand. Let me handle it. Whoever they're meeting with is expecting a dwarf, so . . .'

'That's some sound reasoning, but it's very risky, Master Orenson,' Riordan said, his finger still trailing over the strange schemata.

Tova's expression hardened. 'It is, but I have a bone to pick with Młot. His paranoia killed my parents. I've studied the scroll and know their route. There's been a *massive* increase in mining this past year. I don't know where they're storing the ore, but that much unstable material isn't just dangerous to the miners—it's a threat to everyone.'

Riordan finally looked up, eyes sharp with new interest. 'Then let's work together. Srebrec is not just unstable; it blocks the flow of aether. Creates null zones. With the right instrument, we might detect their storage sites. I'd like to review your findings.'

Tova raised a brow.

Riordan grinned. 'I'll build the enchantments if you craft the device.'

Tova nodded, pleased. 'Deal.'

'Excellent,' Riordan responded. 'Now I need to find an artificer skilled enough to help us put it all together.'

Sana spoke then, her voice soft but steady. 'Tova, promise me you'll be careful.'

She didn't try to stop him, and that alone told me how deeply she trusted him. Her brows drew tight with worry, but her acceptance made the dwarf smile.

'Always, drah'sa. I knew you'd understand.'

Irsha slapped a hand on the table. 'Good. We've got a plan.'

'Not exactly,' Sana said. 'If Tivala's behind this, we need proof. We can't point fingers at men like him without evidence. They don't just fall; they circle the wagons.' She glanced towards the map. 'I'll return to the Brotherhood. Search Jagon's workshop, his rooms—anything that might give us leverage. If that turns up nothing, I'll go south.'

'No.' The word left me sharper than intended, everything inside me recoiling at the thought. If Tivala had dared attack her *here*, what would stop him from killing her *there*?

'You can't accuse him based on a dead mercenary's words and my hunch,' she said, gently but firmly. 'I don't know much about court politics, but I know enough to realise if you touch one of those arseholes, they will all rally against you. What you need is a signed order, something he can't deny.'

She was right. I hated that she was right.

'Sana, if he is behind all this, I'm not going to accuse him—I'm going to destroy him,' I said. 'But you're right. I need time to prepare, and we need to find out what this . . . thing is, what it has to do with srebrec . . . and why the fuck he's been digging into the ground alongside the border.'

Riordan gathered the plans. 'Leave the device to Master Orenson and me,' he said, and I had to fight a grin at the way Tova's chest puffed with pride when he nodded.

'Irsha?' Sana asked quietly, and some understanding passed between them.

'I don't work for free sweetheart, even for you.' He shook his head, but I had a remedy for that.

'Then I'll contract your chapter, just like I did before the rebellion,' I said. 'You'll be my eyes and ears in Truso.'

He smirked. 'You mistake my men for Observers. And I'll have to think about it before I entangle my Blades in a quarrel between the nobles.'

'I don't make mistakes like that,' I said evenly. 'I don't trust the Observers. I trust Sana. That's why I'm hiring *you*, Irsha Vilkor. You'll take my coin—and you won't fail me.'

His eyes narrowed. 'For a man who tried to kill me a couple of hours ago, you have a lot of guts asking me to serve you. But fine. Send your man with the contract tomorrow.'

'Guts? I'm holding a war council in a bloody kitchen. So maybe what I have is a lot of "guts" *trusting* you all with the future of Dagome,' I said, looking at the people gathered around me. 'Though I recognise an opportunity when it arises.'

None of them knew how much was at stake. None of them sat on my royal council or held a military post. And yet—between a dwarf, a half-fae courtesan, and two assassins—I'd received more loyalty, more insight, and more solutions than from a hundred advisors trained in statecraft.

Meeting Roksana had cost me dearly. But now? It felt less like a price and more like fate—like the moment the tide turned, and I was gifted a woman who shifted everything. Including the company I kept.

'Thank you,' I said simply. 'This . . . shadow council has been more enlightening than I could have imagined. Consider yourselves under the Crown's protection. Now, Riordan, draft the letter to the Court of Mages and have it ready for me to sign. I want all their resources at your and Tova's disposal. Irsha, the contract will be sent to your chapter tomorrow. Liliana, I'll assign a handful of my veterans to your establishment. Hire them as staff. I'll cover the cost from my personal accounts. Sana—'

'Will do her own thing,' she cut in before I could finish. 'And right now, her own thing is sending everyone to bed.' She stood and stretched, and Liliana instantly followed, giving a graceful curtsy.

'Thank you, Your Majesty. I bid you goodnight. Sana, come and see me tomorrow. We need to talk.'

Irsha followed her out with very little pretence, and I was fairly certain I knew where he'd be sleeping tonight.

Riordan glanced my way before he grasped Tova's elbow and asked him about his workshop. Both left, giving me a chance to talk to Sana.

'Go home, Rey. I'm tired,' she murmured, leaning against the door-frame.

I braced my hand on the wood above her head, refusing to let the moment slip past.

'You didn't let me finish, Sanika. I'm leaving, and I'm not sure for how long. Tova was right,' I said. 'I need to check on Tivalaran and its borders. Since the accident, I've hidden like a wounded boar, licking my wounds and neglecting my duty while my enemies exploited my weakness. I need to oversee the patrols and check the outposts.'

She nodded slowly, guilt flickering across her features. 'I hope you have a peaceful journey. I'll come with an update when you return—this time in person, I promise. Hopefully, Tova will have found out more about the strange diagram by then.'

She was all formal, distancing herself from me, but I wouldn't leave until she knew exactly where I stood.

'Kiss me, Sanika,' I said, voice low. 'I want to remember the taste of your lips while I'm in my cold tent on the dark fae border.'

Her pupils dilated, her breath catching as she placed a hand on her throat. She shook her head, but her voice lacked conviction.

'I told you it won't work . . . Don't trade one weakness for another. I can't be what you need.'

She turned her face away from me but the flush creeping up her neck and the hitch of her breath betrayed her. I bent down, fingers sliding to the back of her neck, guiding her closer.

She didn't push me away. If anything, she leaned into me, rising onto her toes, and that was enough for me.

I kissed her.

And gods, she *yielded*. Beautifully. Sweetly. Her lips parted beneath mine, and I groaned into her mouth, gripping her tighter as I held myself back by the thinnest of threads. I wanted her so fucking much—all of her—but her heart hadn't chosen me yet.

My tongue traced hers, and the mischievous woman responded wickedly, sucking it between her lips before pulling away just as my hand tightened to keep her close. I nipped her lower lip in protest, a teasing punishment for breaking the kiss before I had my fill of her.

'I didn't come here to make sense or hold a meeting, my light. I just wanted to see you,' I said, gently tracing my thumb over her lips, slightly swollen from our kiss. 'I fought Irsha out of jealousy . . .' I continued, wrapping a strand of her hair around my finger. 'I needed you to understand that before I go.'

Her nostrils flared in frustration as she swatted my hand away. 'And what am I supposed to do with that? You know who I am, what I'm going to do. Why do you act as if there could be something more between us?'

'Because I know what I want,' I said, voice firm. 'I want you to choose me, Sana. But how can you do that if you don't know what the possibilities are?'

Her breath came faster, her pupils blown wide, and I realised I might have pushed her too far. I stepped back, giving her the space she needed even if it killed me.

'When I return to Truso, we'll talk again,' I continued. 'Stay safe, little Viper. I hope you use this time to get used to the thought of being mine.'

'In your dreams,' she muttered, rolling her eyes as she shoved me through the door. I let her push me, a grin spreading across my face. As much as I wanted to stay, she needed to rest, but I couldn't let her have the last word. Not this time.

'In my dreams, we do far more than kiss. When I return, I'll show you just how much.'

The door slammed hard enough to nearly clip me on the way out. I inhaled deeply before striding through the sleepy city, unable to contain my grin.

Fate had pushed us together from the very first moment I'd seen her in the forest.

And like a fool, I had spent the last month tormenting myself, unaware that the woman I sought—a woman who would take a blade for me—had been right under my nose.

Chapter 34

Reynard

Two weeks we'd been trudging through the swamp, and I'd had plenty of time to remember the real drudgery of soldiering. We'd visited every spot that Sana's tinkerer had identified on the srebrec merchants' routes, either bolstering the garrisons with trusted men or, in some cases, building small outposts in the ruins of abandoned villages. Despite the hardships, I found myself standing taller and even smiling occasionally, though I tried to refrain from the latter after seeing the uneasy looks on my men's faces.

My kingly duties still followed me, appearing as if by magic in my tent each night, which is why I found myself once again hunched over a portable desk that sat like a child's toy on my lap. Still, I felt free for the first time in years, with the problems we faced overcome with blood, sweat, and more than a little cursing.

Life, however, seemed to have other plans for me. The latest reports sat before me, their presence bringing my scowl back full force.

Duke Tivala was building an army.

Even if I took the numbers with a pinch of salt, travelling along the border had given me a clarity the palace never could. The villages we visited were filled with women and the elderly. Their husbands and sons were gone—conspicuously so.

'That will be a costly mistake,' I muttered, feeling like a fool. I'd let the enemy arm himself under my nose, dismissing the old duke's antics as someone jostling to improve his family's position. Now, I had to recognise he wanted more than just gaining power through his daughter's marriage—he wanted that power for himself.

'Well, I dodged that arrow,' I said aloud, rubbing the bridge of my nose. The marriage contract still sat locked in my desk back in Truso. When I returned, it would go straight into the fire. Pacifying the South with an alliance was no longer an option.

Is that why he's raised an army? Because I didn't agree to the marriage?

I closed my eye, the dim light in the tent needling at my skull. No—his plans were too far along. This had started before I ever took the throne. *It seems I'm not the only one who'd planned a coup.* Why else would Tivala have asked my predecessor to grant his duchy principality status?

A loud cough interrupted my thoughts, and my adjutant walked in carrying the accounting ledger. *More headaches to come*, I thought with resignation, but it had to be done.

I needed to recall the veterans of the Necromancer's War for the traditional New Year manoeuvres. As king, it was my right to decide which dukedom would host them—and this year, they'd take place beneath the very walls of Ernesto Tivala's castle. A little trick to bypass the law. And when the troops marched out again, the old duke would be in chains. That would silence the whispers of Tivalaran secession for good.

He might have his peasant army, and even the support of some in the Royal Council, but he was still no match for me. Dagome's nobles swayed like grass in a strong wind every time I implemented a new law, and that posed a problem, but I still had the fealty of my army.

Those soldiers were loyal to the man who'd brought them back alive from a war no one expected to survive, let alone win.

I looked down at the ledger, my brow furrowing when I noticed an alarming set of figures.

'I thought we'd stationed troops evenly between the northern and southern borders,' I said, tapping a line on the page. 'So why are the losses here so disproportionate?'

The camp in question guarded the passage to Wreckers Cove, a den of pirates and marauders I'd never managed to fully pacify. Still, I'd kept the main roads open for the sake of the honest few who remained.

'It's difficult terrain,' my adjutant said, 'and there are frequent night raids—small boats, quick strikes. It's rumoured the Tangra Empire is arming them. We've reinforced the output with archers, but it's hard to fight an enemy that comes and goes with the tide.'

I nodded, the tip of my quill tapping thoughtfully against the parchment.

'Write to my brother. Tell him to send a unit of dragon riders to help with the patrols. If it's Tangra, we need to know.'

I had provided Orm with some of my dragon riders to help settle the Ozar Kingdom, but it was time to call them back to service. The idea of Tangra supplying weapons to criminals across the sea sat wrong with me. How had that rumour even started, and why would a distant empire concern itself with Dagome's outlaws?

'The pirates burn their dead at sea,' I said. 'I doubt they'll mind receiving the honour a little early.'

Understanding dawned in my officer's eyes. 'An excellent idea, sire. I should have thought of it . . .'

'Not so excellent, really. Dragons hate the cold and wet. But if we can tempt them with a little extra gold for a few months and rotate the patrol often enough to reduce their discomfort, we might be able to end this threat once and for all.' I paused. 'Any other trouble in the region?'

'Plenty,' he said grimly. 'But all behind Duke Tivala's borders. We've discovered some unusual . . . excavations along the border, and the nearby villages have been swarmed by hostile creatures—biesy,[1] strigae, and worse. It's as if something drove them from their lairs.

'The battle mages there are holding the line, but only just. We could send a company of soldiers, but the duke has refused military assistance. And as the law stands, we can't enter his domain without his permission or the king's order . . . Would you like us to proceed, sir?'

'No. But tell your spies to keep their eyes open. I want to know exactly what he's digging for, and why. Start preparations for the New Year manoeuvres and arrange for enhanced provisions. I want the men ready—for anything,' I said, stretching back in the chair.

The Winter Solstice Ball promises to be an exciting event.

When I'd decided to hold the ball to meet my future queen, I hadn't expected it to turn into a feeding frenzy.

It would be so nice if Tivala were involved in the srebrec trade—then maybe I won't need an army to bring the bastard down, I thought, my lips spreading into a vicious smile. *And I will enjoy telling him exactly who was behind his family's ruin.*

I'd never quite let go of my grudge—not since the old fool had refused to send men to fight against the Lich King.

I was drafting countless plans in my head for preparing for battle and dealing with rebellious lords using political pressure when my guard leaned in through the tent flap.

'Sire, there's a woman here causing a commotion. Claims she rode all day to get here and won't leave without seeing you.'

His words caught me off guard. I wasn't expecting anyone—certainly not a woman. My location wasn't exactly secret, but I'd seeded enough

---

1. **Bies (s.)/biesy (pl.) /pron: b-yes/** — Massive bipedal bison-line beasts with horns and thick hide resistant to most types of weapons. Their habitat is mainly woodland areas, and they are aggressive and territorial.

conflicting reports to keep my enemies guessing. Misdirection had its uses.

'Ensure she's unarmed, and let her in,' I said, gesturing for the scribe to clear the table.

As soon as the scribe left, the flap was pulled back, and my guard ushered in a pale, road-worn Roksana.

'Your Majesty,' she said, curtsying. The display of manners instantly set me on edge.

'Leave us,' I ordered my men. 'Now.'

As the tent emptied, I noticed the tight set of her jaw, the faint tremble in her hands as she clutched her skirt.

'Rey . . .' she breathed.

I crossed the space in two strides, reaching to steady her.

Her breath caught. She tried again. 'Tova's missing.'

'What?' The word came out harder than I intended. 'How?'

'I don't know,' she whispered. 'The dwarven merchants returned two days after our meeting. He went to spy on them and never came back.'

Fuck, I should have someone keep an eye on that damn dwarf, I thought, placing my hands on her shoulders. Her body was stiff with tension, eyes glassy from unshed tears.

'Tova's a tough bastard,' I said softly. 'And you are not alone, my light. Let me help.'

Without a word, she wrapped her arms around me, burying her face against my chest, her body shaking silently. My heart stuttered before beating so hard my blood roared in my ears. We'd shared several intense moments and had had our fair share of bickering, but Sana had never sought comfort from me. The South, the court, everything faded away as I held my Viper close, stroking her hair.

After a few far-too-short moments, she took a deep breath and pulled back. I reluctantly let her go, already missing the warmth of her embrace.

The pale winter sun spilled through a gap in the tent seam, casting her figure in a golden haze while hiding her expression in shadow.

'Thank you,' she whispered. 'I didn't know what else to do.' Her voice wavered, and something twisted tight in my chest. 'I searched everywhere—tore Truso apart with Riordan and the Brotherhood—but it's like he vanished into thin air.'

'Do you think he's still in Truso?' I asked, guiding her to sit in my chair and kneeling beside her.

She shook her head. 'No. That's why I've been trying to get in touch with you. That bloody oath kept me from leaving the capital. If Riordan hadn't pointed out that the city limits extend into the forest, I don't know what I would have done.'

I tilted her chin gently, noting the streak of blood trailing down her neck. I cursed. The city limits might extend into the forest, but they didn't come this far. Roksana must have fought against the oath's compulsion, convincing herself she was still in the city to come here.

'Roksana Regnav, you have fulfilled your oath. You are free to travel as you please.' I blurted out the release phrase, shaking my head at my stupidity, but at least the bleeding stopped 'I'm sorry, Sanika, I didn't think . . .'

'It's only pain,' she said, brushing it off with a shaky breath. 'It doesn't matter. I need you, Rey. Please. I'll do anything if you help me find him.'

She looked so broken, her strength hollowed by desperation. I poured her a drink of fortified brandy and held it out.

Her hand trembled too much to grasp it. The goblet tipped, sloshing over her fingers. I caught it before it spilled further, then knelt again and gently wrapped her hands around it.

'Drink, then give me a moment to issue some orders. I'll find your friend, but I want a front-row seat when you scold him for worrying you,' I said, trying to bring at least a hint of a smile back to her face.

A dainty hand tentatively touched my cheek, her long, delicate fingers caressing the edge of my scar. I leant into it, closing my eye so she wouldn't see the whirlwind of emotion threatening to overwhelm me. That wretched dwarf would be found, even if I had to gut my kingdom to do so.

I needed to see Sana smile again.

'I've hurt you so much, Rey. I don't know how you can stand to look at me, let alone help me, but I swear on my life I'll serve you unconditionally to repay this kindness.'

'I don't want your service, Viper,' I said, laying my head on her lap. 'Or repayment of kindness.'

Roksana's fingers stroked my hair, her touch uncertain at first but growing bolder with each passing moment.

'What else can I offer?' she asked, hissing quietly when I accidentally touched her calf.

'Spread your legs,' I said, lifting my head.

Shock and betrayal burned in her eyes, but she did as she was told, swallowing hard when I rolled up her skirt. My hand trailed over her skin. Just as I suspected, it was red and rubbed raw from the horse's saddle.

'If that's what you want, sire,' she murmured. Her voice was flat and distant, but she parted her knees under my guidance. My Viper was so pale and determined that my chest tightened with pride.

I reached for my pack, pulling out some ointment and dipping my fingers inside. Carefully, I massaged the balm into the tender skin of her inner thighs, slow and deliberate, pausing whenever she flinched. At the worst spots, I leaned in and blew gently to cool the sting.

'I only want to ease your discomfort, my brave Viper,' I said, my voice barely above a whisper. 'You'll never be forced to accept me against your will. The next time you open your legs for me, you'll do so because you want it, not for payment or duty.'

I bent down and kissed her grazed knee, praying to all the gods she didn't see how much I wanted her.

'Be careful what you offer, and to whom, Roksana,' I said, standing up and pouring myself a measure of brandy to calm my racing heart. Her legs slammed shut with a loud smack, and I turned away to hide my smile.

'If you truly want to offer me something,' I added, swirling the brandy in my goblet, 'then promise me you'll never let another man touch you for as long as I live.'

Her head snapped up, and for the first time since she'd arrived, I saw the fire flicker back to life in her eyes.

'So to take a man to my bed, I have to kill you first?' she retorted, a vicious smile teasing her lips as she straightened her dress. 'That's cruel, Reynard. I kind of like you, but you must understand—a woman has needs.'

'Name them, and I'll ensure you're never left wanting,' I said, pleasure warming my chest when I caught the blush on her cheeks.

'You shouldn't make promises you can't keep,' she whispered, blushing even more when I tapped the tip of her nose and challenged her.

'Try me.'

I took a deep breath and reluctantly stepped back. There was one thing I had to do first. With a sharp command, I called for my adjutant. After a brief exchange, the captains responsible for patrolling the northern and southern roads were given new orders.

Sana sat quietly, her eyes brightening when I ordered my men to stop and search every wagon travelling through Dagome. It was a challenging task, but with my enhanced patrols and the swampland now guarded by loyal soldiers, it was doable. After they'd left and I sat on my cot, she chuckled, her entire demeanour changing from despair to cautious hope.

'I'm sorry, Your Majesty. Your word truly is your bond. Shall I kneel and prostrate myself for not believing you, or let you sniff my neck to earn forgiveness?' she said, mischief dancing in her eyes.

There was nothing more I could do to find the dwarf, but my work here wasn't finished, and I suspected Sana needed a break from constantly worrying about her friend.

'You have no objection to me savouring your scent?' I asked, seeing her pupils widen at my question. 'I thought we'd discussed making reckless offers, but I see you enjoy playing with fire. Do you even know why I did that?'

'Yes . . . and no. But I've seen enough at Lilies not to judge,' she quipped, making me laugh.

'While I'm sure Liliana's basement is full of exotic delights, they don't appeal to me. What do you know of the Erenhart bloodline?' I asked, satisfied when she frowned.

'I know your brother, the king of Ozar, was a dragon rider, that's all. Why?'

'My family is afflicted by wild magic. Those who manifest it at a young age become riders. Those who don't are cursed to carry it within them and pass it on to the next generation. The magic is—or should be—dormant.'

'And that means you need to sniff people?' Roksana leaned forward, listening to my explanation.

'Well, not exactly. Its effects are obvious—' I gestured to my body, indicating my large physique. '—but there are less visible differences. Like a resistance to pain, and, as I recently discovered, a sensitivity to certain smells.'

Sana's lips parted, making it hard to resist touching her. My Viper looked so intrigued by the story that I continued sharing more than I initially intended to.

'The magic makes it difficult to control our temper, at least when it manifests. It can trigger the berserker within me, a rage that your assailants in the forest witnessed firsthand. That part of me recognises you. Your magic . . .' My words stumbled into silence when I realised how insane I sounded.

I tried again. 'Ciesko explained it better. Your scent is . . . just, right. But no, Roksana, I won't be sniffing your neck—unless you want me to abandon all reason and ravage you on this table.'

Her breath sped up, her eyes growing wilder when she understood what I'd said. Her lips parted, and I leaned forward, placing my hands on the armrests of the chair, caging her delicious body beneath me.

'Now that you know, are you brave enough to make that offer again?'

I'd intended the words to be teasing, but as they left my lips, I knew I wanted Sana's answer to be 'yes.'

'I . . . why is everything so intense with you?' she deflected, turning away as she fanned herself.

'I don't know, but I'm glad I'm not the only one suffering.'

I smirked and pulled away to ring the bell.

'Ensure my guest is comfortable,' I said when my valet entered before turning back to Roksana. 'We'll be wrapping up our work here soon, then I'll take you back to Truso.'

'I can return on my own. I'll leave you to your . . .' Sana looked around, perplexed, then shrugged. 'Whatever this is, but please let me know if you find Tova. Meanwhile, I'll speak with the Mules. Boyan has regained control of the smugglers—mostly—so maybe I can get a map of any routes we might not know about,' she said, standing up, but I pushed her back onto the chair.

'You will stay here. The garrison is in the middle of a bloody forest. I'm not risking you.'

Her fists tightened, and I wondered whether she'd argue, but much to my relief, she nodded. 'Fine, I'll wait for you, but can I at least walk around the camp? Sitting in a tent with nothing to do but worry is hardly a pleasant experience.'

'Of course. You're not a prisoner, but I'll assign a guard to ensure the men behave,' I said, and she rolled her eyes.

'I can teach them a lesson myself if they don't,' she huffed.

A mischievous chuckle rumbled in my throat at the offence in her voice.

'I know Viper, but I'd prefer my men alive.'

That seemed to appease her, and she didn't protest when I opened the flap to shout for a guard to come in.

'Guard my . . . Lady Roksana. She is welcome to go where she pleases, undisturbed and unbothered by anyone,' I said, voice low and firm. 'If someone pesters her, report them directly to me.'

The soldier gave Sana a wide-eyed look. One glance at my face, and his hands started shaking as I wrapped my cloak around Roksana before they left.

'Have fun, Viper, and try to spare my poor soldiers.'

An hour later, four units had been dispatched, and the only thing I had left to do before heading home was find my woman.

I ordered the guards to prepare the horses and went looking for her. It didn't take long to spot the man I'd assigned her standing by the stables.

Sana sat on a haystack with a scrawny garrison cat on her lap. She looked deep in thought, and I stopped to enjoy the view. Her expression was so serene, her fingers trailing over the animal's back as a dreamy smile played across her lips. Eventually, a horse snorted, dragging her attention back to reality.

'Rey! I-I mean, Your Majesty. Is it time to return?' she stuttered, correcting herself.

I came to sit next to her, but when I reached out to pet the animal, it bolted, using Sana's lap as a launching pad and leaving a deep scratch on her forearm. She hissed, immediately grasping my arm despite the beads of blood appearing on her skin.

'Don't hurt him, he was just scared.'

'I'm not going to,' I said.

What did she expect? That I'd chase after the ragged wretch?

'I'm sorry. The way you talk sometimes. It just . . . made me worry.'

I watched her pull a vial from her belt and pour the contents onto the wound. The blood sizzled, and judging by how her jaw tightened, it must have hurt.

'Will you be alright or should I kiss it better?' I teased, ripping a strip from my shirt and bandaging her forearm.

She smiled and rolled her eyes. 'It's literally just a scratch. As long as it doesn't get dirty from all the dust and horse sweat, it should be fine. But yes . . . you can kiss it better. Actually, I think it would help a lot.'

Roksana's shy smile and luminous eyes were my doom, and when I brushed my lips against her skin, I was sure this wolf had lost his soul to the viper.

I almost killed my sergeant when he came to tell us the troops were ready to go.

Chapter 35

Roksana

The city infirmary, a massive stone building next to the magistrate's office, was busier than the town centre on market day. Ciesko had assigned me to the group of healers looking after those with minor injuries but had failed to mention that there would be so many patients.

Countless people came and went, but after dealing with the injured miners in Wiosna, none of my current patients' injuries were much of a challenge. After several hours, the voices of passing citizens and the stench of blood faded into the background while I worked instinctively.

'My lady, is everything all right?' my patient asked. 'Did you find something else?'

The question shook me out of my stupor as the man on the cot looked between me and his aether-infused wounds, the blood already clotting.

'Everything is fine, but the spell needs time to settle in,' I lied, forcing a smile to my lips. 'Let me suture it, and your arm will be healed in no time.'

My patient quietly hissed when I sprinkled a little nivale powder on his wound, but as the pain-numbing herb began to work, his face smoothed into a blissful expression. I could see the change in him, that hundred-foot stare that always glazed their eyes when the narcotic took effect.

I worked swiftly, closing the edges of his wound while my thoughts drifted to Tova.

Reynard had promised he would find him, and I couldn't fault his efforts. The Observers had reported that patrol after patrol had been sent out, some of which the king led himself. Rey had also engaged dragons in the search.

But so far, they'd found nothing.

And as the days passed, I slowly lost hope.

I wiped my tears with the back of my hand and stood up to collect my tools.

'All done, just remember to keep it clean,' I said to the man before returning to Ciesko.

Today was the first day he'd allowed me to work alone. My healing spells were growing stronger, and my non-magical healing already surpassed his other apprentices. Despite all this, Ciesko resisted, and I had the unsettling feeling he was keeping me hidden.

'I'm finished with the last patient. Do you have any other tasks for me?' I asked as I approached the arch healer, but he only sighed deeply, shaking his head.

'You've done a great job, Sana. Your affinity for healing magic is stronger than I'd thought possible, but you can't do too much too quickly.'

Another refusal, another half-arsed excuse.

Ciesko looked at me with the same benevolent smile he used on his patients, but I had already learned to see past his mask.

'You call this "quickly?" I've barely studied the basics. Why do I have to wait for the geas ceremony?' I asked, my fists involuntarily tightening, rehearsing the arguments in my head.

I'd never realised how gratifying it would feel to work the strands of aether. How a simple tug on a person's energy could change the outcome of a disease, or how purging the corrupted strands could clean a wound and speed up healing.

'You're not ready for more,' he answered.

I wanted to scream in frustration. I studied diligently, barely sleeping at night as I made steady progress through all the books he'd given me, while also juggling my responsibilities in the Brotherhood. But asking Ciesko to show me more, teach me more, was like trying to get blood out of a stone.

'Did you know that I conjured fire yesterday?' I asked, my fingers dancing as tiny flames appeared on their tips.

I'd finally done it. After years of failing, I finally understood the flow of aether enough to manipulate magic I had no affinity for. I had lit a bloody candle, all alone in my eerie, empty house, with no one to share my success with.

Then I'd cried myself to sleep.

Ciesko's pupils widened before he grasped my hand and tightened it into a fist, smothering the flames. The benevolent smile slipped off his features like water, and a fear I didn't expect to see flashed in his gaze.

'Go home, Roksana,' he said, patting my shoulder as he avoided my eyes. 'Get some sleep. You've worked hard enough today. My reputation will suffer if people think I exploit my students.'

He was a mage of vast knowledge and experience. Under his patient guidance, my understanding of the aether had grown by leaps and bounds. I'd have blessed the fates for putting him in my way if not for the fact he was also an insufferable arsehole. I'd seen him soothe a dangerous, half-crazed mage with nothing more than a couple of hastily drawn sigils, yet a few tiny flames had made him send me home with no explanation.

I left to wash my hands in the basin while I calmed my thoughts before I tackled the problem head-on. I returned to the arch healer, knowing I couldn't pretend to be oblivious to his manipulations any longer.

'What's the real reason you're stalling my progress?'

His expression darkened, his brows furrowing as he looked at me sharply, the previous joviality completely gone. This was his true face—stern and powerful. But it didn't matter how much the aether danced around him, I would not back down.

'Roksana. I can't tell you. Not yet. But trust me, I have my reasons,' he said.

I exhaled slowly, calling on all the patience I had left.

'Then I'll ask Riordan,' I responded.

'And end up in the Court of Aether's dungeon until the geas ceremony?' Ciesko shrugged, rubbing the bridge of his nose as he shook his head.

'Roksana, vivamancy is feared for good reason. Some believe it's a blessing that our ancestors eradicated it. We have to develop your skills slowly. Your ability is growing too fast, your power blooming in a way I didn't anticipate.'

He stopped, exhaling slowly, as if our conversation had exhausted him.

'Just . . . promise me you'll only practice under my supervision.'

'I can't promise you that,' I said. 'Tova—'

'Is not here,' he interrupted. 'It's been nearly three weeks since your friend vanished. You have to ready yourself for the worst and not push your magic because you think a more advanced spell may help you find him or save his life.'

Why was he doing that again? Pressing and prodding at the rawest part of my soul. Was he testing how much I could take? Did he want me to throw a hissy fit and give up magic?

I steadied myself, fist tightening until nails dug into my skin, grounding me enough to answer.

'I know all of this, but I believe in Reynard. He'll find Tova, and I'll never give up searching until the dwarf or his body turn on my doorstep,' I said harshly, bracing myself for more insensitive comments.

To my surprise, Ciesko's gaze softened, filling with regret.

'Alright, Roksana, but please get some sleep, child. Otherwise, you won't survive long enough to see your friend return.'

By the time I left the infirmary, the sun was beginning to set. Despite the chill breeze from the river, its rays created a pleasant warmth that had me tilting my face to its radiance.

Winter was coming. It had been three months since I'd arrived in Truso, and in that time, the trees had lost most of their leaves—and I'd lost my friend while trying to save another.

As if mirroring my thoughts, a red Acer leaf floated by on a gust of wind and landed at my feet—a sign that nature didn't care about my woes, the seasons rolling by at their own pace.

The streets were full of traders and passersby as I walked to the Brotherhood's mansion to see Boyan. A nice perk of my healer's training had been the ability to ease the cough plaguing the grand master, an ability I conveniently forgot to tell Ciesko about.

Graveyard cough was fatal, but its victims' prognoses depended on their age and overall condition. As much as I couldn't do anything about Boyan's age, my gentle manipulation of his body's aether helped him cope better with the illness. Lately, I'd been experimenting with isolating portions of his lungs that appeared like black, lifeless holes in his life force.

The sentinels inclined their heads in greeting when I entered the building. Ever since I'd rejoined the Brotherhood, I'd been treated with the respect of my old position. Boyan had even given me a new title—Shadow Mage. But it concerned me. If his current shadow were to resent my sudden rise, I could end up in trouble before I knew it.

Just as I was about to knock on the grand master's door, the sound of quick, light footsteps behind me distracted me. I turned, recognising the runner. It was one of the maidservants Lily had assigned to me, and both the haste and the tension on the woman's face made my heart stutter.

'My lady! Wait . . . Mistress Lily . . .' the girl gasped.

I grabbed her arms, steadying her. 'What? What's happened to her?'

I was almost shouting, shaking the poor girl while my mind came up with the worst scenarios.

'Nothing with the mistress, no, but they found him . . . the dwarf. . . The king sent a message, but we couldn't find . . . Here. That's for you,' she said, passing me a letter.

The poor thing looked like she'd been running all over the city, but the relief and worry I felt at her words overwhelmed me. My knees buckled, and I stumbled to the wall, hiding my face in my hands while trying to calm my breathing before I passed out.

'What's going on here?' Boyan said, opening the door, his shadow falling on the stone floor. 'Roksana, are you alright?'

'They found the dwarf, Grand Master,' the girl responded. 'My lady . . . I think it was too much for her.'

A dry, skeletal hand stroked my hair, Boyan's fingers trailing through the strands.

'Go to the east wing,' he said to the maid. 'Find Irsha—he should be there training his recruits. Tell him I require his presence.'

She bolted to fulfil his orders. Her steps were still reverberating through the corridor when Boyan paused, his hand moving to cup my cheek.

'Roksana, look at me!' he commanded.

I raised my tear-streaked face, and he studied my face before embracing me.

'It will be all right, child. The gods favour those with honest hearts. They won't take your dwarf away from you.'

He took me by the elbow, walking me to his chamber, right to the large, plush sofa.

'I don't even know if he is alive. How could you say it's alright when I feel like . . .'

My breath hitched, and the legendary executioner wrapped his arms around me again, pressing my head to his chest.

'What if all they've found is his corpse, Boyan?'

'Then his killers will lie at the foot of his funeral pyre,' he said with such calm reassurance I felt the choking band on my throat loosen a bit. 'But don't yet mourn a man who may still live.'

Boyan's embrace was comforting, and I wondered why I'd never questioned why the ruthless leader had always shown me more love than my father ever did. I could barely recall the man who'd sired me—only his coldness, the absence of tenderness and affection. His trade kept him away more often than not, and eventually, his face faded entirely, replaced by Boyan's.

Unfortunately, as much as I shamelessly wanted to draw strength from the old man, I couldn't stay like this. The weak were prey in the Brotherhood.

I tensed, gathering my courage to pull away, when Boyan stopped me.

'Stay,' he said, his voice wistful. 'Wait for Irsha. He will escort you wherever is needed. When you return, we'll talk.'

I frowned. 'Talk about what?' I asked, pulling away.

'The past, present . . . the future.' He reached out and took my hand. 'But don't worry about it now. Find your friend but be wary of the king. He's a good man, but even if he's sincere, those like us don't mix well with the nobility. We're like a blend of oil and water—you can shake it and stir it, but in the end, they will always separate.'

'How do you . . .? You had Observers follow me. Was that really necessary?' I asked just as a decisive knock rattled the door.

A moment later, Irsha strode in, still in his training clothes.

'You wanted to see me, sir . . . Sana, is everything all right? You look like you've seen an upiór.'[1]

'She just received a message that her heart's kin has been found,' Boyan responded. 'You'll escort her wherever she needs to go. And Irsha—I trust you with her life. Do not fail me, Blade.' His voice had lost all the gentleness he'd directed towards me.

'Of course. When do you want to go, Sana?' Irsha asked, and I realised I hadn't even read the missive still clenched in my fist.

I unfolded it quickly, noting it was already late, and that the retrieval group was waiting for me to join them next to the city gates.

'Shit, we need to go now. They're all waiting. Fuck, wait. I need a horse. Can I take a horse?' I rambled.

I stood rapidly, a chaotic whirlwind of energy, accidentally bumping the side table. Only Irsha's fast reflexes stopped the small crystal rusalka displayed on it from smashing on the floor.

'Yes, take a horse. Irsha can gather travel provisions and a change of clothes,' Boyan said. He stood up, unexpectedly stopping me to grasp my face in a fatherly gesture. Irsha gaped as I awkwardly stood blinking in confusion. 'Look after yourself, Sana. I can't lose my shadow mage.'

There was more to his tone than a simple goodbye, but I was too distraught to think about it. We left his office in a hurry, and only when we got to the horses did I notice that Irsha was oddly silent, looking at me with a frown.

---

1. **Upiór /pron: u-pi-oor/** — an undead being that arises from one cursed upon their death, appearing as a freshly deceased corpse.

'What?' I asked, annoyed by his covert glances as we saddled the mounts.

'Did you know that Boyan is from the Orcish Steppe as well? The way he treats you . . . It got me thinking.'

'Let me stop you there,' I snapped. 'I know it's a little odd, but maybe I just remind him of someone. Or he knows he's dying, and I'm a convenient target for his affection.'

My hands stilled on my horse's neck.

'I'm sorry, Irsha. I'm not angry, it's just too much to think about, especially now.'

'I know, trouble,' he said. 'Come on. Let's go get your wretched dwarf so I can teach him not to worry you so.'

I yelped when he effortlessly lifted me onto the animal's back but didn't waste any time.

People leapt to the side as we galloped through the streets to the city gates. We rode at a breakneck speed, but it still felt like we were taking too long, and the irrational fear that Reynard would set off without me grew stronger with each passing minute.

I bolted through the gates, pulling on the reins when I noticed the king's strapping figure.

He looked even more imposing dressed in hunting armour. A black warhorse danced beneath him, massive and impatient, turning towards us as soon as the hooves of my mare thundered down the cobblestones.

Reynard didn't wear a helmet, and instead of an eyepatch, a fragment of his wolf's mask covered the scarred part of his face. He looked so otherworldly that I gasped when a stray sunray caught the iridescent blue of his ink-black hair.

He found Tova. Gods, he truly did it . . . for me.

I didn't know how to defend myself from the warmth that flooded my body at the sight of him, but my eyes searched for the dwarf.

'Where is he?' I asked when I reined in my horse, facing the king's guards.

'Calm down. We're heading there now. It's a long journey, but the soldiers who found him are heading back—' he said just as my horse reared under me. Irsha's hand landed on my thigh, and I followed his command, tightening my muscles and shortening the reins to calm the animal.

'Your Majesty,' one of Rey's officers said, 'if we leave now, we can be in Ostrava before nightfall. That is, if Lady Roksana and her . . . eh . . . servant can endure the ride.' He turned to Irsha. 'You can ride at the end of the column, good sir.'

I was about to point out the man's error when Irsha spoke first.

'I'm Irsha Vilkor, Master of the Blades. I'm here at the request of Grand Master Boyan of the Dark Brotherhood to escort the Lady Roksana. And we can both endure the ride.'

I frowned, eyeing Irsha with surprise at his strange formality—but his sharp glare was aimed at the officer, staring him down as if he were questioning the man's intelligence.

The officer shifted uneasily, glancing towards the king. Reynard's brows had climbed so high I half expected them to vanish into his hairline. After a beat, Rey nudged his mount forward until it stood beside mine.

'Master Vilkor, you're welcome to stay, of course, but since my men are here, your skills might be better suited to aiding the grand master in the city,' he said, an amused smirk arching the corner of his lips.

'Perhaps, but right now, my duty is to Roksana, both by choice and by the grand master's command. I hope we won't have this discussion again, sire,' Irsha answered calmly, his expression matching Reynard's.

Oh, for the gods' sake, not this again.

I wanted to bash their heads together for delaying our departure. I was clinging onto my sanity by a thread when Reynard's smirk widened at the challenge, and I wondered when they'd draw their blades to find out who was the bigger arsehole.

'I swear, I'll dose both of you with sleeping powder if you don't stop,' I hissed quietly, before adding loudly for the soldiers' benefit, 'Sire, Irsha is my longtime friend, and I would feel better having him beside me in case the situation is . . . worse than expected.'

I placed my hand on Irsha's forearm, frowning when Reynard's eyes narrowed, the amusement vanishing from his expression.

'Fine, Viper, but your bodyguard will ride with mine while you will travel beside me,' he answered before addressing Irsha. 'I hope that isn't too objectionable, Master Vilkor?'

Reynard was behaving oddly. His gaze lingered on my hand on Irsha's arm, his expression darkening with each passing moment.

'Please do as he's asking,' I murmured to Irsha before moving closer to the king. 'Can we go now, please?'

Reynard's hand landed exactly where Irsha's palm had been on my thigh, thumb trailing lightly over my skirt before he moved away.

'When you visited my camp . . . I should have insisted on your promise,' he said, signalling his men to move. My confusion lasted for a moment before I remembered him asking me not to let another man touch me. But Irsha wasn't a man; he was a friend. Besides, I didn't promise Reynard anything.

'But you didn't,' I whispered, nudging the horse into a trot to match the king's gait.

'And we'll have a talk about that later. For now, we need to go. Are you ready to go faster?' he asked, his eyes on the road ahead.

'Yes. After you, Your Majesty,' I answered, my voice trembling with anticipation.

'No, not after me—beside me, Viper. You'll ride beside me, and you'll keep the pace.'

That was my only warning before the warhorse leapt into a gallop, and I had no choice but to match it.

'I'll find a way to repay your kindness,' I said softly, gazing at his face before staring at the cloak that billowed around the king like black wings.

It would be a harsh ride, but even with stiff, aching muscles and a headache from my sleepless night, I couldn't stop wondering how the man I had blinded had found a way to break through the walls I'd built around my heart.

Chapter 36

Reynard

Roksana was swaying in the saddle, barely upright, when I called for a stop to feed the animals. The dark circles under her eyes had only deepened as we travelled.

I should have left her in Truso, I thought for the hundredth time.

As much as I wanted to spare her pain, I couldn't rob her of a chance to say goodbye to her friend. The scout's report on Tova's whereabouts had warned me to prepare for the worst. And while Sana would insist on seeing him immediately, she was exhausted, and I didn't know how much one woman could take. If only I could ensure the dwarf would survive before I let her see him . . .

My men exchanged confused glances as I issued orders, but my gaze kept flicking towards Irsha, who was constantly by Roksana's side. She gasped when he helped her dismount, catching her when her legs gave way. After she steadied, he led her to sit on a tree stump. Sana laughed, complaining that her legs were numb and tingly at the same time, and the wretched assassin crouched beside her, vigorously rubbing her calves.

The reasonable part of me knew they were close friends, that their bond wasn't romantic—but the berserker in me didn't want to listen to reason. I knew it was just a trait of my personality, but at times like this, it felt like there were two of me—man and beast—fighting for control.

'Perun give me strength. He's going too far,' I muttered when he lifted her skirt to knead her muscles, but my curse morphed into a smirk when my anger gave me an idea.

'Sire?' my officer prompted. I turned to him, but my mind was elsewhere.

The soldiers' voices blurred into background noise. Out of the corner of my eye, I saw Irsha extend a cup of warmed honey water to Roskana. My Viper refused at first—until he dropped to one knee, presenting the dented cup like he was offering tribute to his queen.

Bloody idiot. My fists tightened at the sight. *I should have thought of that first.*

Sana laughed, beautiful and carefree, mischief dancing in her eyes as she accepted the cup with a mock regal flourish. She'd needed a distraction, but if I'd have done that, would she have laughed like that for me?

As if sensing my stare, she turned, still smiling, and raised the cup in a silent toast.

I was on the verge of groaning in frustration. I had to close my eyes for a second before I could plaster a fake smile on my face, pretending I didn't notice that Irsha was now rubbing healing salve on the scrapes on her arm.

'For fuck's sake,' I muttered, my hand drifting instinctively to my blade. Perun, who had forged berserkers in fire and madness, was surely testing me today—I was one breath away from challenging the bastard . . . again.

'Your Majesty?' My officer cleared his throat, dragging me back to the moment. 'You were asking about Ostrava . . .'

'What?' I blinked at him, pinching the bridge of my nose as if the small gesture could help me concentrate on the issues at hand.

'You asked about the situation in Ostrava,' he repeated carefully. 'What are your orders, sire? Shall we make camp here, or continue to the town?'

'No stopping,' Roksana said before I could answer, rushing towards us, hissing with every step she took. As her breath misted in the air, the chill breeze gave her pale skin a luminous glow, making the tiny laugh lines around her eyes even more visible.

'I don't think you can ride any more today,' I told her. 'You can barely walk, Sana. The last thing I need is you toppling from your horse mid-canter.'

'I can manage,' she said with a glint of defiance in her eyes. 'And we can rest when we get to Ostrava. Irsha said that's where we're meeting the group who found Tova.'

As if reeled by an invisible thread, her assassin came closer.

'If you're worried, sire,' he said, gaze flicking to me, 'I'll take her on my horse.' He turned to her, tone softer as he tugged on the end of her braid. 'Don't give me that look, trouble. He's right—you look like shit. The only way I see you riding without holding us back is with someone holding you up.'

That was it. I'd had enough. It was the right thing to do, but if the assassin thought I'd let him ride with my Sana cradled to his chest, he was sorely mistaken.

'An excellent idea,' I said smoothly. 'But as your duty is *guarding* the Lady Roksana, I think it best if she joins me instead. My stallion can carry a man in full armour and a week's supplies. He won't even notice her on his back.'

Before Irsha could reply, I reached for Sana's hand and tugged her gently towards me, sighing with relief when she didn't resist.

'I don't think it's necessary,' she said, though she didn't take her hand from mine.

'I'm not taking any chances, Viper.' I looked at her, then turned to Irsha. 'In fact, in order to keep Sana safe, I require your expertise, Blade. Please ride ahead with the captain of my guard. Make sure our lodgings in Ostrava are secure. We're close to the southern border, and someone has already tried their luck attacking her. I want the area cleared and locked down before we arrive. Make haste.'

The request, though politely phrased, wasn't well received. Irsha wasn't the type of man to be ordered around—even by his king.

'I would be happy to oblige, but my duty is to stay beside Roksana,' he huffed, nostrils flaring as he stepped towards me.

'Well, then, I'll have to insist on camping here until my man reassures me that all potential threats are eliminated,' I said with a smile. My satisfaction was short-lived when I felt Sana's hand slip from mine.

She walked to her friend, and his gaze instantly softened. 'Please, no more arguments . . . could you do it? For me?' she asked.

The bastard had the audacity to take her hand and kiss it as he looked me in the eye. 'For you? Always. Whatever you command, trouble,' he told her, but the smirk was all for me.

'Great,' I ground out. 'We'll rest for an hour to give you a head start.' Addressing my officer, I said, 'Ensure Master Vilkor has the freshest mount and anything else he needs. Tell the captain to get ready, too. Then ensure the rest of our horses are sound and let me know when they've recovered enough to ride to Ostrava.'

The man saluted before walking away, leaving me alone with Roksana. When I came closer, she barely paid me any attention; her gaze still followed the assassin master.

'If fate allows, you'll see Tova tonight,' I said, and she finally looked at me.

'I know. Thank you for this, and for taking me even if I'm a burden.' She sighed. 'But do you really have to behave like such an arse towards Irsha?'

'I don't . . .' I tried to deny it, but she was right. My pleasure at sending the assassin ahead melted away under her stare. 'Come, Viper. You are not a burden, just tired. I won't take you anywhere if you're ready to faint,' I answered, deflecting her question before leading her to the same tree trunk she'd been sitting on and wrapping my cloak around her.

'I don't need your cloak, and I can ride by myself,' she protested with a deep yawn. 'I don't know why you both think I'm such a lady in distress in need of constant attention.'

Leaves crunched under my knee when I knelt, taking Roksana's hand. 'I would never think of you in that way, Sana. You are skilled, intelligent, and so, too bold for your own good, but you are not a warrior. Every single man here has spent years in the saddle, and even they're tired.' I gently tapped her nose, wrapping the cloak tighter around her. 'You can't be the best at everything, so don't argue with your king. Let me be your knight in shining armour, at least for today.'

Her shoulders sagged slightly before mischief teased the corner of her mouth, and I prepared for the worst.

'What if I prefer an orc chieftain with scars that prove his prowess?' Her hand drifted to my cheek, fingers brushing the jagged flesh.

She bewitched me. The early winter sun slipped from behind the clouds and lit the golden flecks in her eyes, mesmerising me. I found myself falling into their hazel depths, the beast inside me revelling at her touch. The air shimmered around her, an invisible force reaching for me, its touch an intimate caress, a breeze on overheated skin.

Sana removed her hand, and I inhaled sharply, as if awakened from a dream. 'Fine, then be my good little killer, and do as you're told,' I said with a soft chuckle that hid how deeply the moment had affected me.

I stood up, patting her head as I imagined one of the orcish brutes would do, until she swatted me away with a scoffing laugh.

'My lady,' someone behind me said, 'Master Irsha requested sustenance for you.'

I spun around to see a squire holding a few travel cakes and a cup of water. The boy meant well, but he was too close, and I was so on edge that I wanted to shove the cakes down his throat and send him on his way with a kick in the rear.

I'm fucking jealous of the squire, now? I thought, listening to Sana thank him for the simple soldier's fare.

'That was thoughtful of him. Ask him to wait, please. I need a word before he sets off,' I said to the boy calmly, unwilling to lose control over a child. 'Once you do that, return and serve the lady.'

Roksana turned towards the forest, closing her eyes as she devoured the rations on her lap. She pulled my cloak up, and I watched in contentment as her face disappeared into the soft fur of the collar.

I promise you, my light, I'll be the man to bring you joy, I thought before walking away to talk to Irsha. After procuring the necessary quill and parchment, I spotted him next to the horses and pretended not to see his eyes roll when I approached.

'What else can I do for you, sire?'

'Take this,' I said, passing him a folded sheet. His eyebrow rose at my private seal on the document. 'It's an order that allows you to command my men. Tova . . . the last report wasn't optimistic, so do what you can to soften the blow for her.'

Irsha's back straightened, and his expression instantly grew serious. 'How bad is it?'

'Would I be speaking to you now without good reason? Do what's necessary to spare her heart,' I said, and he nodded, respecting my unspoken words.

'If I knew you were doing this to protect her, I would have played into your hand,' he muttered.

With a humourless laugh, I replied, 'I'm not that noble, Blade. Remember that next time you decide to lift her skirt.'

He smirked, mounting his horse. 'Oh, I will . . . and I won't forget to invite you to watch either, Your Majesty,' he said, kicking his horse forward before I could answer.

I watched him leave, more amused than annoyed by his arrogance, then walked over to my stallion. He was already grazing when I approached him with a handful of oats. Even after a strenuous ride, he looked fresh and greeted me with a friendly neigh when I patted his neck.

'Behave and smooth your step, my friend. You'll be carrying precious cargo,' I whispered into his ear, and he nudged me with his muzzle.

An hour passed, and I ordered the men to saddle up. As we were getting ready to leave, Sana came to me, my cloak folded over her arm. 'Thank you, I'm feeling much better,' she said, passing me the cloak and turning to leave.

She hadn't taken two steps before my arm encircled her waist, and I lifted her onto my horse. 'No escaping the inevitable, Viper. You're riding with me to Ostrava,' I said, jumping up behind her and pulling her close. I winced as her body stiffened.

'Reynard, this is ridiculous,' she complained.

Why is she so against it? If her objections were genuine, I wouldn't force her to ride with me. Taking the reins, I bent to her ear, asking her a question before deciding my next step. 'Does riding with me repulse you so much that you'd rather risk a fall?'

'You don't repulse me. It's just . . . I remember what you said about my scent and your reaction. I don't want to cause any trouble,' she responded with a small shrug, and I couldn't help but smile.

'I promise I won't sniff your neck. Is there anything else you're worried about?'

Sana shook her head. 'No, if you don't mind your soldiers seeing their king being so . . . gentle and caring. I wouldn't forgive myself if I spoiled your stern war hero image,' she teased with a chuckle, making me feel better than I had in days.

I ensured she was sitting comfortably before easing my stallion into a trot, letting the rest of the men follow.

'How I treat my wo . . . friend has no impact on my ability to lead them or my image as king,' I said, and contrary to my earlier words, inhaled her scent.

Roksana didn't answer, sitting stiffly against me. Still, as my stallion's steps soothed her, she relaxed, melting into my embrace. I felt the tip of her nose touch the exposed skin of my neck.

'You smell like lemongrass and musk,' she whispered as she placed her head on my chest. Her finger traced down to my collarbone, sending pleasant shivers along my spine.

A gentle smile teased my lips as I pressed her closer to my body. 'Be careful, my light, or I'll think you like me,' I teased as she yawned.

'I like you . . . even though I know I shouldn't. And I'm not your light,' she muttered.

I leant down and kissed the top of her head, closing my eyes to savour the moment. 'Oh, sweet lady, but you are. You are the light of hope in the deepest night, my Sanika.'

Sana turned to look at me. 'You shouldn't say things like that,' she murmured. But though her eyes were serious, I caught the smile tugging at her lips.

We lapsed into silence after that exchange, and I watched as she fought a losing battle against exhaustion, drifting off until jostled awake a few times by the ride. In the end, I placed my hand on her cheek, pressing her head to my chest. 'Sleep, you are safe with me.'

I waited until I knew she was deeply asleep so a change of pace wouldn't startle her before pushing my mount into a canter. Sana whimpered quietly, but didn't wake up. I adjusted her position, trusting my horse with the road while I cared for my lightly-snoring bundle.

Gods, she must have been exhausted. Sana's mouth parted in her sleep, and she looked even younger than usual. I risked pressing my lips to her temple, gently kissing her soft skin. I lingered a little longer, savouring her warmth.

Finally, the beast inside and the man in charge were in agreement: She was mine, and woe betide those who dared to defy my claim.

I only had to convince my Sanika that she belonged in my arms.

Chapter 37

Reynard

Several hours passed, and even I was finding the ride hard. The chill misted my breath, and my muscles were stiff from keeping the same pose. The sun hung low over the horizon, blinding us with its last red glow as we crested the hill. Verdant plains, now bare in anticipation of the upcoming snow, framed the lights of Ostrava that highlighted the houses as dusk settled and my unit descended en masse. We were halfway to Tivalaran, and I toyed with the idea of checking the groundworks a report had mentioned.

'Let's go and face whatever fate's prepared for us,' I whispered, nudging the horse onward.

The town welcomed us with nervous bustle, unusual for this time of the day. Many people were still on the streets, likely curious about the sudden arrival of the large group of armed men. The town council was apparently also in the square, the three elderly men squeezing their hats in their hands as if they didn't know whether to drop to the ground or bow their heads.

'My lord, your herald arrived a short while ago. If we'd known you were coming, we would have prepared the town, a welcome. . .' the eldest started, but quickly stopped, looking at his companions. 'We assigned a house for you and your men. He said it would be enough, your herald that is—'

'Herald?' I asked, confused, until I saw the master of the Blades heading towards me with such a thunderous expression that I instantly moved away from the council.

One look at the woman in my arms and he exhaled slowly. 'She's sleeping, thank the gods. We need to talk. Tova . . . he's in rough shape. I dragged a healer over to sort him out before she sees him, but I'm not sure if he'll survive the night,' he said.

I nodded, pulling the cloak tighter around Sana while pondering what to do.

'Her quarters are ready?' I asked, and when he nodded, I slowly, and as gently as I could, passed her to Irsha. 'Take her there and point me to Orenson. I need to see his condition for myself.'

I wouldn't be able to hold her off for long, but I wanted to be ready and ensure the healer spared nothing to save the dwarf's life.

Irsha nodded again, and I clasped his shoulder, knowing he would guard her with his life.

He pointed out the houses. 'Our quarters are in the house by the market—the one with carved flowers and vines on the front. Tova and some of your men are in the healer's house. If you look to the left, you'll see the banner.'

'Good. I'll send someone to bring her as soon as I can,' I replied. 'Try to prepare her for the worst.' I ran a hand through my hair, an old habit in times of stress. I wanted to hold her if the worst came to pass but would not force her affection today. 'She'll take it better if it comes from you,' I said. 'Sana needs a friend more than she needs a king.'

Irsha sent me a questioning look, but I shrugged and looked to the side as he carried Roksana away. I was probably making a mistake by letting her sleep, but I didn't want her rushing in unprepared.

Night had fully settled over the town, covering everything in a grey veil, and the mists slipped in, giving the fae lanterns an otherworldly hue.

I walked to the healer's house, only briefly stopping before the town council. 'Thank you so much for your hospitality. Rest assured we'll be leaving in the morning. No ceremony or special treatment is needed. Just feed my men and give us privacy.'

My brief speech was met with consternation, but I didn't stay to listen to their objections. Soldiers saluted, opening the infirmary door without being prompted. The stench of decay was so strong I stopped. Even being used to the smell of death on the battlefield, I gagged.

A young woman appeared, wearing the uniform of an apprentice healer, stained with blood and other fluids. She bowed, and didn't straighten, her whole body shaking.

'Don't be afraid. Just tell me where the patient is,' I said, and she gestured to a heavy oak door carved with healing ivy.

I entered, covering my face with a sleeve in a vain attempt to block some of the odour, only to see my men holding down a crazed dwarf. His eyes were glazed with fever, and the healer was standing in the corner, clutching a vial.

'What's going on here?' I demanded.

'He's delirious, sire,' one of my men answered. 'He shouts and fights as if he were still locked inside the cage we found him in.'

I approached the haughty dwarf, now reduced to a shadow of himself, and looked at his emaciated face.

'You . . . I know you . . .' he rasped when his gaze landed on me.

'Let him go,' I ordered.

He instantly jumped off the examination table and grabbed a metal instrument, holding it like a weapon.

'Tova . . .' I said, approaching him with caution. 'Sana is here. You want to see her, right?'

'My drah'sa?' he asked, lowering the metal tool.

'Gods, he listened . . .' The healer rushed towards me, pushing the vial into my hand. 'Make him drink this, Your Majesty.'

'Yes, your drah'sa,' I said, taking another step towards the dwarf and wondering whether I should give him a chance or grab him by the scruff of his neck and force him to drink whatever potion the healer had given me. 'She came for you. But first, you need to drink this medicine. You don't want her to worry.'

'Is she worried?' he asked, calming as if the mention of Sana alone was enough to bring him back from a mindless rage.

'She is. Your Sana was looking for you. She told me to find you, but you must drink this before you see her,' I told him, and, in a moment of inspiration, added, 'Your condition is dangerous for her.'

That was the right thing to say. As soon as I mentioned a danger to Roksana, he reached out, snatching the vial from my hand and emptying it in one gulp. I stood frozen, realising where the stench came from.

Three fingers of his right hand were mutilated beyond recognition, pus oozing from broken bones and torn muscles, with maggots writhing in the mangled flesh. Tova didn't seem to care, as if he no longer felt any pain there.

I recalled the words of the army healer when I had argued against amputation in the past: *There are wounds no magic can help. All you can do is remove the rotten flesh before it kills the soldier.*

I nodded to the healer. 'Do what you must.'

Tova pushed the vial onto the table and staggered, taking a step back before landing heavily on his rear. 'Tell her . . . Młot sent men to kill her, the mages, the kingdom is falling apart, and he blames her . . . Wiosna, the miners . . . all dead; it's a fucking tomb.'

He fell back, head lolling to the side, and the healer sprang into action.

'Put him on the table. Quickly!' he said, and my men rushed to assist him. 'The sedative won't work for long. I have one chance to save him.'

The healer's apprentice stepped in, and together, they began preparing the dwarf.

I stepped aside to allow the medics to work and beckoned to one of my soldiers. 'Tell me what happened, and as soon as the healer finishes, send someone to bring his friends from our quarters.' A part of me knew I should call Sana now, but I didn't want to delay a procedure that could save Tova's life.

The man briefed me, and I discovered it was pure luck that my men had stumbled upon the wagon returning to Wiosna. Its wheels were stuck in the mud up to the axles, and the dwarven merchants had argued whether to unload the merchandise and dig the wagon out or abandon it.

'We found him in a pig crate, my king,' the soldier said. 'Rotting in his own filth. I don't think they cared if he were dead or alive when they handed him to Młot, as long as there was a body.'

My jaw tightened. I wasn't Tova's friend, but for the pain his imprisonment had caused Roksana, I would ensure Młot paid for this. My thoughts of revenge stopped abruptly when the heavy door was thrown open and Sana walked in, freezing in the doorway.

I moved to intercept her, but as if my movement spurred her to action, Roksana sucked in a lungful of air and rushed towards the still figure on the table.

'Tova! I'm here. I found you, tinkerer. Please . . . please open your eyes. Please, talk to me . . . Tova!' Tears streamed down her face as she wrapped her arms around the dwarf, cuddling him as if she hadn't noticed his dirty clothes and the layer of filth that covered his body.

'Please step away, my lady,' the healer said, gently pulling her away from the table. 'We need to prepare him. His hand needs to be removed if he is to live.'

'What?! Removed?' Sana stared at the healer in horror. 'But his work
. . . He needs both hands. You can't just chop one off.'

'If I don't, he will die.'

The man was blunter than I'd like, but Sana didn't struggle when he
pulled her away, thrusting her in my direction. I instinctively wrapped
my arms around her. She was shaking, but as I tried to take her to a
different room, she looked at me in such a way that I instantly knew not
even a dragon could force her to leave.

We watched as they stripped him of his dirty clothes, leaving only a
modesty wrap around his hips. Hot tears fell on my hands as Sana silently
cried, her gaze sliding over his swollen flesh covered with colourful bruises. Tova had been beaten, starved, and gods knew what else, and the more
injuries that appeared as they removed the filth from his skin, the more
Sana stiffened in my embrace.

When he was prepared, and the healer had placed his instruments on
the table, drawing sigils to aid in the procedure, the shimmer of aether
caught my attention. My skin prickled in a wave of goosebumps, but
it hadn't come from the healer. Small jolts of energy sparked where I
touched Roksana's bare skin. It felt like the air before a storm, heavy with
tension, and my heart sped up with the prickle of fear.

'Sana?' I whispered, tightening my grip.

She raised her head, looking at me with eyes that had lost all humanity.
I'd seen that look once before—the day she'd struck me with the hairpin.
I wasn't even certain if she could see me as green fire danced in the depths
of her eyes. Her breath came in laboured pants while something moved
around us, an invisible tide shifting, pushing me away when she took a
step forward.

The healer frowned, looking around in confusion before shaking his
head and leaning down to make the first cut, hissing when a red welt
appeared on his hand as if a whip had struck it. My ears popped, briefly

muffling all sound, but it did nothing to ease the pressure of her magic filling the room.

'No!' Her voice echoed around us, hollow and emotionless, freezing us in place.

The sound of steel hitting the stone reverberated in total silence when the healer dropped the knife. He retreated in haste, eyes wide and filled with terror as she approached the examination table. Sana took the mangled remnant of the dwarf's hand in hers, and the scent of lilac and honey overpowered the stench of decay.

The pressure dropped, letting us move. I stepped towards Roksana when the clattering of falling instruments snapped my attention to the old man. The healer pressed his hands to his chest, looking at Roksana as if she were a monster come to devour us, his pale lips whispering a single word.

'Vivamancer.'

Chapter 38

Roksana

The healer's clinic should have smelled different. With all the ingredients on the shelves, a polished wooden table for patients, and meticulously scrubbed floors, it should have been a place of peace and healing, but right now, it was anything but. With so many people crammed inside, it was pure chaos.

Tova's hand hung limply from mine, the slimy flesh peeling under my touch. I didn't know what to do, but I couldn't let him lose it.

He's resilient, and the healer said it'll save his life.

The voice in my head sounded reasonable, but I was past reason. Tova would eventually adapt and overcome the disability, but I couldn't stand another man losing a part of themselves because they'd helped me.

'Not fucking happening,' I whispered through my tears.

The power that had awakened inside me once again silenced the voices in the room, allowing me to focus on my injured friend. I may not have known what to do, but the aether surrounding me felt almost sentient as it seethed.

I recognised the emerald inferno that had stopped the healer. It was the pressure I'd felt all my life—the desire, the need to touch the power, to feel it coursing through me . . . and now, for the first time, it had answered my call.

Tova's hand twitched in my grasp before his fingers hung limply again. I looked down, battling the stench of gangrene threatening to overpower my senses.

If I can purge the pus seeping from his wounds, it would stop poisoning the rest of his body. Poisoning . . . If I treat this like it's poison . . .

An idea emerged, and I didn't question the inspiration. Anything was better than sitting here uselessly watching him die. I inhaled, shaking with an emotion I couldn't identify, and focused on Tova's life energy. It felt wrong—corrupted by the sickness that consumed his flesh. I called to it, following my instincts, accepting the poison as my own, welcoming it, but the putrid liquid resisted.

'Fuck. No, not like that . . . I need to merge with it first,' I muttered, preparing myself. I wove my aether into the tainted strands in his body, just like I had for Jagon's apprentice.

Agony burned through my chest, my free hand squeezing into a fist so tight that my nails drew blood, and I stifled a moan. *I can control this. I'm no longer a clueless, uneducated apprentice. Pain will not defeat me,* I told myself over and over again until my despair gave way to sharp focus.

I searched my memories, trying to recall everything Ciesko had taught me, everything I'd learned from Jagon and the dusty volumes I'd studied during my time in Wiosna. My fingers weaved all the sigils I remembered, desperate to find one that would help.

'Sana, please, let the healer work,' Reynard said, appearing behind me and placing a hand on my shoulder.

I shrugged him off. 'Step away,' I snarled, focusing on my task while the power inside me strengthened, spreading its tendrils until I understood what to do.

Reynard's grasp tightened for a moment, but he let his hand drop and took a step back.

I concentrated completely on the aether, marvelling as it changed from barely visible threads to solid, interwoven strands that filled the world with life-giving energy. They were bright and powerful everywhere except for Tova's hand. I could still see the traces, the echoes of what had been, but the aether there was a mess of blackened, withered fibres, the emerald streaks of my power flashing within.

'Come to me,' I whispered, calling on my power. The flashes transformed into pulses, growing in strength and anchoring the damaged strands. They flowed towards my hand, twisting and weaving with my essence, becoming a part of me. They resisted at first, refusing to detach from Tova, but soon my magic overwhelmed them, and they peeled away from his flesh.

My breath hitched when I realised it had worked. Tova moaned, jerking in response, but the flesh, now free from the rot, warmed under my touch, telling me exactly what I must do.

I briefly looked at Reynard. 'Hold him.' I issued the curt command, uncaring that I was ordering a king.

Rey put his hands on Tova's shoulders, pressing him down.

'If you know what you're doing, I'll help the best I can,' he said, 'but Sana, don't let him die because you're worried he'll blame you. As long as he survives, he won't—just like I don't . . . at least not anymore.'

His voice was so calm, so reasonable, but I could barely hear him as I was worked like a woman possessed. Broken strands were cut away, and as I whispered beneath my breath, new strands blossomed into life. My mind directed and wove them into the damaged areas, creating new, healthy prongs and supporting those weakened or crippled.

As I worked, something happened. Tova's breath deepened, his heartbeat steadied, and the tissue, which, moments ago, looked rotten, started bleeding. Fresh, brownish dwarven blood replaced the foul slime, while fragments of bone and flesh fell to the ground, pushed out by strong white bone and pinkish flesh.

'Zivie, Mother of Healing, help us. What are you doing, woman? This is forbidden magic! You can't transform his essence. He is a sentient being. Stop it—you are creating a monster!' The healer behind me was frantic, trying to pull me away.

'Take him away and ensure he doesn't disturb her,' Reynard snapped, and the commotion that followed nearly distracted me from my task. I worked as fast as I could as the healer continued to shout, still struggling with the guards.

'You may stem the infection,' the old man said, 'but his hand will never work again! There's too much bone and muscle missing. You will condemn him to a world of suffering where even a touch of wind will cause him pain!'

The healer was determined to stop me, but his words had the opposite effect.

'And how is chopping his hand off any better?' I sneered, but he was right. I'd removed the gangrene and its corruption, but though the flesh now looked healthy, it was still broken and torn. Unable to feel any sort of triumph, I felt a sob trying to break free.

Tova would live, but his hand was more a pointless outgrowth than a working limb, useful for his inventions. Worse, I didn't know how to stop the bleeding. The rejuvenated tissue oozed profusely, but I didn't trust the healer to ask him for advice. I suspected he wouldn't be keen to help, anyway.

'Fuck!' I cursed, slamming my hands on the wooden table. Aether spread over the surface like green lightning, hitting the dwarf before sinking into his body, which absorbed it like a dry sponge.

Tova moaned softly, his spine arching, eyelids fluttering as whatever sedative they had given him wore off. Whatever my outburst had done to him, he no longer appeared to be on the brink of death. Colour returned to his face, his muscles tensed under my touch, and I faced the dread of telling him he might never have use of his hand again.

How does anyone give this kind of news to a friend?

I shut my eyes, squeezing them so tight my head hurt. My hands tightened on the wooden planks, digging into its surface so hard a splitter pierced the sensitive pads.

I knew no one could create flesh out of thin air, but had anyone ever tried?

Tova groaned again, the remaining fingers of his mangled hand twitching on the table. If he were awake, he would tell me not to worry, that he would build himself a prosthetic—

That's it.

I didn't need flesh, but something that could replace it. He was a tinkerer—he didn't care for a pretty hand, but he needed it working.

But what could replace the missing tissue . . .

My mind latched onto a memory: Tova bounding into my infirmary, waving around his newest invention, a contraption I didn't understand, but remembered commenting that it looked just like a light elf's hand.

The power inside me responded, weaving itself around my hand and his, seeping into the table. The wood swelled, glowing and changing, becoming pliable as it enveloped my friend's ruined hand. I bit my lip while the aether flowed like water as it merged with Tova's life force, the wood transforming into bone and tendons. I watched with perverse fascination as it became whole, a seamless fusion of fibre and flesh.

Thought made form. I'd imagined his hand whole, the memory of his invention brought to life by my magic. I blinked, seeing veins on the back of Tova's new hand. *Did that just pulse? Did I . . . ?*

'Monster!' the healer howled, startling me. 'You're a godsdamned monster!'

The power I'd used for this miracle slipped from my control. The dwarf's hand tightened into a fist, the three perfectly formed wooden fingers moving in unison.

I didn't have time to admire my work. Tova's eyes flew open, and he screamed my name. His dark pupils held an ocean of suffering, but when I tried to withdraw my aether, I couldn't. Panic flooded my mind as the power grew angrier, unwilling to return to me. Untamed and restless, it sought a new target.

'Sana, stop! Please stop!' Tova shouted, pulling his hand away, tearing the connection between us.

I tried, but I couldn't. The precarious control I'd had over my magic was gone, and I became the tool of my power rather than its master.

'Get him away from me,' I hissed through clenched teeth, unable to look at Reynard, begging fate for him to understand.

I cried in relief when Tova was dragged away, and I watched helplessly as the table came to life, growing new branches, each one reaching for Reynard and his burden. I now understood why Ciesko wouldn't teach me vivamancy, why the healer called me a monster. I didn't wield the power of creation; it wielded *me*. It was as if the aether possessed my mind, and it wanted to change, to transform, to shape life into countless fresh forms.

I was helpless to stop it.

'Leave! I can't control it . . .' I muttered, bent over the table, coughing up blood while I desperately attempted to restrain the flow of power. Pressure built in my head as blood dripped from my nose, staining the wood. My knees buckled, and I would have crumbled to the floor if Reynard hadn't caught me, hissing when the emerald magic reached for him.

'Don't touch me!' I screamed, afraid of what it would do to him, but he didn't let go.

'Tell me what to do! How can I help you? I'm not leaving you, Viper. Not even your power can cast me out.' He grasped my chin, forcing me to look at him, but all I could see was his eye glowing gold with wild magic.

The berserker took the reins. I looked into the soul of a beast, knowing he stood with me against this monstrous force, but in my attempt to save Tova, I'd doomed us all.

'I don't know . . .' My throat was so tight that even those words barely escaped. I used all my energy to stop the magic from reaching for him, directing it inwards.

Let it be me. If you need to tear something apart, let it be me. Don't hurt him, please, I cried, bargaining with a force I didn't understand.

A crash shook the room, the door bouncing off its hinges as Irsha stormed in, roaring my name like a raging bull, his face still marked with traces of my sleeping powder. He looked me in the eye, shock twisting his face into a terrifying mask as he rushed towards me.

Reynard shouted a warning, but Irsha was faster. Before the king could stop him, Irsha grasped my neck with well-aimed pressure, and I fell into a welcome oblivion.

Chapter 39

Roksana

'You're a healer. Why aren't you more concerned about your patient? It's been two days, and she hasn't woken up.' Irsha's voice broke through the fog enveloping my mind.

'She's no patient of mine. I refuse to have anything to do with such an abomination. The only reason you're alive is because that . . . that *thing* used up all her aether. The gods know what else she would've done. You saw what happened to the dwarf—what kind of degenerate king would allow her to live?'

'Clearly a wise one, you prejudiced bastard. If you weren't the only healer in this fucking town I'd snap your neck for those words.' Irsha was seething. I heard his steps as he moved, which surprised me into opening my eyes. 'Guards! Take this fool and lock him up, then report him to the king. This fucker wants to murder the king's woman!'

'Your king can't silence me! I've already reported it to the arch healer and the Council of Mages. She needs to be detained, not coddled and cared for.' The healer's high-pitched screeching made me wince and motivated me to sit up.

'Oh, shut up, you idiot,' I groaned.

Sitting up proved harder than I expected, but I wanted to be ready in case someone followed the illustrious healer's advice.

'Oh, for fuck's sake.' The unmistakable *swish* of a thrown dagger fused with a pained squeal before a large, calloused hand landed on my forehead. 'Lie down, trouble. Anything I can get you?' Irsha's voice made me smile, and I turned my head to look at my friend. He was sporting an impressive black eye that hadn't been there when I'd left him snoring on the bed.

'What happened to you? Where's Tova?' I asked.

'Your bloody king happened. The arsehole thought I was killing you, and before I knew it, he'd punched me in the face so hard I hit the wall and didn't get back up. And Tova's on his third breakfast right now—three fucking chickens back-to-back and a dozen scrambled eggs to go with it. If we stay here any longer, I worry for this town's winter supplies.'

'So, he's fine, then.' I sighed with relief, briefly closing my eyes. My misadventure with vivamancy might have been a catastrophe, but as long as Tova was alive, I didn't care. I would deal with the consequences as they came—and judging by the healer's reaction, they would come sooner rather than later. If the other mages reacted like him, then Ciesko's prediction of being locked up in the Court of Aether's dungeon might come true.

'Fine?' Irsha said. 'Damn dwarf's more than fine. Looks like your magic didn't just bring him back to life but gave him the energy of three men. He hasn't slept, is constantly eating, and thoroughly enjoying his new hand.'

'Well, you can't say I do things half-arsed.' I chuckled as my friend fluffed my pillows. 'Irsha, I'm . . . I'm sorry I drugged you, but you know better than to try to stop me.'

'And I thought I taught you better. Never disarm your protector, Sana. Never. What would have happened if I hadn't woken up and helped you get out of this mess? Your kingling had no idea what to do. He was just staring into your eyes like some lovesick buck.'

'He's not my . . . anything,' I said, straightening up, feeling strangely rejuvenated despite the incident.

'Are you sure? Because you called out to him in your sleep, and he sat here two whole days, barking at anyone who came too close. Besides, no man—not even the king—punches an assassin master in the face unless the woman in his arms is more important than his life,' Irsha said, helping me to sit. 'So tell me what's going on between you.'

'Nothing. I'm a dark sister and he's the king of fucking Dagome. There's no reality where there'd be something between us.'

'And if he wasn't the king?' Irsha wouldn't let it go, and I sighed heavily because it was the question I'd asked myself a thousand times.

'It's complicated. Without him . . . you saw how he found Tova.'

He rolled his eyes. 'What a perfect nonanswer, but that's not you, Sana. Have you forgotten how to trust me during your time with the dwarves?' he asked, tapping his chest. 'Come on, trouble, your secret is safe here.'

'If he weren't the king, I'd climb him like a damn tree. Is that what you wanted to hear? He is different than any man I've known . . . No offence, Blade, but even *you* think twice before ordering me around—he just does it. But he is also so gentle. Like he wants to make things better for me even if he has to force me to accept it. And he keeps saying things that make me . . . melt.'

I bit my lip, unsure if I should say more, but somehow the words came out of my lips. 'I like his touch . . . I like when he is firm with me.' I lowered my head. 'I know that's not right, but I can't help it.'

Irsha's eyes brightened, and he cupped my cheek. 'There is nothing wrong if both of you enjoy it. But you're refusing to give in to this. Why?' His voice was gentle, his hand stroking my back, encouraging me to be honest with him—with myself.

'Because I'm scared that whatever this is, or could be, will never be enough for me. I can't share him. I can't be some sort of . . . royal mistress. I will not be some dirty little secret, hidden and ashamed. Yet . . . I'm tired of resisting. Sometimes I want him to overwhelm my senses, leave me no choice but to take him. How insane is that?' I stopped suddenly, smacking him in the chest. 'That's not something I should be telling you anyway. For fuck's sake, you used to be my lover.'

Irsha chuckled, pulling me closer. 'That's exactly what you should've told me, sweetheart. Now I know when he barks around you like an overgrown guard dog, I don't have to think about sinking a knife in his heart. Trust me, I really wanted to during this journey.'

'You're impossible.' I laughed, ruffling his hair. 'Don't touch my king. I like him . . . a little?'

'I'm glad to hear I don't have to worry about a knife in my heart—and to see you awake, Sanika. Master Vilkor, would you give us a moment, or should I call the guards to arrest you like the healer?'

I stifled a moan at seeing Reynard standing in a doorway with a tray, glaring at us. I recognised that expression. He meant every word.

Irsha stood up and bowed theatrically. 'Of course, sire. I was only reassuring Sana that no one could force her hand,' he said, marching towards the door. For a moment, I thought he was going to collide with Reynard, but with a grin, he slid to the side and left.

The door snapped shut behind him, but my eyes were on Rey, whose jaw was so tight and sharp you could cut bread with it.

'Next time he crawls onto your bed, I'm going to chop off his hands,' he said casually, placing the tray on the table and sitting beside me. 'I come bearing gifts. Mind you, I had to fight off a very hungry dwarf to get them.'

I cursed under my breath, believing his threat while a blush warmed my cheeks. I wondered how much of our conversation he'd heard.

'So, you stole the last crumbs from a starving dwarf? It's a miracle you are still alive,' I quipped, hoping to distract him.

'I wouldn't come with crumbs. The ladies of Ostrava take it as a point of honour to provide us with enough baked goods to feed an army. I snatched an apple crumble for you because a little—well, not so little—bird told me it's your favourite.'

I gasped, only now realising the mouthwatering aroma was winter apples with cinnamon and honey.

'Oh . . . you didn't.' I stuck my finger in the crumble, scooping up the delicious goodness and putting it in my mouth. My eyes closed, and I moaned with delight as sweet rapture coated my tongue.

'Sanika . . .' Reynard's voice, low and husky, turned the pleasure into need.

My eyes fluttered open as he took my hand and lifted it to his mouth. He licked my finger clean, tongue expertly teasing the confection from its surface, lips opening to draw it into his mouth. I watched, hypnotised. His eye burned with savage hunger, a golden halo slowly overtaking the grey iris.

'Rey?' I moaned.

Gods, did I just do that?

I swallowed back a nervous laugh, looking down at the sound of ripping linen. Reynard's other hand had grasped the bedding so hard that the fabric tore.

He's trying to restrain himself . . . for me, I thought, feeling him move back. I gave in to my instincts, leaned forward, and wrapped my arms around his neck, pulling myself onto his lap.

He stiffened, but only for a moment, then his arms locked around me, crushing me to his chest before he exhaled, tension melting from his frame. I'd only wanted to stop him from withdrawing, but as my world disappeared in his embrace, I sighed, closing my eyes and placing my head on his shoulder.

The world won't end if I cuddle the king, will it? I asked myself as I nuzzled the crook of his neck.

Reynard had become so much more than a means of destroying Jagon and securing the Brotherhood's future. I couldn't allow myself more than a few stolen moments, but I craved his touch, enjoying the strength it gave me.

Rey shifted, his breath more ragged as his embrace tightened into an iron band that allowed no chance of escape.

'I can't . . . I—Sanika, you looked so forlorn that I felt real fear for the first time in . . .' Reynard shuddered, then took a deep, steadying breath. 'How do I even say this? When you saved Tova with your magic, I was amazed, but gods, the look in your eyes when you lost control? I've never been so frightened. I thought I was losing you,' he said quietly, his voice breaking.

I felt something flutter in my chest and reached up, stroking my fingers through his dark hair. Gripping the silken strands, I pulled him close, my lips trailing over his ear. 'Thank you, Rey. For finding Tova, for escorting me here . . . even for the apple crumble, you thoughtful, magnificent brute of a man,' I said, kissing his sensitive earlobe.

I shouldn't have done it, but Tova's near-death experience, the eruption of my magic, and Irsha's words made me reckless. Too soon, we'd return to Truso, and he'd once more become the king, and I, his servant. But here and now? I wanted to feel him, to know what could have been if our worlds weren't so far apart.

'Kiss me . . .' I whispered. 'Please.'

He grasped my braid, pulling it until my spine bowed, exposing my throat. His nose trailed over the pulsing artery in my neck as he inhaled deeply, teeth grazing my skin. Even through his tight leather trousers, I could feel the strength of his affection.

'I can't,' he groaned, his mouth leaving a trail of fire that burned with the most exquisite torment, stealing my breath away. 'I won't be able to stop if I do.'

'I won't ask you to stop . . . not today,' I breathed, pulling him closer and pressing his mouth just above my collarbone, where his breath travelled down my gown, reaching the sensitive skin of my breasts.

'Gods help me. I want more than a day. A lifetime won't be enough to savour you,' he muttered, sliding my nightgown off my shoulder, exposing more skin. I arched under his touch, giving myself to this ruthless man who became gentle for me.

Reynard's mouth captured my nipple, tongue swirling around the sensitive peak, making me moan.

'Do you like that, my light? You are so fucking perfect,' he murmured, sucking it into his mouth, then grazing his teeth over my flesh, causing my stomach to clench with a jolt of pleasure.

Rey's hand drifted upwards, calloused fingers trailing along my inner thigh. My grip tightened in his hair, pressing him closer, encouraging him further while whimpering softly from my building excitement.

'Are you in pain, little healer?' he teased, a playful smile ghosting over his lips while his hand wandered under my chemise. 'Is it hurting here?' he asked, fingers brushing my folds so gently I barely felt it.

I rocked my hips, pushing into his hand, but he withdrew.

'Tell me you want this, Sanika, that you need my touch. I could never live with myself if I ever saw that look in your eyes again. I would rather die than force myself upon you.'

His voice was so raw that I opened my eyes. I met his gaze, only now realising how my accusation from that night must have hurt him.

'Please, Rey, touch me. I want you.' I guided his hand between my thighs, the heat of my desire pulsing beneath his palm as I moved against him with aching need. 'I want you so much. I'll beg you if I have to . . . please.'

With each word that came out of my mouth, the uncertainty faded from his gaze, replaced by searing desire. The civility he wore like armour crumbled, those luscious bow-shaped lips curving into a dark, wicked smile.

'That's not how you beg, my light. I'll teach you how to beg properly, how to form the words with my cock deep in your throat,' he said, hand pressing to my sex, covering it completely. 'But not today. Today, I'll take my fill.'

He nudged me onto my back before kneeling in front of the bed. 'Spread your legs, Sanika,' he commanded gently, pressing on my knees. A shiver ran down my spine as my legs parted, giving in to his demand.

'Such an obedient little Viper,' Reynard murmured, caressing my thighs. His hand slid up, fingers parting my folds, and I arched, crying out from the pleasure. 'And soaking wet for me.'

'Rey, please,' I begged, reaching towards him. I wanted more—so much more. 'Stop tormenting me.'

'Tormenting?' He bent lower, his breath drifting over my skin. 'Torment is your scent robbing me of sleep.' His tongue trailed along my sex, then swirled around my sensitive bud. My back arched as bliss set me ablaze. 'Torment is seeing another man make you smile.' Another long lick that wiped my mind clean of any other thoughts but him. 'That's the real torment. This is just a taste of what I'll do to you, Roksana. So find something to bite because I'm going to make you scream my name.'

I'd barely grabbed the pillow when he started, his mouth hot on my sex, tongue lashing viciously, expertly wringing every drop of pleasure from my body. Reynard alternated between long, languid strokes and harsh flicks before sucking on my clit while I cried into the pillow, muffling the sounds he forced from my throat.

The tension built to impossible heights. This man, this berserker, owned me with his tongue, demanding my bliss as if he knew exactly what I needed. My pleasure crested in a release so powerful that my body shook, muscles tensing, forcing tears from my eyes.

I fell apart under him, uncontrollably sobbing as I realised nothing would ever be the same. I felt him move onto the bed and lift me up before he cradled me in his arms, stroking my hair.

'Why didn't you . . .? You're still hard,' I said when I could control my voice, his shaft beneath me a stark reminder he'd denied himself.

'Because you haven't accepted me yet. Your body has, but deep in your mind, there is still a barrier I must conquer, and I won't take you until every part of you welcomes all of me,' he replied, kissing my forehead. I opened my mouth to protest, but he placed a finger on my lips. 'I don't mind it, my light. I like a challenge.'

'So, what was this?' I asked quietly, confused.

'A promise, a sample of my prowess and a small payment for all those nights I couldn't sleep, wondering how you'd taste. Now, when you go to bed, you can touch yourself while thinking of me,' he said with a mischievous grin. He playfully nipped my neck before straightening my chemise. 'Also, you needed a distraction. You were too tense, and I can't think of a better way to release the tension.'

'Oh, you're a bloody menace.' I laughed, smacking Rey's shoulder and pushing him onto his back before straddling his hips. 'I'll show you prowess,' I said right before the door creaked open.

'Irsha told me you're awake, so I came with—Lada's tit, Roksana! Why are you riding the king?' The words preceded the draft from the corridor. 'I thought you hated him!'

Tova stood in the doorframe, his eyes as big as saucers, holding a steaming mug in his transformed hand, and I realised two things. First, I was indeed riding the king, straddling his hips like a bloody stallion. Second, as Tova's voice trailed down the corridor, there was more than one person who now knew my little secret.

'Master Orenson, you have an ill-begotten sense of timing, so please give me one good reason not to send you back to Młot,' Rey said, grinning like a fool as I scrambled off him, muttering quiet, colourful curses.

'I told you she likes apple pie—it seems to have taken you places. Besides, if you want to stay in my drah'sa's good graces, you won't lay a hand on me,' Tova said with a shrug, coming closer.

I gasped, looking at Reynard, but instead of anger, a mischievous smile lifted the corners of his lips as his finger dived into the warm centre of the pie.

'Bold words, Master Orenson.' Rey smirked, licking the sweet, warm filling with the same gusto he'd used on me a moment ago. 'I'll forgive you this time, as it *did* give me the chance to bring this radiant smile back to her face.' His gaze challenged Tova to comment on his wordless statement. Tova's mouth gaped open, and I groaned when he understood the meaning behind it.

Someone please get me a shovel so I can bury myself and my embarrass-ment, I thought before taking control of the situation.

'Get out, you dreadful duo. I need to dress.'

Chapter 40

Roksana

'You can't just barge in here. I don't care who you are!' Raised voices woke me from my sleep, so I sat up, stifling a yawn, trying to work out what was happening.

We returned to Truso last night after a journey that had technically lasted two days—but felt like a lifetime, thanks to the men around me. This morning, all I wanted was to stay in bed and let my aching muscles recover. But apparently, the world wasn't going to allow that.

I sighed and rubbed my eyes. That trip was destined to haunt my nightmares. I couldn't even blame Reynard—especially not with how Tova and Irsha had taken turns testing his patience, behaving like two overprotective brothers offended at catching him deflowering their innocent sibling. My being exhausted didn't help. So when Rey lifted me into his saddle, insisting on looking after me, a huge argument broke out. It only ended when he'd banished them to the rear, where they spent the rest of the ride choking on road dust and horse farts.

The journey had taken even longer thanks to Reynard's relentless need to dote on me. How he managed it, I'll never understand—but there was the bouquet of winter berries, the skittish rabbit he produced from gods know where, and even a cinnamon bun from a village baker where we'd stopped for the night who swore the king had saved his cousin's life during the war. Eventually, I released the rabbit back into the wild and gently pointed out that even the soldiers had started whispering about his reluctance to return home.

I pressed a pillow to my mouth and groaned, knowing I had myself to blame. I'd kept him at arm's length for so long, only to succumb to his touch in a moment of weakness. Still, I couldn't bring myself to regret it. The only question now was what would happen next. Rey seemed to share my feelings, which explained the many delays. We should have discussed the future on our way back, but every time I tried, his little kisses, the nips that left faint marks on my skin, left me without a care in the world.

The thought of those moments led, inevitably, to the memory of our encounter, and with it came the pulsing desire between my legs. I squeezed my thighs together, pressing the pillow to my belly.

You can't want the king, Sana. This isn't some fairytale where the blushing orphan becomes his queen, especially not if this queen plans to train in magic and become the next poison chapter master.

The realist in me knew that it couldn't be—we lived in two different worlds. Rey had to choose a queen that the court would accept. But my heart always guided my knife, and it seemed it had already made its choice.

Can I truly enjoy these stolen moments only to face heartache when it all ends? Or should I cut ties now, when it wouldn't hurt so much? Another sigh slipped out. *Gods, it's already going to tear my heart out. Would losing him now or later be any different?*

The commotion outside intensified. I got up to help Tova deal with our uninvited visitor when the door crashed into the wall and a silhouette appeared, framed by the light from the corridor.

'Take her,' he said, snapping his fingers, lighting up all the fae lights in my room.

'I don't bloody think so,' I said. I reached under the pillow, but as I gripped the handle of the dagger, his fingers danced in the air, and with the simple sigil, a strand of aether flew from his hand, wrapping itself around mine.

'Roksana Regnav, by order of the Court of Aether, you are under arrest. Surrender willingly and you shall be treated with all due respect. Resist, and you'll be dragged through the city, bound and gagged,' he said with a grim expression.

My eyes finally adjusted to the light, and I recognised the uniform. *A battle mage enforcer.* That could only mean the incident in Ostrava had come to light, and I had no choice but to face the consequences.

'Right, of course,' I muttered, standing up and pulling the covers around my body. 'Would you give me a moment, please?'

'Get the fuck out of our house! Sana, stay where you are. I'm sending a message to the king.' A tousled head appeared behind the mage, and the flash of light from his axe was enough to frighten me.

'Tova, no. I have to go. But please make sure Riordan and Ciesko know.'

It was the Court of Aether. As tempted as I was to appeal to the king, quarrelling with the Council of Mages on my behalf would only cause him trouble. This was my battle, and I hoped the two men who'd introduced me to magic would have my back. Hidden behind the privacy screen, I hastily dressed in my most comfortable gown, but as I reached for my alchemist's belt, the battle mage's voice stopped me.

'No need for violence, Master Orenson. However, if you wish to use the blade, you are welcome to try, but please be sure you can stand your ground against the captain of the Court of Aether's enforcers.'

The viciousness in his voice as he goaded Tova was enough for me to put the belt away. We had no chance when facing a mage whose only task was to kill monsters and subdue other wielders of the aether, but Tova was not so easily discouraged.

'I'll do more than stand my ground, you arrogant—' he said, stopping when I rushed out from behind the screen to stand between them.

'I'm ready,' I said to the mage while gesturing to my friend. 'Tova, remember when we discussed my magic? I told you this might happen,' I said, hoping he still remembered the conversation on our return to Truso.

He was fascinated by his new hand and referred to his fingers as 'living wood,' claiming they felt as if he'd never lost their original counterparts. His enthusiastic acceptance had made me hide how terrified I was—not just of the reaction of other mages, but also of my absolute lack of control over the power that had continued creating life, even against my will.

'Fine, but . . .' Tova hesitated. 'I don't trust him. I'll go see the king's mage. He'll know what to do.'

The mage rolled his eyes at Tova's stubborn expression. 'You can go wherever you want, Master Orenson. Do me a favour—once you meet Riordan, tell him he is expected at the hearing.'

I followed the battle mage out and inhaled the crisp, early winter air that had swept in with the frost, painting the window in ephemeral flowers. It was refreshing, but my empty stomach rumbled, demanding sustenance. My custodian didn't seem to notice the sound, and at the sight of a large black carriage with barred windows waiting for us, my hunger miraculously vanished. I swallowed hard, stopping in my tracks.

The mage sighed heavily when he noticed my hesitation. 'Mistress Regnav, please, let's not make a scene on the streets.'

My jaw was so tightly clenched that I could only nod.

I climbed in when he opened the door, wincing as it slammed shut. I sat curled in the corner, barely breathing as I thought through every possible outcome while we slowly travelled through the streets of Truso. The silence that stretched between us felt too heavy.

'Does the king know about this?' I asked.

He looked at me, his hands tightening on his armrests before he shook his head. 'His Majesty clearly isn't objective. Besides, he has no dealings in the disciplining of mages.'

'I think he has plenty of dealings—and keeping him in the dark to cover your ill-deeds will come back to bite you and your esteemed council in your distinguished arses. So, are you going to tell me where you are taking me, or should we see if my magic can turn you into a talking tree?' I said, readying myself for whatever came next.

'I'm taking you to be interrogated by the High Council,' he answered. 'Given that they're letting you live, maybe you'll even survive to have your geas ceremony. And I'll pretend I didn't hear your threat.'

'Let me live? It was just a small magic flux. It's not like I can shatter the kingdom. I'm just a potion-mixing commoner,' I said, trying to convince myself more than him, especially since this man would likely have no say in the council's ruling.

'You are anything but common, Mistress Regnav. You changed the strands of aether so completely that a dead object became alive. You think you just repaired your friend's hand, but what you did was create what commoners call a monster—a hybrid entity blended so perfectly that it cannot revert to its original parts. How do you think biesy, manticores,[1] or harpies[2] came to be?' he asked, his expression earnest. 'Only the gods

---

1. **Manticore (s.)/manticores (pl.)** — beasts with a lion's body, human head, and scorpion tail that love to eat their victims whole after paralysing them with their scorpion's venom.

2. **Harpy (s.)/harpies (pl.)** — Rapacious monsters described as having a woman's head and body and a bird's wings and claws; depicted as birds of prey with women's faces.

should create new life, and you are no god. Vivamancy was eradicated for a reason.'

'So, it's submit to the geas or death?' I asked, weighing my chances if I were to jump from the carriage. But that would mean being on the run, away from my friends, from Truso, never certain I wouldn't wake up ensnared in magic.

'Yes. Twelve mages have worked to energise the wards of the geas hall, as the council didn't want to wait for the solstice ceremony. All for you. So at least some of them think you're worth saving.'

'Thank you for letting me know,' I said with a shrug, hoping he didn't notice how much I was trembling.

Calm down, I told myself. *The last thing you need is for them to see you acting unhinged . . . Calm as a cucumber, Sana. Just be as calm as a cucumber.*

I wasn't sure why that particular vegetable came to my mind, but realising how much my mind drifted to ease the fear made me chuckle. My reaction must have surprised him because he frowned, looking at me as if he were assessing an exotic curiosity from a foreign land.

'You are . . . not what I expected,' he said.

I shrugged, falling back onto the carriage pillows, still shaking with quiet laughter. 'Yeah, I hear that a lot.'

We didn't enter the Court of Aether through the main doors. Instead, I was taken to a strange back entrance that led to a heavily warded chamber. As I drew a shaky breath, I noticed the strands of aether weaving and wrapping themselves around the walls in hypnotic, swirling patterns as Ciesko walked out and gave me one of his benevolent smiles.

'Welcome, Roksana,' he said. 'You've caused quite a stir. I wish you'd followed my advice when I said not to disclose your skills to anyone until you went through the geas ceremony.'

The battle mage choked and spluttered. 'You knew?'

Ciesko waved him off, taking my elbow. 'Of course, I knew. I discovered her,' he responded, completely untroubled, as if he hadn't just admitted to hiding vital information from the council. 'Come, child, let's get it over with. The geas hall will be ready for you momentarily. You know you have to do it, right?'

'Yes, Arch Healer, thank you for arranging this,' I said. If he hadn't, I would've begged him to do so as soon as possible. Even if giving my geas would leave me enthralled to the Crown, anything was better than worrying what might happen if I lost control of my magic without someone like Irsha there to stop me turning everyone into monsters.

We entered the room, and four other mages turned to observe my arrival. I wasn't sure what to do, so I curtsied the best I could.

'Greetings, esteemed council members. How may I be of service?' I said, desperately trying to recall all the court protocols I'd learned as an assassin when training to infiltrate the nobility.

'We are not here for your service, girl, but to establish if you should live,' one man answered with a sneer.

'Girl? My name is Roksana Regnav. I'm no youngster, but I'm sure you can see that, Mage. What name do you go by?' My anger rose at his attitude, but Ciesko snorted his amusement at my sharp-tongued reply.

'His name is Marius, a master artificer. I can only assume my esteemed colleague is sour because the way you repaired your friend's fingers reminded him of his own limitations,' answered the man who walked into the chamber behind me. He looked so much like Riordan that he could be his father. 'Why was I not invited?'

'Riordan the senior, I assume,' I said before realising I'd spoken out loud. 'I mean, Royal Mage Riordan, how good it is to see you.' It wasn't pretence—I was genuinely happy to see him, especially since he was directing his ire at the arsehole who sneered at me.

'I didn't think it necessary,' Marius responded. 'You know the law. Vivamancers are dangerous and need to be neutralised.'

'That law was written before we had the geas ceremony, Marius. Let's not draw hasty conclusions. I, for one, am curious as to what she can do,' a woman sitting next to Zenon, the provost of the University of Magic, chimed in. 'I am Anora, head of the battle mages,' she said for my benefit, and I had to school my face not to smile with satisfaction at the angrily pulsing vein on Marius' neck.

'Neutralised?' Ciesko jumped in. 'Only a fool like you would consider Roksana dangerous. I've worked with her for a month. I've thrown every obstacle into her path, hurt her with harsh words, exhausted her, belittled her and judged her character all the way. Roksana can control herself, and she is not prone to emotional outbursts. Teaching her is as safe as any other mage.'

Ciesko came closer, placing a hand on my shoulder while I stood gaping at him like a fish out of the water. All this time I'd wanted to murder the patronising prick, and he was quietly testing me? His hand tightened as if he could read my thoughts, and his slight nod confirmed my suspicions.

'From the drivel that healer sent me,' he continued, 'it was clear she pulled Master Orenson from the brink of death and restored the salvage-able flesh before repairing the missing tissue with wood. Roksana didn't use her power to create life but to preserve it.'

The vein on Marius' neck pulsed faster. 'You conveniently forgot to mention that she lost control of her power, which started transform-ing everything in reach until the Dark Brotherhood assassin ended the threat. How is that safe? How can you be so fucking blind?' Spittle flew during the master artificer's outburst, and I jumped when he hammered his fist on the table.

'Language, Marius,' Ciesko said. 'I'm not blind. You can't blame her for that. We all made mistakes at the beginning of our training. Should I remind you of yours? All we need is her geas, and you can sleep the night knowing you're safe in your bed.'

'I don't care about my language. Ciesko, for fuck's sake, you can't train a chaos mage!' Marius was beside himself, jerking from his seat with such force that his chair fell back with a thud. I gasped, looking between the two, unsure of what was going on.

'She is not a chaos mage. Is it simply your lack of knowledge, or have you become so senile that you cannot remember that one has to be a conduit to manipulate chaos? She can't channel limitless spells or feed off destruction. We have a pure vivamancer, an extinct trait, and we've been given a second chance to nurture this beautiful ability instead of trying to destroy it.'

Ciesko looked around, and whatever he saw in the council's faces tightened his lips. 'I'm calling for a vote.' The old mage's voice hardened as he pulled me to his side. 'And be mindful of how you vote because I won't stand idly by if you make the same mistake as our ancestors.'

And I thought you were a prick . . . I thought, ashamed at how many times I had cursed his name.

'Vote it is,' the Royal Mage stated. I looked between the council members, shocked at how fast it had come to this. 'Nothing that can be said or done will change the fact that Roksana is a vivamancer who has manifested her power. It is our job to assess if we're willing to risk the kingdom or even the entire continent's safety.'

'You're ready to decide?' I asked. 'How is this fair if no one wants to hear my opinion on the matter?' I grabbed Ciesko's hand, but he shook his head.

'What could you say, Mage? You are who you are. As much as I want to give you the benefit of the doubt, not a single vivamancer has resisted the pull of their power, becoming its mindless tool in the end,' Anora said before raising her hand with a heavy sigh. 'My vote is no. I'm curious about vivamancy, but the risk is too great to allow the history of the Mad Mage repeat itself.'

My heart skipped a beat, panic tightening my throat when Marius raised his hand with a smirk. 'No, but let's ensure her death is painless, especially since Master Ciesko claims she has merit.'

I looked at Ciesko, then at the doors, wondering if I could dash to safety, but I was surrounded by the most powerful mages in the country. Even if I made it past them, there were battle mages outside trained to subdue any threat, ready to jump into action. And I refused to play into Marius' hands.

'My vote is yes,' Ciesko said. 'Roksana will live, surrender her geas, and train under my supervision. I'm ready to take full responsibility for her.'

I swallowed hard, looking at the other two—the royal mage and the university's provost. Riordan Senior looked at me with a gentle smile and nodded his head.

'It looks like your mishandling of Annika Diavellar's[3] case taught you nothing, Marius. I have the testimony of another mage offering to vouch for her character: My grandson—who, as of tomorrow, replaces me as royal mage,' he said, smiling at me. 'I vote yes.'

---

3. **Annika Diavellar** — a conduit mage whose efforts won the Second Necromancer's War for Dagome. After the death of her first Anchors, the council planned to force her into a new Anchor bond, but she faked her death and ran away.

'If you plan to retire, you shouldn't vote,' Marius snapped before turning towards the provost, who sat there, a silent enigma, not saying a word. 'What say you? Be reasonable and stop this madness.'

My survival hung by a thread, or rather, on the decision of someone who didn't know me at all. I looked at him, cold and distant, unsure if I should drop to my knees and beg. A single tear fell down my cheek when our gaze met.

'Decisions guided by fear are never wise. I read the report, and I found no evidence of wrongdoing. If we punish mages for deeds they hadn't yet committed or lack of training, you, Marius, would never have survived your studies. Let her live. I vote yes,' he said, and I felt able to breathe again.

My knees buckled, and I crumbled to the floor, hiding my face in my hands when a silent sob shook my body.

'Stand up, child,' Ciesko ordered, but I didn't know if I could. My body felt boneless and uncooperative, the suddenness of my reprieve stripping me of my strength. He must have noticed because he gestured to the mage who arrested me. 'Take her to the geas chamber and wait for me there.'

He lifted me as I took a breath, still dazed after regaining my life, and carried me along a dark corridor to a massive door, its frame carved with countless runes. The entrance stood open, but all I could see were shadows surrounding a huge stone block with heavy, metallic manacles fused to its surface.

Atavistic fear boiled to the surface. As soon as the mage put me back on my feet, I turned, seeking a way to escape, but the only exit was blocked by Ciesko, who nodded towards the door.

'Enter, my dear, that's our price for your life,' he said, and with a shuddering breath, I turned to face my fears.

Chapter 41

Roksana

I walked into the Geas Hall, wondering at the grand name for such an obscure cave. The stone block was stained the colour of old blood, and the shudder that travelled down my spine left me feeling vulnerable.

Two men emerged from the shadows, looking at me with unsettling indifference. The older male drew a sigil in the air, the symbol flickering briefly before the runes on the doorframe lit up as if struck by lightning.

'Should I come closer?' I stalled, the severity of the situation catching up to me. I knew it was inevitable, but I couldn't stop shaking. I wiped my sweaty hands on my kirtle, trying to control my breathing, but I couldn't even manage that. The fear of the unknown, of the pain I expected, got the better of me.

'What must I do?' I whispered, wishing I were brave enough to face it with dignity.

'Just survive.' Ciesko patted my cheek in a fatherly gesture, concern and sadness mixed in his expression. 'The man on your left is a geas custodian. He will witness and record the words that define you. Don't worry, he will never speak it—both of them are mute. The man on your right is your judgment, a broken mage who won't stop until you reveal the secret of your soul. The rock behind you, the Veil Stone, will unveil your past, revealing who you truly are. Humans are rarely prepared to see the reflection of their soul, but still, try not to resist if you can,' he said before he gestured to the men. 'I leave her in your hands.'

That was the only explanation I received before he walked away as I stood frozen in place, at the mercy of the stone's guardians. I observed them warily, clenching my jaw so they couldn't see my teeth clattering. The geas trial was a mystery. No one talked about it because the survivors preferred not to remember the scars left on their souls, while those who performed it were made mute to protect the mages. Ciesko's words were the first bit of genuine information I'd been given, but it didn't make me feel any better.

The hollow thud of the door sounded like the slamming of a coffin lid, and the surrounding symbols flashed brighter, blinding me. When my sight returned, the door was replaced by a smooth rock wall.

'How?' I asked, releasing the breath I'd been holding, but there was no answer.

The older man touched my shoulder before gesturing for me to undress. His touch was gentle, his eyes kind, but I had no illusion that if I didn't comply, I would be forcibly stripped.

So I did, removing the layers of clothing until I stood in nothing but a thin chemise, the contours of my body clearly visible beneath the thin linen. When I reached to take it off, the older man stopped me, then motioned to the rock. I followed him, my heart beating so hard I could feel it in my throat.

He positioned me next to the stone, and my shivers intensified when my back touched the cold, moist surface that looked like a strange vertical altar.

Like a lamb to the slaughter, I thought when he fastened a collar around my neck, forcing me to lean back. The manacles followed, and as the heavy metal settled against my skin, the other man came over. Both mages began casting an elaborate aethereal design, weaving the threads in intricate symbols. Once complete, the energy alighted over me and sank into the stone.

The Veil Stone awakened—its hungry consciousness probing my mind, seeking answers, as if I was an enigma to be unravelled. Its magic burrowed into my brain, parasitic and hungry, while I panted hard under its merciless touch that threatened to strip me of my sanity. The manacles rattled as I jerked in pain, but despite doing my best to calm my breathing and not resist the invasion, my body didn't want to listen.

You survived the steppe, the beatings in the Brotherhood, and the times Jagon forced you to drink poison just to see how it worked. It can't be worse than that. It just can't . . .

The broken mage approached me then, his cloudy blue eyes seeing through me. Not with hate or compassion, but with the cruel gaze of a child who wondered how many legs they could pull from a bug before it finally died.

I looked on in horror as he took a small blade from his belt and drew a thin line on my skin. It was so sharp it barely registered at first, but the stinging sensation soon followed. His gaze met mine, and he pressed his hand to the wound.

A curse died on on my lips, as power flooded through me, and I screamed.

I was wrong, so very wrong.

It was so much worse than any beating, any poison I'd ever ingested. The pain was . . . I struggled to form a coherent thought. It felt as if my soul was being forced into the stone, and what returned was . . . oh *gods*. Every memory, every hidden feeling and thought—the stone fed upon them, gaining strength, forcing me to relive every moment.

The broken mage carved my skin over and over, each cut an ice flame spearing me to the stone. But it didn't matter how much I screamed—there was no respite or hope, only endless darkness filled with memories and torment. The worst moments of my life assaulted me one after another.

My mind shattered, shredded by the eager power of the stone while my body thrashed, harried by the broken mage's corrupted aether. Blood flowed from my flesh, weakening me, but I fought back, my raw, hoarse voice declaring my defiance.

It was futile. I fled from the torment, protecting the small child I had been—the innocent, beautiful core that was untainted by the killings and the desire for survival. But the broken mage was relentless. His voice rang clear as a bell in my mind as he promised that the pain and torment would end if I only told him who I truly was.

But how could I put into words what I didn't even know myself?

All I knew was that I killed, and maimed, and schemed. That child on the steppe had been tainted by the deaths of many—some deserving; others, not so much, even if I'd tried to ease their suffering.

The answer came to me and filled me with bitterness and pain.

I'm the Deadly Nightshade.

But I was wrong. That was not it, and the will of the Veil Stone pressed down upon me even more, forcing me to face my demons.

The pain lessened with the scent of lemongrass and musk, only to be ripped away, replaced by the filthy hands of men tearing at my clothes. I once again ran from Młot's kingdom, drowning in an ice-cold mountain river, fighting to keep my head above the water as my body bumped against sharp rocks.

I'm regressing . . . I thought as the magic of the rock spun me, stripping away more layers.

Turn.

Countless little deaths in Jagon's workshop, my magic fighting to keep me alive while his poison destroyed my insides, making me cough up bloodstained foam.

Turn.

My arrival in Truso, fighting with other apprentices, earning bruises and broken bones until Irsha stepped in, taking me under his protection.

Turn.

I was back on the Orcish Steppe, running towards my ancestral house, the flames engulfing it. I fought the mercenaries, desperate to reach the blocked door to tear it open, but I was too weak. I could only scream as I heard my family's fading cries while the roaring inferno consumed them.

Turn.

Suddenly, I was free. Time slowed down, releasing me from the endless rotations, and I was small, so small I fit in a traveller's chest.

This was my favourite hiding place; even my mother didn't know this one. As I waited for her anger to abate, someone entered the room and I risked a peek through the crack, recognising my mother's skirt. She was with someone, but it wasn't my father.

'*Lower your voice* or my husband will hear.' My mother's angry whisper made little sense, but I kept silent and listened.

'Why would I care? Just give her to me, Dobra. He wants his daughter back. In exchange, he'll let you and that thief live.'

The voice sounded strangely familiar, but to my younger self, all men sounded the same.

'Sana's too young to leave her home. His ambition is dangerous—dragging her back to Truso, to that viper's nest, will destroy her. Her power will flourish here, where her roots run deep. She needs the steppe beneath her feet, the endless sky above her, the wind in her lungs, the freedom no city can grant. Please . . . tell him to wait.'

My mother's desperate plea was a stark contrast to the cruel laughter that followed.

'Oh, Dobra,' the man drawled, amusement laced with malice. 'I can pass along your message, but tell me, what do I get in return for my help? Will you bear a child for me as well? A pretty little girl whose bloodline is touched by the divine? I always wondered why he chose you until I saw you out here. You're a vila. Can a lady of the forest truly love a human?'

A cold weight settled in my chest. Tears burned my eyes, blurring the memory and freezing it in time.

From a distance, a deep, firm voice cut through the moment. 'Dobra, who's there? The workers said we had a guest. Is it the merchant I told you about?'

My father's voice faded, replaced by even harsher pain. The cuts continued, the bloodletting weakening me further. My strength was waning, but the pain brought clarity to who I was and why my magic was as green as a spring meadow.

Power emerged, whipping out of the countless wounds on my body. Emerald strands coiled around me, the aether sealing my flesh, a net of silver scars covering my skin. I was a budding flower, opening to embrace the world. My soul grew, sinking into the rock behind me, and even the Veil Stone hesitated.

'Stop . . .' I whispered. 'Please, I can't control it.'

The broken mage gasped, his dagger clattering on the floor. I felt a moment of relief, my heart beating loudly in my ears as thumping reverberated throughout the chamber. I frowned. *Am I doing that?* I wondered, but no, my heartbeat was much faster than the heavy echoes.

Even through my tears, I saw the door shimmer into existence as the room shook again, debris falling to the ground. A masculine roar formed words I couldn't quite understand, but I knew it . . . That tone, that timbre—it was my salvation.

It calmed me, and my power retreated. But if I thought the ordeal was over, I was mistaken.

The broken mage attacked once again, corrupted aether flooding me. My body seized, every nerve an inferno, reducing me to a shrivelled, tormented knot, no longer caring for the world as I prayed for the pain to stop. The magic in my blood responded, exposing my deepest memory—one I shouldn't have been able to remember: the moment of my birth, when the aether filling our world had blessed my first breath.

Words formed in my mind, and I realised what they were: Everything I had been, everything I was, and everything I would ever be. The simple phrase that anchored my soul to existence.

S'eteto te sue me carer lumiere, verites a met ser viller laner.[1]

My geas.

As I whispered them, ashen lips forming the words, the Veil listened. The entity within, finally satisfied, slowly withdrew, releasing its grip on my soul.

I sighed with relief, taking one last breath as my heart stuttered to a halt.

---

1. Clothed in twilight, bearer of the dawn, her touch changes how fate is drawn.

Chapter 42

Reynard

The door bounced off the wall of my office as Riordan burst in, Tova in tow. 'You must stop them. That bloody healer's lost his mind, hiding this from me!'

Distracted by the sudden interruption, my hand shook, and a massive drop of ink fell from the quill onto the trade agreement with Lumivitae, the light fae kingdom. I hastily threw blotting sand on it, hoping to salvage the document, before looking at the two expectant lunatics standing before me.

'Could you spare me the hysterics and explain what's going on?' I said, wondering what had prompted their dramatic entrance.

'They arrested Sana and took her to the mages, so shift your royal arse and get her out of there!' the dwarf shouted.

'What are you talking about? Who took her?' I frowned, questioning whether I'd understood him.

Sana has been worried about the consequences of losing control in Ostrava, but I hadn't thought the council would do anything with Ciesko pushing so hard for her geas trial.

'The council decided to take action after the Ostrava incident,' Riordan replied. 'They're putting her on trial! I've already sent for my grandfather, but only you can contest the verdict. Gods, you knew she was a vivamancer, and you didn't tell me?' He gave me such an accusatory glare that I nearly shrank back. 'Rey, if they see her as a threat, they're going to *kill* her.'

The rustling of a piece of parchment falling on the floor was the only sound as I rose from my chair, hands crushing the precious document I'd tried salvaging a moment ago. My lips curled in a snarl so vicious that the two men took a step back.

'What . . . the *fuck* are you talking about? What trial?' I carefully enunciated every word, holding back the berserker's rage by the thinnest of threads. If I went there now, I would kill every soul blocking my path and let the necromancers ask questions later. 'Explain. *Clearly*. Before I drown that wretched council in molten srebrec.'

Riordan's eyes widened as he took another step back, and I scowled at his flinch when I reached for my sword and buckler. I shouted to the guard manning the door, my voice echoing as I methodically fastened my weapons, 'Tell the stables to saddle three horses!'

'Rey, you can't storm over like this. You can't attack the council,' he started, but I raised my hand, silencing him while reaching for a set of daggers.

'No, Ri, if there's one thing I can't do, it's lose her,' I said. 'Everything else can burn.' A threat to Sana's life from the people supposedly helping her was my breaking point in this political death trap I'd found myself in. 'I'm done doing my damnedest for all these people who think they can rule this kingdom better than me. I'm the War King of Dagome, and if they won't bend to my will, I'll enjoy watching them break.'

'Fucking finally,' Tova muttered, and when I looked at the dwarf standing quietly by the door, he had a hand on his axe and an eager expression on his face that didn't bode well for those threatening his drah'sa.

Riordan looked at me in horror. 'Rey, don't let your the wild—'

I thrust a half-filled goblet of wine into my flustered friend's hands. 'This isn't the berserker speaking, it is the king. A king who wanted to be loved, not feared—but as I can't achieve the first, I'll excel in the latter. Now tell me all you know, and start making sense, or I swear I'll punch you.'

'Yes, sire.' Riordan bowed, then drank the wine while I drafted an order.

Send the garrison to the city. Surround the Court of Aether.

A few simple words to the captain of the guard, ensuring the mages understood me.

As we walked out of my office, I passed my orders to the guard before gesturing to Ri.

'Talk.'

'Vivamancers have always been treated like abominations despite their magic being rooted in life. There are rules—laws that forbid the creation of new life, but no one has seen a vivamancer in centuries,' he said, his robes rustling with each step he took as he rushed to keep up with me. 'You should have told me as soon as you knew. Those old pricks are out of their depth, and I don't know what they'll do.'

I tightened my fists at Ri's quiet rebuke, briefly pausing on the stairs to look at him.

'How the fuck could I have told you if I only learned about it in Ostrava myself? It was past midnight when we got back, and I thought it could wait until the morning.' My jaw flexed at my lapse in judgement. 'Besides, Sana told me the geas would help. She wanted reassurance . . . I thought Ciesko had set everything up for her.'

'When did she tell you that?' Tova asked, taking the stairs two at the time to keep up with my pace as I rushed towards the courtyard.

'On the journey home. Discussion can wait. I need information,' I said, and he dared to roll his eyes at me.

'Of course. You talked while Irsha and I inhaled road dust at the rear,' he grunted. 'That's why she didn't fight them . . .' He shook his head. 'I should have stopped them. She told me not to, but I should've ignored her.' The guilt in the dwarf's voice echoed my own.

'That's not the point,' Riordan said. 'She's a vivamancer! Even with my grandfather and Ciesko there, those arseholes could still execute her. Or she could kill them . . .' He trailed off as we walked through the courtyard. 'Gods, what else don't we know? What if she's a chaos mage? She could destroy the fucking city or turn it into a primaeval forest if we torture her for her geas,' he muttered to himself as we reached the horses.

My stallion's forehoof dug into the courtyard, the large iron horseshoe striking sparks as it hit the granite stone. He stopped when I put my foot in the stirrup. Before I could mount, Riordan's hand landed on my shoulder.

'If, for even a moment, they think she's a chaos mage, your authority might not be enough to save her,' he said. 'If that happens, I'll set up a ward so you can take her out of Dagome. Maybe she'll be safe at your brother's court.'

'They'll shackle you in augurec if you take the side of the king against your kin,' I said. We both knew that was true. They would place him in a collar that would cut him off from the aether, condemning him—a high mage—to a life worse than death.

'I'm not siding with the king. I'm siding with a friend and the woman he loves. You would do the same for me.'

'It won't happen,' I said. 'Besides, chaos mages don't exist anymore.'

But what if . . .

A sudden wave of fear washed over me, making me stumble back until I grasped the pommel of the saddle.

Fuck, what if I'm already too late?

Even during the war, I hadn't felt such fear. My hands shook violently before tightening into fists. My mind blanked, and for a split second, I felt as if I was seeing my city from above, my focus centring on the white ornate building of the Court of Aether.

No. I shook my head. Whatever this strange feeling was, I couldn't allow the berserker to take control, not now. I was surely going insane because I felt something ancient sweep through me, dissipating as quickly as it came, but with its passing, I was once more in full control.

In the blink of an eye, I was on the horse, surging forward into a gallop while those in my way jumped to the side. I didn't look behind to check if anyone followed.

I needed to get to Roksana. They would not strip me of the only light in my life. I swore to the gods right then and there.

If they hurt my Sanika, I would bathe this city in blood.

The sleek fae arches and opulence of the Court of Aether passed by unnoticed as my instincts guided me onwards. When I heard the screams, my legs were already propelling me from the saddle, the impact as I hit the ground nothing compared to the pain I heard in each agonised cry. My snarling face emptied the corridors as I rushed towards the sounds until Riordan caught up and guided me in the right direction.

'*Where is she?!*' My roar fused with the torment in Roksana's voice and the thunder that rumbled through the sky as a dragon's shadow swept overhead.

Her voice, so clear even through the thick walls, unravelled my sanity. We practically flew, jumping down several steps in our desperate rush into the bowels of the building until Ciesko blocked my way, pacing back and forth with a worried expression.

'You'll pay for this,' I growled, grasping the collar of his robe and dragging him up into the air.

'It was the only way, sire.' He didn't fight me, his face filled with regret and sorrow. But even my rage at his betrayal wasn't enough to snap the neck of the defenceless old man.

My gaze drifted to the door. I dropped the healer to the ground and reached for the brass handle, yanking on it.

'The doors are sealed by magic. None can enter until it's done. Trust me, Your Majesty. Roksana will survive. She must,' Ciesko babbled as my fists hammered against the solid wood, hoping the pain would ground me enough to remove even a fraction of my fear.

Another torturous scream shattered the silence.

'Trust you? You've lied to me for weeks. All this time, you knew the council would seek her life!'

'But they didn't,' he said. 'I gave us the time to build a defence and demonstrate her principles. Once we gain her geas, no one can touch her. The council—well, the majority—voted to let her live.'

Instead of calming me, his statement angered me even more.

'If anyone has shown their principles, it's you and that damn council,' I snapped at him, pushing against the door before I hammered my fist on it. 'Open it! In the name of the king, open the bloody door!'

Nothing happened. The screams only intensified, followed by sobs.

'They can't stop it now,' Ciesko said, falling back when he saw the fury in my eye. 'The Veil Stone won't allow it. Its power over this place vanishes only if she surrenders her geas . . . or her mind shatters. We must wait, sire.'

'It's only stone and wood,' I said. 'Let's see how your spells handle this.' I rammed into the door, the massive frame creaking when my shoulder smashed into it, but it held. In the next breath, Tova was beside me, hammering his axe into the lock. I nodded, matching his unyielding determination. Again and again, we hit the door, battering the impervious material, but nothing seemed to work.

Suddenly, everything went silent; the spells etched into the doorframe shimmered and died. A click, loud in the eerie quiet, focused my attention, and I yanked the door open. The metallic scent of blood filled the dark space. The only noise was the sound of my boots as I charged inside, panting like an enraged bull.

Two men silently met my gaze, one so old he looked like a dried prune holding a quill, and the other as dispassionate as a corpse, showing no emotions one could appeal to.

Hanging from a stone altar like some bloodied sacrificial offering was my Sanika. Her head was bowed, knees bent, arms stretched out by the shackles holding them in place, her wrists looking more like raw meat than human flesh. She must have suffered so much while the blood slowly gathered in the pool beneath her feet. My beautiful, defiant woman had been reduced to scraps left to hang, forgotten and uncared for.

No, Sanika . . .

My light, look at me . . .

The Void swallowed my mind, my roar filling the chamber. I rushed to her side, gently cradling her to my chest before grasping the metal chains and ripping them from the stone. Her body felt so light in my embrace as I knelt on the floor, my voice cracking when her head lolled to the side. Ciesko rushed towards us but halted when confronted by my fury.

'Sire, let me help, please.' He approached slowly, arms wide, palms up, and I had to fight the urge to push him away. A quiet whisper in the back of my mind reasoned to let him come closer, that she needed him, and that I had to rein in my anger and let the healer do his job.

I nodded, breathing slowly as I tried to control the beast that howled for blood inside my soul. Ciesko placed a hand on Sana's chest, and the aether swirled around him. I couldn't see it, but its energy raised the hair on my forearms when he drew arcane symbols on her bloodstained chemise. For an excruciatingly long moment, nothing happened until he uttered some words, and Roksana choked in a breath.

The moment Sana's eyes snapped open, her gaze fell on my face.

'Rey . . . you came.'

Her quiet voice shattered my heart. There was so much pain in it, I instinctively tightened my embrace, pressing my forehead to hers. She threw her arms around me as silent sobs shook her body.

'It's alright, my light, I'm here. No one will hurt you anymore,' I whispered, rubbing her back, pointing the healer to all the wounds I could see.

To his credit, Ciesko didn't stop. He kept muttering his spells, fingers dancing over her skin, symbol after symbol drawn using Roksana's blood.

So much blood . . .

My teeth clamped shut, stifling a growl. For Sana's sake, I held still, only allowing myself to stroke her hair gently.

Eventually, Ciesko said, 'She'll be fine now, my lord. She'll probably only need a couple of days to recover. I knew she was strong enough to survive the ceremony.'

He offered me a reassuring smile, but I closed my eyes, unable to stomach the sight. I took a deep, unsteady breath as I held Roksana close, unsure which of us was trembling more.

A hollow laugh escaped my lips.

'You . . . "knew."'

Gods, this mage was testing my patience, and at the worst of moments.

'Is there somewhere she can rest?' I asked through clenched teeth. I needed time to organise a carriage and prepare her old room in the palace. I didn't want her to travel like this, barely conscious, on horseback.

'I'll take her home,' Tova said as he approached slowly.

I shook my head. 'No, Master Orenson. Roksana will stay with me.'

He looked at me as if I'd just slapped him. 'You'll force her?' he asked, his accusation provoking another humourless laugh.

'Force? I'll beg her to stay if I have to, but until she recovers, Sana will stay with me . . . Please, Tova, don't fight me on this,' I said, knowing I couldn't bear to be apart from her, not when my emotions were still raw and churning inside me.

Something akin to understanding flashed in his eyes.

'She won't be happy,' he said, reaching for Sana's hand. 'But I'll prepare the house so that you can bring her back when she's ready.' I stood like a statue, observing as she opened her eyes, a faint smile ghosting her lips when he pressed her palm to his cheek. 'Do you want to go with him, drah'sa?'

I held my breath, relaxing slightly when she nodded. I understood Tova's concerns, and when he stepped away, I was grateful to the dwarf who had more strength than I did.

'I'll look after her, I give you my word.' I didn't need to give him that reassurance, but the loyalty of this man commanded respect. And to my surprise, I'd discovered I actually liked him a bit—either that, or I'd just gotten used to his antics.

'I'll come by tomorrow,' he said. 'Don't let him order you around, drah'sa.'

'It is customary to ask if you want to see it, Your Majesty,' Ciesko said after the mute custodian handed him the sealed envelope that held the key to my Viper's soul.

I pulled away as if it would bite. 'No, take it to the geas vault and put it in the deepest, darkest hole you can find. Nobody must see it . . . ever.'

My brother had used his wife's geas, and even if it *had* saved the kingdom, it'd almost broke them apart. I would not repeat his mistake.

'Very well, sire,' he responded. 'We have a room upstairs set aside for those who have undergone the geas trial. Lady Roksana will be comfortable there. Please, follow me.'

Ciesko led us through the meandering corridors until we arrived at the rear of the building. The room was small but spotlessly clean. A large bay window overlooked a garden that, even in early winter, surprised me with its vibrant Acer trees, pines, and winter berries. Soft throws and coverings in natural colours added to the feeling of tranquillity. Refreshments were already on the table, and I wondered how many mages had been carried here, broken by the harshness of the ritual.

'She can rest as long as she requires,' Ciesko said. 'Some mages recover quickly—a few hours or a day, maybe two—but for others, it may take a while. Don't rush it, sire, but if you need to leave, I'll personally look after her.'

I sneered. 'Forgive me, Arch Healer, but my trust in your words—not to mention your *judgement*—is severely damaged. I'll stay with Sana until she is strong enough to make her own decision.' The old healer flinched, but I had no mercy. 'How could you let them pin her to that rock? How could you let her suffer?'

'That's the price of her power, as it was mine, Your Majesty. I did all I could to ensure she would survive. Even if some of those measures were drastic.'

'So the ends justify the means?' I couldn't hide the disdain from my voice, but there was no point in arguing with him. 'Does she need more healing?'

'I should ask the same, seeing the soldiers posted around this building,' he said. 'But no . . . Her body is fine. She didn't sustain any lasting damage, and she will quickly replenish the blood she lost.'

I looked down at the pale woman in my arms.

'I'll stand my men down the moment we leave this place.' I sighed. 'Thank you, Arch Healer. I'll send for you if you're needed.'

I saw the hesitation in his gaze, but I waved him away, leaving him no choice.

I was finally alone with my woman, and I had no idea what to do.

Chapter 43

Reynard

I carefully lowered Roksana onto the bed and sat beside her, unsure, hesitant. She looked so fragile, curled in the foetal position, conscious but quiet and withdrawn as her tears silently fell.

'Sanika, tell me what to do. How can I make it better?'

She didn't respond at first, not until I moved to get her some water. Her hand darted out towards mine, grasping it with a strength that contradicted her defeated appearance.

'Stay . . . I need you here.' Her voice, hoarse from screaming, tore something inside me. I'd never wanted anything so much as I wanted to raze the entire court to the ground.

'I'm not going anywhere,' I said softly, stroking her hair. 'But let me bring you some honey water. You'll feel better if you drink something.'

Sana nodded, releasing me, but when I returned to her side, she was half asleep. Still, she needed to drink, and muttering encouragement, I urged her to take a sip.

'The memory of you was the only one that didn't hurt.' The words were wisps on the wind, yet they hit me like an avalanche. The clink of the glass sounded like a bell tolling when I placed the cup on the bedside table. I turned towards her, swallowing hard when my gaze met the green inferno of her power blazing within her eyes.

'We'll make more memories, so they can protect you when I'm not by your side.' I reached out to smooth the frown between her drawn brows.

'I'm sorry, I didn't know they'd make you go through this without me . . .' I said, wondering if I'd ever forgive myself. 'I should have been there.' Sana didn't answer, but her hand gently squeezed mine, and I lifted it to my lips. 'Sleep, my light. You need it. I'll be here when you wake.'

I meant every word. Hammering against those bloody doors while listening to her screams made me realise I couldn't be without her. That if she'd died, Dagome would have lost another king to madness. Roksana had given her geas to me and the kingdom, and I'd given her my heart in exchange. I just hoped she was ready and willing to accept it.

Roksana's breathing evened out, but I still stroked her back. The slow, languid movement relaxed her tense muscles until her mouth opened slightly, and she fell into a deep, healing sleep. Only then did I move and ask a servant to bring the captain of the guards to me. After a few curt commands, I had soldiers guarding the door and someone retrieving the documents I'd left on my desk.

I persuaded Riordan to placate the mages who were less than pleased by the military within their walls. I didn't know how long her recovery would take, but I was prepared to stay by her side as long as it took, even if that meant governing the country from Sana's bedside.

Roksana didn't move or say a word for an entire day. I continued working on my daily tasks, taking breaks to relay commands to awaiting soldiers before sitting beside her, ensuring she was warm and coaxing her to drink small sips of water each time she woke.

As the sun set, I stopped writing to sit beside her again. Maybe it was the gentle glow of the fading light, but the dark shadows under her eyes seemed less visible. I trailed my finger over her cheek, and she sighed, her eyes opening ever so slightly, her gaze more focused than before.

'Welcome back, little Viper,' I said, smiling when her eyebrow arched. Sana seemed to be more aware, and that little change made me sigh in relief. The only thing that didn't match her recovery was the bloodstained chemise.

I opened the door and asked the soldier to fetch some female maid-servants, requesting fresh clothing for Sana. The man saluted, rushing to fulfil my order, and half an hour later, two female healers stood in the door looking like they wanted to be anywhere else but here.

'Good evening, sire. The arch healer sent us to help with your . . . I mean, Lady Roksana,' the taller one said.

I gestured them in. 'Thank you. I'll leave you to help her wash and . . . go to the privy,' I said, raising my eyebrow when the younger girl giggled. 'Is there a problem?'

'No, it's just that men rarely think of such things,' she said.

I smiled. 'I'm used to seeing issues from every angle.' I stood up and took a few letters from the desk. 'I'll go to the garden. Just open the window and call for me once you're done.'

The garden welcomed me with the rustling of leaves and an evening frost that painted the tree trunks in every shade of grey. The slight chill in the air sent a shiver down my spine, but I welcomed the refreshing breeze. The bench directly beneath Sana's window was perfect for keeping an eye on the room, even if all I could see were shadows moving behind the curtains.

With a deep sigh, I delved into the letters. Most required only brief answers or decisions that didn't weigh on my conscience or cause a strain on the kingdom. Later, putting the letters down, I sat on the bench for a moment longer, watching as my breath misted the air while I thought about how to handle the discontent when I announced my choice of bride. I knew the nobles would oppose it as soon as they realised their daughters wouldn't be sitting on the throne, and my thoughts briefly drifted to Inga Tivala, my almost betrothed.

What am I going to do about the Winter Solstice Ball?

I'd briefly considered calling it off, but it was the perfect opportunity to gather all the old families under one roof and determine who truly supported me as king. Introducing Roksana as my chosen could be the catalyst to gauging the reactions of those who'd only used me as a tool to win the war.

'If she agrees,' I muttered to myself. As much as this strategy would benefit me, I wouldn't use her, not without her knowledge. 'Well, the only way to find out is to ask.'

The shadows in the window disappeared, and a short while later, a mage gestured for me to return. With the night drawing in, I gathered the rest of my paperwork and headed inside.

Sana looked so much better. Her remaining cuts were healed, and with the blood scrubbed away, her skin glowed. I sat on the bed, brushing a stray lock of hair from her face.

'I thought you'd left,' she said, and I huffed in denial.

'As if I could leave. I need to stay by your side or who knows what might happen next time,' I quipped. She frowned, and a hint of anger flashed in her gaze, but it quickly dispersed when I grinned. 'Didn't you hear? There's a madman trying to knock down the walls.'

'You're impossible,' she said, and I loved the eye roll and the blush that tinted her pale cheeks.

'And you are the most treasured woman in this kingdom. Tell me what you need, and I'll see it done. Should I call for Liliana? Tova?' I asked. As much as I wanted to be the person by her side, what she wanted mattered most.

Her eyes narrowed on me. It was a strangely vulnerable look, one that made me feel unsettled. I wanted to wrap my arms around her, tell her that the fear of losing her had driven me insane. That she had taken my heart with her to that damned chamber and that I was lost without her smile.

'May I hold your hand?' Her quiet voice broke through my stream of thought.

'You already hold my heart, Viper. My hand is all yours.'

A soft chuckle escaped her lips, and I congratulated myself on the little victory, even more when her dainty fingers entwined with mine.

'Did Tova give you lessons in smooth talk?' she said. 'You're too suave for your own good.'

'Tova? Oh no, Lady Roksana. It is pure admiration and natural talent. Besides, as king, it is my duty to welcome you to the ranks of Crown mages and provide for your every need,' I responded, placing a hand on my chest and bowing gallantly. Her lips twitched, and warmth spread in my chest when she turned away to hide her smile.

'If that's how this works, then you'll be very busy during the Winter Solstice when the other mages go through their geas trials,' she said, and I realised my blunder.

I was out of my depth. My experience with women was limited to lust or politics. In my time as lord marshal of a disgraced military, they came to my bed expecting to be fucked by a brutal, cunning beast, not for banter or charming words. When I became king, it was even worse. But in a way, I was happy that they'd come and gone, never occupying my mind for longer than it took to remember their names.

Sana had turned my world on its axis, making me regret never learning how to care for a woman. Orm, despite the wild magic roaring in his blood, was so much better at showing affection. Still, thinking of my brother and the surprising way he'd gained his mates gave me an idea.

'May I lie beside you?' I asked hesitantly, and her eyes brightened, the corner of her lips lifting a little.

'Should I expect you to share a bed with every Crown mage?' she teased, shifting slightly to make space for me. 'I don't think I'd like that.'

'No. You see, only a vivamancer can enter the king's bedroom. We kings should have *some* standards, you know,' I answered with a wink, pleased at the blush that painted her cheeks. Its colour deepened when I whispered in her ear, 'There will be no one else but you, Viper.'

The bed creaked when I changed position to lay my head on the pillows, but as I moved, I gathered Sana into my arms, pulling her closer until her head lay on my chest. She sighed, wrapping herself around me, and the world finally felt right.

'Your heart is racing,' she said, her ear on my chest while her hand tapped the rhythm on my skin.

'I'm a man in bed with a beautiful woman. Cut me some slack.' I laughed, acutely aware of her proximity and my body's response.

Her eyebrow lifted, but she didn't pull away. 'Oh, is that so?'

'Yes, it's that simple.' I buried my face in her hair and inhaled deeply. 'Standing in front of those fucking doors, knowing you were in pain . . . I've never been so scared in my life—and I've faced the Lich King's army.'

She nestled in closer, her hand drawing circles on my chest—slow, mesmerising movements that made my muscles tense. I watched, fascinated, as her hand continued down my abdomen, fingers playing with my belt, so close to my bulging hardness that I struggled to breathe.

This mischievous woman knew what she was doing. If the smile that teased the corner of her mouth wasn't proof enough, her hands were.

'Rey . . . did you mean it when you said you're all mine?' she asked.

I groaned when her hand drifted upwards to tug the laces of my shirt loose, one after another.

'Every word, my light. Feel free to explore,' I said, proud of how casual my voice sounded when all I wanted was to growl my frustration at her moving away from my shaft. Still, if she wanted to touch me, I'd endure her teasing, afraid that a random sound, one badly-placed word, would spoil the moment.

It wasn't my first time with a woman, but the anticipation rising with every stroke of her dainty hand made me feel like it was. My body was taut with need for her. Pent-up desire burned through my veins, urging me to take action. I hadn't felt like this for years, and I didn't want it to end. I wondered if I should shift and capture her lips; they were so close that if I turned my head, I could kiss her.

No, that isn't why I asked to stay. What bastard thinks with his cock when the woman he loves has just been tortured? I scolded myself, acutely aware she'd snuggled so close to me that there was no gap between her body and mine.

Sana's hand slid under my shirt, fingers playing with my old scars in the most exquisite of torments. I forced myself to think about military rations and dwarven petitions just to stay in control, wanting so much more but fearing to ask.

'What else is included in this royal treatment?' she murmured against my skin, lips brushing my neck as her hands slipped even lower.

'Whatever you want, Viper,' I groaned, my hands nearly tearing the sheets when her teeth grazed my skin.

'How noble of you, rescuing a damsel in distress, then letting her do what she wants,' she said, straightening slowly, dragging a single nail down my chest until it reached my belt. Her gaze met mine—and whatever she saw there made her smile. 'Don't move, Your Majesty.'

'Fuck, Viper . . . *yes.*' My voice broke on a groan. 'I'll be as noble as you want, grant you every indulgence, but have mercy, I'm just a man—'

A guttural sound escaped me as she pressed her hand over my cock, squeezing it through my breeches. 'Sana, please . . . more.'

Her pure, bubbly laugh lit my soul even as my hips bucked, body arching, desperate for more of her touch. But when I reached for her, she stopped me with a hand to my chest.

'No?' The word rasped out of me, tangled in confusion. She was the one guiding this—*why push me away?* I searched her face for an answer, fighting for control, trying to understand. Maybe this wasn't the time. Maybe I'd misread something. I grasped a shard of my sanity and forced myself to be still.

'Rey, I . . . I was helpless, so bloody helpless. I-I want . . . I need . . .' She was as lost as I was, but her stuttered words gave me the strength to stop, to yield to her needs. My Viper could have all the damn power she wanted. If it helped her forget the geas trial, I would let her tie me to the bed and use me as she pleased.

'I understand, my light.' I smiled, easing back and placing my hands above my head in surrender. 'I'm at your mercy. Touch me, little Viper. All is yours to take.'

And as her eyes darkened, hungry and hesitant, I knew my torment was only just beginning.

Chapter 44

Roksana

Despite the gentle smile playing on his lips, Rey's intense gaze lingered on my face. Golden light swirled in his eye like molten sunfire, and beneath it simmered something far more primal: hunger.

'Are you sure?' I asked, but he didn't move. Still lying in the same pose, his chest rose and fell in shallow, rapid breaths, hands clenched above his head as if I'd tied him to the bed.

You make loving you easy, Rey, I thought.

How could I not, when this man would face mages for me—when he would give himself so completely, so unflinchingly, to whatever I needed? To be taken as I wanted.

A shiver of anticipation ran down my spine.

This was my choice, my decision on how far I would take this, and gods, I wanted it all. The darkness that had sat heavily in my chest since the ceremony melted, dissolving in the heat of his gaze. My sins and pain may have been stripped bare, but so too had my feelings for this giant of a man.

It was Reynard I thought of when everything else fell apart. He was my shelter, a safe port in the storm, and I wanted him to unravel under my touch.

Tension filled the air, fuelled by the heat building in my body, an unfulfilled desire driving me onwards.

'I won't be gentle,' I said, pulling off his shirt. 'Or shy,' I added when he moved, letting me drag the fabric away.

He held back, a soft growl escaping his lips as I lay my hands on his chest. They looked small and pale, contrasting sharply with his tanned skin. The hard muscle flexed beneath my touch, and I spread my fingers, diving into soft, dark hair, the alluring pattern that begged to be caressed.

'I can take it,' he said, his gaze trailing after my hands as they slid down to his stomach.

'Can you?' I chuckled, accepting the challenge, loving Rey's groan as his hips bucked before he forced himself to still. His muscles tensed as I traced the hairline that narrowed the lower I went until it disappeared into the waistband of his trousers.

'May I, my king?' I bit my lower lip in a coy smile.

The swift lift of his hips made me laugh again. Reynard was as keen as I for this exploration to continue, his gaze begging me to pull down his trousers.

'I'll take that as a yes, a *very* enthusiastic yes,' I said, already working the loosened belt. My hands moved fast, tugging at the waistband, eager to see what waited for me.

His cock sprung out, making me gasp before a nervous chuckle escaped me. I wrapped my fingers around him, feeling him pulse and swell with the first gentle stroke.

'You have a lot to give, Your Majesty,' I said, shifting closer to him, adjusting my grip. Like everything else about him, he was large. But with a bit of effort, I could accommodate him.

'I'm sure my Viper won't shy away from the challenge,' he breathed, his eye squeezed shut, moaning quietly when I stroked him again.

Watching this powerful man come undone at my touch was intoxicating. I couldn't help but smile.

'I think I like you,' I said, my finger trailing over the thick vein on his shaft. 'I think I like you *a lot*. And I bet you taste divine.'

'Perun, give me strength . . . Sana, *please* . . .'

His voice cracked on my name, breath trembling, body tense. His breathy moan when I wrapped my fingers around him tighter and slid my hand down only encouraged me. The bed creaked ominously, and when I looked up, I saw Rey grasping the headboard like his life depended on it, the wood bowing in his grasp.

How much control does he have? I wondered, my gaze not leaving those luscious bow-shaped lips. *Will he snap if I take him in my mouth?*

I bit my lip, heart racing, sending gentle tremors through my body. But the last of my fear melted like the first snow as I watched him. It vanished under the weight of his restraint—this man moaning softly with every stroke, every scrape of my nails, fighting his own instincts for my sake.

'Roksana . . .' he groaned, his hips rocking as he fucked my hand, 'you're testing my sanity.'

I didn't know what aroused me more: that I was in control or that my touch unravelled him.

'You call this testing?' I purred, mischief mixing with the desire. 'Grab that headboard a little tighter, Your Majesty. The real test is just beginning.'

Before he could answer, I bent down, taking the head of his cock in my mouth and swirling my tongue around the flared edge. His body shuddered, muscles spasming when, with deliberate slowness, I took him deeper, inch by inch, until the tip hit the back of my throat.

I liked the way he tasted, but more than that, I loved the sounds he made. Those deep, guttural moans were their own kind of music, and I wanted to get drunk on every note. My hand drifted between my legs, finding the sweet, aching place already pulsing with need.

At this rate, I was going to climax from the sheer pleasure of sucking him dry.

His shaft twitched in my mouth as the headboard creaked. My head moved with a slow, teasing rhythm while I moaned softly, using the vibration to heighten his pleasure. He was close—I could *feel* it in every tense muscle, every sharp breath.

Then a sharp *crack* split the air.

I startled, pulling back instinctively as Rey's cock slipped from my lips. The headboard had shattered—solid oak, split clean in his grip. His eyes flicked from the ruined wood to me in disbelief, wild and blazing.

He'd broken the bed trying to hold himself back.

And suddenly, I didn't care who was in control anymore. I just needed him inside me.

The man I loved. *The berserker king.*

'Touch me, Rey,' I whispered, swallowing hard.

He froze. A low, feral rumble rose in his chest—the sound of a sleeping beast awakening. Then, with one swift motion, he tossed the broken wood aside and reached for me, yanking me into his arms as his mouth crashed onto mine.

'Say it again,' he demanded, gripping my braid, pulling just enough to force my eyes up to his.

'Touch me, Rey,' I whispered. 'I want you. *All* of you.'

'Fuck, Sanika . . .' he growled, his chest heaving, the pulse in his neck thundering. 'It's too strong. I want to devour you—I *need* to—but I'm afraid I'll hurt you if I touch you now.'

Yet even as he said it, his mouth was already on mine again, locking us together in a kiss so searing it set my body ablaze and wiped my mind of any doubts.

He tasted like winter apples, sweet and tangy and so intoxicating that my lips parted, letting him in. My body and mind yielded, giving in to the desire I'd so long resisted.

'I can't live without you, my light,' he said, his lips landing on my collarbone, teeth scraping oversensitive skin, leaving a mark. 'I've never wanted someone so much, so desperately. Until I saw you in that forest, I thought that women like you only existed in dreams. My forest goddess, my vila, give yourself to me.'

'I'm real,' I breathed, arching into his touch.

He smiled—a savage, reverent thing—and kissed me again.

'Then let me taste you, let me fuck you so hard that reality becomes a distant memory. Then, when I'm deep inside you, maybe you'll understand how much I need you.' His hands grasped the collar of my nightgown and tore it open in a single movement, the fabric falling away in scraps. 'I claim you, Sanika,' he groaned, inhaling deeply. 'You are mine and always will be.'

The sudden exposure sent a chill across my skin, my nipples tightening—but I didn't care. Not about the cold. Not about the possessiveness in his voice. Not even about the claim he'd just made.

Because when Rey looked at me like that, like I was sacred and sinful all at once, I didn't want to run.

I wanted to *stay*.

It had been too long since I'd lain with a man, and Reynard's unbridled desire, wrapped up with his brutal strength, was exactly what I needed.

Make me forget the world outside your arms, I thought as his teeth bit sharp enough to leave a mark. I arched into him anyway, offering my breasts to his mouth, because every whispered word, every worshipful murmur of praise, sent sparks down my spine and a pulse of heat between my legs.

'Yours . . .?' I teased, nails dragging over the muscle of his arms. 'But will I be able to tame this ravenous beast?'

His growl was low and dark, curling heat in my belly. 'Tell me you're mine and you can put the fucking collar around my neck yourself.' His fingers tightened on my hips. 'Tame the beast. Play with fire. Let it burn your name into my skin.'

That was the essence of his claim, not to own but to cherish. The simple beauty of it tightened my throat with a swell of emotion.

Reynard hissed when my nails raked down his torso. I gripped his shaft, circling the slick head with one finger, teasing him, claiming him in my own way.

'I like the fire,' I said, voice husky. 'I'm not afraid of you. Do your worst, my Wolf.'

He groaned, hips jerking at my touch. 'My worst? The things I want to do to you . . . no honest man should want them.'

'But you'll do them the moment I say I'm yours?' I asked sweetly, tightening my grip and stroking him until he moaned, his self-control unravelling in my hand.

'Say it,' he panted, golden eye blazing as something shifted in him—his restraint cracking, the berserker rising. 'Say it and find out.'

'I'm yours,' I whispered, catching his groan with my lips, swallowing it down. My breath hitched as his hands slid around me, and with a strength that took my breath away, he flipped me onto my back. 'I want to be yours.'

'My Viper,' he rasped, kissing my neck, his voice and plea and a promise, 'my sweet, forbidden poison. I'll destroy your enemies, I'll wage war for you, I'll defy the fucking gods—but please, *please*, my wild desire, open your legs for me. I cannot take it any longer.'

His mouth trailed heat down past my collarbone, and when my fingers tangled in the thick waves of his hair, I parted my thighs for his questing mouth.

'Like that?' I breathed, lifting my hips towards him.

'Exactly like this,' he said, no longer pleading. 'Now tilt your hips and grab your knees.'

His voice was a command now, firm and possessive. Never before had I allowed a lover to speak to me like this while his head dove between my thighs. Never before had I allowed a lover to dominate me. And yet, with him, it was perfection—to be at his mercy, to trust him with this much of me.

Rey's breath teased my sensitive skin when he whispered another command. 'Tell me what you want.'

My blush heated my exposed skin. *He wants me to talk? Now?*

'Tell me,' he repeated, and this time he pinched my nipple—just enough to make me gasp.

A startled yelp escaped my lips, and something inside me snapped free.

'Taste me,' I whispered, breath ragged. 'Take me. Fuck me *hard*.' I arched beneath him as his hand covered my sex, his thumb circling my clit with slow, deliberate pressure. 'Oh yes, *yes*. I need you to fuck me, Rey. *Please*.'

'That's my little killer,' he growled, voice thick with lust. 'I like it when you beg . . . Do it again. I want to hear my name on your lips again before I lose myself in you.'

Sweat gleamed at his temple. His fingers flexed against my thighs as he lowered his head between them, every movement agonizingly controlled. And then—gods help me—his tongue parted me.

I opened my mouth to tell him I didn't need preparation, that I was already aching for him. But when his lips sealed around me, tongue sliding between the folds, all I could do was scream, clamping my legs around his head.

'Reynard!' I cried as he pried my thighs apart again, eyes lifting to meet mine, searching for permission. 'Please,' I gasped. 'Do it again. *Don't stop.*'

A wicked smile curled at his lips.

'Good girl,' he murmured, then licked me again—slow and devastating. 'Say my name again.'

He sucked gently on my clit, and my entire body jolted, the pleasure so sharp it stole the breath from my lungs.

'*Please* . . . Rey . . . fuck me,' I panted. 'I'm ready. I'm so—*so* ready.'

A dark, satisfied chuckle vibrated against me, sending sparks shooting through every nerve.

'Not yet,' he said, voice like velvet over steel. 'A queen must be patient. Take your pleasure, Sanika. Show your warrior how to worship you.'

He's going to kill me. It's too much—but gods above, I'll die happy, I thought. *Breathe, Sana . . . Fuck, it's too much!*

My hips moved, my mind falling apart under his lashing tongue. Reynard was methodical and merciless, alternating between long, languid strokes and sucking on my sensitive bud. He waged a war with my pleasure, determined to pillage it all before he conquered me. My legs shook violently, but I refused to give in, edging myself until the strength to resist washed away.

'Oh no, Viper,' he growled, his groan vibrating against me just as his hand smacked my arse. 'Don't you dare hold back.'

The world disappeared into ecstasy, and I screamed out his name, so overwhelmed that tears flowed down my cheeks.

'My beautiful Sanika,' he murmured. 'You're finally ready for me.' He stalked forward, every movement exuding control and purpose. 'Now wipe those tears away because I haven't finished with you yet.'

He gripped my knees, spreading me wide, settling between them with the focus of a man claiming something holy. The heat between my legs still pulsed from the last peak of pleasure, and I was barely back in my body when he slid the tip of his cock through my soaked folds.

'Look at me, sweet poison,' he said. 'I want to drown in your eyes when I take you.'

I forced myself to open my eyes, locking onto his gaze like it was my only tether to reality. My body trembled, not from fear but from sheer, aching need.

'You're mine, Roksana,' he said, pressing into me with slow, relentless pressure. 'And here or beyond the Veil, I'll always be yours.'

He stretched me wide, filled me to the point of delirium—he was not just long, but *thick*—the kind of fullness that that bordered on unbearable. But gods, it felt divine.

A moan tore from my throat as I writhed, hips rolling to take him deeper until he pinned me down with one hand, holding me still.

'Too much?' he asked, voice tight with restraint.

I shook my head, breathless. 'Just right—but gods, I need you to *move.*'

My walls clenched around him, and I watched his jaw go rigid, the struggle evident in every line of his body. His breath escaped in shallow pants, but he refused to move until I started begging again, grabbing his hips and dragging myself onto his cock. I didn't care that it was awkward, only that it felt good.

'You're driving me crazy, Viper,' he said, finally beginning to move. 'How can someone be this perfect?'

He rocked into me—deep and hard—making me cry out.

'Fuck, Sanika . . . I don't think I'll be able to stop.'

Reaching towards his discarded clothes, he retrieved a dagger and set it beside me. His gaze met mine, blazing with intensity.

'Stab me if you need to,' he rasped. 'Because I'm going to fuck the soul out of you.'

I nodded, lifting my hips to meet his, tilting the angle to take more of him. His wild roar echoed through the room, and Reynard unleashed his beast.

I felt him *everywhere*.

His hands branded my skin. His mouth left trails of fire. His teeth grazed sensitive places, and his fingers mapped the curves of my body with reverence and raw need. I came. Then I came again—screaming his name, writhing beneath him—but still he didn't stop.

He pounded into me with primal power, sweat glistening on his chest, each thrust stealing my breath. The room blurred and sound narrowed to his groans, my cries, the frantic rhythm of our bodies colliding.

His cock swelled inside me as his hands fisted the sheets. '*Sanika!*' he snarled, hips jerking as he spilled into me—hot and deep, his body shuddering above mine.

That final thrust pushed me over the edge again. The world detonated in stars behind my eyelids, my body convulsing in total, uncontrollable bliss. When I could breathe again, I found myself wrapped in his arms, my trembling body draped over his.

He rolled us onto our sides, keeping me close, pulling me to his chest like I was something precious. He didn't speak, just kissed me—softly, gently—before reaching for the covers and tucking them around us. The warmth of his skin, the weight of his arms, the rise and fall of his chest—*this* was the peace I hadn't known I needed.

'Oh gods above and below . . .' I breathed, voice hoarse with satisfaction. 'That was . . . something.'

I chuckled weakly, even as the cooling mess between my thighs made me shiver. Rey wrapped himself tighter around me and bent to kiss my temple.

'It was,' he said, exhaling against my skin. 'I don't think I'll ever get enough of you.' He grinned, pulling the ribbon from my hair to release the tangled braid into a spill of golden waves.

I loved that smile. It softened his face, soothing the harsh angle of his jaw. I reached up, tracing it with my finger, letting my thumb stroke his lower lip. He caught it, sucking gently, making me laugh.

'You're impossible,' I sighed, nuzzling against his chest.

I found the perfect spot, tucked above his heart, and settled there. His hand stroked lazily up and down my spine, and I hummed in contentment, fingers curling in the soft hair on his chest. My berserker was falling asleep, but my mind had just awakened. As the haze of pleasure receded, reality seeped in like a slow tide. The fragility of what we had—the risks, the impossibility of forever—wrapped around me like a second skin.

Still, I didn't regret a thing.

'I'll be by your side for as long as the world allows,' I whispered, kissing my sleepy king who, despite being mine, could never fully belong to me.

Chapter 45

Roksana

I woke to find myself wrapped around Rey so completely that it looked like I was climbing him like a bloody tree. He was fast asleep, nose buried in my hair, one large hand possessively cupping my rear. With a roll of my eyes, I attempted to wriggle free—only for the randy sod to crack his eye open and tighten his grip.

'Sanika, where are you going?' His voice was husky with sleep, but his gaze sharpened, sweeping the room with sudden alertness.

I sighed theatrically and leaned in to press a kiss to his forehead, my other hand reaching for his discarded shirt at the edge of the bed. Luckily, it was large enough to fall to mid-thigh on me.

'No man should ask where a woman goes first thing in the morning,' I said, shrugging into it. The smile returned to his face, and he pulled me back, smacking my naked rump.

'Fair enough, little Viper. But be quick about it. There's a particular kind of . . . agony men wake up with, and your presence might be quite helpful.' He arched a brow and tilted his head towards the obvious tent in the blankets.

'You don't need me, you need a handmaiden,' I shot back, laughing as I ducked the pillow he tossed. 'I won't be long. Unless they make me beg to get my dress back. I need to go home, and since you tore the only thing I had on . . .'

I darted from the room, nearly startling the guard into drawing his sword when I asked him to send for the servants to return my clothes. Then I dashed off to the privy, where I washed up quickly, eager to return and help Rey with his so-called affliction.

When I returned, Reynard was standing by the window beside a tray of breakfast and a jug of water. My kirtle lay folded beside it.

'The servants brought your dress,' he said. 'But must you return to Tova?'

I froze, frowning at the note in his voice.

'Well, I *live* there, remember?' I chuckled, trying to lighten the moment. 'And if I don't go home tonight, I imagine Tova will be here soon enough, shaking his axe at your head.'

He didn't laugh.

'You could come with me. To the palace.'

'And do what there?' I asked, blinking. 'My life is here. I can finally learn how to use my power properly and help Boyan get the Brotherhood in order. We're getting so close, Rey. If I can push the Mules into revealing their routes and pressure Jagon into exposing his backer, we can eliminate the threat to your throne.' I picked up a piece of bread and popped it into my mouth.

'You could still do all that,' Reynard murmured, moving to stand beside me and sliding an arm around my waist. 'But from the palace. With me. I know it's a change . . . but we'll figure it out.'

I swallowed a small canapé that suddenly felt dry and tasteless in my mouth and reached for my kirtle. As tempting as it was to wake up by his side every morning, Dagome wasn't ready for that—and neither was I.

The geas trial had revealed more than just the key to my soul. It cracked open a truth I couldn't ignore: I needed to find out who my real father was.

My suspicions pointed towards someone high-ranking in the Brotherhood, but I wouldn't accept it without confirmation from the grand master himself. Being the daughter of an infamous assassin, on top of finding out I wasn't entirely human, wasn't something I could leave unchecked to simply move into the palace.

'Rey, there's so much I have to tell you . . .'

Before I had a chance to finish, a decisive knock disrupted our conversation.

'Oh, go away!' Reynard shouted, just as I said, 'Enter.'

The door opened, and Riordan stepped into the room. He glanced between Reynard and me, frowning at the tension. I hoped he wouldn't try digging into my mind because I didn't want anyone learning what I'd discovered in the Geas Hall before investigating it myself.

'My apologies for the intrusion, Your Majesty,' he said, voice taut. 'But some problems have arisen that require your immediate attention.' He hesitated, gaze flicking to me. 'Though perhaps we can discuss them at the palace—'

'Whatever it is, you can say it in front of Sana,' Reynard cut in, tugging me closer.

Riordan's mouth tightened. Whatever news he brought, it wasn't good.

'I can step out, if that makes things easier,' I offered, but Rey's grip on my waist only firmed.

'I trust you with my life, Roksana,' he said simply. 'Why wouldn't I trust you with my country?' He turned back to Riordan. 'Spit it out.'

The mage braced himself before inhaling deeply. 'Fine,' he said. 'A messenger arrived from the northern garrison—Młot's finally lost the last of his marbles. His army's crossed the border. Two villages are gone, possibly more; I'm not sure. That was the situation when the rider left for Truso.'

'What?' Reynard's voice cut sharp and low. Then a dark smirk curved his lips. 'That fool attacked us?' He huffed, shaking his head. 'If he wants to play stupid games, I'll give him exactly what he wants.' But then his tone shifted, and he gestured to Riordan. 'You said *problems*. Plural.'

The mage looked like he'd swallowed a bug that was trying to crawl its way back out to freedom.

'I'm not sure if it *is* a problem,' Riordan hedged, 'and I really don't think we should discuss it now . . .' He paused. 'Your scribe found a letter.' His fists tightened, and I didn't need to be a psychic mage to see he was growing more agitated with each passing moment.

'And that is important, why?' Reynard looked puzzled. So was I.

Riordan passed him a small envelope sealed with the Tivala family crest, and as I looked at it, a feeling of dread washed over me.

Had the old duke found out about Lily? If Jagon told him, I'd kill the fucker.

'Rey, whatever he wants, you swore to protect Lily. I'll take the blame if needed,' I said, tightening my fists as he broke the seal.

Reynard said nothing as he unfolded the letter, but I could see the way his jaw tensed the more he read. His brows furrowed, his lips thinned, and his entire body wound tight with fury I recognised far too well.

Then he snapped.

'That bloody bastard thinks he can blackmail me?' he growled, slamming the letter down on the table. 'Not bloody likely.' He stormed to the door, yanked it open, and barked at the guard outside. 'Bring me my scribe. Now!'

I knew I shouldn't have, but my curiosity overcame politeness. If Tivala was using Lily as a bargaining chip, I needed to know. I picked up the vellum. The letter was heavily embellished, more like an invitation than a threat, and as I looked at the ornate handwriting, my mouth dropped open, unsure if I was reading it right.

'What?' I shook my head, my thoughts a jumbled mess. I looked from the letter to Reynard, then and back again, trying to make sense of it. The letter was dated two days before the kidnapping attempt at my home.

Tivala's attack on my home, I could understand. But *this*—a whole betrothal? Worse . . . Rey didn't even look surprised.

My chest tightened, threatening to rob me of breath. Reynard rushed over, arms outstretched, but I took a step back.

'Were they all lies? Just pretty platitudes to get me to open my legs?' My voice sounded hollow even to my own ears. 'I know you need a queen, I'm not stupid. But if you were already planning to marry some-one, why sleep with me? Was I meant to be your last little tumble before settling down? Or'—my voice broke—'should I expect an offer to be your dirty little secret?'

'I didn't plan anything,' he said quickly, voice rough. 'Please—let me explain.'

'Explain?' I snapped. 'What, did you accidentally fall on the quill and sign your name before sneezing your seal onto the marriage contract?'

I clenched my jaw, squeezing my eyes shut so he couldn't see how close I was to breaking. I knew this interlude would have ended eventually, but why did he bother pretending to care?

'Roksana,' Riordan cut in gently, 'I can confirm Rey never wanted to marry another woman.'

His voice startled me—I'd forgotten he was still here. Heat flared in my cheeks. Having an audience for my humiliation made it worse.

'Leave us, Ri,' Reynard said without looking at him. 'Please.'

The moment the door shut, Rey knelt before me.

'This happened because of my complacency,' he began. 'Ruling Dagome has always been a balancing act. On one side, the people. The other, the nobles. And Tivala . . . well, that bastard's the worst of them.' He exhaled sharply. 'He sent a proposal months ago. A contract promising his support for my reforms—*if* I married his daughter. It was . . . politically sound. So I signed it.'

My jaw tightened.

'But that was before I knew you,' he said. 'And even then, something about it felt off. So I locked it away. I should've burned it the day you walked into my life.' His voice broke slightly. 'But idiot that I am, I didn't. I forgot. The gods as my witness, I forgot.'

He bowed his head, dragging both hands through his dark hair, frustration radiating off him in waves.

'I'm not asking you to believe me without proof,' he added. 'That's why I called for my scribe.'

He rose to his feet slowly, reaching out—but I took another step back, pretending not to see the desperation in his eyes.

'Sana, look at me.'

His voice held weight, the kind that demanded to be heard. Against my better judgement, I met his gaze.

'The night you came into my room,' he said quietly, 'and told me that wild story about a woman on the run who had made a mistake and blinded me, but never wanted to hurt me . . . It sounded so farfetched. But even then—*even then*—some part of me believed you.'

His voice softened to a whisper. 'Isn't there any part of *you* that believes *me*?'

'There is, but . . .'

I was suddenly engulfed in Rey's embrace. I bit my lip, desperate to hold back my tears.

'Then please,' he murmured, his voice raw, 'give me a chance to find out what happened and fix it.' He held me so tightly, it felt like he was scared I'd disappear into thin air.

'Will it change anything?' I whispered. 'The contract's still in Tivala's hands.'

Part of me wanted to believe him, *needed* to believe him, but having my worst fears realised made it so, so difficult.

A signed and sealed marriage contract was nearly as binding as a blood oath. Even a marriage itself was easier to dissolve than the promise often used to end wars and bring prosperity to the land. Breaking one didn't just ostracise you. It marked you. *Oathbreaker.*

And even kings weren't immune.

I didn't want to be the reason Reynard wore that stain.

The next half hour was the longest of my life. It didn't matter how I looked at the situation—Reynard had no choice but to marry this woman or risk all the nobles rallying against him . . .

Unless the contract vanished before it became public knowledge. My fists tightened as I watched the king pace the room, responsibility weighing down his shoulders.

He is mine to protect. Mine. And I won't give him up, not like this.

At last the scribe arrived, breathless and red-faced, only to go pale the moment he caught sight of Reynard's thunderous expression. A sombre-looking Riordan entered behind him, positioning himself close to the doors as he traced the truthseeker sigil. Our eyes met, and he gave a small nod. He would get the truth out of the scribe, even if it meant dissecting every though the young man had.

'M-my king—what happened? What can I do?' the scribe stammered, his high-pitched voice frantic.

'Did you seal and send a signed marriage contract to Duke Tivala?' Reynard asked calmly, but even I felt the weight of his words.

'*No*, sire!' The scribe's fear and confusion were so evident that Rey cursed, but it only made the poor boy stutter more. 'I-I beg your forgiveness. I'm still learning. If you tell me where it is, I'll send it immediately. I'm s-so sorry. My predecessor left without warning, and he didn't explain everything, and I-I should've asked for a list, I know, I know—'

I blinked. Still learning?

What predecessor . . . ?

'When did you start in this role?' I asked quietly.

The scribe turned to me, trembling under the king's stare. 'My lady, I w-was promoted t-two days after you tried . . . when t-they said . . . when you c-came to t-the palace.' He was practically vibrating with nerves, and I knew the truthseeker spell was difficult to deal with.

Riordan nodded. 'He's telling the truth. He hasn't sent anything—hasn't even *seen* the contract. Looks like Roksana's arrival forced our little spy to cut and run back south . . . with a gift for his master.'

I groaned, thumping my forehead with my fist. 'That's it! I think I know what happened.' The memory of my night in the cell flashed in my mind's eye. 'Jagon's accomplice—the southerner boasted about having the king's seal and scolded my old master for acting against the king.'

Reynard frowned.

'Why kill the king,' I said dryly, 'when you can just marry him off? Rey . . . your previous scribe, I'm sorry I didn't think of it earlier.'

He nodded grimly. 'I suspected something when he left so suddenly, but—' He turned to the scribe. 'You may go. Not a word about anything you heard today. Return to the palace and draft letters to all the garrison commanders. They are to prepare for war.'

The scribe bowed so fast he nearly stumbled, bolting like demons were snapping at his heels.

Once the door clicked shut and only the three of us remained, Reynard turned to Riordan.

'Postpone the ball until Gromnitsa,[1] two months from now. The celebration of Makosh on the Day of Thunder is the perfect moment to reveal that Sana is my chosen. Młot's insane actions have given us the perfect excuse for the delay,' he said, placing a steady hand on the mage's shoulder. 'I know you never wanted this, but in the face of war, I have to appoint a regent . . .'

'The old nobles won't like it,' Riordan warned.

'They'll suck it up,' the king said with a snort. 'Unless they'd prefer chaos in the kingdom and their daughters dancing on the front lines. Don't worry, Ri, I'll return—but while I'm away, I need someone I trust here.'

Rey walked towards me.

'It's all just pretence, my light. I need to keep Tivala guessing while I fight Młot.' His hand brushed my cheek, his gaze searching mine for understanding. And I did understand, all too well.

If Tivala revealed the agreement and Reynard refused to accept it, the nobles would overthrow him. Not even the threat of the dwarven

---

1. **Gromnitsa** — a holiday marking the midpoint between the Winter Solstice and the Spring Equinox.

axemen infantry could hold the kingdom if the aristocracy branded him an oathbreaker.

'I know,' I whispered, kissing the inside of his palm and leaning into his touch. 'What do you need me to do?'

I knew what I had to do. I had to retrieve that damn contract and burn it before it caused more problems, but that wasn't something I wanted Rey to know—at least not yet. Riordan's head whipped around in my direction, and I immediately shielded my thoughts. The mage sighed, his shoulders drooping, before he slipped out of the room, leaving us alone.

'Stay safe, my light. Learn your magic and wait for me,' Rey murmured, pulling me into his arms. A gentle tremor ran through his body, a silent sign of the pressure he was under, before he whispered, his lips brushing the shell of my ear, 'How do you feel? Please tell me you trust me. I need to hear it, Sanika. I can't go to war worrying I've left only ashes of my woman's heart.'

I exhaled through a tangled knot of emotion. 'Right now? I feel a whole lot of worry and a healthy dose of anger. But yes, Kingling. I trust you. How could I not? You've seen the worst of me—and still had the courage to bed me,' I teased, trying to relieve the tension.

Reynard smiled, tenderness crinkling the corner of his eyes when he took my palm and brought it to his lips. 'Maybe I should add a viper to my banner. As a reminder to our temperamental neighbour that I have a very personal grudge against him.'

I rolled my eyes. 'Like he'd know what it means.' Then casually, as if it meant nothing: 'Before you leave, could you grant me free entrance to the palace and permission to attend Privy Council meetings? I don't want to have to sneak around every time I want to talk to Riordan.'

Rey narrowed his eye but eventually nodded.

'I trust you won't do anything to put yourself at risk. Whatever's on your mind—and I know there's something—' he said, tapping my nose, 'please wait to act until you hear from me. I may need your help in Wiosna . . . And as much as it pains me to ask, please bring Tova with you.'

I could almost see those invisible gears turning in Reynard's head.

'Fine, I'll wait . . .' I sighed. 'Just don't cosy up with any other assassins while you're away.'

He laughed, then lifted me into his arms, sealing my lips with a kiss.

'I mean it, Viper,' he whispered, breath brushing my lips. 'I can't fight if I'm worried about you being involved in anything dangerous . . . I love you, Sanika.'

My heart skipped a beat at hearing those quiet words spoken with tenderness and reverence. This man, my berserker, had seen past the pain I'd caused him and still offered me his heart.

But I couldn't be honest with him. Not yet. Not if I wanted to help him.

I smiled, resting my head against his chest, the steady rhythm of his heartbeat grounding me as I made my silent vow.

I needed Jagon to get into Tivala's home, and I'd force my former master to help—even if it cost me my soul.

Because the man holding me in his arms was worth everything.

He might be the War King of Dagome, and I might not be able to be his wife or his queen, but *nothing* would stop me from being the King's Shadow.

Glossary

Alkonost — a legendary woman-headed bird that has a healing touch, an otherworldly beautiful face, and a mesmerizingly alluring voice capable of making anyone who hears her forget all their sorrows and worries.

Amare — the title given to a secondary male in a dark fae household, meaning 'beloved' and showing a meaningful bond between males, contrary to the term 'servus' that showed a submissive, subservient role.

Augurec /pron: au-gur-retc/ — an alloy of silver, iron, and copper produced by artificer mages with the ability to disrupt the natural patterns of all aether; magical shackles.

Bies (s.) /pron: b-yes/ biesy (pl.) — a personification of all the undefined evil forces in nature. Once, they were placed amongst the most dangerous and oldest demons in Central and Eastern Europe. They were massive bison-like beasts with horns and hooves that were hostile and resistant to most types of weapons.

Borovio—one of the seven dukedoms of the Dagome kingdom, governed by the Erenhart family.

Domine—the official title of the primary(alpha) male in a dark fae household responsible for the protection and external affairs. His authority is almost equal to Domina's.

Domina(s.)/dominae(pl.) — a lady of her own domain. Dark fae title for the head of the household.

Drah'sa /pron: Dra-sa/ — a dwarven term of endearment meaning 'little sister,' used for one considered a family member.

Draugr /pron: drow-gar/ — a revenant awakened in his grave that retains some mental capabilities. Their primal reason for existence is to protect their treasures, but they can be tethered to the necromancer's will.

Falchion /pron: falkion/ — a broad, slightly curved sword with a cutting edge on the convex side

Geas — a form of magical compulsion, curse, or obligation. Those under a geas are required to follow certain conditions or orders, risking death for disobedience.

Ghoul — minor Vel demon. A male with pale bodies, sharp fangs and poisonous claws that feasted on dead bodies, preferably freshly killed.

Gromnitsa — a holiday marking the midpoint between the Winter Solstice and the Spring Equinox.

Jarylo — god of fertility and spring, exceptionally well endowed.

Kirbai — a hybrid of the horse and snow leopard created by Cahyon Abyasa before he was corrupted by foul magic. The animal is known for its intelligence, fierce nature, and loyalty. It can survive in the harshest environments and climb almost vertical walls.

Kirtle — a dress similar to men's tunics. They were loose and reached to below the knees or lower. Slits on the sides were pulled tight to fit the figure. Kirtles were typically worn over a chemise or smock and under a formal outer garment or surcoat.

Kupala's Night — an ancient holiday celebrating the summer equinox with high fires and fertility rituals.

Lanara poison — a potent poison invented specifically for the mages. It suppresses the ability to connect with aether and, therefore, cast the spell.

Latawiec(s.) /pron: Lata-vi-etc/ latawce (pl.) /pron: latav-ce/ — shapeshifting demons. They flew in the currents of the wind. Their physical bodies were similar to large birds, with sharp claws and colourful feathers, but they had human heads. They could temporarily shift into human shape to tempt the victim with their song, and when they sang, those who heard it clawed their bodies, ripping the flesh as an offering for the ravenous demons.

Mamuna — a female swamp demon in Slavic mythology known for being malicious and dangerous.

Makosh — goddess of family and females, sometimes called the mother of gods.

Morgenstern — otherwise known as Morning Star flail – mace with a chain ended with a spiky ball.

Navia — an afterlife where all spirits come to rest after crossing the Veil that divides the spirit world from the living.

Nyja /pron: Ni-ya/ — goddess of War and Death, guardian of the souls that died a violent death.

Obraka — a slow and sensual dance relying on physical touch and showcasing the male's strength to lift their partner.

Olgoi worm /pron: ol-g{oi}/ — giant blind earth worm with rows of serrated teeth, famous for drilling tunnels in the dirt and rocks. They rarely hunt sentient beings, but during periods of starvation, they can migrate to the surface and prey on warm-blooded animals.

Peasant's crown — a traditional crown-like braid for women

Psoglav /pron: p-so-gwav/ — a demon with a human body with horse's legs, a dog's head with iron teeth, and a single eye on the forehead. They live in caves or in a dark land that has plenty of gemstones but no sun, and they love to eat people, especially fresh corpses

Raróg /pron: ra-roog/ — fire demons coming in the shape of horse-size falcons with beaks and claws made of burning embers and wings that start fires while they fly

Rusałka — a nature spirit affiliated with water and streams. Often in the shape of beautiful maiden with green or bluish hair. Similar to vila it has capricious nature and can be both helpful and obstructive to the humans. Often asociated with luring young men to their deaths in the waters.

Skeins — length of thread or yarn, loosely coiled and knotted

Spectrae — Ghost-like creatures created from tortured and fractured souls. They feed on the life force of other beings attempting to regain their solid shape and restore themselves. Particularly attracted to the life force of the dragon.

Srebrec — unstable ore similar to silver, with magical properties. The ore is able to siphon and store aether especially from the living beings. Mining it requires magical protection. Due to its instability it needed to be smelted into an alloy such as augurec to under the risk of explosion.

Striga — a female monster born from violent death. They hunted those who wronged them, and once their vengeance was completed, they hunted for any human. They looked like skinny females with two rows of teeth, large claws, and leather-like hair.

Strychnos — a highly toxic shrub whose bark and berries can cause seizures and imminent death.

Svarog /pron: S-va-roog/ — god of fire, patron of blacksmiths and metalworkers.

Utopiec(s.)/utopce(pl.) — spirits of human souls that died drowning, residing in the element of their own demise. They are responsible for sucking people into swamps and lakes as well as killing the animals standing near the still waters.

Upiór /pron: u-pi-oor/ — an undead being that arises from one cursed upon their death, appearing as a freshly deceased corpse. An upiór draws its strength from drinking and bathing in the blood of the living and can kill with its shrieks.

Vambraces — forearm guards are tubular or gutter defences for the forearm worn as part of a suit of plate armour that was often connected to gauntlets.

Vila /pron: vi-wa/ — a beautiful female nature spirit who dwells in pristine corners of the natural world, from forests and meadows to rivers and lakes. They possess supernatural healing abilities and the power of shapeshifting. Their eyes and dance can bewitch men who often perish from unrequited love.

Vjesci /pron: vi-yes-chi/ (s./pl.) — (originally from Polish folklore adjusted to the lore) An undead demon that retained the thoughts, personality, and body of the person. As their body slowly cooled down, the cheeks and lips would have a bright red colour, and blood could be found underneath the nails and on the face, while their limbs remained supple.

Vyraj /pron: vi-ray/ — an afterlife paradise for those who deserve it and warriors who have fallen in battle.

Wlok /pron: w-wok/ (s./pl.) — a major Vel demon that looks like tumbleweed made of bones. It rolled over the roads and fields, killing any living creature that had bones inside, adding them to its "body" in its constant need to grow.

Żmij (z- as in English: vi_si_on -me-j)— a powerful demi-god associated with water and marshlands, a giant, three-headed viper with large wings. He can be called from the void between the worlds, and his favour can be obtained by offering him a sacrificial woman. Once the żmij makes a deal, he will protect the city to its death, only to be reborn in the void.

CLASSES OF MAGIC USERS:

HIGH MAGIC ORDER

Vivamancer

Once practiced on the continent of Tir ha Mor, Vivamancy was eradicated due to its deep ties to Wild Magic and the inherent difficulty in controlling its chaotic power. A Vivamancer is a mage who manipulates the essence of life itself—able to reshape the magical blueprints of living beings. They can transform one creature into another, create entirely new entities, or even forge hybrids capable of producing viable offspring.

Healer

A mage who channels aether to influence the body's natural processes. While primarily focused on restoration and healing, a Healer's powers can also induce biological alterations or trigger unnatural mutations in living beings.

Enhancer

A mage is able to take the power in objects and other mages and weave it into patterns that enhance the effectiveness of what spell is being used.

Illusion

A mage who manipulates light to craft vivid, lifelike illusions. Beyond mere visual trickery, a skilled Illusionist can sense a person's surface thoughts, using that insight to anchor their attention—drawing focus to the illusion and away from their true surroundings.

Psychic/Psionic

A mage attuned to the subtle currents of aether within the soul, able to perceive and interact with thoughts and emotions at a fundamental level. Their influence ranges from subtle persuasion to direct mental manipulation, often shaped by their empathy and ability to connect with others. Psychics frequently find roles as advisors within noble houses or as interrogators in judicial systems.

Artificer

A mage skilled in crafting artefacts that channel and execute magical spells by manipulating the flow of aether through physical objects. The creation process is complex, often involving multiple stages and the infusion, melding, or etching of intricate glyph diagrams into the artefact's structure.

PRIMAL MAGIC ORDER

Paladin

A mage of the warrior class, the Paladin seamlessly blends martial prowess with magical discipline. Trained in traditional combat techniques, they channel aether to enhance their physical abilities, fortify their defenses, or empower their strikes. While many follow the path of the battlemage, Paladins often stand apart through their dedication to duty, discipline, and the mastery of both blade and spell..

Elemental

A mage who harnesses and directs the raw forces of the elements in their magic. They may specialize deeply in one element or exhibit versatility across multiple, shaping fire, water, earth, air, or other primal forces to suit their needs.

Animage

A mage gifted with the ability to communicate with animals and shapeshift into their forms. Those with minor talents often assist in animal husbandry, while those with greater skill can commune with aether-marked creatures such as dragons, gryphons, and manticores.

Seer

A mage gifted with the ability to glimpse future events and uncover past memories tied to a person or object. Often sought after as advisors or investigators, their role and allegiance vary according to individual affiliation.

FOUL MAGIC ORDER

Necromancer

A mage tainted by foul magic, the Necromancer commands the flesh of the dead, extracts the spirits of the living, and manipulates life essence through dark and forbidden means. Among their ranks, Blood Mages form a feared subclass—practitioners who perform blood rituals to bind aether and reshape both living and dead flesh into undead abominations.

Summoner

Often shunned by the mage community, Summoners or otherwise called a Velcallers wield foul and wild magic to pierce the Veil and summon Vel demons from their native plane. They frequently collaborate with necromancers, corrupting the aether of dead bodies to anchor these entities in the physical world, giving form to twisted, demon-bound vessels..

Cursegiver

Cursegiver mages lack strong aether manipulation but possess a rare talent for disrupting the aether in people and objects. Their magic manifests as misfortune, sabotage, or decay—often mistaken for mere bad luck. They are also known for crafting cursed items, or *fetishes*, which carry lingering disruptive effects.

Dreamwalker

To become a Dreamwalker, a mage must possess foul magic in their blood. Though controversial, dreamwalking is often classified as a subset of psychic magic, as it involves manipulating a sleeping person's thoughts and emotions within the dream realm. Skilled Dreamwalkers can go beyond mere influence—invading the mind, seizing control, and plunging their victim into a waking nightmare.

About the Author

Olena Nikitin is the pen name of an indie UK-based couple who share a love of fantasy and paranormal romance. Their series, Season's War, Broken Bonds, and Amber Legends are set in rich, vibrant worlds, their exciting storylines based on Slavic myths and legends.

Both in their books and out, they love down-to-earth humour and have a visceral approach to life, striving to write realistic romances filled with the passion and spice people always dream of experiencing.

Meet the minds behind the magic:

Olga—Polish-born and raised, brings Slavic soul and dark gritty humour to the page. An emergency physician by day and fantasy writer by night, she can't resist ensuring every injury detail is as close to reality as possible. She's proud of being a crazy cat lady, and together with Mark, owns five cats.

Mark is the quintessential English gentleman, armed with a dry charm and mad tinkerer skills, with enough roguish swagger to make Olga cross a continent for him. When he's not fixing syntax or spinning tales over a glass of good whisky, he's probably telling (and embellishing) the story of how he got shot. Spoiler: it's a good one.

Olena Nikitin loves hearing from their fans and critics alike and welcomes communication via any platform!

For more information or to follow them on social media, check their website: www.olenanikitin.uk

For updates and to sign up for their newsletter, click here: Newsletter Form Sign-Up

Also by

Epic Fantasy Romance (completed series)

In a land where the Old Gods still walk on earth, the antihero, the harbinger of Chaos, and the daughter of Autumn, Lady Inanuan of Thorn has to face her magic and choose between power and the life she has always wanted.

While for many, she is known as Striga for her explosive temper or Royal Witch for her role in the kingdom, she is just Ina, a woman of many colours who wishes to live her life free without too many expectations.

Unfortunately, because of her rare Chaos magic, she becomes the centre of a power struggle between those who desire to rule the world with her hands. And when her life gets tangled with Marcach of Liath, and Sa'Ren Gerel, her heart has to choose between them . . . even if her magic has already claimed them both.

Amber Legends

Do you know the place where your night-mares exist, the Nether? A realm shifted in time, a shelter for those hunted to almost extinction by iron and silver, a place where the gods rule and monsters thrive? The place where magic flows freely?

No? I thought so. It was separated from the mortal plane for a reason, but it is still there. This hidden world that lurks in the shadows, caught in the periphery of your vision when you speed your steps, afraid of the darkness.

What you saw in your dreams is real. What you see in your nightmares is even more because now the Gates are open, and danger no longer hides but barges into your life, demanding nothing less than your soul.

Walk the cobbled streets of Gdansk, where the living stone, amber, measures the magic of time and the guardians of the Nether ensure that unsuspected humans don't discover the existence of those for ages considered a myth . . . unless they are tonight's prey.

Amber Legends is a series of standalone books inspired by Slavic mythology and the legends of Pomerania. They are dark paranormal fantasies with profanity. Audience: 18+ years of age.